Portr

MW01193862

"This historical novel is the richly imagined life of Annie Shaw and the Paris she came to call home. A chance introduction into the Bohemian world of artists offers Annie the chance to shrug off her confining identity as the aging widow of Robert Shaw and the caretaker of her extended family. Among the artists she meets, Annie discovers in herself a spirited and generous-hearted woman ready to defy the social norms of her class. This smart, deeply engaging book showcases Harold's depth of research and her thrilling use of dialogue among a large cast of characters. The language races along, conveying both the inner life of Annie Shaw and the Bohemian world of artists in *fin de siecle* Paris."

—Meredith Hall, author of
Beneficence and the memoir *Without a Map*

"An engaging, moving and witty novel, filled with fascinating characters and a vivid sense of the exuberant, risk-taking artistic world of late nineteenth century Paris. Annie Shaw is an appealing character, honestly and lovingly drawn, in her yearning for a freer and more creative life, beyond her role as faithful Civil War widow, sister, aunt and daughter-in-law. As Annie starts to discover her own path toward self-expression and love, she offers crucial support for those around her who break away from society's restraints of race, gender, and sexuality."

—Harriet S. Chessman, author of
Lydia Cassatt Reading the Morning Paper

"In *Portrait of an Unseen Woman* Roberta Harold gives us Paris in 1892 from the point of view of an American woman of means who has lived in the city for decades but never let herself be her own woman. Deftly, Harold traces over the course of a few months Annie Shaw's education, one that includes Americans and Parisians and that recognizes painful entanglements and conflicting mores. As suits the setting, which is wonderfully depicted in one adroit detail after another, no easy answers emerge, but the recognition of the creative spirit shines through steadily. Annie, the widow of the Civil War hero Robert Gould Shaw, comes to a deeply felt fictional life in these pages. The reader feels that a great debt of recognition to an 'unseen woman' has been handsomely paid."

— Baron Wormser, author of *Some Months in 1968: A Novel*

"*Portrait of an Unseen Woman* evokes the fashions, cuisine, music, and, above all, painting that made Paris such a dazzling destination at the end of the nineteenth century. For the long-widowed protagonist Annie Shaw and the other Americans in her expatriate community, this time and place represented both escape from the strictures of privileged lives in New York and Boston and a crucible within which to encounter both personal and national confusions in the aftermath of the Civil War. Harold's vivid descriptions and nuanced dialogue make reading her novel a highly absorbing experience, while the subtlety of her denouement opens a new vista of possibility for her characters and her readers alike."

—John Elder, author of *Reading the Mountains of Home* and *Picking Up the Flute: A Memoir in Music*

"Roberta Harold knows how to put a good story together. Annie Shaw, who has endured half her adult life in the shadows as the widow of Robert Shaw, a revered Civil War hero, is struggling to shed the suffocating role society has assigned her and find her own identity. Harold follows her into the brash and heady art world of Paris during its Golden Age where the real-life Annie Shaw disappeared into history and completes her story. The food descriptions will make you ravenous."

—Mary Hays, author of *Learning to Drive*

Portrait of an Unseen Woman

A Novel of Annie Shaw

Portrait of an Unseen Woman

A Novel of Annie Shaw

by

Roberta Harold

Rootstock Publishing

Montpelier, VT

Portrait of an Unseen Woman: A Novel of Annie Shaw
©2024 Roberta A. Harold.

Release Date: May 20, 2025.

All Rights Reserved.
Printed in the USA.

Paperback ISBN: 978-1-57869-194-4
eBook ISBN: 978-1-57869-195-1

Library of Congress Control Number: 202590303

Published by Rootstock Publishing
an imprint of Ziggy Media LLC
Montpelier, VT 05602
info@rootstockpublishing.com
www.rootstockpublishing.com

Book Design by Eddie Vincent, ENC Graphic Services.
Cover Art: "Girl Standing on a Balcony" by Carl Vilhelm Holsøe (1863-1935), The Athenaeum, Public Domain, via Wikimedia Commons.

For permissions, or to schedule a book club visit or reading, contact the author at rah53@comcast.net.

For Wayne, after all this time.

There you stood with your indefinable charm.
Because so little
is known about you from history,
I could fashion you more freely in my mind...

—C.P. Cavafy, "Kaisarion"

Cast of Characters

Anna Kneeland Haggerty (Annie) Shaw, American expatriate living in Paris, widow of Civil War hero Robert (Rob) Gould Shaw, colonel of the 54th Massachusetts Infantry, one of the Union's first Black regiments.

Clemence Haggerty (Clem) Crafts, Annie's sister, wife of notable chemist James Mason Crafts, mother of Annie's four nieces; recently returned to the US after years as a Paris expatriate.

Julia Shaw Greene, American expatriate, aunt of Robert Gould Shaw and Annie's aunt by marriage, widow of social reformer William Batchelder Greene.

George Kneeland, Annie's cousin on her mother's side, her first and deepest love, died of consumption in 1859.

Sarah Blake Sturgis Shaw, mother of Robert Gould Shaw, formerly a leader of the Abolitionist movement; Annie's former mother-in-law.

Catherine Lorillard Kernochan (Mrs. Kernochan), parishioner and committeewoman of the American Cathedral in Paris.

Roland Burwell, scion of a South Carolina plantation family, unsuccessful suitor of Annie Haggerty.

Jackson Burwell, Roland's son, an aspiring artist who comes to study art in Paris and is commended to Annie by his father.

Adèle Fourget, Annie's housekeeper, native of Martinique.

Henrietta Reubell, wealthy bohemian whose weekly salons are a cynosure for French and expatriate artists, musicians, writers, and public figures.

Comte Bertrand de Leiningen, Alsatian painter and instructor at the Académie Julian and the Ècole des Beaux Arts of Paris.

Alice Mason Hooper Sumner (Mrs. Mason), a childhood friend of Annie's in Lenox, notable beauty in earlier days, most recently the mistress of Junius Spencer Morgan.

Henry Ossawa Tanner, American artist studying in Paris to escape racial discrimination in his native Pennsylvania.

Thalia (Tallie) DeKuyper, bohemian artist, art student at the Académie Julian, and sometime artists' model.

Lydia Burwell, a young woman with a forbidden connection to Jackson Burwell.

Carlotta Russell Lowell (Lotta), Annie's niece by marriage, granddaughter and traveling companion of Sarah Shaw; daughter of Civil War hero Charles Lowell and social reformer/ philanthropist Josephine Shaw Lowell.

Harrison Bird Brown, notable Maine landscape artist, moved to London to live with his daughter after the deaths of his wife and sons. One-time painting instructor for Annie in her youth.

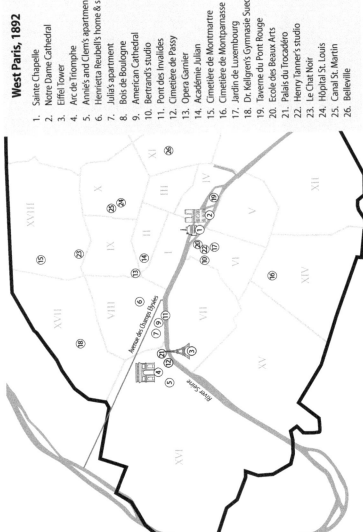

West Paris, 1892

1. Sainte Chapelle
2. Notre Dame Cathedral
3. Eiffel Tower
4. Arc de Triomphe
5. Annie's and Clem's apartments
6. Henrietta Reubell's home & salon
7. Julia's apartment
8. Bois de Boulogne
9. American Cathedral
10. Bertrand's studio
11. Pont des Invalides
12. Cimetière de Passy
13. Opera Garnier
14. Académie Julian
15. Cimetière de Montmartre
16. Cimetière de Montparnasse
17. Jardin de Luxembourg
18. Dr. Kellgren's Gymnasie Suedois
19. Taverne du Pont Rouge
20. Ecole des Beaux Arts
21. Palais du Trocadéro
22. Henry Tanner's studio
23. Le Chat Noir
24. Hôpital St. Louis
25. Canal St. Martin
26. Belleville

Chapter 1

unlight slanted through the lancet windows of the Sainte-Chapelle, splashing rainbows on a small, stooped woman in gray seated near the front of its narrow nave. To Annie Shaw's eye, the medieval chapel the Baedekers called a jewel-box seemed itself made of jewels, its thousands of tiny panes glowing in lacy columns of sapphire, ruby, emerald, and amber. Impossible not to feel the Divine presence in such a place, cool and perfumed after the early summer warmth outdoors. On one side of the altar, a fountain of white roses and stephanotis sprayed over its pedestal like a bride's abandoned bouquet.

Anna Kneeland Haggerty Shaw, fifty-six years old, widowed for nearly thirty, was Mrs. Annie Shaw to her expatriate American circle, Madame Robert Gould Shaw to strangers and authorities. The relict of a young, seraphically handsome hero of America's Civil War, Annie had lost everything she loved most by the time she turned thirty: her small brother Oggie, sweet-natured heir and hope of her mercantile Haggerty clan; George Kneeland, the cousin she first meant to marry, and Rob Shaw, shot through the heart on the walls of an island sand-fort two months after their wedding, leaving her only his name. Even his child was denied her, miscarried amid civic upheaval in her native New York days before word came of her beloved's death. *My love is cursed,* she had concluded. *It kills everything it touches.*

She chose a rickety chair just off the center aisle, the better to watch the fingers of the pianist, the young composer Debussy, fly and hover and caress the keys. And here he came, tugging nervously at his maroon cravat. Perhaps thirty, perhaps younger, shock-headed, like a little boy in Sunday clothes who had escaped his mamma's ministrations and gone rough-housing with the family terrier. Yet something masculine and compelling in the gaze he ventured around the small audience, the dark eyes glancing for a thrilling instant off hers before he sat, bounced a few times on the stool, and let his fingers drop, gentle as rain, onto the keyboard.

The beauty bursting so suddenly from silence triggered a flow of tears, as it often did for Annie. The feeling kept building—the composition simple yet exquisitely melodic, and when the third movement, which he had titled "Promenade Sentimentale," began its glissandos and arpeggios, she closed her eyes. The notes melded into the sparkle of moonlight on the old Stockbridge Bowl near Lenox, and she felt again the soft eddies of an August breeze, a tug in her belly of youthful ecstasy—was it beloved George Kneeland who had rowed the little boat that night, or some later, soon-discarded beau? Only the sensation of her fingers trailing in the silky black water remained.

She rummaged for a handkerchief. Foolish to dwell on vanished joys with this new one unfolding in her ears. But perhaps they were all of a piece. Music pierced defenses, erased time's boundaries. She closed her eyes again and drifted on its lovely ripples. Debussy played another piece of his own, lyrical and haunting, and then a strange, deceptively simple trio of short pieces he called "Gymnopédies" by "mon ami, Satie."

The spell broken by hearty applause, she felt bereft, only wanting to lose herself in it all over again. But the composer rose, bowed, and withdrew with a shy, triumphant smile. She blew her nose and rose stiffly, retrieving her cane and stepping into the aisle.

"Annie Shaw, isn't it?" said an American voice behind her.

She turned to see a tall, white-haired woman heading toward her, her face alight with pleasure. She looked familiar... of course!—Rob Shaw's aunt, Julia Shaw Greene, his father's younger sister.

"Madame Greene?"

Her sister-in-law Effie Lowell's letters had mentioned that "Tante Greene" lived in Paris, but neither she nor Annie had sought out the other, and their paths had not crossed until now. Reed-slim in aquamarine silk, Julia Greene carried an elegant ebony cane that seemed merely decorative, her movements easier and more vigorous than Annie's own. Her bright blue eyes—so like Rob's—sparkled. For a moment Annie's throat tightened.

Julia caught up and laid a hand on her shoulder. "We'll have none of that 'Madame'—it used to be Aunt Julia, but 'Julia' will suffice now—we're still family, aren't we?"

Annie suppressed a wince. Having her reasons for resisting the Shaws' persistent attempts to claim her as family, she had

evaded the clutches of that insatiably idealistic tribe only by
removing permanently to Paris with her own. Might the need to
proselytize everyone in one's orbit be a familial trait? "We are,"
she managed finally. "Please call me Annie. Didn't I hear from
Effie Lowell that you're living in Paris now?"

"I've lived here for years, near my son Will and his wife—I'm
four times a grandmamma." Julia hesitated. "Would you have
time for a *café*? Or a lemonade, since the day's turned so warm?
Or must you be off somewhere?"

Annie hesitated in turn—only inwardly, she hoped. Four
grandchildren—a potentially stultifying catalogue that could
take days, all too familiar from Colony teas. And Julia's late
husband, Colonel William Greene, had been a notorious
utopianizer, beloved of social revolutionaries everywhere. But
his widow's eyes held a glint, not of fanaticism but of the wicked
humor Annie had seen in the eyes of the Shaw she had loved.
And in the days from their engagement until the end of all
hope for Rob's return, the lively and at times scandalmongering
wit of Julia's letters had brought respite from the Shaw clan's
abolitionist preoccupations.

"I should like that," she said finally.

"I know a nice little spot on the Île St. Louis, if you don't
mind the walk."

They set out eastward by the north quays of the Île de la
Cité, cooler near the water and free of the touristic hordes who
swarmed around Notre Dame Cathedral to the south. Julia
Greene slowed her vigorous pace to match Annie's.

"You find me newly sans famille—I think you met my younger
sister Clemence, before she married James Crafts? She and her
daughters left for Boston a week ago. My brother-in-law has

taken a chemistry professorship there."

"They went without you?" Julia searched Annie's face and nodded. "I shouldn't care to live in Boston again myself. I've spent more than enough time in that suffocating little hamlet."

Annie roared at the thought of that in the ears of James Crafts, a devoted son of his native city. "I've spent little time there. Only when Rob was training the regiment—you remember. In any case, it didn't appeal."

There had been more to it than that. For years Annie had played mother's helper, nursemaid, and listening ear to her four nieces. She had even thought herself of some little value to James; despite joining in the girls' teasing about his foul chemistry experiments, she was the one member of the *ménage* with any interest in scientific matters. She remembered with a pang the episode of accidental eavesdropping that had led her to stay in Paris—James asking Clem, with a weary note in his voice, *What are we going to do about Annie?*

She had another reason for avoiding Boston: the sculptor Saint-Gaudens was at work on a huge bronze bas-relief, to stand on Boston Common, depicting Rob and his Negro troops on their triumphal march through Boston, less than a month after their wedding and the last time Annie saw Rob alive. She had stood with his family on his cousin Loulie's Beacon Street balcony; when he passed them, superb on his black horse, and raised his sword in salute, his eyes burned with a martyr's flame, and she knew she'd already lost him. With the unveiling of the statue would go any chance Annie had of being seen by Boston society as anything other than the hero's grieving widow, a role she had no wish to play any longer and, considering her first passionate opposition to his taking the regiment, one to which she'd never felt entitled. Each time she saw it, it would bring back the sorrow and anger she'd felt as she watched them march away.

"I may yet end up there, once my various infirmities catch up with me," she conceded.

She colored under Julia's rapid appraisal, trying vainly to straighten herself from a stoop that had become habitual. "You should be a long way from worrying about that," her companion said. "I, for one, am glad to know you stayed." Would anyone else in Paris have said that?

They traversed the quay behind the Hotel-Dieu, whose grim walls and narrow windows gave it the look of a penitentiary rather than a hospital. It was a relief to emerge into sunlight and cross the bridge to the Île Saint-Louis, the elegant little island upstream of the great Cathedral. *I could live here,* Annie thought. *In the real Paris.*

The red awnings of the Taverne du Pont-Rouge welcomed them at the first corner, and a smiling waiter with a splendid mustache bowed them to a marble-topped table alongside the bar, open to the summery air. "Mesdames aimeraient une boisson fraîche, peut-être?"

"Une demi-bouteille de Pommery, s'il vous plaît," Annie found herself saying, smiling at Julia's raised eyebrows. "My treat. Unless you'd rather have lemonade," she added. "That music made me think of champagne, which one daren't drink alone. " She watched the waiter whisk a dozen empty glasses onto a tray and steer it deftly through the crowded tables. "Nicely put-together young fellow, isn't he?"

"He is at that. Champagne in mid-afternoon! The Bostonians would be horrified." Julia's laugh showed off her still-splendid teeth. "Fie upon lemonade. Now, tell me everything. How long have you been in Paris? Where are you living?" Graceful and regal, framed by a trellis of salmon-pink roses, she sat in her cane-backed chair like a ballerina at rest.

"On the avenue Henri-Martin, in the Sixteenth—due west from the Trocadéro."

"Passy's nice, but isn't it rather far from everything?"

"Hopelessly suburban. It was my brother-in-law's choice. He's something of a—valetudinarian. There's a famous mineral spring, and he swore the water was good for his digestion." James Crafts was a life-long hypochondriac, a trial to his family with his insistence on the unhealthiness of French cuisine and the benefits of herbal infusions and vegetable fiber. Annie envisioned James' old-fashioned muttonchops rising and falling like pistons around an unbuttered slice of graham toast. *Thank God I won't have to deal with that anymore.*

"We came to Europe, for my father's health, about twenty years ago—"

"I liked Ogden. He was a delightful man."

Annie sighed. "He was that. Though he and my mother—" She cut herself off; no need for Julia to hear of the estrangement that had led her mother to wander the capitals of Europe, with Annie in tow, in the last years of her parents' marriage. "He died in '75. Heart failure. By then James—James Crafts, my brother-in-law—was researching with a senior colleague at the École des Mines—over by the Luxembourg. His work was the reason we all stayed on in Paris. I'm still in the apartment next door I used to share with my mother."

Julia Greene's smile faded. "Your mother died too? I hadn't heard."

"Four years ago. She'd been declining for some time— *dementia senilis*, the doctor said. What Shakespeare calls 'second childishness and mere oblivion.' The mere oblivion part took years. Pneumonia, at the end, and peaceful enough."

"And you looked after her. That must have been difficult." Julia laid a light hand on Annie's arm. How rare, to be touched so, for affection's sake.

"I had help—but, yes, it was."

The waiter arrived with the champagne and two etched flutes, silently uncorking the bottle and pouring the golden bubbles expertly down the sides. His perfect teeth flashed Annie a dazzling smile, which she returned.

Julia raised her flute in a toast. "To happy reconnection!"

"And handsome waiters."

The glasses chimed; Julia closed her eyes and sipped the wine with a beatific sigh. "*So* much better than lemonade. Tell me, what are your plans?"

"Plans?" Annie was enjoying the cool tickle of the bubbles against her nose.

"Now that you've been emancipated from your protector?"

"I can't imagine Dr. Crafts in that role—isn't it rather an— improper position?" Annie pictured her brother-in-law at his morning toast, and grimaced.

Julia's guffaw drew stares from neighboring tables. "Not *that* sort of protector! But we females are supposed to have one, aren't we? The household head. Especially in France. Father, husband, brother-in-law—my son qualifies in my case, I suppose. I'm across the hall from him, on the rue Bassano, near your American Cathedral. But you're avoiding my question."

Annie hesitated. "For so long I was the deputy mother—the

family chaperone. I won't miss that. You know, an unmarried sister—a spinster or widow—becomes superfluous eventually, doesn't she? When the children grow up.

"I hadn't thought of having plans—of my own, I mean. I had them with Rob; we were going to have a house in the country—near Lenox—and children..." her mind went back to the day when all her plans evaporated. Rob and she in her father's library on Bond Street, after she learned that—at his mother's behest—he'd accepted command of the 54th Massachusetts, the first Union black regiment, without waiting to hear the thoughts from Annie that his letter had requested of her. That meant three more years of enlistment, with all its risks—she knew the odds, the target he would become as leader of a Negro regiment, and had been resolved to break off their engagement. At twenty-eight, she had already lost too many beloveds.

And then he came in, his fair hair gleaming against the dark blue of his new uniform, the rosebud of those now-familiar lips under the soldierly mustache, the blue, blue eyes of him, the slender neck. Oh, God.

"You are angry with me, Annie."

"You have a keen grasp of the obvious, Captain Shaw. In this instance at least. How could you? You must have known what I would say, if you had waited for my answer."

"If I had thought—"

"If you had thought!"

"I didn't come to apologize for what I've done. Only to explain—"

"What good is explanation now? It's done, and past mending."

"It's not Mother's fault. It was my decision."

"The gentleman protests too much, methinks." She knows very well that Sarah Shaw is the reason Governor Andrew asked Rob

to head this regiment. A prominent and fanatical abolitionist, quick to remind her children what they owed her for all her maternal sacrifices. Including, apparently, their lives...

Later, though, when she's vented her anger and let his arms steal around her waist, his lips nuzzling her neck in that particular spot he's found, she gives way to resignation and agrees to marry him in spite of it all...

"And I would paint," she went on, pulling herself back to the present. "I used to love to paint. Later, after the War, Father was so ill, and Mamma needed me. And after he died, I fell in with whatever Mamma or the Crafts had in mind. When you are part of a family, and they need you—"

"—or want you, or have a use for you?" Julia gestured to the waiter, who picked up the bottle and topped off Annie's glass. "You can drift through a whole life that way. Most women do—it comes with having children, usually. And then you outlive your usefulness. It's not just aunts, you know."

"That's why I stayed!" It burst out suddenly. "I felt—surplus to requirements. An encumbrance. And I wanted to—I want to—" Annie felt her eyes filling, set her lips in a tight line and dropped her head. Stupid tears again. What was wrong with her today? Julia Greene was looking at her with something like understanding, which wasn't helping.

She took a breath and went on, her voice lower. "I stayed because I still have little dreams of my own. I want to belong here! In Paris, I mean. I want Paris to be my home, and I want to have friends of my own here—not Clem's friends, who only think of me as this poor invalid widow— and go to the theater and opera and salons and have conversations—"

"About—?"

"I don't know. Something besides babies and marriage prospects and how much cheaper things are here than in the States. And hear wonderful music like—" she waved a hand back toward the great Cathedral's island, "—today's, and perhaps help a struggling artist or writer or composer or two, as my father did. I have the money, I might as well put it to good use—" She stopped, out of breath again. "And get back to a little painting of my own."

"That all sounds reasonable enough."

"But I haven't the slightest idea how to go about it. I hardly know anybody."

"Your French is good, isn't it?"

"Well—yes, I thought that was important. I don't know how people live in a country for years and refuse to learn its language. There's a reason it's called the American Colony—it could be anywhere. Charleston, or—or Milwaukee, even."

"Milwaukee? Heaven forfend! You've been consorting with the wrong sort of Americans."

"And too few of the French," Annie sighed. "The condition I'm in—" she waved a hand down her bodice—"doesn't help. It's been hard to get out and about. I should so love to start going to the Opéra again—it's been years. And the theater. Before I fell ill, Mamma and I went everywhere—"

Julia fixed her in a warm blue gaze. "How long were you ill?"

"Five—no, six years. Seventy-five to...eighty-one. The Paris doctors said surgery would be dangerous, but finally decided the beastly thing would suffocate me if they didn't operate. I wish they'd done it three or four years sooner."

"A tumor, was it?"

"A cyst, of the ovary. An exceptionally large one, they said, but benign, thank God—or, at any rate, it hasn't returned."

"But you're not altogether well now?"

"I know the surgery saved my life, but it didn't heal well. The doctors were rightly pleased with their work—but the scar on my belly keeps me from moving freely. If I try to stand up straight, or wear a corset, it pulls and hurts." Annie hoped she wasn't whining like a typical invalid, but Julia was right; every day she woke to pain that sometimes doubled her over and sometimes exhausted her, resisting all her attempts to keep busy enough to ignore it.

"You're wearing corsets now, aren't you?" Julia winced sympathetically. "I noticed you seemed a bit stooped, though."

"It may be permanent, I'm afraid." Annie bit her lip. "The truth is—I'm not so bad-looking, but I've let myself go. I didn't mean for it to happen." They paused to watch the waiter deliver a pair of ornate pink-and-white ice cream concoctions to a slim woman in a feathered bonnet and her bowler-hatted companion.

Annie brightened. "How on earth does she keep her—and for that matter, how have you—"

"Kept my sylph-like figure?" Julia smiled. "Not on vegetable roughage and mineral waters. I'm out and about a good deal, which helps."

"When I was ill, and after the surgery, I stopped feeling like—like a woman. A tumor like that turns your skin yellow and your breath foul—" she paused. "But the urges come back, sometimes. I'd meet someone at my sister's, or at a Cathedral function—usually married, unfortunately."

"You certainly show no signs of all that now. You're older than when I saw you last, but you still have those lovely cheekbones and that rosy complexion—"

Annie smiled and ducked her head. "You are kind to say so. I've looked worse, certainly—but there didn't seem much point in struggling against the forces of nature. My circumstances, with the family obligations and so forth, weren't conducive—"

"You must have had some chances to remarry. I wondered why you didn't."

"No one else wondered," said Annie bitterly. "Least of all the Shaws. Can you picture me telling Sarah I was marrying again? Who could possibly live up to our dead hero?"

"Surely you wouldn't have let that stop you." Julia signaled the waiter and pointed to the confections being devoured at the nearby table. "Deux de ceux-ci, s'il vous plaît. My treat this time," she added in response to Annie's raised eyebrows. The waiter grinned, raised an approving eyebrow and went off to the kitchen. "They didn't come more lovable than Rob, of course—but that wasn't the reason, was it?"

Annie didn't respond at first. She and Julia might be related, but they'd had no contact for decades. And then: "My heart healed, as hearts do—grief without end becomes madness, don't you think? Like Queen Victoria, since Albert—I'd been twenty-eight, not even three months married. And there had been another—I lost him long before Rob and I met. It was so hard—"

Julia nodded. "I wondered at the time why a rich and pretty girl like you hadn't married long since."

"Crème glacée aux fraises, mesdames!" The waiter set the tulip-shaped glasses on their table with a little flourish. "Bon appetit!"

Scenting the fresh strawberries, Annie felt a laugh bubbling up. "If James Crafts could see me now!" She excavated the concoction with a long-handled spoon and closed her eyes in bliss.

With the treat half gone, she put down the spoon. "For a while, after the War was over, it seemed something might happen. I wanted it to. I went to Washington, with friends. It was such an exciting time—so much hope, even after Mr. Lincoln's...all those energetic, good-hearted men bent on changing the world—but the stars never quite aligned. Perhaps it was just as well, since I became so ill, and what husband would've wanted to deal with that?"

That wasn't how Annie had felt at the time. There had been expressions of mutual interest—Colonel Nelson Miles, as he was then, before the Army put stars on his shoulders, and before Annie learned his true character and banished him. Schuyler Colfax, the House speaker who steered the Thirteenth Amendment to passage and went on to be Grant's Vice-President—but whenever Annie seemed on the verge of a conquest, her old Lenox friend Alice Mason, the belle of post-war Washington, seemed compelled to step in and charm away the object of Annie's attention. Indeed, Annie and Senator Sumner had been growing fond of one another, but Alice couldn't resist dazzling the old abolitionist crusader into what turned out to be a disastrous, short-lived marriage. The friendship had rapidly cooled over what Annie saw as Alice's cavalier, cruel treatment of her elderly husband.

Julia dabbed ice cream from the corner of her mouth. "An agreeable and pleasant-looking woman with a little fortune is always marriageable."

"I don't care so much for marriage. Indeed, I relish the prospect of being my own mistress at last! Though it does frighten me a little. But a bit of masculine conversation—not dinner-table pleasantries—would be stimulating from time to time. Oh, that sounds so rude, especially as we've only just met again, and I'm so enjoying—" And it was a more splendid afternoon than she could have imagined when she left the avenue Henri Martin.

Her aunt-in-law's smile widened, and she squeezed Annie's arm. "I couldn't agree more, my dear! Present company is delightful, but in general I find mixed company the most entertaining. In terms of sex, nationality, occupation, interests— what you will. I'm quite done with talk of babies and marriage prospects and the dollar exchange rate."

"I have a house in Cannes, and thought of holing-up there for a while. Summer doesn't seem the best time for building one's circle of acquaintance in Paris."

"D'you know, there are many interesting people in Paris who don't feel the need to decamp every summer? Some of us even enjoy the relative calm of the city when le Tout Paris are in Biarritz and Deauville."

"Are your interesting people French, or Americans?" Annie felt a flutter of hope.

"Some of each, with a few British and Germans and the odd Scandinavian. Some remnants of Madame Mohl's old salon— how I miss that lovely old eccentric!—but I've come to know some younger folk as well—a good thing at my age, since one's contemporaries are forever dying off. There are even a few habitués of your Cathedral, I believe. Shall we walk a bit?"

They fought over the bill briefly and finally went halves, resuming their eastward stroll down the rue Saint-Louis-en-l'Île, the island's narrow, cobbled main street.

They passed a florist whose wares spilled out into the street in baskets and galvanized buckets, a patisserie, its windows like an edible version of the jeweler's next door, a greengrocer's with its colorful ranks of fruits, a milliner's with its riot of extravagant summer hats. "Now this," said Annie, "is my idea of the real Paris." Catching her reflection in the shop window, she touched her old straw bonnet self-consciously.

"I first grew fond of our Monsieur Debussy's work at Henrietta Reubell's, for instance," said Julia, picking up where she had left off at the café.

"Miss Reubell? Why, she's an American Colonist—"

"But Retta's half-French, which makes all the difference. She attracts a rather fascinating circle. Are you acquainted with her?"

"Acquaintances only. I've seen her some Sundays at the Cathedral. My sister knew her. I believe Clem introduced her to Henry James—they're good friends now, I've heard. But Clem doesn't seem to approve of her."

"If I had marriageable daughters, I'm not sure I would either," Julia said with a sideways smile. "She's considered somewhat of a misleader of youth, particularly of females. I find her charming, intelligent, an excellent conversationalist— she brings that out in others too. And she has a knack for discovering talent. She holds court on Sunday afternoons. She's an heiress, of course," she hesitated a moment and cleared her throat, "but her crowd is a little less—well to do on the whole. Starving artists and such. Should you like to come there with me on Sunday? Or do you share your sister's disapproval?"

Annie thought a moment and smiled. "I haven't any marriageable daughters. Might you procure me an invitation?"

"Forgive me if this inquiry is indelicate—" Julia waited

for Annie to nod encouragement. "Were you serious about improving your physical condition? Your, ah, mobility?"

"I certainly could be," Annie said, nettled, "if I had the slightest idea of where to start."

"If you haven't the energy to move about freely without pain, you'll never be able to enjoy Paris life as you ought. It's a city meant for walking."

Annie sighed as if to confirm her verdict. "I'm afraid it may be too late. My gears have seized up and I don't see how I can get them unstuck."

"Ah, there you're wrong. Look how well you've done on our little walk, even with the cobblestones." It was true; Annie felt looser-limbed than she had in some time, and they had walked all the way across the two islands to the Pont Sully with its splendid view downstream to Notre-Dame and the quais of the Rive Gauche. "And then there's the masculine company angle," Julia added. "Freedom of movement is such an asset to one's social encounters with the opposite sex."

"I've had hardly any of those in years," Annie laughed. "Men, in general, seem to require some business or professional reason to interact with an unattached female. It's amusing, really, since I'm hardly a prime target for prospective adulterers—"

"You'd be surprised, my dear, how many younger men in Paris desire the company of an accomplished woman 'of a certain age,' as they say."

"You must introduce me to some of those—I'm quite unchaperoned now." Annie realized that she hadn't been entirely joking, and felt a flush creeping up her face.

They reached the eastern tip of the island, stopping for a rest on a park bench. "What were—are—the medical issues, exactly?"

"There were complications from the surgery. Adhesions, some nerve damage. Painful spells—"

"Still?"

"Not much to be done, I'm told, except spa-bathing. I can't abide spas. The conversation is so morbid—"

Julia's laugh, Annie noted, had a delightfully mannish quality—deep and hearty. "It would have to be! Illness being the only thing the invalids could be sure to have in common."

"The medicos call them 'organ recitals.' And the food is revolting." Annie shuddered at the memory. "Porridges, gruels, overcooked vegetables, milk puddings—enough of this! You, on the other hand, appear to be in the pink of health. How do you do it?"

Julia smiled and gave a little shrug. "Keep moving, I always say. Find a pleasant companion and take long walks."

"A gentleman companion would be nice," Annie ventured.

They crossed the northern span of the bridge in search of a fiacre. "Miss Reubell's salon, then, for a start," Julia said, "You know she's a Sapphist, don't you?"

"I supposed that was why Clem didn't seem to approve of her. Afraid she might lead one of my nieces astray."

"The Sapphists don't bite, as a rule," Julia replied, "unless you've given indication of interest. But I may know just the gentleman—well, that may be misusing the term—for your purpose." She smiled as if at some private joke. "He has a title of sorts—perhaps he's in the market for a wealthy American himself. You'll probably meet him at Retta's." She waved an arm. "Ici, mon brave homme!" A horse-cab clattered to a stop.

Chapter 2

s she rose and dressed the next morning, Annie felt a twinge of guilt at having left Julia with the not entirely truthful impression that the Crafts had consigned her to Parisian exile. Had she wanted to return to America, she needn't have lived anywhere near them. But over Boston, as over New York, loomed the prospect of being boxed back into the weed-clad persona of Mrs. Robert Gould Shaw, widow of the gallant Civil War colonel. That was bad enough in the American Colony, which didn't seem to know what to do with her otherwise. She wished she were simply Madame Shaw, with no pathetic history attached. Someday, if the friendship with Julia grew, Annie would tell her all this and she might understand.

She wouldn't tell her about George, though. She'd dreamed of him again, her broody, poetic cousin, who had never attempted to tame his dark, Byronic locks and whose contemplative indoor life had left him bony and pale. From childhood, George and

Annie had known each other's quick minds as no one else had; known, too, and loved each other's flaws: his cutting comments about his intellectual inferiors—practically everyone—her prickly resistance to showing any unguarded emotion, her unbridled bookishness. They'd howled with sacrilegious laughter over Patmore's interminable poem, *The Angel in the House*, which everyone else seemed to have gone misty-eyed over.

"A creature you haven't a prayer of becoming, my love," George had told her. "Thank goodness."

However unsuitable as a marriage prospect, George had Annie's heart, and still owned it years after he died—the only man in her life she'd felt understood by, seen by, Rob Shaw not excepted. In their love had been a deep friendship as well as the charm, the thrill of a necessarily concealed romantic connection. Though Rob eventually won her heart, her soul remained her private property.

"We should elope and be done with it," Annie had told George once. "I don't need a fancy wedding."

And then in 1858, when Annie was twenty-three, George's sister Joanna died of a virulent consumption, and all talk of romance and marriage was set aside in deference to her family's grief. Uncle Charles had been inconsolable; George himself, remorseful and subdued, seemed to have lost some vital force.

Hardly had that blow been absorbed when the worst followed—George, too, gone forever, eight months after his sister, from the same cause. Annie, helpless and angry, had watched him dwindle and fade, the flesh falling away until only skeleton and skin remained, the life drained out of him as by some night-stalking, blood-drinking beast.

"We waited too long, Annie love," he tells her toward the end

of it, propped up on a mound of pillows, his voice a raspy whisper.
"Should've whisked you off and married you in '56." His head falls
to the side, and he closes his eyes for a moment, his fingers slackening
around hers. The lids flutter slowly open again and he looks at her
with infinite sadness. "There might've been a child by now. I'd have
liked that..." A tear that would have mortified him six months
earlier rolls unchecked down the deep furrow the disease has carved
on his cheek.

Annie turns away, unable to reply.

After he's gone, she tells no one of their love, their secret engagement,
their blighted hopes. The sapphire ring he gave her when she accepted
him still sits in a velvet-lined box, taken out and polished and, years
later, occasionally cried over.

She was startled from her reverie by the clatter of footsteps
on the staircase, and left her flat to investigate. Monsieur le
Poste, as she called him to his apparent delight, beamed at her
beneath his dark blue képi. "Madame Shaw! Je vous trouve seule
aujourd'hui?"

"Oui, enfin seule, monsieur!"

It was an old joke between them. He paid court to her as "la
veuve Américaine riche et belle de mes rêves," but so frequently
found "en famille" that his pursuit was impossible. He had
the twinkly eyes and blond whiskers of a mouse-hero from a
children's tale, as well as "un petit chou" of a wife and a handful of
children near the Marché St-Quentin. She gave him a flirtatious
smile, one fine eyebrow arched. If she was not a beautiful widow
now, she was a well-to-do one, and if he cared to dream of that,
he was welcome.

"Des billets-doux pour vous—" He held out a bundle of
letters, something from her American bankers on the rue Scribe;

a typically thick epistle from her mother-in-law Sarah Shaw who lived with her philanthropist daughter Josephine Lowell in New York; a note from Clem, hastily scrawled and postmarked from Le Havre, and another on fine cream stationery with "the favor of a reply requested" prominently inscribed. An invitation?

Sarah Shaw's letters always induced a state of mild trepidation, with their invariable attempts to draw her into Sarah's wallowings in the role of Spartan mother who had sacrificed her only son on the altar of Abolition. It galled Annie that she had fulfilled Mother Shaw's gloomy prophecy that she would never remarry, though not for lack of interest nor undying devotion to her martyred husband, as Sarah still chose to think.

You should come home to New York and live with us, dear Annie, the new letter said. *You are much too good to live among the French, I am sure—Effie is so preoccupied with her charitable committees that I am quite starved for company, and dear Lotta would benefit from the influence of an aunt who has seen something of the world.* Annie's sister-in-law, an industrious practitioner of Good Works, had herself been widowed by the War, but left with a daughter for solace. Goodness, Carlotta would be twenty-eight already…

Saint-Gaudens' progress with Robert's monument is positively glacial, the letter continued. *With Rob's poor widow among us, he might feel obliged to devote more effort to the project.* Saint-Gaudens' studio was only a few blocks south of Mother Shaw's Manhattan townhouse. Annie imagined, with a shiver, her mother-in-law's damp breath on the poor man's neck, and gave silent thanks for her own decision to remain in Paris. The prospect of Mother Shaw's ravenous appetite for one's company was too fearsome to contemplate.

The ivory letter requesting a reply came from Mrs. Kernochan, a New York heiress and stalwart of the Dorcas Society who had called on Annie with a trio of fellow Cathedral ladies a few days after the Crafts' departure. Charitably intended, and no doubt undertaken at the behest of a guilt-ridden Clem, it had been an awkward little gathering, with her sister's family almost the exclusive topic of conversation. The visit had pulled Annie away from happy immersion in von Humboldt's *Cosmos*, a gift from James. The ladies cheerfully professed ignorance of the eminent scientist and explorer, and with no vote and no husband to influence, Annie could not share their preoccupation with the forthcoming American elections.

I've always found Annie Shaw a little...odd, haven't you? she pictured one of her visitors telling another as they rode home. And nods all round in the carriage.

In the course of the visit, Mrs. Kernochan had mentioned a distant connection to Roland Burwell, scion of a Georgia cotton plantation, a gallant but unsuccessful suitor of Annie's both before the War and afterwards when she was a Union widow. Soon after her second refusal, Roland had returned to his family's plantation, married, become a father, and in time been widowed himself. He had sent Annie Christmas greetings at irregular intervals in recent years, which she had reciprocated politely without much thought. Roland, Mrs. Kernochan revealed, had still made occasional inquiries "about dear Mrs. Shaw" until his death this past February. When she and the other ladies had taken their leave after making dubious assurances of frequent visits and of Annie's continued welcome in the Dorcas Society, their hostess had retreated to her study and given way to a small and inexplicable storm of weeping. Though she hadn't loved the knightly Roland Burwell, his death saddened her.

Today's letter from Mrs. Kernochan introduced the younger of Roland's sons, one Thomas Jackson Burwell, newly arrived in Paris to study art, who wished to do himself the honor of calling upon Mrs. Robert Gould Shaw at a time convenient to her. "I rely in this request, dear Mrs. Shaw," she wrote, "on the knowledge of your friendly acquaintance with my late cousin Roland, of whose sad passing I informed you at our last meeting."

Curiosity compelled an affirmative response. Annie rose with her little bundle and went to her escritoire to find pen and paper. She wrote a reply and rang for the concierge.

She read Mother Shaw's letter again. She could not think of living in New York as long as Sarah Shaw was there. Besides, she'd heard, it was much changed from her childhood and her father's heyday—overrun with nouveaux-riches who had built huge vulgar mansions up and down Fifth Avenue, and with ragged swarms of immigrants from the most backward corners of the globe. And how to escape entanglement in the Good Works sure to be urged upon her by Mother Shaw and Effie Lowell?

Paris, then! It was fear she'd been feeling, not loneliness—fear of having to make something new of herself, and of not having the slightest idea of what it should be. The honorable status of war hero's widow, and of invalid, had been her identity for so long, sparing her the necessity of choice. Perhaps a Sunday afternoon among Paris bohemians would open a new path forward. And the aspiring young artist from Georgia, Jackson Burwell: how agreeable it would be to make some introductions for him, once she knew some artists herself.

But here came her housekeeper Adèle, her halo of black curls accented by her madras *tignon*, a fresh baguette protruding from a round basket on her arm covered with a blue-and-white cloth. The kitchen was already filling with the aromas of good strong French coffee and efflorescent cheese from the Marché de Passy. And was she smelling croissants?

The sculpted features softened into a wide smile at the sight of her. "Voilà, Madame—j'ai déjà trouvé des framboises!—" A native of Martinique, Adèle at that moment looked like the goddess Pomona, pulling the cloth back to reveal tiny nubbly spheres of scarlet raspberries, and larger, smoother ones of orange, bronze and pale green. Annie reached in and plucked a perfectly ripe nectarine, a green leaf still on its stem. It exploded like juicy fireworks on her tongue.

"Oh, that's heavenly. And are those what I think they are?" Annie pointed to a white paper bag. Adèle extracted two warm, crisp croissants and placed them on plates with curls of butter and tiny ramekins of raspberry confiture. She poured a cup of coffee for Annie and, by long habit and permission, one for herself.

Annie gestured for her to sit. "Tell me, Adèle. What kinds of fruits do they grow in Martinique?"

Chapter 3

confirmed smoker, Miss Henrietta Reubell scorned the usual rules against tobacco in one's salon. A blue-gray miasma hung over the room, a beautiful *salle* with turquoise brocade chairs and pier glasses augmenting the light from long windows. Gold velvet draperies matched the luxurious sofas.

Conversation buzzed in French and English, amicably argumentative, producing an agreeably cacophonous effect. A gray-haired, dissolute-looking fellow perching on the arm of a sofa tousled the hair of a young blond man holding forth to a circle that included two short-haired women in trousers. One of his male listeners had kindly dark eyes and a pointed mustache. Goodness, it was the poet Mallarmé! Annie recognized him from his photograph on the frontispiece of his collected works. What should one say, if one were introduced? No doubt he heard gushings of "I adored *The Afternoon of a Faun*" every day.

Her hostess was easy to spot, with a topknot of reddish-blonde hair that gave her an air of height when in fact she had only an inch or so on the diminutive Annie. She wore shadow-striped turquoise silk and large rings on all her fingers. Nothing of the virago about her despite her reputation, unless one counted a not unpleasant raspiness in her voice.

She took Annie's hands warmly in hers. "*Dear* Mrs. Shaw! I'm so pleased that Julia persuaded you to join us." Julia smiled and twitched an eyebrow. "I've thought of you often since your sister left. Henry James was asking about you in his last letter, and now I'll have something to tell him. He's always thought you quite interesting, you know," she added, registering Annie's surprise.

"I was merely his friend's sister, as far as I knew. Why on earth—?" Annie felt her cheeks coloring.

"'How a woman goes on—after a tragedy like hers,' he said." Henry's brother Wilky, Rob's adjutant in the 54th, had been badly wounded in the assault on Fort Wagner and had died young without ever recovering his health. Almost as tragic as her own Rob's story. But why would Mr. James wonder particularly about how a *woman* would go on after a tragedy? Could it be so different from his own experience of bereavement?

Miss Reubell swiped two wine glasses from a passing waiter and handed them to her new arrivals. "Your Comte is here, Julia, back from settling his Alsatian estates." She waved them toward a tallish, powerfully built man in a ruby smoking-jacket, his elbow resting casually on the white marble fireplace. "Bertrand! Madame Greene est arrivée!"

He excused himself from an older man and beamed at the two of them, moving vigorously and swiftly through knots of guests to join them. Late thirties, early forties at most—*too young for me*, an unbidden thought flashed. A wavy lock of light brown hair fell over one eye when he bowed to kiss Julia's hand. His head was large, the facial features full and mobile, even boyish, with an almost androgynous softening around the jawline and lightly cleft chin. Julia raised him by his chin and kissed him on both cheeks, turning to her new friend.

"Madame Shaw—Comte Bertrand de Leiningen, my artist friend, and the closest thing I have to a scapegrace nephew."

He grinned and took Annie's proffered hand. "Enchanté, madame. Everyone should have one of those, don't you think?" He bent and brushed her hand with his lips. His hand was fleshy though firm, adorned on its fourth finger with an onyx seal-ring.

"Even if they're not actually related," Julia agreed. "Besides being a painter, Annie, Bertrand instructs the young ladies of the Académie Julian."

"I have male students too," the Comte protested. "Though in general *their* work is less...ambitious." There was a hint of accent in his excellent English, rather a blurry "continental" than the French one might expect. A touch of German, perhaps.

"Shaw," he mused, gazing at Annie. "Wasn't that your nom de jeune fille, Madame Greene?"

"Mrs. Shaw is my nephew's widow. We're recently reacquainted, I'm happy to say."

His glance swept Annie's bare left hand, his eyebrows rising in an inquiring fashion which for no reason she could name induced a tug in the belly reminiscent of her response to Debussy's moonlight melody.

"It was nearly thirty years ago," she blurted.

His face was all sympathy, suddenly. "How young you must have been—ah, le jeune héros, ce neveu-là tué dans ce gaspillage horrible d'une guerre?" He turned to Julia Greene, who nodded, then back to Annie. "Et vous êtes une Parisienne?"

"I've lived in Paris for some time," she said, barely managing a smile and suppressing a flash of annoyance at being introduced once more as a Civil War widow. Comte Bertrand's view of that war as a ghastly waste resonated with her own, but she had met no one who spoke of it so bluntly on short acquaintance. "Someday I hope to qualify as a true Parisienne. I understand you're newly returned to town, Monsieur le Comte."

"My condolences on your father's death," Miss Reubell said.

For a moment Bertrand looked as if he did not know who was being spoken to. "Oh! Thank you. The old fellow had been tottering on the lip of the grave for years. Never the same after Maman died. I sha'n't miss him greatly, I confess—he never approved of me."

Miss Reubell tapped him on the wrist with her fan. "And who could blame him? If you'll excuse me—" She went to talk with a large elderly man overflowing an armchair.

"Forgive me, mesdames, I must have sounded callous. But several weeks of winding up the family estate—what's left of it—have left me in a less agreeable frame of mind than usual."

"You needn't apologize, Monsieur," Annie said. "My mother passed on four years ago, and only now are we filing away the last of the estate papers. It was even more of a trial when my father died—he being an art collector whose tastes had—well, gone out of fashion."

The eyebrows rose again. "An art collector!"

She felt Julia's hand on her wrist. "Annie, dear, Retta is calling us over. Will you excuse us, Bertrand?"

The venerable gentleman seated beneath Miss Reubell began to heave himself up, but she motioned him back. "I'm sure the ladies will forgive your not rising, Henri—Madame Greene, Madame Shaw, I present to you my friend the poet Monsieur Legrand." The portly, amiable-looking fellow wore a prodigious set of whiskers that made Annie think of General Burnside, in command at Antietam where Rob's first blood had been drawn. He made as deep a bow as a sitting man could and glowed as though he'd just been introduced to two of the three Graces.

A balding man with an enormous nose and aggressively waxed moustaches sprang from his spot next to M. Legrand and bowed to them. "As for me, Mesdames, I am a firm—Americanophile, is that the term?"

"You're Jean Béraud, the painter, aren't you?" exclaimed Julia in delight.

No one could have appeared a more quintessential Frenchman. He clicked his heels and bowed. "À votre service!"

"Ah, you're the one—" Annie began. He had done a large painting of the Christmas congregation outside the American Cathedral on the rue de l'Alma, with a hint of satire in his rendering of the overdressed American ladies awaiting their carriages. She had found it enormously amusing. "Should you like to go to America, Monsieur Béraud? Your talents in rendering the haute monde would find much scope in New York these days."

"Alors, I leave American themes to the distinguished Monsieur Bartholdi," the painter said with a smile. "You know of him, perhaps?"

"I visited his studio when the Liberty was under construction. We had a most interesting conversation—"

Several heads turned in Annie's direction.

"I found him charming, but perhaps not so, ah, aware of the realities of liberty as currently practiced in America."

"And what of the work itself, Madame Shaw?" Comte Bertrand had perched on the arm of Legrand's armchair.

"Magnificent, of course—a tour de force in every sense—"

"—but?—"

"I told him that it must reflect our country's aspirations rather than its accomplishments." Her hearers looked a little shocked— Bertrand, however, grinned and raised an admiring eyebrow. "I hope that someday soon I shall be proved wrong," she added.

Annie had surveyed the great statue in progress at Bartholdi's workshop near the Parc Monceau, before it was disassembled and shipped to New York. Its title, "Liberty Enlightening the World," struck her as sadly ironic. Her colored friends and correspondents, survivors and widows of the 54th Massachusetts, kept her abreast of the realities of daily life for Negroes—living in poverty and subjection, harassed by authorities, reviled and barred from full citizenship—and not just in the South. She treasured those friendships. Her brief time with Rob and the regiment, however opposed she had been to his taking the command, had engendered a deep sympathy with the men, an appreciation for their humanity and the daily struggles of their existence. For all her fervent abolitionism, that was something Sarah Shaw would never understand; her work was done, she believed, when the slaves were freed. When Annie saw Negroes on the streets of Paris, striding confidently with heads high as they still could not do in America, she still scanned their features for someone she might have known in long-ago days.

Julia waved away a plate of tiny puff-pastries. "Bartholdi's Alsatian, isn't he, Bertrand?"

"From my birthplace, in fact—Colmar. He casts a long shadow among his compatriot artists. Even in bronze, his command of expression and emotion is beyond that of *most* portrait artists," the Comte replied, "present company excepted, naturellement."

Béraud shrugged and smiled.

"You have to know the subject's milieu to make a good portrait, wouldn't you say, Monsieur Béraud?" Miss Reubell said. "That's why your Parisian depictions are so delightfully apropos. America would be another matter altogether."

"Béraud lurks for hours in taxicabs to get his street scenes," said the poet Legrand with a wheezy chuckle that rather endeared him to Annie. "For not being a Frenchman, Sargent managed to get *you* right, don't you think, Retta?" He gestured to a doorway beyond which, Annie assumed, there must be a portrait of Miss Reubell.

The lady shrugged. "It's only an aquarelle, and he's a friend. And we're both part American, after all. Madame Greene here, *she* would be a worthy subject for him—but I don't expect him back in Paris soon."

"Oh, heaven's sake, Retta, who'd want a portrait of this old biddy?" In her chartreuse figured-silk dress—a color most women would not dare attempt—and puff-sleeved over jacket, no one could look less like an old biddy than the slender Julia Greene. "Now Mrs. Shaw, here, has a face that would interest a portraitist."

Annie laughed and shook her head. Béraud eyed her, his chin between finger and thumb. "Oui, en effet," he said at length. "Des pommettes remarquables. Et les lèvres... except that it is difficult for the painter when the sitter does not wish to be seen."

She flushed and dipped her chin as if to prove his point.

"I quite agree about the cheekbones," Comte Bertrand crossed to her, and she felt the momentary brush of a hand on her shoulder. A man's touch, fleeting, spontaneous. How long had it been? "As for the reluctant sitter—portraiture is a form of seduction, don't you think, Béraud?"

"Your Sargent seems to practice that, *certainement*," Béraud replied, smiling. "But it must never proceed to actual love, or the work is ruined."

"You're telling me you can't paint someone you're in love with?" Comte Bertrand's tone was ironic. "Many masterpieces would have been lost if that were true."

"Ah, oui! I did not say I have not done so. But my work is society, not the individual, and I would defy anyone to identify the object of my affections in any particular work."

If Béraud's aim with this remark was to provoke his listeners' curiosity about his love-life, he succeeded—though his dandified Paris flâneur type had never appealed to Annie. She found herself more curious about the Comte Bertrand's. She was finding the notion of being seduced into yielding up a portrait more intriguing than was strictly proper, and wondered what form it typically took. Perhaps she was simply starved for attention.

"One must, I think," Comte Bertrand was saying, "feel love for one's subject—or at least some affection—to do a portrait full justice."

Annie thought of Sargent's infamous portrait of Madame Gautreau in her low-cut Félix gown. The coldness in that depiction said nothing to her of affection, much less love. "Perhaps," she ventured, "all that's needed is that the artist finds something *attractive* in the sitter, if only visually—even if he dislikes him or her. I'm thinking of the Sargent from the '84 Salon."

Comte Bertrand narrowed his eyes thoughtfully and

nodded. "I wonder if the scandale that provoked had to do with his obvious dislike of his subject in that instance. What came to me when I looked at it was his desire to—expose her."

"Almost to the point of violation, might one say," Béraud agreed. "Forgive me, mesdames."

"*Desire* is the operative word, I think," said Miss Reubell. "Men often don't feel the slightest affection for their objects of desire."

"And what of women in that regard?" Béraud said.

"We're as capable of desire as any man," said Julia, "but perhaps less inclined to separate it from the warmer and deeper feelings that should accompany it."

"What I saw in Sargent's painting," Annie said, overcoming her hesitation, "was judgment—an unfavorable one—of a woman who acts on her desires."

The Comte Bertrand nodded rapidly. "And a woman who is unusual—they say—in being capable of the separation of feeling of which Madame Greene speaks."

"So, how does Sargent feel about his Dr. Pozzi?" M. Legrand challenged.

Béraud chuckled. "A handsome devil in that red robe, no denying it."

"How could anyone doubt that the artist of that one is in love with his subject?" said Comte Bertrand. "It radiates from the canvas. And not just because of all the red, which was a choice of genius. I wish I'd done it."

"Perhaps his portrayal of La Gautreau came from jealousy," said Miss Reubell. "She and Pozzi had got farther with each other than Sargent did with either, on dit."

Julia and Annie exchanged looks. Béraud hastened to say,

"Sargent's affection for the subject is apparent in his portrait of *you*, Miss Retta."

She laughed and shrugged. "Then it's rather unfair of me to be gossiping about him, I suppose." A waiter handed around a tray of smoked salmon canapés.

"Didn't I meet Pozzi here a couple of years back?" the portly Legrand said from the depth of his armchair. "He made quite an impression on *some* of your female guests."

Miss Reubell washed down her smoked salmon with a healthy swig of Sancerre. "He's moving in more rarefied company these days—do you know Dr. Pozzi, Madame Shaw?"

"We've, ah, met once or twice," Annie replied, deciding not to add that Dr. Pozzi had seen a good deal more of her than she of him. It was he who had removed the hideous tumor a dozen years ago and, she was convinced, saved her from a miserable end. Charming and handsome, certainly, but more important at the time were his reputation and reassuring demeanor. *Repose en paix, Madame Shaw. J'ai fait beaucoup de procédures de ce genre.* One vivid memory came back to her in dreams, of his great dark eyes looming over her as the chloroform was taking hold. She'd felt as if she were floating softly down into warm, fathomless pools.

"I've wondered," she went on, "whether there's a difference in quality between a portrait the artist takes the initiative to do—of a subject he admires, or loves, or has sought out—and one for which he's been commissioned."

"An excellent question!" said Béraud. "Yet I am not sure the artist himself is qualified to answer that. What do you think, de Leiningen?"

"In an ideal world—which ours is not—the two coincide," said

Comte Bertrand. "For me, the artist's relationship with his subject is more important to its success than the painting's genesis."

From behind them, a distinctively American voice said, "What's all this? Do I see Annie Shaw, of all people, holding forth among the artists?"

Annie rose rapidly and turned to face the speaker, whose voice was all too familiar.

"Alice Mason. Fancy meeting you here after all these years."

Alice was a magnificent figure, tall and regal in a purple brocade afternoon gown not unlike, Annie thought, the gown in which Sargent had painted her. Fascinated gazes, male and female, followed her around the room.

Retta Reubell appeared at Annie's elbow. "I was going to introduce you, but apparently you've met."

"Long, long since," said Alice Mason, in a tone suggesting it would have been impolite to inquire as to exactly how long. "Annie and I were practically playmates, back in our Lenox days." She gave Annie a rapid up-and-down appraisal. Despite herself, Annie flushed. She had acceded reluctantly to Julia's suggestion that she wear something "a little fancier than your usual," and found an old dress of her mother's, a brown silk with black lace trim, old-fashioned in cut and perhaps a touch too short in length. Brown was not her best color. Such details would never escape Alice's eye.

"I heard your sister and brother-in-law had gone back to America," Alice said. "What on earth would keep someone like you in Paris on her own?" Her glance flickered down to Annie's hands. "Still no husband, I see. Evidently even a fortune can only get an invalid so far. Or are you still mourning your boy soldier?"

Out of the corner of her eye, Annie saw Bertrand's look of

admiration at Alice's magnificent figure change rapidly to one of bland neutrality.

"I'm quite well, thank you, and I dare say I've moved on from being widowed in the War as much as you have, Alice," Annie said sweetly. "You have several grandchildren, I hear?"

Alice scowled but recovered rapidly. "On my way back to Britain to see them all. My daughter married well..."

"One of the Dollar Princesses, wasn't she? An English lord?"

"Lord Balfour of Balbirnie, as it happens," said Alice, a touch of frost in her tone. "A Scotsman, with a country estate in Fifeshire."

"Always lovely to have one of those to go to."

"Shame you don't have one yourself. I heard you sold Vent Fort to the Morgans."

"You're remarkably well informed." Thanks to the Reverend Morgan, dean of the American Cathedral, Annie had reluctantly sold the Haggertys' Lenox estate, with all its memories, to the dean's brother George and their cousin Sarah, sister of the tycoon J.P Morgan. "Speaking of Morgans, do you still have your Monte Carlo place, or did that end when Mr. Morgan Senior passed away? My condolences—I hadn't your London address at the time."

Alice's liaison with Junius Spencer Morgan had been the talk of the American Colony over several seasons, and even Annie, for whom most gossip was a bore, had been intrigued to hear of her old schoolmate's involvement with one of the wealthiest men in America.

"Oh, Monte Carlo. It's overrun now, with American nouveaux riches. Don't you have a place near there? Or is that your sister's as well?"

"I have a home in Cannes," Annie said, "My sister's never been to it."

She had once thought of Alice as a friend, but her Washington sojourn after the war, when she and Clem had stayed with Alice and Senator Sumner, had put an end to that.

"You must come and see me if you ever come to London," Alice was saying. "I agree with Henry James—London's not crawling with Americans as Paris always seems to be." Her gaze fell on Bertrand, who was regarding her now with reluctant admiration. "Aren't you going to introduce me to your friend?"

"I have seen and admired Sargent's portrait of you, Madame," Bertrand said. "An introduction would be superfluous on my part. I am, however, honored to make your acquaintance."

"Comte Bertrand de Leiningen, who is himself a portrait painter," Annie began. Bertrand bent over Alice's hand as he had Annie's. Annie felt a stab of disappointment.

"Really? And a Comte too. Perhaps you could improve on that Sargent. I thought he made me look like a murderess."

"I'd always thought Sargent was known for capturing the essence of his subjects. In that instance I was evidently mistaken."

Annie turned away to stifle a smile. When she turned back, Alice had moved on to another part of the room.

Two men stood framed in the salon door.

"Pardon," said Retta Reubell, smiling and heading toward them through the parting crowd. Annie broke away in turn and followed her progress. The younger of the two, who stood hesitant in the doorway, was a Negro, though light-skinned; his race had not been obvious at first glance. He had a long, thin face, ascetic and scholarly, and wore rimless glasses and a neat Van Dyke beard.

"Mr. Anshutz!" said Miss Reubell. "I'm so pleased you've brought your friend!"

The distinguished-looking white man to whom she had spoken inclined his head. "Mam'zelle Reubell, may I present Henry Tanner, who came here last year from Philadelphia. We knew each other at the Academy there, and we find we're both studying at Julian's—"

"Mrs. Shaw, come and meet a pair of your compatriots!" Miss Reubell put an arm around Annie and guided her into the little group. "So, this is the gentleman you were telling me about, Tom—welcome to my little Palace of Art, Mr. Tanner. Mrs. Shaw—Mr. Anshutz and Mr. Tanner, two of our American art pilgrims."

Annie held her hand out to the young Negro and he took it with a brief, light touch. She put her other hand over his. "I'm happy to know you, Mr. Tanner. We've just been talking with the Comte de Leiningen, who I understand teaches at Julian's?"

The two faces lit up in smiles. "Comte Bertrand's here?" Tanner said.

"Over there, talking with Monsieur Béraud. Have you heard of his work?"

"Béraud? I should say so!" said Anshutz. "His street-scenes capture the very heart of Paris. What d'you say to that, Henry—will you introduce us, Mam'zelle Reubell?" Young Mr. Tanner's skin was light enough for his blushes to register, and Annie wondered whether he might be scared off by too warm an enthusiasm and too many introductions at once.

Miss Reubell handed each man a glass of wine from a passing maid. "Do come with me," she said, "we'll toast to your studies and your success! Mrs. Shaw, will you bring fresh glasses for yourself and me?" She towed her new guests over and made introductions. Annie followed with their two wine glasses. Something in that little request made her feel like one of Miss Reubell's regulars, and wish that it might prove so.

Chapter 4

ho was that horrid woman you were talking to?' Julia Greene asked on their walk home. "I take it you'd known one another for some time."

They had refused several offers of carriage rides; the air was sweet and cool, the afternoon light golden and crystalline after the fug and intensity of the crowded salon. They decided to cross the Seine at the Pont des Invalides, walk along the Quai d'Orsay, and re-cross on the Pont de l'Alma for its fine view of the Tour Eiffel and the golden dome of the Invalides before catching their separate trams for home. Annie, her head still fizzing from wine and conversation, was feeling the strain of the walk, but pressed on; it was too lovely a day to ride.

"That was Alice Mason, the belle of Lenox back in my youth, and the bane of my existence for a time. I hope she's not planning to spend much time in Paris."

"Alice Mason as in Sumner?"

"The same. She has a nasty habit of moving in on any male in her orbit, particularly if he's showing an interest in oneself. Friendly with Henry James, she tells me."

"Well, *that's* not likely to do her much good. Wait—wasn't she

Junius Morgan's *inamorata*? Shame he got himself killed in that carriage accident—I wonder if they'd have married."

"He'd had six years to do it after his wife died, but it never happened. Didn't want to end up like poor Senator Sumner, I suppose. I heard he left Alice something in his will, though."

"For services rendered, I dare say," said Julia. "She looks like a man-eater. And seemed to feel a need to interrupt your *tete-a-tete* with Bertrand before he got too interested in you—"

"Surely he wasn't interested in me," Annie blushed again. "What is he a Comte of?"

"He doesn't much care for the title," Julia replied. "Some hold-over from the Holy Roman Empire—Alsace was part of that. Once you've met him another time or two, it'll just be 'Bertrand.'"

"Is it a good idea, do you think—going to his studio?" The invitation as he walked them out from Reubell's had been casually delivered, and seemed to Annie's ear sincere enough, though she wondered if it were a sort of restitution for Alice Mason's taunts.

"To see the Paris artist in his natural habitat, complete with a demimondaine model or two? You did say you hoped to become a true Parisienne."

"Well, I must say Retta's salon was an eye-opening experience. Thank you for taking me there, my dear—I hope I'll be invited back."

"Oh, I think you fit right in," Julia smiled, inducing a wave of pleasure in Annie's heart.

"Speaking of fitting, Julia, I'd welcome your advice in the matter of couture. I looked like a dowdy sparrow compared with Alice in her finery."

They stopped in the middle of the Pont des Invalides and

rested their forearms on the parapet, watching the busy bateaux mouches glide to and fro under its arches. "The navy blue and the brown I've seen you in are, since you asked—on the dull side. Colors worn by someone who, to echo Monsieur Béraud, does not wish to be seen—"

"But I do!" It came out as almost a wail. "I've no one left to blend in with. The ladies at Reubell's—well, the ones who weren't dressed à la garconne, anyway—wore such charming patterns and colors—"

"It's only in the avian world that the female plumage is drab—and a less severe *coiffure* would enhance your fine features. They're right about the cheekbones. Your eyes change color, you must have been told that—sometimes gray, other times more green or blue. Remarkable. As to your dimensions—I should say, if you'll forgive me, the concern is rather that you move like an invalid—and don't move enough. It makes for a less graceful silhouette." She paused, watching her friend absorb the confusion of compliment and critique. Annie opened her mouth to protest, but Julia was quite right, and after all, she *had* asked.

"I dare say it's a pattern you fell into when you *were* one. I wish these doctors would realize their job is to restore the patient to full vigor. With women, they think their work is done if they sew her up and she doesn't die of infection afterwards. She could languish on a fainting-couch for the rest of her life, and it wouldn't trouble them a bit."

"But they saved my life—"

"And a good thing too—but they didn't save your health. What do you know about Swedish gymnastics?"

Annie hunched farther over on the parapet. "They sound

like something practiced by Swedes with a thirst for self-punishment."

"You kindly remarked on my prodigious mobility for one of my ancient vintage," Julia said, "not in so many words, but your meaning was clear. I attribute it to following the precepts of Dr. Henrik Kellgren."

"He's not that Swedenborgian fellow, is he?"

"Goodness, no! This is about the physical, not the metaphysical. Though no doubt there's a connection—it's hard to be in good spirits if one's body is suffering."

"So much for the 'cheerful invalid' theory," Annie said. A querulous-looking specimen rattled past them in a Bath chair along the bridge's walkway, pushed by an unhappy-looking young nurse. He looked up sharply and frowned as if Annie had been talking about him. She beamed at him, and they clattered on.

"No such thing," Julia said crisply. "Play-acting martyr, is all *that* is. There is a good deal of hard work involved, and it's quite uncomfortable early on. But the cost pales in comparison to the benefits."

"If they can help me move better with less pain and even—" Annie hesitated, "look a bit slimmer and straighter, I'm willing to consider them. It's tiresome being short. It takes so much less of life's bounty to turn one stout and frumpy."

"It is rather unfair, at that. What did you think of Mr. Tanner?"

Annie turned from watching a pair of racing shells glide below the bridge. "Sensitive, serious—perhaps, having grown up Negro in America, he's afraid to be at ease. As if he can't allow himself to believe that it's different here for gens de couleur. I'd like to see his work."

"According to Bertrand, he 'likes his Bible'—and folk-scenes from his childhood," her companion said. "Quite good technically, but old-fashioned subject matter."

"Which may be an advantage in some quarters, as far as prospective sales are concerned. The South, for instance—as long as they don't find out he's black."

"He's had a lot of training already, and he's a diligent student, says Bertrand. Anshutz told me he was the solitary Negro in a class of two hundred at the Pennsylvania Academy."

"In this day and age, in the cradle of our democracy? Abominable. I'd thought Philadelphia one of our more enlightened American cities."

"Sadly, it may well be," Julia replied. "Another reason I choose to live in Paris."

Tanner's vulnerability and pride had brought to Annie's mind some of the younger members of the 54th: the direct gaze, the stiff back that spoke of refusal to be condescended to. What if he did 'like his Bible'? Any artist up through the Baroque must perforce have 'liked his Bible,' that being the acceptable subject matter; nonetheless, many delivered up dramatic, compelling scenes without a grain of sugar in them. Annie found some of Caravaggio's, for instance, positively sinister. She liked the Bible herself. Though she hadn't necessarily joined in the socializing which at times seemed the main reason for the existence of the American Cathedral, she was a faithful communicant there.

"Well, I look forward to seeing his work. And your Comte Bertrand's as well." They resumed their walk northward.

"Oh, he's not *my* Comte Bertrand. He's not anybody's anything, as far as I know."

"Speaking of which," Annie said, "you must come and meet

this Jackson Burwell I was telling you about. The son of my late admirer. He's due for tea on Wednesday."

"Named for Stonewall?"

Annie sighed. "He must have been. They'll never let it go, I'm afraid."

Chapter 5

hen young Jackson Burwell presented himself for inspection and tea, it could have been Roland come back to life as he was in Annie's youth. Fair as his father, with the same Apollonian curls and air of gentility—though taller, and slighter of frame.

"I'm honored to meet you at last, Mrs. Shaw." He took the hand she offered and smiled at her with keen interest. "My father spoke of you often."

"I was so sorry to hear of his death. Were you very attached to him?"

"We all were, ma'am, particularly since my mother died so young." She introduced him to Julia Greene and they took tea in Annie's little library. He delved happily into a pear tart, drank three cups of tea, and told them of a small flat he hoped to rent in the rue des Saints-Pères, which was to let for only a few francs.

"You mean to stay a while in Paris?" Julia asked.

"Yes, ma'am, I've been dreaming my whole life of coming here." The Georgia drawl was in evidence, but his diction was perfect. "I'm an artist—an aspiring artist, anyway. Along with every other American my age in Paris, I guess!" The blue eyes surreptitiously scanning Annie's bookshelves held a spark of humor that had been missing in his father's.

Perhaps Roland had told him of the Haggertys' once-famous art collection. Since the nouveaux riches of Annie's generation had begun acquiring European Old Masters wholesale, Ogden Haggerty's Cranches and Doughtys and Cropseys now languished in the Manhattan cellars of Knoedler's, to which his daughters had reluctantly consigned them after the sale of Vent Fort to the George Morgans. Annie wondered if Jackson had ever seen a Cropsey.

"I was given an introduction to Mr. Carolus-Duran," the boy was telling Julia. "I'm hoping for a place at the École des Beaux Arts."

Annie smiled. "You've been practicing your pronunciation."

"Yes, ma'am, but then I grew up with French. My mother's people were from Louisiana—one of the old Creole families."

"How long is it since your mamma passed on?"

The cheerful face clouded. "It'll be ten years ago next month. And Father left us this past February, as you know. Died in his sleep, which was a blessing. He hadn't been well for a couple of years. That's why I asked to see you."

His words began coming out in a rush. "I think Papa knew he wasn't long for the world. About this time last year, he sat me down and said, 'Jackson, there's a thing I'd like you to do for me, when the Lord calls me home.' And I said, 'Papa, Edgar's the eldest'—that's my older brother—'maybe you should be talking to him?' And he said 'no, if you really mean to go to Paris and be an artist, there's an errand I'd like you to attend to, when you get there.'" He looked momentarily sheepish, which Julia took as a cue to excuse herself.

Jackson leaned forward with elbows on knees and hands steepled together. "Papa told me, in confidence, about a Northern lady he'd paid court to, back before the War Between the States, and then again after. A lady he couldn't get out of his mind. He told me that a couple of years after Mama died, he set out looking for you in New York. Mr. Draper, Mr. William Draper, told him you'd gone to live in Paris."

Annie sat back in surprise. Her cousin Will Draper had never mentioned the contact in their desultory correspondence. "I never heard from him. Your father, I mean."

Jackson sighed. "I believe he got, ah, timorous about trying to renew the acquaintance. He talked about visiting Paris, but, see, his sister, my aunt Alice—I think you knew her—was so ill, he didn't feel he should leave her. Oh, she's still alive," he said, catching Annie's concerned look, "though an invalid. She was widowed in the War. Her husband was an old family friend, a major in the Twenty-Fifth Georgia, died in the defense of Atlanta—" he paused.

"So many promising young men lost on both sides," Annie said kindly. "Your father was in that regiment, wasn't he?"

Young Burwell's face brightened. "You have an excellent memory, Mrs. Shaw. He was an aide-de-camp to General Henderson. That's what kept him from getting shot, he always said."

"Your aunt—had she any children?"

"Well, that's the really sad thing, ma'am—twin boys, born in 1864—but one died as a baby, not long after his daddy, and the other wasn't but four or five, and she lost him to diphtheria. She lives with my brother and his family now."

"Will you give her my regards, when you write? She was a

sweet young lady, and I enjoyed your family's visits. They were quite frequent—back before the war." Roland Burwell, when he came calling on Annie in Washington after the war, had not mentioned his sister's tragedies.

Annie recalled Alice as a shy, fair-haired young girl of sixteen, on one of the Burwells' last visits to the Haggertys and Kneelands, not quite able to conceal her tender feelings for George Kneeland. Both families, ignorant of Annie and George's love, had hoped for a romance between them.

"*Simpering plantation belles aren't my style,*" George had said unkindly when Annie teased him on the subject. "*Neither are dynastic alliances with slaveowners, and besides, I'm spoken for.*" He'd drawn her into his arms...Jackson's voice pierced the fog of memory.

"Why, she asked me to do the same, ma'am, if I was to see you here. And my father—not long before he passed, he gave me this, and asked me to give it to you, if I should meet you on my travels." Jackson reached into a breast pocket and brought out an envelope. "Perhaps you'd rather read it later, Miz Shaw—"

She took it from him, reached for a letter-opener, and slit the envelope open, donning a pair of reading-glasses. She smiled at Jackson, who looked as if he were awaiting a revelation.

My dear Mrs. Shaw, began Roland Burwell's letter from the grave.

I hope you will forgive a dying man's presumption in thus addressing you. Having learned from your cousin Mr. Draper of your long residence in Paris, I make bold to commend to you my younger son Jackson, by whose hand you will have received this missive.

My approaching end bids me speak plainly in expressing for you, dear Mrs. Shaw, the highest regard and the most tender feelings which in all the years that have separated us have never abated. Had

I won your hand on either of the two occasions I was bold enough to ask for it, I should have been the happiest of men. Alas, our youth in the first instance and, perhaps, the circumstances of History in the second contrived to rob me of that happiness.

Annie suppressed an exasperated sigh. Poor Roland couldn't accept the fact that she was never in love with him. Fond of him, certainly, in the way one is fond of a relative or old family friend, as she thought of Roland still. She would not have been the happiest of women had she accepted him, momentarily tempted though she had been in Alice Sumner's Washington parlor when for the second time he dropped to one knee and, boldly for him, seized her hand. The War had left few enough eligible men to go around, and she was hardly averse by then to the prospect of re-marriage. But he wasn't right for her then either, and not only because he was a Southerner. Amusing to think of that now—the plantation scion proposing to her in the home of one of history's most eminent Abolitionists.

I was most fortunate, Roland's letter continued, to find in the late Mrs. Burwell, a distant connection on my mother's side, a faithful and loving wife who bore me three lovely children and whose passing I mourned deeply. My children were left orphaned at a tender age without their dear mother's gentle, guiding hand to see them safely into adulthood—

Annie looked up from the letter. "Mr. Burwell—how old were you when your mother died?"

"I'm twenty-two now—I'd just turned eleven. Edgar would've been thirteen, I think."

Roland, she noted with a mixture of relief and chagrin, had not wasted time mending his broken heart in the arms of another after her second refusal. Like the heir of an old English demesne, he would have felt obliged to marry and have sons to whom the estate would pass. He must have married within the year, and gone right to work on producing an heir. She was glad. Perhaps it was natural that in the enveloping loneliness of widowerhood on an isolated plantation, he might delude himself that he had never lost his passion for his first love, the Yankee lady who had broken his heart.

My dear sister Alice, the letter continued...

whom you may recall from our visits, was kind enough to assume, insofar as she might, the tender duties of a mother, and I am pleased to think that, with her guidance, my sons have emerged into the world as men of honor and decency.

It is in this hope that I commend to you my younger son, Thomas Jackson Burwell, who comes to Paris to pursue a course of study as a painter. It is, you will understand, not necessarily the path a fond parent would choose for his offspring, but the young of today are less patient of constraint than we were (I must speak only for myself, I suppose!)—goodness, perhaps Roland had had a sense of humor after all—The boy exhibits, to my untutored eye, a pleasing level of proficiency in his chosen vocation, and our family means, while not lavish, are adequate to support him in those modest circumstances which I am told constitute at Paris as large a component of the artist's education as the formal instruction of the atelier. He can't bring himself to picture his son starving in a Montmartre garret, Annie thought.

Should it be within your power and inclination, dear Mrs. Shaw, to render my beloved son any small service in the pursuit of his aims, such as introductions to the artistic circles of that great City so renowned for its art, or to those of your acquaintance who might take an aesthetic interest in the products of his brush and canvas, know

that you will have the deepest thanks and eternal esteem of—your
devoted friend, Roland Wadsworth Burwell.

As Annie folded the letter, something fell out of the envelope—a dried, brown sprig of white lilac blossom, which she held close to her face, inhaling aromas that swept her back to a warm May night in Lenox, some thirty-five years ago. Feeling flirtatious that day, and trying to make George jealous after some paltry disagreement, she had plucked the spray of blossom and tucked it into Roland Burwell's buttonhole. Like a bridegroom's boutonnière, she had realized belatedly, and perhaps it was that which had emboldened him, a day or two later, to ask whether he might speak to her father. Her eyes misted over, and she felt a constriction in her throat.

"Mr. Burwell," she asked, "do you play the piano?"

"Why, yes, ma'am, I do—"

"Are you familiar with Chopin's third étude?" Annie gestured toward the small parlor piano near the fireplace, recently retuned since she had started playing again.

The boy's smile was a mixture of pleasure and sadness. "The *Tristesse*? It was one of Papa's favorites. So, I learned it pretty early. I haven't played it in a while, though."

"You'll find the sheet music near the top of the stool."

He played like his father—sure-handed, and with a delicacy of expression that seemed to embody all that was loveliest in that dark world of the Old South. She felt Julia, who had joined her on the divan, scanning her face as the piece went on. She bit her lip and looked away, the faded scent of lilac and the music taking her back to the verandah at Vent Fort, the sweet notes wafting into the moist night air. A tear rolled down her cheek. Goodness, she was growing lugubrious. She felt Julia's hand on hers.

"How young we were then," she said, before realizing that Julia would have no idea what she was talking about. She took in air in a great sniff. "I'll tell you later." What if Roland *had* sought her out? Perhaps time hadn't been kind to him either. He'd have lost his hair—all blond men did, Papa included. What would it have been like, to find quiet companionship, all question of romantic passion gone—*for at your age, the heyday in the blood is tame, it's humble, and waits upon the judgment...* well, that's all young Hamlet knew. In any event, there had been no one in years for whom she had felt that stir in the belly, that quickening of the pulse, so evoked by George Kneeland and then, so briefly, by Rob Shaw. *And wilt thou leave me so unsatisfied?* Romeo's line had come to her as she watched the *DeMolay* pull away from Battery Wharf, Rob's silhouette on the deck dwindling to a black dot, vanishing forever.

She opened her eyes. Jackson Burwell was looking at her, puzzled, expectant.

"How that piece transported me. You play so beautifully—I thought of your father."

The boy gave a little bow from the neck and smiled shyly.

"Now, tell me about your art."

"Rather a melancholy destination, don't you think?" Julia closed the heavy iron gate of Annie's apartment building at 30 Henri Martin and brandished her walking-stick toward the Cimetière de Passy. "And the stairs are steep—"

"The stroll will do me good." Annie adjusted a small paint box tucked under her arm. "I need to clear my brain of its sentimental fog. Jackson's father was a suitor of mine."

"But you weren't in love with him?"

"How shrewd you are! But I was fond of him, and I'm sorry he's dead. Under other circumstances, a marriage mightn't have been out of the question."

They skirted the edge of Place Trocadéro and its grandiose Moorish Palais, heading for the cemetery gate. Julia cocked her head back toward the Palais. "Hideous pile, ain't it?"

"Like someone's idea of Kublai Kahn's 'stately pleasure dome'—executed under the influence of too much laudanum."

"Of course, Roland was a Southerner."

"I didn't hold his Southern-ness against him, so much as his lack of a sense of humor. I had no politics in those days. Only my heart's inclinations, which were elsewhere—"

"With our Rob?"

"Not till later on. Before Rob, there was another—who also died much too young. Though not in war."

"Intriguing! And after the war, your Mr. Burwell was married—"

"Indeed, no. He renewed his suit, in the most considerate and respectful terms, when I went to stay with Alice Mason in Washington in '67—Mrs. Sumner, as she briefly was then."

"But you were still mourning Rob—"

"Honestly, Julia—no. Naturally I'll always mourn him—-but I wasn't averse to making a new life for myself. And by then I did hold Roland's Southern-ness against him—can you see me as a plantation mistress, especially *after* the War? But that's not why I refused him. I just couldn't love him. Poor Roland…"

"…who, nonetheless, married shortly afterwards, or this estimable young fellow couldn't have knocked upon your door."

"Nothing so easy as catching a heart on the rebound—didn't some English author say that?" Annie pushed open the cemetery's wrought-iron gate and they made their way up the steps.

Julia laughed. "I heard that whispered when I accepted dear William. The world thought I'd been having a love affair with the famous—or infamous—Reverend Parker of Roxbury."

"And you hadn't?"

"I found Theodore's free-thinking and intellect compelling—and vice-versa, I suppose—but I couldn't reciprocate his romantic passion. Which didn't save me from being depicted as the Scarlet Woman who seduced the poor fellow away from his wife. I suppose I shouldn't blame the gossips—I refused to abandon our pleasant woodland discourses just because someone thought ill of them."

Before Rob Shaw introduced his fiancée to the Greenes, he had told Annie the old scandalous story about his aunt, then a golden-haired Nordic goddess, having enchanted the Unitarian heretic. The beauty and the élan were still there, though the hair was white now and the skin lightly wrinkled. Easy to see why men would have been foolish about a younger Julia.

They strolled down a gravel path lined by the ubiquitous Paris chestnuts, pausing before a column topped with a man's head in bronze with a forked beard, gazing benignly eastward.

"Who's this?"

"It's Manet, the artist, and his brother Eugène who just died—Berthe Morisot's husband," Annie read from the granite slab at their feet. "It took me a long time to warm up to Manet's work, but it was worth it."

"I've never got there myself," Julia said. "What does Manet

do for you?"

"It's hard to put into words. He—wakes me up, somehow. He paints real people in real places, but he makes you see them as extraordinary. You can feel them, feel *with* them, in a way you can't with the old Biblical and Classical heroes. At first glance the work isn't so different, but when you get closer you can see he's not trying to—hide the seams, or pretend it's real and not a painting. And it's got more feeling, more immediacy, because of that."

They perused the bust, trying to read Manet's face. "I think he's unhappy about something," Julia said at length.

Annie took a sketchbook and pencils from her little paintbox. "That looks more like a smile to me—subtle, but—give me a minute here. Just a quick one, I promise." She perched on a nearby table-tomb and sketched rapidly, darting looks toward the bust.

"I mean young Jackson," Julia said. "Excited about being an artist in Paris, but he's left something—or someone—behind."

"You're not just being Romantic—as usual?" Julia Shaw's generation, obsessed with the Sublime, had shaken up the tidy, rational world of their grandparents with tales of unbridled passion, awe-inspiring landscapes and tempestuous music.

"Of course I am, but that doesn't mean I'm wrong."

Annie closed the sketchbook and they strolled on. "We could plant ourselves here." Julia's walking-stick swept in a half-circle. "The view's fine, and it would be lots less trouble than being pickled and crated and shipped off to America."

"Julia, I'm shocked to hear you say that! Would you abandon poor Uncle William?"

Her friend paused to sniff at a pink rosebush adorning the

tomb of a young woman, sculpted in white marble, who lay smiling and lovely on a pillow with a baby at her breast. "Paris has been home for so long. And Will and his family are here," she added, as if in afterthought. "It would be different if Bessie—" Her voice quavered, and she turned her head away.

With a lurch of the heart, Annie recalled the fate of the cousin by marriage she had never met. She laid a hand on Julia's shoulder. "Goodness, yes—the *Schiller*..." Bessie, only twenty-eight, had died in a great shipwreck off the Cornwall coast in 1875, the year Ogden Haggerty's heart failed. Ogden's wife and daughters had been preoccupied then with futile rounds of Alpine clinics to find him a cure. Annie had sent the Greenes a condolence letter, shaken her head at the tragedy of it, and gone back to her father's dying. "And her friend gone too—a lady doctor?"

A nod, and another sad smile before Julia raised her head. "Our daughter-in-law, as we thought of her. Susan Dimock. *Her* body was recovered—we buried her in the family plot, and William next to her when he passed on, all too soon afterwards. They never found Bessie. For a time, we deluded ourselves that she had survived and must be wandering around Cornwall with amnesia. The mind plays odd tricks..." Like Annie's own mother, Julia had lost two children in infancy. Only William Jr., the youngest, had survived to make her a grandmother. She laid a hand on Julia's forearm.

"You're right, Annie," Julia said at length. "It would never do, would it, to leave William all by himself among the Puritans. Besides, I'll be dead and past caring."

Rob Shaw, infamously, had been buried with his black troops in a trench on the beach of Morris Island, where they had fallen while storming the walls of Battery Wagner. Annie had pictured him washed away in the sea: *Those are pearls that were his eyes: Nothing of him that doth fade/ But doth suffer a sea-change/Into something rich and strange*—and had taken comfort in that. But months later, victorious Union troops had excavated the burial trench and interred the remains, long past individual identification, in the new Beaufort National Cemetery. Among the rows of stones marked "Unknown, 54th," one marked the last resting place of Rob's bones.

Annie heaved a breath. "Enough of these morbid preoccupations!" she said brightly.

"Quite right!" Julia followed her down the path toward the stairs of the cemetery entrance. "We have a studio visit to plan."

Chapter 6

"t voilà les chaperons!" Bertrand de Leiningen greeted Annie and Julia at the door of his studio, a wet paintbrush in his hand. "Too late to save my models' reputations, I fear…"

He bowed them into a high, bare space redolent of turpentine, linseed oil and stale coffee. Its concrete floor and walls were painted a cool gray, with a wall of black-framed windows on its north side, whitish-gray rectangles that rose from three feet above the floor almost to a high ceiling. An unseasonable spell of cold, rainy weather had set a radiator hissing and clanking in one corner, making as much noise as heat, it seemed. The ladies had squelched through a grassed-over yard—the place must have been a warehouse or workshop in the past—with the backs of other, dilapidated-looking industrial factories beyond.

A Japanese silk screen blocked the view from curious eyes that might peer in the windows. Bertrand's two models lay in front of it quite naked, on what looked like a pair of récamiers pushed together and covered with silken drapery in an indefinable vegetative print. The girls could not have presented more of a contrast—an olive-skinned, sloe-eyed Amazon with a cascade of black hair, and a small-featured, pink-cheeked gamine with a froth of blonde curls and a sharp chin. "For God's sake, Bertrand," the latter was saying in an accent more New York than Paris, "you might have warned us."

Oh, we've come at a bad time—" Annie began.

"Never!" said their host. "Madame Greene said you wanted to see work in progress, and I wanted you to meet my fair and dusky Muses." The young women were hastily donning Oriental-looking robes retrieved from the floor.

"These are ladies," the little blonde protested. "It's one thing showing us off to your fainéant friends—"

"Madame Greene, Madame Shaw," Bertrand cut her off with a courtly sweep of his hand, as if unveiling something, "I present Madame Fernandez, and Mademoiselle DeKuyper who, if it weren't obvious from her speech, is a countrywoman of yours. My Esprits je Juin et Mai."

A huge canvas angled away from them on a paint-splotched, oversized easel. On what might be a mossy bank of flowers, the outlines and some of the colors of the two young women were roughed in, Miss DeKuyper appearing to be lying down to sleep, Madame Fernandez, an arm thrown over and one leg entwined with her companion's in a sensual posture, propped on one elbow and gazing upward as if just awakening. The "bank" from which the models had arisen was comprised of green draperies, buried cushions and strewn clusters of silk blossoms over the two narrow couches—cramped for two, surely, even with one as diminutive as Miss DeKuyper.

"*Spring dies for summer,* I may call it," said Bertrand, submerging his brush in a jar of turpentine.

"It's Tallie," said the little blonde, apropos of nothing. "And this is Sofia." She rummaged in a black cotton reticule, extracted a small tin box of tobacco and began rolling a cigarette. "Want one?" she asked her companion, who shook her dark locks. Tallie struck a match, inhaled deeply and blew the smoke up in a tight jet.

"Are these the Brahmins you were telling us about, Bertrand?" She looked the pair over with catlike curiosity. There was something feline about her quick, delicate movements, an economy and grace like a dancer's.

"Tallie fancies herself an artist as well," said Bertrand. He strode to a paint-spattered sink and filled a kettle, which he set on a gas ring.

"But I have to do this for the rent," said Tallie with a petulant little moué, "and your exorbitant fees at Julian's. D'you know," she told Annie and Julia, "they charge women more than the men, for a fraction of the studio space?"

"Your studio-mates are the best women art students in Paris!" Bertrand protested. "You were lucky to get in."

Sofia pulled her black satin robe more tightly around her and eyed Tallie with mild resentment. "I was told *you* came from money."

"If only! Uncle Julius owns half of lower Manhattan. We're the poor relations. Papa lost what little we had gambling," Tallie added offhandedly. "And I wasn't 'lucky' to get in, Monsieur, I got in because I'm good. As you well know."

Bertrand gave her an indulgent shake of the head, dropped a pair of rickety-looking chairs behind the visitors and settled them in. "Assayez-vous, mesdames—it's the best I can offer, since the ladies won't relinquish their couches."

"He doesn't want us disarranging his mise-en-scène, he

means." Tallie tapped ash into a tiny dish and turned a dazzling smile on Annie. "You're new to Paris?"

"Is my French so bad as that?" Annie returned her smile. "I've lived in France for eighteen years, Madame Greene even longer."

"Her French is better than mine, though," Julia settled herself in the unforgiving chair. "What do you paint, Miss—Tallie?"

"Very little at present, except for classes when I can afford them. I like portraits, and people in landscapes. Real people in real landscapes—not this myths-and-Bible stuff they're still so fond of here." She sighed. "Perhaps I should take up sculpture. People seem to feel immortalized if they're done in marble."

"Oh, come!" said Bertrand. "There's been nothing new in sculpture since—who was it you said? Caesar Augustus?"

"My father had a sculpture collection," Annie recalled, "shipped from Italy, though the sculptors were mostly American. Have you met Saint-Gaudens?" The name Augustus must have triggered the association.

"The name's familiar," Bertrand said. "Not in Paris, is he?"

"Not at present."

"He's at work on a monument to my nephew and his Civil War regiment," Julia said.

"Madame Shaw is the Colonel's widow," Bertrand told his models, who regarded her sympathetically.

"Shaw," Tallie said. "Oh! The famous colored regiment—" Annoyed with Julia for raising that subject, but realizing she had only herself to blame, Annie nodded.

Tallie's eyes widened. "He was awfully young, wasn't he? I saw a bust of him—Edmonia Lewis, she was a colored lady herself, wasn't she—will it be marble?"

"Bronze, I'm told, like most of his work." Annie had exchanged letters with Saint-Gaudens, parting with a few precious photos he had promised to return years ago. He was employing a dozen or so Negro models for the infantrymen on the bas-relief, there being few to no photos of the regiment's members. Having long since exhausted his fee from the Memorial Committee, he now viewed the monstrosity as a "labor of love," which apparently meant something he worked on between paying projects.

Tallie and Sofia paced the floor, barefoot, stopping to stretch cramped limbs from poses held too long. Tallie clasped hands behind her back and bent backwards into an acrobatic arc, nearly reaching the floor.

"She could do a bust of your husband, Sofia." Bertrand grinned wickedly.

The Levantine gave him a passing look of annoyance. "I haven't seen him in months. I don't know where he is. Fortunately, he remembers to send money."

"Just as well," Tallie straightened up and waved toward the easel. "He'd hardly approve of this."

"Ha! His latest conquest has done a good deal of—modeling, I've heard. But Ranulfo doesn't paint."

"We've got some wine open." Bertrand took a cloudy pair of stemmed glasses from a shelf. "May I offer you ladies a glass?"

Annie and Julia exchanged dubious looks, but Julia said, "Why not?" The models looked at him hungrily.

Bertrand filled the glasses and handed them to his guests. "We have to treat prospective patrons well," he told the models. "You may have tea if you like. Otherwise, the rest's over, ladies— back on your flowery bank, please. Mesdames, be comfortable, as much as you can. Perhaps someday I'll be able to afford an upholstered chair or two." He gave them a faux-sycophantic smile and reached for his paintbrush.

Annie sipped at the harsh, cheap claret—perhaps Bertrand's circumstances were indeed as straitened as he claimed. Young Miss DeKuyper—Tallie—looked about her niece Marian's age; in different circumstances it could be the headstrong Marian, a trial to any chaperone, reclining on some couch like an odalisque instead of this worldly elf-child. Tallie had surely abjured any thought of a respectable marriage, much less a reputation; perhaps it was impossible for a woman to live as an artist and be concerned about such things. Annie thought of polite, naïve Jackson Burwell and wondered what his father Roland—or Jackson himself—would think of walking into what looked at first blush like a den of vice.

Bertrand darted back and forth in front of his canvas, placing tiny dabs of paint here and there. Tallie and Sofia lay like sunning leopardesses, the loose, languid poses held still by some prodigious but invisible muscular effort. An occasional stifled sigh issued from the mossy bower, but never a movement.

Along the far wall were canvases in various stages of completion. A Byronic head caught Annie's eye—Bertrand, in a breathtakingly good self-portrait. He had managed both to render his own features with near-photographic accuracy and to suggest some dissolute, even diabolical quality in the tilt of his head, a glint in the eye—no more than a dot of white paint—and the hint of a one-sided smile, as if he were about to offer the viewer some wicked suggestion. A bright red cravat, carelessly tied, and a burgundy background reinforced the not unpleasantly infernal quality of the composition. She thought again of Doctor Pozzi as rendered by Sargent, and felt a spasm of worry for Tallie—for which, she was sure, she would get no thanks from that insouciant young person, draped along the couch as if in an opium dream. Sofia, she judged, was past such concerns.

She still had the reflexes of a bourgeois aunt, Annie realized. But Tallie had lain there in her winsome nakedness before their arrival, with her equally naked companion, and would do so whenever occasion demanded. To intervene on behalf of bohemian girls' virtue would only deprive them of needed income.

"Let me see a bit more of that right hand, Mam'zelle," Bertrand said. Tallie made a small movement in response. "No, palm still down, please—there, that's good." He turned from his easel. "If you'd care to stay, I should run out of steam in twenty or thirty minutes—"

"I think," Annie said, with a side glance at Julia, "that we should tiptoe out and leave you to the Muse."

"Comme vous voulez," Bertrand said with the hint of a shrug. "The ladies will have to rely on their own virtue to maintain their reputations, it seems."

Tallie caught Annie's eye and gave her an amused, what-can-you-do look.

"Perhaps, Monsieur le Comte, you and your lovely models would join us for dinner next Tuesday? I'm eager to learn more about what it's like to pursue such interesting occupations, and there's a recent arrival from America, I'd like you to meet." She meant to invite Jackson Burwell in pursuit of her obligation to his father, along with Bertrand's student Henry Tanner, the grave young Negro who had so intrigued her at Retta Reubell's.

"Madame Shaw is on intimate terms with the best butcher in the Sixteenth, "Julia put in. "It will be worth your while."

"We need no further inducement than Madame's kind invitation," said Tallie, who had grown suddenly alert and propped herself on an elbow. The girl was well-bred, for all her bohemian affectations.

"Mademoiselle!" Bertrand scolded. "Your pose—please. Well, if my ladies here will consent, I don't see how I could refuse." He walked Annie and Julia to the door and bowed them out. "Till next Tuesday, then."

"Well, now!" said Annie. "That wasn't quite what I expected."

Her companion laughed. "He did say something about working on a paganistic theme. I might've realized it would involve a minimum of clothing." When they reached the Quai Voltaire, they hailed a fiacre.

"What did you think of his models?" Julia asked over the rumble of carriage wheels on the cobblestones of the Pont du Carrousel.

Annie considered. "The dark-haired one? A grande horizontale, I'd think. The little blonde interests me strangely—"

"Because she's American?"

"Because she's an artist herself. These young women, with their bicycles and cigarettes and bloomers—I wonder what my own life would have been, had I been born thirty years later, and here instead of America. I used to paint quite a bit—I've only recently started dabbling again—"

"My dear, you'd have been chaperoned within an inch of your life, and married off to some cantankerous old Count, quite independent of your own preferences!"

"Is it so bad as that, still? I didn't say I'd be French, or aristocratic—but if I'd grown up here, as an expatriate—"

"Ah—like your nieces. Or my Bessie." Julia turned toward the carriage window.

"I wish I'd known Bessie," Annie laid a hand on Julia's. "She was delightfully unconventional, Rob said. And vivacious."

"That she was," Julia smiled. "It's been a long time—but, oh, Annie, I miss her so much, even now! Sometimes it just comes over me in a wave..." she turned away to blow her nose.

"A mother's pain—I can't imagine it would ever stop." And a memory assailed Annie too.

Her little brother Oggie at four or five months, his face turned toward her, eyes big with alarm as she hefts the big tabby cat in her plump little arms—she feels the warm fur and the muscled weight— up and over the edge of Oggie's crib. She's heard that cats will suck the breath out of babies. She wants him gone. Mamma dotes on him as if he were a perfect little angel, when of course he howls all the time and grabs greedily at her bosom so she's always having to leave the room to feed him.

It was so nice before he arrived. She wants Mamma back. Maybe the cat will do the dirty work for her. But then the fearful blue eyes in Oggie's little pink face stare at her with such appeal, with such reproach, that she scrambles in panic over the lip of the crib and grabs the cat out and away from the little boy, for whom she's suddenly flooded with love and wants only to protect from the cat's scrabbling claws. She climbs back into the crib and holds him till he stops crying.

Her first love, this little brother, who grows into a sturdy, ruddy playfellow. Until at age seven he turns chalk-pale, then begins to waste away—a 'liver complaint,' Mamma tells her—till at last he can't even stand up any more, and then there is the little coffin and the suffocating scent of white roses in the parlor and the still little body that looks like a doll and won't wake up when Annie shakes his shoulder. This is her punishment for that evil wish when he was a baby. Mamma in a chair by the bier, silent and still, her hands over her face.

Nearly fifty years, and still she feels the pain. How could Julia have gone on after losing her only daughter? Annie, stricken, reached out a hand to touch Julia's cheek. Sunlight poked through the clouds as the cab rattled north past the Jardins des Tuileries, a light wind scattering the chestnut blossoms. Their honey scent wafted through the partly open windows.

But Julia had recovered her composure. "Tallie doesn't look a bit like her. Bessie was tall and dark-haired. But something about her reminded me too—the vivacious and unconventional part."

"What did you want for her, when she was Tallie's age? Husband and children and so forth?"

Julia took a minute to respond. "I assumed, as attractive as she was, that she'd have a host of male admirers and marry one of them. But she repelled all boarders, and then when she went to the Boston Women's Hospital for her knees, she met our dear Susan Dimock, who was a doctor there. After that her life was all about caring for poor women and children, and her devotion to Susan. Whom we grew to love as much as she did."

"I wonder how young Tallie ceased to care about having a reputation," Annie said, "or a husband. Perhaps she has enough faith in her own talents to think she can earn a living. We can interrogate her, tactfully, when she comes to dinner—*if* she comes."

Julia smiled. "Oh, I think she will. She seemed quite interested in you—perhaps she'd like to paint you."

"Or perhaps it was your reference to my estimable butcher. She probably hasn't had a decent meal in weeks." Annie herself had been constantly hungry at Tallie's age. "As for painting me," she added, "I still don't see why anyone would want to. But since Sargent hasn't come knocking on my door—"

"Good heavens, who'd want him after what he did to La Gautreau? If you're setting up for a patroness, shouldn't you see what young Jackson can do?" The fiacre circled the Place de l'Étoile.

"Why not have both of them paint me, and see who does it better?"

Julia smiled and slowly shook her head. "I believe you're serious."

"And Bertrand too, if he wanted." Annie was feeling mischievous. "A temporary branch of the Atélier Julian. But I sha'n't take any clothes off, never fear."

"Which reminds me," Julia said as the carriage slowed on the avenue Henri Martin, "I must set you up with Dr. Kellgren's. Sorry—that was tactlessly put. But I long to see you moving about happily and comfortably. You'll invite me to this dinner, I trust? As a chaperone?"

"That goes without saying—that is, if you've nothing better to do! But no chaperonage necessary. Come in with me and have a glass of wine. I'm so glad I stayed in Paris!"

When they were settled, Annie said, "how do I enlist in your Swedish gymnasium?"

"I shall tell you. But you might consider the disadvantages of growing fit and mobile—no more excuses for not paying calls."

"I hadn't thought of that." Bodily limitations were an excellent excuse to avoid the tedious rounds of calling and receiving among American Colony ladies that had laid waste to so many of her mother's and Clem's days. Conventional, superficial conversation, endless tea—such an insipid beverage, which was the point, she supposed—fretting over whether a dress had been worn too recently to make a repeat appearance. She could think of no worse hell than an everlasting round of committee meetings for the Welfare of the Poor and the Redemption of Fallen Women. She had been careful to continue giving the impression of fragile health, which typically went unquestioned in females, particularly one past middle age.

But a salon—all that unused space in the Crafts' apartments, with its balcony view sweeping down the avenue Henri Martin to the Trocadéro and the Eiffel Tower. What if she and Julia convened a small circle—musical, conversational, literary, and of course the artists? They wouldn't have to be famous—not yet, anyway—Annie was more interested in up-and-comers like Tallie and the young ladies of Julian's.

She did miss the youthful energy of her nieces—but not the role of social shepherdess and enforcer of parental constraints. The girls had taken little interest in what made Paris the cynosure it was—the creative ferment of the studios and music-rooms and ateliers, the bookshops and galleries.

Perhaps Tallie DeKuyper embodied a future in which women could develop their talents without regard for the old proprieties. It still could not be easy to forgo the security and comforts of conventional living and cast oneself adrift on the tides of chance—particularly for a female artist, whose work would be assumed to be inferior to men's and whose approved subject matter was limited to the decorative and the domestic. But there they were in Paris, Tallie and hundreds like her, no doubt often failing, as much for lack of support as for lack of talent. What they would fall into after failure didn't bear thinking of. But there were successes too—like Mary Cassatt and Rosa Bonheur...

Ogden Haggerty, Annie's father, had been a godparent of sorts to the young artists of his day. Perhaps she could do that for promising young women in Paris who might otherwise fall by the wayside. What if she invested in a couple of Bertrand de Leiningen's 'ambitious' young women painters? It would bring the satisfaction of lending a needed hand, perhaps eventually of knowing her patronage had helped launch an artistic career or two. For that matter, Jackson Burwell seemed to have been left short-handed by his father, and might welcome more substantial help than introductions.

After Julia's departure she let herself into the Crafts' apartment, shaking her head at all the bare spots left on the walls by paintings shipped to Boston. Had she any business refurnishing it with art of her own choosing? There was so much to investigate—Mr. Tanner's work, Comte Bertrand's—he too might welcome a patroness—and the ladies of Julian's, whose work might become the focus of a modest new collection.

It felt urgent, suddenly, like a mission to be undertaken.

Chapter 7

urveying her lace-draped table, Annie felt a glow that rivaled the soft gold light slanting in the long windows, now melding with candlelight to give the dining room a romantic air. Her first dinner-party as an independent hostess included Henrietta Reubell, Julia Greene, Jackson Burwell, Henry Tanner, Bertrand de Leiningen and Tallie DeKuyper, whose couch-companion Sofia Fernandez had sent regrets. Here were a few artists who might be useful guides to Jackson in his new world—as indeed might Miss Reubell. Inviting her had been an inspiration, Annie decided, watching the lively red-head appropriate Mr. Tanner and put him at ease.

Tallie had followed suit with Jackson, who'd seemed momentarily surprised to find a colored man in the drawing-room but initiated a cordial handshake. Tanner's brow had creased at the Southern accent, but the young Georgian's warmth quickly melted the frost. The younger men's attentions to his pretty little model seemed to arouse Comte Bertrand's competitive instincts; his back stiffened when Jackson offered Tallie his arm to go into dinner, and when Tallie and Henry Tanner began laughing over a shared joke, Annie could have sworn she saw Bertrand pout. She caught Julia's eye and watched her suppress a knowing smirk.

"I've been reading a young artist's diary," Annie began, amused to watch dismay flicker across the four young faces. "Consciously intended for publication, I should add." Comprehension dawned on Bertrand's face.

"La belle Russe Bashkirtseff?" He regarded her expectantly.

"Ukranian, I think. Madame Greene and I were walking in the Passy cemetery and came upon her tomb—the day you came to tea, Mr. Burwell. It intrigued me into reading her diary."

"You could support all my students for a year—with decent room *and* board—for what that monstrosity must have cost," Bertrand said. "But then, the girl's vanity was legendary—"

Tallie's eyes flared. "I think her a fine artist. It's clear from her portraits that she understands tone and composition—"

"How would *you* know?" snapped Bertrand. Adèle, who was removing his soup plate, startled at the rudeness. "Pardon, mam'zelle," he said, laying a hand on her wrist. Adèle snatched her hand away.

"Well," said Tallie into the momentary silence, "you thought the one I did of you was—what was your word?—creditable."

"I should like to see that," Julia said.

"You may have, Madame, when you visited the studio. It was propped against the wall, gathering dust with some of his own work-in-progress."

Annie remembered the Byronic portrait that had impressed her. "I saw that. A fine work, I thought. I assumed it was a self-portrait, and—one that seemed to capture its subject." Judging by Bertrand's scowl, quickly erased, that was the wrong thing to have said. She felt herself redden, thinking of the conversation at Reubell's about portrait artists' feelings for their subjects, and recalling the impression of Bertrand the portrait had left her with. An attractive touch of the diabolical—had Tallie seen that in Bertrand too?

With a sideways smile, he drawled, "I wouldn't stop modeling yet, if I were you."

"Well, you're not, are you," the girl said, stung.

"I thought the notion of a studio as monument rather brilliant," Annie said. "It reminded me of the Pharaohs, being buried with everything they might need for an afterlife—"

"Now, there would be a fine ghost story," Miss Reubell put in, "the paints, the brushes, the empty canvas—but every morning, as the sexton makes his rounds, he looks through the glass doors and sees a painting beginning to take shape. I must suggest it to Henry James. He should write more ghost stories. The crypt is locked, I imagine?"

"With a heavy padlock." Julia said. Adèle began to lay out plates of pork tenderloin in a red-currant glaze.

"It would do me fine as a studio," Tallie said wistfully.

"I don't mind you using mine," Bertrand said, magnanimous now. "You do show promise, my dear, if you work hard at it and devote the time—"

"I appreciate it, really I do," Tallie said, relenting and giving him a brilliant smile, "but a studio of one's own!" Jackson and Henry Tanner nodded enthusiastic agreement.

"The only thing!" said Jackson.

"Well, I do have my own studio," Tanner said, "though it's a damp little cellar on the rue de Seine. I wondered why it was so cheap until the walls begin to seep after a heavy rain."

"You could catch your death of consumption!" Miss Reubell cried.

"They're my living quarters too."

"You must have some hangings for your walls at least," Miss Reubell said briskly. "I just changed my library portières and you shall have them—they're a pleasant shade of green and quite thick, if a bit bland, which is why I replaced them."

"Oh, I couldn't possibly—"

"Make me a little oil-sketch. A small still-life, a vase of flowers. And then I'll be able to say, he painted something for me, just before he grew famous."

Tanner smiled and bowed his head. "Well, in that case—you're very kind."

"What will you have for a studio, Mr. Burwell?" Julia asked.

Jackson sighed. "A couple of other fellows have a little space up in Batignolles, but by the time I'd get there from my lodgings, and with the classes and all—"

"You're at Julian's too?"

"I am—but I'm hoping to hear soon from the École des Beaux Arts," Jackson turned pink.

"When will they finally admit ladies, I wonder?"

The three men looked mildly shocked. "The École provides free education," said Bertrand, "and since they'd have to have separate life-classes, it would be too expensive—"

"Why do they have to be separate?" said Tallie, indignant. "Women are far more respectful of the models than the men are—and, yes, Bertrand, I speak from experience. Do they think we're going to fall into bacchanalian orgies if we study together?"

Annie pictured Clem reacting to the news that one of her daughters was taking a life-drawing class with a mixed group.

"I suppose the mammas are worried their daughters would be ruined socially."

"Too late for me!"

"It wouldn't have taken a life-drawing class to ruin *you*, my dear," Bertrand said into another awkward silence.

"And how would you know?" Tallie's tone was a slap to the face.

Julia arched an eyebrow. "My goodness! We've fallen in among the bohèmiens!" This drew the laughter she had intended.

"Don't worry," Tallie said to Jackson, who was looking worried. "There's a good deal more talk than action where these, ah, extra-curricular ventures are concerned. How long have you been in Paris, Mr. Tanner?"

The talk took a benign turn and moved on. Clearly the girl could handle herself in social situations. To be thus in Paris, unchaperoned, Tallie must have made a break with her family that would bar her from being received in the decorous American Colony. Paris beyond that was a different matter. Here, her presence felt to Annie as natural as a daughter's, or a niece's. Tallie wore a serviceable dark green twill dress, with a little Belgian lace, probably machined, around the collar. Annie and Julia had forgone evening-dress, surely an unaffordable extravagance for their younger guests.

She worried for them already, for Tallie and Jackson and Henry Tanner. Distinguishing oneself from the hordes of talented artists in Paris couldn't be easy. The Americans who had competed successfully with the natives, whose blood seemed to run cadmium red, could be counted on one hand. And there were hundreds of others from elsewhere in the world—Britain, Scandinavia, the Balkans—who had come in search of the

Muse. That's why the neighborhood south of the Seine, where so many of them now strove and starved in their garrets and cellars, was called Montparnasse—where the Muses dwelt. Jackson was sharing a small suite there with a college friend.

She wondered where Tallie lived. She shouldn't be sharing workspace with the likes of Bertrand, who clearly cared nothing for young women's reputations, though Tallie herself seemed indifferent on that subject. Annie recalled episodes of rescuing her headstrong niece Marian from scrapes that would have ruined her prospects had they come to light. Marian was her blood-kin, almost a daughter—

But Tallie intrigued her. Perhaps it was the novelty of the acquaintance. Marian might play at being a scapegrace, but at bottom she wanted what all young women were supposed to desire: a suitable husband, and the combined freedom and respectability that marriage to the right man would bring. One might dismiss Tallie as the typical demimondaine modeling for artists, like so many of her kind with pathetic pretensions to their own artistic talent. But she had evidence, in the portrait of Bertrand, of Tallie's genuine skill as an artist. What was "Tallie" a nickname for—Thalia? The comedic, pastoral Muse. That rather fit Bertrand's present subject matter…

"How goes your spring-and-summer allegory, Monsieur le Comte?"

"I'd be honored if you called me Bertrand, Madame."

"Told you," Julia said.

"We are making good progress, wouldn't you say, Tallie? It should be ready for vernissage in another week or ten days. I'm thinking of entering it in the Salon." Annie wondered if acceptance of his work in the annual Paris exhibition was something Bertrand could take for granted.

"Nothing's guaranteed, of course," he added, as if reading her thoughts, "but they've been receptive to my work in recent years."

"Bertrand, such false modesty. You're one of their habitués." This, wistfully, from Tallie.

Bertrand shrugged, conceding the point. "It helps to have friends and colleagues on the Jury."

Retta Reubell waved her hand toward the hallway and the Crafts' apartment. "Forgive my nosiness, Madame Shaw, but— have your sister and her family given up their lease?"

"Please—call me Annie, if you'd like."

Miss Reubell beamed. "Certainly—and please call me Retta!"

"To your question—not as yet, perhaps not at all. They're keeping the lease in case the Technology Institute doesn't suit James'—Professor Crafts'—professional requirements. Clem says they plan frequent return visits, and they didn't want to burden me with neighbors who might prove disagreeable. In the meantime, they said I must treat the place as my own, though at present everything's draped in dustcovers. It looks funereal in there."

"We'd thought of a little salon there," Julia told Retta Reubell. "There must be one time of the week not already spoken for—"

"Who would I invite?" Annie said.

"Why, the up-and-coming artists and intellectuals of your acquaintance," Bertrand said. "You have a nice little nucleus around your table."

"I won't let you take advantage of Madame Shaw's hospitality, Bertrand," said Miss Reubell with mock severity, "foisting your bohemian ne'er-do-well friends on her for the food and drink."

"Thus speaks the voice of bitter experience," Bertrand

grinned. "What would *your* salon be, Mademoiselle, without the aforementioned wastrels?"

"A good deal less costly," the lady replied good-naturedly. "But I admit to drawing a more than usually interesting assortment from la vie de bohème. Some of you may be famous someday, and repay my substantial investments in your entertainment."

"Some already are," said Julia. "Goodness, you had Mallarmé, Béraud—"

"I wouldn't presume to invite *them*," said Annie, who was warming to the idea of a salon. "I'm intrigued with the notion of gathering young people like you—" she gestured a circle around the table, "—who are making their way in the world of art and music and so forth. I'd be intrigued to see what happens when they're all together."

"Be careful what you wish for, Madame. You may never get rid of us," Bertrand said. Tallie and the others smiled at her, dubious and hopeful.

"I'll take my chances." Annie stood, her heart rising at the prospect. "Shall we adjourn to the library for port and Roquefort? Mr. Burwell, will you play for us again—and perhaps one or two of you would care to sing?"

Henry Tanner's glance darted around the table. After long hesitation, he spoke. "Mr. Burwell, I don't suppose you know any, ah, Negro spirituals?"

Jackson's head jerked up—'like a guilty thing surpris'd,' Annie thought. "I know one or two. I heard them a good deal, when I was younger—"

"How charming!" said Miss Reubell. "Do let's hear you. It's an aspect of American culture in which I'm sadly deficient. That's what comes of having spent one's whole life in Paris."

Responding to an eager look from Tallie, Tanner said, "Perhaps Miss DeKuyper would care to harmonize?"

Tallie looked momentarily shy but gamely said, "I'll give it a try."

Tanner's warm baritone on "Swing Low, Sweet Chariot" brought Annie back to the barracks of the 54th at Readville, to the choruses that had come together spontaneously in the evenings after long, exhausting days of drills and maneuvers. Jackson proved a skilled accompanist, modulating volume and tempo to highlight the young Negro's voice and the sad, hopeful lyrics of the piece. Tallie's higher tones blended effortlessly.

Annie saw tears glistening on the cheeks of Retta and Julia. Eager as she had been back then for precious private time with Rob, she hadn't been able to tear herself away from the beautiful melodies. He had felt the same way, letting out a soft sigh and squeezing her hand as they stood just out of the men's sight in the dim spring evenings. And now, in this little room in Paris, through a blur of her own tears, she saw a gleam on Jackson Burwell's cheeks. Home-sick for Georgia?

Jackson Burwell had turned from the piano and was now regarding the singers with an expression Annie could only interpret as troubled. Did he think the duet improper? No, that wasn't it. It was sorrow, perhaps even grief, as if for something lost whose memory the voices had recalled. Julia gave Annie an upward flick of her eyebrow, question and confirmation in it. She had noticed it too. Jackson stood up, forcing a smile. "Well, that took me right back to last summer in Georgia. Guess maybe I'm a little homesick after all."

Annie poured him a little glass of port. "A sad song for such a lovely evening. Though it does seem to fit with the way the light turns gold, doesn't it? This time of day is a little melancholy, I always think, especially in summertime."

"Ve *must* loosen up zese muscles!" pronounced Fröken Johansson, in tones that could charitably be described as authoritative. "You haff been holding zem cramped for so long, you have frozen up like a machine viss no oil!" She laid Annie's arm on a padded table and began batting it with the sides of her hands as if tenderizing chicken breasts.

But machines don't feel pain. Annie wished for an oil that could be applied directly into her suffering joints. When the Swedish masseuse seized the back of her neck and began pummeling it as if punishing a miscreant, with alarming cracks and pops for accompaniment, she bit her lip to keep from screaming aloud, letting only a little moan escape.

"Ja, it vill hurt a lot at first," her tormentor said, "until ve get you loosened up, Madame Shaw. It has been a long time and it vill not be easy. But I vill give you some meadowsweet extract. Take it vith food, and you vill feel better."

When the lady began applying her considerable strength to the middle of Annie's back, what had gone before felt mild in comparison. Her entire body throbbed with pain, and it sounded as if her vertebrae were cracking and falling to bits.

"I can't do this," she whimpered. "Really, it's too much. Please stop—"

"You must trust ze prozess, Madame. In five weeks, I promise you, you vill start to feel like a new voman. Your friend Madame Greene was much as you when she came to us."

"Really? — aagh—" More blows rained on Annie's back,

clad only in a thin cotton camisole and something resembling bloomers.

When Annie had arrived at the Gymnasium Suedois de Dr. Henrik Kellgren, Fröken Johansson had insisted on her removing all her clothes. "Ve must see vhat ve have to work vith!"

The critical ice-blue eyes had swept her patient's stooped, naked frame. "Please to stand straight up, Madame!"

Shivering and humiliated, though the room was warmed by a coal boiler, Annie had uncurled herself like a hedgehog, stopping well short of the vertical. "This is as far as I can get," she'd heard herself whine.

The Swedish woman's gaze had stopped abruptly on the scar left by the surgery that had saved Annie's life. "Ah, I see. You haff had—what? Ze gallbladder?" The livid line ran from Annie's breasts to her pubic bone.

"A tumor in my ovary," she said, swallowing hard. "I'd had it for five or six years before they went in for it. It was huge—" she gasped as the woman's cool fingers ran the length of the scar. "This makes me feel like a giant baseball—" Fröken Johansson's eyes narrowed. "—oh, never mind."

"You haff adhesions, perhaps?"

"I suppose—it just seemed to contract, as it healed."

"And zey did nothing? No massage, no oils, no stretching exercises? Idioter! No vonder you haff difficulty!" She shook her head. "Perhaps ve can do something here. These doctors! But it vill take time. Perhaps a long time. You must follow the steps I prescribe. It is not just the area around the scar, Madame. Your whole body has cramped itself around ziss scar, to hide it, you think. But one cannot hide such things. One must *vear* them. Like a soldier!"

Perhaps this was what war-wounds felt like, at that. "Well, I'm hardly going to—"

"Not literally, Madame," said the masseuse, with the first glimmer of a smile. "I mean in your bearing, your valk. You must stand tall, you see? Ve vill vork on this together, to loosen up zese poor tissues. When you are away from here, you must valk, stand straight, stretch yourself—until it hurts, but not too badly. And you vill come twice a week, without fail, ja?"

"How long will I need to do this?" Annie gasped as the pummeling began on her thighs.

"Perhaps six months, perhaps a year. I think you vill be amazed, when you look back, at how much better you vill be moving. You vill be taller, also. That is a nice thing. Ve haff a machine also, to stretch—"

Good Lord, a rack? What next, an Iron Maiden? "Madame Greene," Annie got out between blows, "when she came to you, she was—like me?"

"Stiff and slow, stooped over. Vith her it vas mostly bad habits. And grief, perhaps. Grief is a weight on the body."

"I hadn't thought of it so literally," Annie said, then remembered a letter she had written to a friend after Rob's death, talking of "the weight of grief that is to last so long." So much longer than she had imagined, apparently. How much worse for Julia—her only daughter drowned, her husband gone three years later. It must have taken courage just to get up in the morning.

"Ze Dowager's Hump, the English call it. Madame Greene had the beginning of one, as you do also. Tell me, when you read, do you lean your head forward?"

Annie frowned, reflecting. "I suppose I do."

"That you must stop. If you need stronger glasses, you must get them, so you haff not to peer so far. Remember you are a soldier—head up, shoulders back!"

Fröken Johansson gave Annie a bottle of meadowsweet tincture, instructing her to put it in a ginger or chamomile tisane and to eat something with it.

"One question—" Annie ventured on the threshold of the clinic. "When you're finished with me, will I be able to dance?"

The masseuse gave her a sly smile. "Zat depends, Madame. Could you dance before?"

When she first came out of mourning, James Crafts had taken her out on the dance floor sometimes—as a favor to Clem, she assumed. She had loved to waltz, to dance reels and schottisches, quadrilles and cotillions, to whirl from one partner to another until the music stopped and they stood there, breathless, red-cheeked, laughing. She hadn't had to worry about putting on weight in her dancing days, she loved it so. Somewhere along the way, the dancing had stopped. It would be nice to know that if she wanted to, she could start again.

She pictured herself at Tinta's wedding the previous August, in the wheelchair they'd got to help her up the steep Swiss paths, watching her eldest niece in the arms of her lovestruck young husband, catching his passing glance of pity at the sight of her invalid aunt. How lovely it would have been then, to get up and dance. How lovely it would have been, to have been asked.

"I shall come twice a week," she said firmly, trying to stand as tall as she could and wincing with the effort. "I will drink my tea—" she patted the little package, "and change my glasses, and keep my shoulders back. If I were able to dance again, just a little, it would be worth it."

"Ja! Zat is the spirit. Ve vill do the best ve can with you."

That evening in her usual chair, Annie realized she was bending forward to read. "Adèle, would you fetch me a firm cushion—no, wait, I'll do it myself." The meadowsweet tea helped a little, but every muscle and joint creaked and howled in protest as she rose from the armchair.

Adèle looked alarmed. "Madame, please, do not trouble—"

"Don't tell me that!" It was sharper than she'd meant, but the pain that shivered through her hips nearly felled her back into the chair. "Forgive me—I must move as much as possible, says the clinic lady."

"Forgive *my* saying, but when you came in, you looked like a cripple. Are you sure—"

"You mean, even more like one." Annie smiled. "It has to get worse before it gets better."

"But, Madame, how do you know—"

"I don't." Annie placed a square pillow at the back of the armchair. "But I look at Madame Greene, who is eighteen years older than I—" Adèle's look of disbelief told her all she needed to know. "The Swedish lady says that when she came to her, she looked like me. And could not move very well. But you see how well she does now."

"When you came in, I thought you had been run over by an omnibus."

"Well, that's what it feels like at present." Annie re-settled herself gingerly and picked up her book. "But I'll have to be careful. If the Colony ladies find out I'm no longer an invalid, they'll be dragging me off to their committees and teas."

"Horreurs!" Adèle smiled. "But you don't have to tell them, do you? You can pretend, when you go out to church."

"Let's hope it comes to that!"

Chapter 8

Jackson Burwell was thinner since his last visit; Annie was sure of it. The rims of his eyes had the pink of insomnia, his cuffs looked frayed, and his coat bore the marks of too many brushings. Surely his allowance from home was ample; could he be gambling? Using drugs? But he brightened at the sight of her, or perhaps of the dining-table replete with plates of sandwiches, bowls of fruit, and tiers of cakes and pastries. She took him by both hands.

"How glad I am to see you again! Come sit and tell me how things go for you."

He returned the pressure of her hands and dipped his head shyly. "It's real nice to see you again, Mrs. Shaw—say, you didn't put all this on just for me, did you?"

Annie waved him to a chair. "I grew fond of high teas when I visited London as a child. It's a civilized transition from afternoon to evening, and Cook loves to show off her skills as a patissière. So you'd better do it justice, or she'll be crestfallen." She poured tea, added a few drops of meadowsweet extract to her own and sipped at it.

"What happened to that flat you mentioned, in the rue des

Saints-Pères?"

"Unfortunately, someone beat me to it. May I have another?"

"Help yourself—that's what they're for." Annie nibbled a triangle of pâté on toast. "You're still in that place in the Fourteenth?"

"I'm afraid so." Jackson avoided her gaze. "I won't get my results from the Beaux-Arts exams for a while, so I signed on at Julian's to tide me over—"

Julian's was expensive, but surely the boy could afford its fees along with a decent semblance of room and board. Was his brother holding back on what his father had intended to keep him in decency and comfort? Was there some disapproval of the young man's course on the part of one who held the purse-strings? Annie grew indignant at the thought.

"Mr. Burwell—Jackson—your father as much as asked me to look out for you, and it pains me to think of you crammed into a slum in the Fourteenth—that's all they have there, from what I hear. It doesn't look as if you're taking good care of yourself. I'm sorry if I'm overstepping bounds, but—I'm concerned."

The young man's lips tightened. "I shouldn't have come. It's sponging, taking advantage—" He half-rose.

"To accept an invitation to tea? To please your hostess and flatter her cook with a healthy appetite? Really, I—" Annie stopped, noting with dismay that Jackson's eyes were brimming. "I don't mean to pry, but if you'd tell me what's troubling you, you may be sure it will go no further." Had he been dissipating his funds in the Latin Quarter?

Jackson cleared his throat, took a deep breath and squared his shoulders. "My father's provision for me is generous enough. However, it was not calculated to stretch to the support of a wife and child."

It was the one response Annie hadn't anticipated. "You're married?"

"In the eyes of God, Mrs. Shaw. In the eyes of the law, we're not—we aren't allowed to marry. Her name is Lydia. She is—a colored lady. My son is a colored boy."

Annie was silent for a moment. "What's his name? How old is he?"

"Ben. Benjamin Franklin Burwell. His mother's grandmother was—ah, one of the plantation workers, a house-servant—back before the War."

A slave, that meant. And her granddaughter married to one of the plantation's heirs.

"He's nine months old now," Jackson's words sped up. "We went to a colored preacher, and made our vows before God, and lived apart by day. I hoped, somehow, there would come a time when we could live together as husband and wife. I thought of moving North, and finding work, but what work would there be for someone like me, and I'd always planned to be an artist—"

"Did your father know?"

"He got it out of me, not long before he died. He said I wasn't the first young man to get ensnared by a pretty colored girl—those were his words—but as for my being married, that was absurd, and I couldn't let this ruin my life or my chances as an artist. I must go to Paris—"

"—and what of your wife? Your son's mother?" Any residue of sentiment Annie had felt toward Roland Burwell was dissipating rapidly.

"She'd look after herself, they always do, he said. I didn't tell him who she was, and he didn't know about Ben—" Jackson's lips twisted in a bitter smile. "'And live on what? The air?' I said. 'You must go and forget her,' he said. So, he sent me away. I don't come of age, under the will, until I turn twenty-five. So, I thought, I *shall* go to Paris, and work as hard as I can, and send most of my allowance back to Lydia—and some day, when I succeed, as by God I intend to, she and I and our son will be together again. As a family."

"How did you tell her?" Annie's words came out flat, half-choked.

"She knew. When I came to her that night she said, 'he knows, doesn't he, and he's sending you away.' And I picked up my son from his cradle, and—" long-suppressed tears were trickling slowly down the boy's cheeks. "I'm sorry, I never meant to—" He pulled out a handkerchief and dabbed at his nose.

"She said 'I release you. I knew it would come to this. I should never have let this happen.' And I put down my son and took her in my arms and said, 'You can't—you're my wife before God, and this is my son, and I'm not letting either of you go.'"

"But you came away," Annie said softly.

"I had to. And I *will* succeed as an artist and I *will* be reunited with them. In the meantime, I send them as much as I can—it's little enough for a mother and child, God knows—"

"—hence the garret in Montparnasse."

"Don't pity me, Mrs. Shaw! It was my own doing." Jackson blew his nose vigorously then looked over the handkerchief, eyes full of apology.

"How could you think to survive?"

Jackson gave her a rueful smile and shook his head. "Paris is so cheap, everyone said. But I hadn't counted on the fees at Julian's—and what if I don't get into the École?"

"Oh, I think you will, in time. The question is how to get you out of this quandary. Now, bear with me a moment—what could you afford, if you were not supporting a wife and child?"

"Well, something quite decent," Jackson said, "a little house, even, with one or two bedrooms and a studio, on the edge of the city, but—"

Annie set her teacup down with the air of a lawyer who has clinched an argument. "Then why not bring them to Paris?"

"Lydia? And Ben?"

"Did you know that French law does not recognize distinctions of race?"

He stared at her. "It's never come up—it wouldn't, of course, I've told no one but you, and I'm sorry—"

"I'm very glad indeed that you did, though you didn't mean to, I know. What a sad and cruel situation! It is not to be borne." Annie's own eyes filled and she reached for a handkerchief.

"It has been hard." Jackson bowed his head.

"How do they fare? What do you hear from her?"

"Oh, she's very brave—and good," he said with a broken smile. "Everything goes well, she says, Ben grows so fast, which means that he needs new shoes, which she can't afford. She's a dressmaker, a very good one—but sometimes she works so hard on things and her customers, ah, 'forget' to pay her, or give her less than was agreed, and there's nothing she can do—"

"Because they're white, I take it—" Annie said grimly.

"Oh, Mrs. Shaw, I'm so ashamed!" He dropped his gaze again, but Annie kept hers on him until he looked up again and saw the sympathy in her eyes.

"Of what? Of falling in love, of making a promise—"

"—of leaving her so! We should have gone North together, I

should have found work as a clerk, or—something, anything—"

"Things might not have been much better there. Some of the Northern states—the states whose men fought and died to free the Negroes—have laws against intermarriage as well. And even if they don't, I'm told life for couples like you and your wife can be very harsh, even in a place like Boston."

Annie was thinking of Silas Campbell, one of the 54th's drummer boys. She had taken a motherly fancy to him at Readville, and he wrote her a letter every Christmas, telling her of his doings. He had gone back to his native New Bedford and married a white girl from a Quaker family. Taunted, threatened, jeered at, their children bullied at school, the family had fled west, settling in racially tolerant Oberlin. But they missed the sea and the port city where they had been raised, and he'd never have chosen farm work…he dreamed of returning home someday.

Might it be hard for this young wife, however constrained her life in Georgia, to leave that native ground for an alien world like Paris?

"I've heard stories," Jackson was saying. "But we love each other, we thought we'd find a way—it would be all I'd ever ask of this world if we could be together again."

"Would she come to Paris? If you could bring her here?"

"It would be a lot to ask of her." Jackson rose and paced in front of the fireplace. "Her parents are gone, but there's an aunt—"

"An aunt is nothing to a husband. I speak from first-hand experience."

"My brother sided entirely with Father. At least he doesn't know we're married—Father didn't tell him, since he thought the idea so absurd—much less that the little colored baby he must sometimes see in town is his own nephew. I know he's asked Mrs. Kernochan—the lady who introduced you and me—to keep him informed on my doings—"

"He asked her to spy on you?"

"That's why I beg you to keep this in confidence. I don't feel safe even telling my friends—I've already learned what a small world the American Colony is, and if it got back to my brother, that would be the end of my allowance. My only hope is to work hard and make a little money, doing portraits, perhaps, and when I'm twenty-five and get my inheritance, Lydia and I—"

"You can't wait that long. If she will come, and bring your son, I can help you."

I'm doing it again. Faced with a fellow being in a state of abject misery, I'm going to set things right for him. This, as Clem has rightly scolded me, has got me in trouble on past occasions. I've allowed myself to be taken advantage of. A rich woman is an easy target for the unscrupulous, particularly one with no husband to look out for her and keep her naïve generosity in check. This 'wife' of Jackson's could be a mere adventuress—ensnaring him, just as Roland had said, preying on his tender feelings till she got him trapped in a web of guilt and obligation—exercising the sensual charm for which women like that are known—

"Oh, Mrs. Shaw, if you knew her, you'd love her as I do!" Jackson sat on the edge of the loveseat, leaning forward, his hands outspread, his fervor negating the unworthy thoughts that only race-prejudice could have put in Annie's mind. Well, even Rob hadn't been free of that...

"Tell me about her."

"She's tall, and has a long neck, and long wavy hair. Skin as smooth as satin, and the fine strong features of a queen. What

I first noticed was the grace of her movements—like a dancer, or, oh, a deer," he finished lamely, and flushed, smiling, at his own foolishness. "She's shy, quiet, not one to draw attention to herself. I found her one day, sitting outside one of our 'cropper's cabins,' reading to a group of small children from the Bible. She was wearing a yellow calico dress with lace at the neck. I was out riding, and when they saw me, they started up, and the book fell at her feet, and I just jumped off the horse and grabbed the book and handed it back to her, and asked her pardon for startling her and the children so. And just for an instant, her eyes met mine, and then fell away, and she thanked me and went back to her reading. I asked her if I might stay and listen, and she said, very quietly, 'Well, I guess so, sir, if you want.' So, I sat a little away from them, under a tree, and listened to that sweet, clear voice talking about Jesus raising up the centurion's daughter from the dead. And when she got to the part about the father saying 'Lord, I'm not worthy to receive you,' I thought to myself, I'm not worthy of her, but if she'd only say a kind word to me—"

Jackson's voice quavered again and he took a breath. "And she did, eventually. I kept coming back, and bringing her books—it was Stevenson's *Child's Garden of Verses*, for the children at first, then some I thought she'd like—poetry and such. I didn't plan to fall in love with her."

Annie smiled. "We never do, do we? It just happens. And it doesn't matter what our parents think, about who might be suitable and who comes from a good family—"

"Ah, she does, you see—one of the most respectable *colored* families in the county. The colored branch of the Burwells." The boy's lips twisted. "We figured it out once—we've got a great-great grandfather in common. Which makes us third cousins.

Most of us don't even know any of our third cousins, do we?"

"My mother was friendly with one of hers, back in our Lenox days," Annie said, thinking of dear old Mr. Charles Sedgwick, who had welcomed the Haggertys, one of the first families of 'summer people,' in part because of her mother's Sedgwick antecedents. They had cemented the relationship over Elizabeth's famous milk punch. "But they'd have got along regardless. Like you and your—Lydia. She sounds lovely."

"I can go for days, you know, running around Paris, preparing my canvases and doing my oil-sketches and going to the cabarets with the fellows from Julian's—and then suddenly her sweet face will—" Jackson's voice broke.

"It must feel lonely."

"And I've never so much as looked the wrong way at another woman," Jackson declared. "She worries about that. She thinks Paris is a den of vice compared to home."

Paris *was* full of temptations for the young—for anyone, really. Celibacy was a lot to expect of a young, healthy fellow like Jackson Burwell. Annie didn't doubt him, but wondered how long he could hold out before loneliness, and envy at all he was forgoing while his companions indulged themselves, overcame whatever vows he might have made in all sincerity. A vivacious, charming life-model, for example—a lady painter at Julian's, a serving-girl in a café—someone like Bertrand's exotic Sofia would be hard for any man to resist, if she decided to test him— and since no one knew about his wife, what would hold them back?

"We must bring her back to you," Annie said, her declaration as firm as Jackson's. "Your marriage will be valid in France—a civil ceremony will make it legal, but then you'd be married in the eyes of the world—on this side of the ocean, at any rate, and no one will be able to keep you apart. There's always work in Paris for a good seamstress—we can start with the Cathedral ladies, while she learns her French—"

"But I don't have—"

Annie raised a hand. "I will pay for her passage, and Ben's. And the train journey to New York, or Baltimore—whatever you decide is best. You can meet them at Le Havre. In the meantime, you can find a place for the three of you to live—not too far from the Beaux-Arts, since that's where you'll be much of the time."

The boy's face was like a sky after a storm, clearing but not without clouds still. "I couldn't repay you until I'm of age—"

"I'm a bit of a gambler, Mr. Burwell. I'm prepared to make a modest bet on your success. If I lose, I will at least have had the satisfaction of seeing Romeo and his Juliet reunited."

Jackson gave her a sideways smile. "Mrs. Shaw, what you are is a bit of a romantic."

"Oh, more than a bit. This will take some planning, of course. I have a channel to Mr. Coolidge, the new American Minister to France—his son-in-law is my cousin by marriage—we must seek his advice about passports and visas and that sort of thing. If you'd permit me to let Mrs. Greene know about this as well, she may also have some influence with Mr. Coolidge."

Jackson looked dubious. "As long as she understands she mustn't tell anyone else about it."

"Julia loves a good gossip," Annie said, "but I'll personally guarantee her discretion on this."

Chapter 9

"**H**e's *married* to her?" Julia Greene turned in her carriage seat and stared at Annie.

"As near as a white man and a colored girl can get in that locale. Let's get out and walk to the Grande Cascade, shall we? The terrace will be lovely on a day like this." Annie tapped on the carriage roof and the driver pulled over near a small bridge. Spring was turning to summer, the green of leaves darkening to lushness, the sky a deeper blue, and the Bois de Boulogne had an idyllic air—Annie thought of Tallie and Sofia, luxuriating on their artificial foliage in Bertrand's studio. She and Julia leaned on a bridge, watching swans glide on the slow-moving water below.

"The poor fellow practically reeks of unhappiness. And to be here in the midst of this feast of art and music and companionship to be had for the asking, and be as determined as he is to be true to her, with no idea of when he'll see her again—it's just too sad!"

"It's rather a lovely story, especially given his origins. Do you think he can succeed as a painter? Thick on the ground as they are?" Slim and vibrant in a light crimson silk, Julia would have caught any painter's eye.

"Perhaps not till he, or some of his work, goes back to America," Annie said after a pause.

"Bertrand's seen some of his work," Julia said. "Some nocturnes, with ghostly figures in them, which he says are quite good—they have an unusual dreamlike quality."

"Plantation ghosts? That whole country must be haunted. I made an appointment with Mr. Coolidge, to see what needs doing about travel documents and such. I hope he won't be sticky about the circumstances—they couldn't have been legally married, of course. If necessary, I'll remind him of his fellow Harvard man's gallantry and sacrifice—seeing we're almost related."

Julia smiled. "That will be the first time I've known you to play the war-widow's card. Didn't my nephew Fred Sears marry his daughter? Poor Marian's boy—I can put a word in too, if necessary."

"It's a rotten shame Mr. Coolidge is married. He's awfully handsome."

"Has he pictures of the girl? And the child?"

"What—oh, Jackson, you mean. Not that he showed me. She sounds quite a beauty—a bit like Bertrand's Sofia, perhaps." Carriages rattled by them on the Allée de Longchamps, with dandified men in top-hats and women in pastel dresses and hats like huge flowers.

"Will she be able to adjust, d'you think? I can't imagine the reverse—being transplanted from here to a Southern plantation town, away from all my connections."

"If it were the only way to live freely with the man you loved—"

Julia flicked her skirts around a little puddle. "Perhaps. But I should have to love him a great deal. Still—better a wrenching change in this direction than the other, I suppose. But what if it doesn't work out? What if they're unhappy?"

Annie held up a hand. "Stop a minute—I'm not up to your level of stamina yet." She caught her breath. "Why borrow trouble? He loves the lady. They have a child to seal their bond. Here in France, it may go well. There, it's simply impossible—if not downright dangerous."

"True. It's just that—"

"That what?"

"The way young Tallie was looking at him, over dinner. Stared at his face 'as she would draw it,' as the Bard says." Julia took Annie's arm and they walked on together.

Annie raised an eyebrow. "You think she's developing a tendre for our young cavalier?"

"We'd best keep an eye on them. Or tell her he's married—just in case. Maybe she *does* just want to draw him."

"We can't tell her. I promised I'd only tell you. He's terrified of it getting back to Mrs. Kernochan, and then his brother. That would be the end of his allowance and any chance of getting Lydia here. But Tallie mightn't wait for an invitation."

Julia looked thoughtful. "Bertrand seems to take a proprietary interest in her. That may be all in Bertrand's mind, but these bohemians view the world differently from you and me."

"You'll want a hat to go with that—a flat brim with straw and a drift of flowers, I think." Julia, backing away from the dressmaker's little platform, gave Annie an approving once-over.

"You don't think it's too—young? Girlish?"

"Everyone's wearing pink this summer, n'est-ce pas, Mademoiselle?" The couturière, kneeling with her mouth full of pins, nodded enthusiastic agreement. "Even relics like myself. The only lace will be on the bodice, so it won't be too frilly. The ivory stripes break up the pink nicely."

"It looks—fresh," Julia concluded. "More of a peach, really. Airy and floral but not fussy."

Julia had used up a substantial portion of her goodwill with a favorite dressmaker on the rue de la Paix to persuade her to see Annie about a summer wardrobe. As the cycles of fashion dictated, the modistes were long since working on their clients' autumn and winter selections.

"Stripes are slimming, I suppose," said Annie, a little dubiously. "The bell skirt will certainly be an improvement on the bustle—I need to get rid of those. I haven't had anything this colorful since—since before I was married."

"High time, then. You're not Queen Victoria—mourning needn't be your standard. Why so many widows feel compelled to follow her unhealthy example, I can't think."

"Heavens, I haven't worn black all the time," Annie said. "But the colors have been pretty dull, I'll admit."

"Proper, staid, and matronly—as un-Parisian as it's possible to get! If you're going to set up for a salonnière, you need something to be noticed in."

"Like Retta Reubell?" Annie held her arms out for the dressmaker's tape.

"Ha! One Retta Reubell is quite enough. We'll avoid turquoise—why invite comparisons?"

Annie scanned the little room, its walls lined with bolts of silks, cottons, and summer wools in every hue and print imaginable.

"Let's have a look at that celadon, once we're done with this."

"That's the spirit!" Julia fingered the bolt Annie had spotted. "The silk's a bit heavier than the one you've got there—maybe more of an evening item. What about an organza overlay, with some roses on it? You should have at least one evening gown in case we get invited to a musical soirée."

"I sha'n't be baring my shoulders till Fröken Johansson says I've got rid of the dowager's hump." Annie shook her head ruefully. "I'm making progress, but I still felt crippled the morning after the last torture session. Still," she smiled, "it's something to aim for."

"Madame, veuillez rester immobile?" the dressmaker reproached.

"Bien sur—desolée. How about a little straw turban to go with the ecru cotton? Navy blue, to match the embroidery?"

"With a bird's wing or two to liven it up. We'll ask Madame Reboux what she thinks when we get there."

"I'm going to be quite unrecognizable," Annie grinned. "I rejoice in the prospect." She had a vision of Comte Bertrand's surprised face the next time they met, and was startled to realize that it had been guiding her choices all day.

"I'm trying a little painting on my own," she told Julia. "Will you come with me next week to Merlin et Denis, for some supplies? If the weather's fine, we might have a promenade in the Luxembourg."

Bringing in tea and lemon thins for the ladies after their shopping trip, Adèle nearly dropped her tray at the horrified expression on Annie's face, her hand slackening around a sheaf of mauve stationery.

"What is it?" Julia half-rose from her seat across the library fireplace. "Has someone died?"

"Mother Shaw is on her way to Paris," Annie croaked.

Julia opened her mouth and closed it again. "Sarah?"

Annie nodded weakly. In her too-frequent letters, her mother-in-law had occasionally mentioned wanting to see "dear old Paree" again, but had not accompanied any of her family members on their European forays. With Sarah now in her late seventies, Annie had felt safe that the threat would not materialize. Yet here it was, and soon. Mother Shaw would arrive at Le Havre on the *La Bretagne* in a week. *Your dear sister,* the letter ran...

with whom I had the pleasure of a brief visit when she arrived at New York, kindly offered me the use of her apartments for however long I may stay. Since I contemplate the possibility of a permanent residence in the City of Light to pass whatever remaining years our Creator has allotted me—you must pay no heed to my jocular references to its deficiencies in earlier letters—I told Mrs. Crafts that I should of course find my own place at whatever time I might make that decision...You will be pleased to know that despite the rigors of her voyage she is looking as well as I remember her...She has been concerned for you, dear Annie, an invalid all alone in a strange city, and saw at once the benefits of having a loving family member nearby...

Mother Shaw. Not only in Paris but across the hall. What in God's name had Clem been thinking?

"How could she?" said Julia aloud. "She knows how you feel about that woman!"

Annie shook her head. Ties of family and civility, and Annie's affection for Rob's sisters, had dictated continued, if limited contact with the woman whose emotional manipulations had sent her son to his death and destroyed Annie's future. And who, far from acknowledging the wrong she had done her daughter-in-law, expected Annie to live out the role of the martyred hero's widow, as she herself made a career of playing the *mater dolorosa*. But until now, Mother Shaw had been a safe three thousand miles away.

Annie's stomach seemed to have fallen into her shoes. "And Clem tells her she can stay next door as long as she wants!"

"As to that," said Julia gloomily, "you know Sarah. Likely she simply assumed Clem would be eager to accommodate her. And that you and I—there'll be a letter waiting for me at home, no doubt—could wish no greater joy in life than her—" she shuddered, "permanent companionship."

Adèle picked up the teapot. "Mesdames would prefer a tonique nerveux?"

"Thank you, Adèle, that would be lovely."

"Oh-la-la!" Adèle headed toward the kitchen, shaking her head.

"It's possible she has grown less insufferable since we last met," said Julia, "though I shouldn't care to wager much on that."

"Do you correspond?" Annie stuffed Sarah's letter beneath a book as though it might be made to disappear.

"Irregularly. Always at her initiative. She has inquired after you on a few occasions, but since we were not reacquainted until recently, I could tell her nothing. I see you're glad of that."

"I am," Annie admitted. "Nor have I mentioned you in letters to her—or to Clem. It's not that I have anything to hide, but—

Sarah has a way of seeking to *own* one. It's part of the reason I made Rob burn my letters—"

Julia's eyebrows raised. "That was a hard thing to ask of him, surely—"

"He wrote to me once, from Fredericksburg, telling me of a house they commandeered after they took the town. Of going through the desk of the owner, reading and laughing over the man's love-letters, and I thought, what if his camp were overrun and the enemy read *my* foolish letters to *him?* For their collective amusement, around a campfire? I couldn't bear it."

Adèle returned with the new pot of tea and looked inquiringly from once face to the other. Annie reached for the teapot.

"Deux minutes de plus, Madame."

"Merçi, Adèle. And then," Annie continued, "if he were killed, I knew she would want to publish his letters—to and from—to immortalize him as a martyr for the Cause—"

"Which in fact she did." Julia reached for a lemon thin. "You didn't want the general public reading your correspondence."

Anger flooded over Annie at the memory. No one's private life had been safe around Sarah Shaw; she assumed the right to do as she wished with anything that fell into her hands. "I didn't want *her* reading my correspondence. As it was, she published the letters he sent *her*, in the newspapers. Before the 54th even. He protested, but she kept doing it. When he was made Colonel, she blanketed her circle of friends with photographs of him in his Colonel's uniform. He was mortified." Annie poured the tisane. "When I explained my reasoning, he took it to heart. And I don't think he disturbed anyone else's private correspondence after that, unless they were considered a threat to our side."

Julia set her cup down. "I should have felt as you did."

"Do you think she'll take to Paris?"

"She's not a flexible person." Julia stared thoughtfully at a small Durand near the fireplace, a scene of a rocky woodland glen which Annie had kept from her father's collection. "She likes to have things arranged to suit her, and the daughters have danced to her tune all these years. They're all in the City, aren't they?"

"Susie Minturn is spending most of her time at Point-à-Pic." The middle sister who had introduced Rob and Annie, widowed three years since, had four eligible daughters and a little son to chase after. Her summer home on the upper St. Lawrence was conveniently distant from Mother Shaw. "Effie Lowell hops all over the country to her philanthropic meetings. And poor Anna is nursing her George, who's said to be quite ill—"

"Mr. Curtis? I hadn't heard."

"Effie's letter mentioned it a few weeks back," Annie said. "I hadn't thought to tell you—and he your nephew by marriage too. Ellen's Frank Barlow is poorly as well. Something to do with his kidneys."

"So, Mamma is lacking in devotees at present." Julia refilled their teacups. "Mmm, this is helping a little. Now, what are we going to do about this menace?"

"She does need to have everything her way, doesn't she? Paris *per se* will not accommodate that. She'll expect us to smooth her paths—"

Julia's eyes took on a mischievous glint. "What if we strew some rocks instead?"

"She'll want you to accompany her to church," Annie said. "Thank God I'm Episcopalian, which is decadence personified in her eyes. She made such a fuss against us being married at Ascension."

"She didn't try to convert you, surely?"

"She wanted the wedding at the Staten Island Unitarian church she and Mr. Shaw had helped found. Rob set her straight there. He said, 'It's always at the bride's church—how would you feel if Susie had married Bob Minturn at *their* church?' The Minturns being Episcopalians too—she couldn't argue with that." Sarah had wanted Rob to wear his colonel's uniform to their hastily planned wedding, but he had refused. If only he'd refused her on things that mattered, like taking the regiment.

"I don't feel the need of church. To experience the sacred, I go for a long walk in the Bois—" Julia looked thoughtful. "You could flee to Cannes, pretend you'd gone before the letter came—"

"She'd just follow me there— Cannes is an invalid Mecca, and you'll recall she's always describing herself as an invalid. No, I think we must find a way to stand our ground here—or I must, anyway..." The thought of being abandoned to the Gorgon was dispiriting. Julia eyed her keenly and set down her cup.

"I wouldn't do that to you! So formidable a foe requires a collective attack. What's worse, like so many of our vintage, she conceives of the younger generation as servants to the whims of the elder, never mind that the younger generation is, at this stage—"

"Well into its fifties," Annie finished.

"Might we set her up with one or two of the more, ah, adhesive old ladies from the Cathedral set?"

"Why do you think I don't mind being known as an invalid? I could produce a sick headache on cue if they arrived at my door.

It used to get me out of Clem's Dorcas Society gatherings—
Adèle and I had a system of codes."

Julia puckered her brows. "Could we produce a suitor for her?
An unwelcome one?"

"That may be worth pursuing." Annie sipped her tisane. "Ha!
Poor old Doktor Finkelmann from the École des Mines—a
former colleague of James.' A devotee of Wagner, with a
prodigious case of halitosis and a habit of sitting too close to
one on sofas. He came to call a couple of times, but I managed
to get rid of him—"

"How old?"

"A hundred and five, I think. Widowed young, so he thought
we might have something in common. Certainly old enough
to pay court to Mother Shaw. He's passionate on the subject of
American slavery, now I think of it—"

"Aha! She can pour out the story of her gloriously martyred
son."

"I doubt she could resist a new victim. Knowing Herr Doktor,
he'd bone up on everything he could find about the 54th, to
dazzle her with his erudition. To quiz someone who was
practically an eye-witness—he'd fasten on her like the Old Man
of the Sea—"

Julia clapped her hands together. "They'd deserve each other—
it's almost too much to hope for! Have you others in reserve?"

"There's Capitaine LeBoeuf, who led an ignominious retreat
at Sedan, though in his version it was the most prodigious feat of
gallantry since the Spartans at Thermopylae. He has enormous,
waxed moustaches and fancies himself the ladies' man. A wealthy
widow like Mother Shaw might be his cup of tea."

Julia rose and stared out the window into the courtyard as

though expecting Sarah's coach to come bursting through from the building's front hallway. "What if she *liked* one of them?"

"Little chance of that. Morbid as she is, clinging to the memory of the Sacred Dead—"

"There is a difference, isn't there? Between genuinely mourning those we've loved and lost, and deriving social advantage as a Tragedy Queen. I'm surprised poor Frank lived as long as he did. I thought she'd have eaten out his substance long before."

Annie brushed cookie crumbs from her lap. "Was he unhappy, d'you think?" There had always seemed a veil of sadness around the gentle Frank Shaw, even before his son's death, tempering Annie's anger at his role in Rob's tragedy with pity and a lingering affection.

"I don't know that she'd left him enough will to know. He was so...forceful in the public sphere, but of course he was pursuing the shared ideals that had been the basis of their marriage. Lord knows it couldn't have been her looks!"

Annie howled. "Julia, how wonderfully *feline* you are at times!"

Julia grew thoughtful. "What does a woman like Sarah find repellent?"

"Vulgarity. Anything that smacks of sensual indulgence—the Sturgises are old Puritans, after all—"

"As are the Shaws, but I got away from all that. Worldliness, urbanity—"

"Paris is the last place she ought to be comfortable, then." Annie drained the last of the nerve-tonic, which seemed to have done some good. Her mind felt more focused and clearer. "But the bonds of kinship, however tenuous—if she's worn out her welcome with more immediate family members—"

"Or perhaps she's just bored. That woman hasn't had enough

scope for her immense—what does Nietzsche call it?—will to power? She should have been a general in the War, or a captain of industry. And since she's female, she tried to get there through the men in her life. Frank was a grave disappointment to her, poor fellow. She told him he lacked the faith in himself to aim for greatness—difficult when your wife is bent upon the surgical removal of your, ah, manly parts."

Annie stifled an unseemly snort, then grew sober. "She convinced Rob she had sacrificed everything in life for his sake. She was horrified when she learned he was courting me. I wasn't at all what she had in mind for him—good Lord, if she's looking for an outlet for her Will to Power, what do you suppose she has in mind for me?"

"You'll be the kindly caretaker for the invalid she professes to be—when she's no more an invalid than that racehorse I bet on at Auteuil, and he's paid my millinery bills for the last two years. If there is a Deity, I wonder he doesn't punish all these fainting cases with the bad health they seem to crave."

"You can threaten her with your Swedish exercises, if she limps over the threshold in a state of imminent collapse." Annie felt herself straightening up as if hearing Fröken Johansson's voice in her ear; it was becoming a habit, as stooping had been previously. Progress. But the prospect of Sarah in her vicinity made her want to curl up like a hedgehog.

"These young Bohemians of yours…" Julia began thoughtfully.

"Bertrand and Tallie are *your* young Bohemians. I'd never have met them—"

"—but Jackson's yours. Could we induce them, d'you think, to some sort of egregious misbehavior—"

Annie's eyes widened. "Mother Shaw arrives to find Jackson

and Tallie *au naturel* in Clem's grand salon, with Bertrand painting them as Eros and Psyche—"

"Not a bad start!" Julia bounced to her feet, eyes gleaming. "'Oh, dear, what a shame, Sarah—your letter just reached us today, and we'd promised them the use of the Crafts' flat as a studio...'" Her fan bounced up and down on her palm.

"When is the *La Bretagne* due at Le Havre?"

Julia made some mental calculations. "Next Tuesday, I think, if the weather's been favorable."

"Apollo and Daphne might be even better," Annie mused. "Unbridled male desire in action—well, we'll give Bertrand his choice, or perhaps he'll have an idea of his own—"

"Jackson could do *him* as Hades, carrying off Persephone," Julia warmed to the subject. "He'll have to paint in a beard, perhaps little horns..."

"We'll have to see if Tallie recoils from this prospect in horror. I certainly would."

Julia reached for her parasol. "Are you sure? In her current circumstances—"

"I'll have to make it a paid commission, of course," Annie said.

"I have it!" Julia dropped the parasol and clapped her hands. "Tallie paints Jackson and Bertrand—both quite naked—as Jacob wrestling with the Angel."

Adèle, gathering the tea-things, looked from one to the other with suspicious severity. "*Mesdames?*"

"I mightn't mind painting that myself," Annie grinned.

Julia's laugh was an unladylike roar. "Going native has taken you no time at all. What would your sister say?"

"Nothing," said Annie darkly, "if she knows what's good for her. She deserves whatever she gets—paint-spots on the carpet, the furniture, naked men cavorting about the *grand salon*—we may have to smash a Sèvres vase or two just for vengeance—"

"Oh, that's going too far!"

"All right, we'll put the Sèvres out of harm's way. And drop-cloths on the floor. Clem may have some notion of making this abomination up to me, though I can't imagine how."

"Look here, are we really going to do any of this?"

Annie rose to walk Julia to the door. "We've got to do *something*. Let's see what the young folks have to say."

Chapter 10

udging by her portrait, Jackson Burwell's Lydia was a beauty: swan-necked, olive-skinned, with huge dark eyes and a long, almost Norman nose. The infant at her breast had a light dust of gold in his curls; the mother seemed lost in reverie.

"You're wondering how I could have left her," Jackson said. The painting transformed Annie's mantelpiece into a sort of shrine.

"You hadn't much choice, but this helps me appreciate all the more what a wrench it was. What do you hear from her?"

He looked away, biting his lip. "They're well. She's doing her best to convince me they're getting on splendidly without me, but—" he shook his head. "She doesn't sound herself. She's holding back—trying not to upset me. And she seems afraid that I'm going to leave her for some Parisian temptress. As if I could ever—"

Annie handed him a plate of sandwiches. "Have you told her about the plan? To bring her here?"

"I hadn't dared mention it yet. Unless—until you—"

"Ah! Mr. Coolidge. He came back from America last week. I

have an appointment for tomorrow, and I'll lay it all before him. You must have been wondering whether I were serious after all. I'm sorry I didn't apprise you of the delay."

His brow cleared. Some people's looks were improved by brooding, but Jackson's gold hair and blue eyes were made for happiness. The lovely boy he had made with Lydia would grow into an Apollo.

"This would ornament any church as a *Madonna and Child*. Had you thought of doing a version to exhibit, with her wearing a mantle? I think the Salon would find it entrancing."

Jackson looked doubtful.

"Don't you see—Mary was a Jew from the Middle East. She couldn't possibly have been the insipid blonde with dolly features as she's so often depicted. Your Lydia makes a splendid Madonna. The Christ child wasn't a pale-skinned doll either. I'm honored you brought this to show me, Jackson. It fortifies my resolve for the meeting with the Minister." Annie passed him a plate of jam tarts.

"I am, however," she said after an interval, "facing a truly fearful prospect. My sister has seen fit to lend out her apartments to a woman I had hoped never to see again in this life. A woman I would readily label a Gorgon."

Jackson paused in mid-bite.

"My erstwhile mother-in-law, Mrs. Francis George Shaw of Staten Island. She'll be here within the week and proposes an indefinite stay. Next door."

"Your Colonel's mother? The abol—"

"The same. The reason he became the Colonel, and the reason I was widowed. I loathe the woman."

"She's coming alone?"

"She didn't mention companions. There may be a servant or two. She proposes to throw herself upon the hospitality of her family, as she claims to think of us—myself and Madame Greene, who's the sister of her late husband—"

"But you're not blood family," Jackson protested. "I thought the Colonel had sisters—"

Annie took the painting from the mantel, propping it carefully against Jackson's armchair. "She's been living with one of them—Effie Lowell, a war widow, as I was, but left with a daughter. My sister-in-law is a professional practitioner of Good Works. Her letters teem with accounts of committee meetings for the improvement of this and the reform of that, and train-journeys all over the country, and encounters with the good and the great. If I were Effie, I'd absent myself as much as possible too. I believe Mother Shaw is feeling neglected, and has decided on a change of scene."

"Your sister—Mrs. Crafts—didn't consult you about this?" Jackson looked charmingly indignant on Annie's behalf.

"Mother Shaw enmeshes one in her assumptions as does a spider in its web. All my sister would have had to do is acknowledge that she had kept the lease on the apartment, and Sarah would have pounced. I can't exonerate Mrs. Crafts, however. In the circumstances I'd have had the ingenuity—and the motivation—to dissemble. But I've had a lot more practice with the woman."

"She thinks to make her home here in Paris? She doesn't sound—"

"—like someone who could possibly appreciate the place. Indeed, when she spoke to me of her travels when her children were small, she described Paris as dirty, smelly, and immoral, and its inhabitants godless and surly. However, it's been—what do they say?—'Haussmannisée' since then. No doubt the reports from visiting Americans have grown more favorable."

Jackson rose and returned the painting to its leather portfolio.

"Mrs. Shaw, you are arousing my chivalrous instincts. I must do something to save you from this dragon in human form." He tapped his forefinger against his lower lip.

"Even someone who dislikes what makes Paris Paris," Annie said gloomily, "can find refuge in the American Colony."

"True—I've already met many people who never venture beyond their own few streets, or the English reading-rooms, or the Munroe Brothers offices—" Jackson paused. "Would she be going to the Cathedral?"

"She's a Unitarian, and militant in that creed, so she'll go to the American Church in the Seventh. She hasn't any French, as far as I know—the book sort, perhaps, but not the conversational."

"So, she plans to rely on you as translator—if she interacts with the natives at all."

"We thought of connecting her with a few of the more tiresome Church ladies, the dowagers who feel it their Godly duty to call upon poor invalids such as myself—"

"But you're not—" Jackson began.

"Hush, lad! Do you know how many committees I've been spared from serving on, and how many rounds of afternoon calls I've avoided, by being thought an invalid? I was one, for quite some time—long enough for the impression to be engraved in the minds of the good ladies of the Colony. And I've pled an attack of something or other, when they came calling to offer me the comforts of piety. Young and male as you are, you have no idea of the danger faced by women of my age and circumstances—of perishing in agonies of boredom at the hands of the earnest and well-intentioned."

Jackson shuddered. "I was trapped a few times when Aunt Alice was entertaining such ladies. I felt like leaping out the window. And is this senior Mrs. Shaw such a person?"

"If only that were all!" Annie rose and paced the fireplace. "It's worse. She assumes that whatever surroundings she finds herself in are duty-bound to conform immediately to her wishes and plans. Paris will be in full spring bloom; Madame Greene and I will welcome her as thirsty desert travelers do water—and our sole topic of conversation will be the tragic and glorious martyrdom of her son in the Great Cause, and the monument in progress to honor him—" she paused, registering the shock on Jackson's face.

"Oh, my dear," she said, patting his hand, "his death *was* tragic and glorious, and—saving your ancestry—in a great cause. But there is heartfelt mourning, and there is self-dramatization, with its assumption that all one's interlocutors should be both fellow players in their assigned parts—I'd be the grieving widow, for instance—and infinitely patient audience."

Jackson grinned. "I'd thought that only happened among the ladies of the Decoration of the Graves of the Glorious Confederate Dead. Poor Aunt Alice—all the losses she'd suffered, and she was expected to sit like Patience on a monument while Mrs. Colonel Such-and-Such went on about the treacherous Yankee attack on Fort Somewhere or Other."

"Ah, then you've already met the likes of Mother Shaw." Annie's tone became conspiratorial. "Madame Greene and I were wondering if we might enlist a few of you young people in a scheme of deterrence. But only if you think you might have fun doing it."

Jackson rose and bowed, sweeping off an imaginary plumed hat. "I shall be honored to assemble the Queen's Musketeers! Name your players and their parts."

"I suppose you've come about Mr. Deacon," Thomas Jefferson Coolidge, the American Minister, perused Annie over his coffee-cup. Mr. Coolidge's slight physique and sea-blue eyes, full of weary amusement, were distracting; he looked as Rob might have, had he lived.

Annie searched her brain for his reference. Of course: the American who had murdered his wife's French lover in a Cannes hotel last February. She put down her cup. "Goodness, no!"

The Minister's shoulders dropped with relief. "You've no idea how many Colony ladies are agitating for me to get the fellow released, or pardoned. I'd have thought a year's imprisonment for murdering a man more or less in cold blood was getting off very lightly indeed."

"The French seem to think so. I wonder what the ladies would think if it were a Frenchman murdering his wife's American lover. By all accounts Deacon was a dreadful husband, and she had been—ah, less than discreet for quite some time. That's what one heard in Cannes, at any rate. Why didn't they just divorce?"

"To avoid scandal, I suppose." The Minister's eyes brightened with merriment. "D'you know, Mrs. Shaw, it's surprising we haven't met before now. My son-in-law Fred Sears is a cousin of your late husband's—his mother, who died giving birth to him, was a younger sister of Mr. Francis Shaw's."

"Poor Aunt Marian!" Rob had told her of his beautiful aunt, youngest of his father's siblings, gone at twenty-seven. "Rob— my husband—said she was more of a playfellow than an aunt. I met Fred once or twice. He would only have been eight when Rob died."

"I knew him, you know." Coolidge's face clouded. "Not well, but enough to remember—Bob, we called him then. A charming, golden-haired lad. Just as well, since he was rather a troublemaker at school."

"So he told me," Annie smiled. "What a tiny world it is. Have you met Mr. Sears' aunt, Mrs. Greene? We're recently reacquainted, though we've both lived in Paris for years. I wish I'd known her sooner."

"I mean to, soon. Fred and Nora are looking forward to calling on her."

"She'll enjoy that, I know. Especially if Fred's nice-looking."

"My daughter evidently thinks so. Tell me how I can help you, since you've afforded me a respite from the prevailing preoccupation."

Annie told him.

"The lady is colored? And your young friend wishes to marry her?"

"He is, in fact, married to her," Annie summoned a reserve of smiling patience, "in the eyes of God, and they have a little son—for whom his father pines, naturally. But you know as well as I do the laws of the Southern states—"

"—some Northern states have them too." As a Boston Brahmin descended from a slave-holding Southern President, the Minister was perhaps conflicted regarding sectional distinctions.

"Exactly. Which is why she must come and join him in France. They may marry here with perfect legality."

"So they would become landed immigrants in France, even citizens..." Coolidge frowned. "Is the young man ready to renounce the land of his birth?"

"Surely non-citizens may marry in France? Perhaps they contemplate returning to America, if its policies regarding the personal choices of its citizens ever become more enlightened. In the meantime, he will finish his artistic studies, and she is a skilled seamstress who has been earning her own living."

"You're quite right—the French will let them marry, and stay as long as they don't become public charges. You're sure this is what he wants? Burwell—weren't they one of—"

"The Fuhst Families of Vuhginia," Annie finished, the voice of Mrs. Edgar Burwell echoing in her head. "Sorry! I heard that phrase once too often from his grandmother, in my own youth." What stuck in her mind, though, was her beloved George's devastating imitation of the Burwell matriarch's plummy phrasing.

Coolidge failed to stifle a laugh. "You sounded just like my mother. Who was quite the Southern belle, and the apple of her grandfather Tom's eye. So this young Burwell is good-looking, well-spoken, comes from a bit of money? There must be a lot of, ah, talented ladies in Paris who'd welcome him into the bohemian fraternities—"

"That has already happened, but he's a veritable Galahad— pure of heart and devoted to his little family." Annie thought suddenly of Julia's assertion that Tallie seemed to be developing a tendre for Jackson, and his reports of Lydia's insecurities about his fidelity.

"The Southern cavalier," Mr. Coolidge mused. "That's what got that damn—that benighted war going. All that feudal claptrap about knights and fair ladies and faithful dusky retainers, born and bound to the land as the Lord intended. Seems I heard somewhere his father was a suitor of yours—if I'm not being too intrusive?"

"Good Lord, the Colony is far too small." Annie felt herself blushing. "You'll have heard this from Mrs. Kernochan, I suppose."

"She stopped in to commend her young artist kinsman to my attention," Coolidge smiled, cocking an eyebrow. "She seemed to think he warranted keeping an eye on—and I suppose she was right."

"Oh, please—I must ask for your absolute discretion. If Mrs. Kernochan were to hear of this, she'd feel honor-bound to report it to Edgar—Jackson's brother, and the controller of his purse until he turns twenty-five."

"And he'd cut the boy off?"

"There's no doubt of it. To your question, yes—heartless woman that I was, I refused Roland Burwell's suit."

"Because he was a Southerner?"

"Indeed, no! My family on both sides was connected to the cotton trade. There were more Southern swains around our dining-table than Yankees. I simply couldn't reciprocate his feelings. Though it would have taken an overwhelming passion to induce me to become a plantation mistress. What a provincial life it must have been!—except for your great-grandfather, of course," Annie added hastily, fearful of having given offense. "Monticello is something else altogether, I'm told."

"M. Carnot congratulated me for following in his footsteps as

Minister to France," Coolidge smiled. "In that respect, at least, I hope to emulate him. Your young lady—Mrs. Burwell?—has spent her whole life in the South, hasn't she? I wonder how she'll adjust." Coolidge put aside his coffee cup, and Annie took the hint to retrieve her reticule.

"It's hard to think a young Negro lady from the South would not rejoice in the prospect of broader horizons—but we do cling to what's familiar, don't we, however confining it might seem. We'll give her a proper welcome—have you met Mr. Tanner?"

Coolidge's face looked blank, then brightened. "The Negro painter? From Philadelphia. Not yet, though I look forward to it."

"Mr. Burwell's made a friend of him. That's a small start."

"You seem to be arranging matters very well. I foresee no difficulty with the formalities—and I will keep this confidential." Coolidge went behind Annie and pulled back the chair as she rose. "And now that we're personally acquainted—you perhaps know that Mrs. Coolidge is an invalid, and that my daughter Mrs. Sears is serving as my hostess. Since she is, after all, your cousin by marriage—"

Annie smiled. "How pleasant to think of that!"

"—I'll suggest that she call on you, and that you might be included in a few of our more, ah, intimate social gatherings. Along with Mrs. Greene, should she be amenable."

"I can safely say we would both be delighted." Annie rejoiced inwardly; she had no aversion whatever to further social contact with the Minister, who was rather handsome in that fine-boned Brahmin way. "Forgive me, but you have me curious now—what do you think to do about Mr. Deacon? I assure you I have no recommendation whatever."

Coolidge's face fell. "I suppose I shall have to intervene on his behalf. I can't say I'm looking forward to it."

"Perhaps it would be best," Annie added as an afterthought, "if you were not to disclose Mrs. Burwell's—ah—heritage, unless of course it's necessary to the documentation."

"I doubt it will be necessary, Mrs. Shaw." Coolidge smiled, showing her out.

Annie wondered about Mrs. Coolidge, and whether her "invalidism," like her own in the past, served the useful function of limiting her societal obligations. And then wondered if that might leave Mr. Coolidge free to pursue other connections.

Bertrand's eyes gleamed at Annie over the rim of his brandy-glass. "Why not include yourself in this lovely *tableau*?"

"Me? In what possible capacity?"

Jackson and Tallie exchanged smirks.

Bertrand's gaze wandered around the Crafts' grand salon, to which the group had removed after dinner to assess its potential as a studio. "You're a Shakespearean, aren't you? I'm thinking of that scene in *Pericles* where the hero's virtuous daughter is offered by the wicked Procuress for the delectation of the male population of—Lesbos, was it?"

"Bertrand, that is a shocking proposition even from you. Are you envisioning Madame Shaw in the Procuress role?" Julia twirled her sherry glass.

"Unless Madame Greene would rather take it on herself," he replied with an undisguised leer. "I shall be Boult, of course, and Monsieur Burwell the prospective, ah, client, with a golden ducat in his hand. We shall all three—" he gestured toward Tallie, who was looking slightly fevered—"take turns in executing this *magnum opus*. A collaborative effort—"

"'From the School of Bertrand de Leiningen,' the art historians will label it," Tallie said.

Bertrand nodded. "An amusing test of our capabilities, don't you think?"

"It will be something of—a copying exercise?" Jackson said, "for me and Miss DeKuyper? There must be a unified style—"

"We shall all engage in a copying exercise." Bertrand rose and clapped his hands together. "In the style of Caravaggio. Like one of those tavern scenes, with the ladies overblown and half-falling out of their dresses, the gents ruddy-faced from drink—"

"This may be going too far even for you, lad," Julia said. "As the closest to a figure of parental authority among you, I'm not sure I can countenance—"

"Oh, it'll be all right!" Annie heard herself saying. "We did Shakespeare scenes here all the time, when my nieces were younger—I was the Nurse in *Romeo and Juliet*, which isn't so far off from this dame."

"But no one was painting you," Tallie noted. "What will your Cathedral ladies say?"

"It's what the senior Madame Shaw will say that I'm interested in."

Bertrand twiddled a cufflink. "I shall count it a success if she faints dead away on the spot."

"As will I!" said Julia.

"Does she expect to be met at Le Havre?" Jackson looked worried.

"Some agent of the Sturgis family will meet her and see her conveyed to my doorstep," Annie said.

"She's a Sturgis by birth," Julia added. "The American Medici, they've been called. Made fortunes in the China trade—as did my own father, in fact. Financial tentacles over half the globe. Father was greatly disappointed when I rejected the hand of Miss Sturgis's brother."

"Wasn't he your cousin?" Tallie said.

"As were Sarah Sturgis and my late brother Frank Shaw. It was encouraged in our circles—keeping the money in the family, marrying a known quantity. Like European royalty, I suppose. It used to be quite the thing—though, happily, not by the time Miss Haggerty came into society."

Julia raised her glass to Annie, who mused that someday she must tell her about cousin George Kneeland.

"This all sounds like too many clothes." Tallie took a demure sip of her cordial. "Wouldn't it be more shocking if we were all half-naked?"

"That lets me out," Annie said.

"Still," said Julia, "something in the nymph-abducted-by-satyrs line would add considerably to the shock value."

"We can work Mesdames into the background." Bertrand rose and leaned an arm on the fireplace, a favorite pose of his. "Burwell, how do you feel about shaggy legs and cloven hooves?— I suppose I could do the abducting and you can accompany me on the Pan-pipes."

"How long can you hold me up before you drop me?" Tallie said.

"You reckon without my twice-weekly visits to the Turkish gymnasium, my dear. Those clubs must weigh seven or eight kilos each. We'll do my head on your body, Burwell—that'll give you some practice in portraiture while we're about it.

Tallie can work on the ladies—"

"No, indeed, I need more practice on the male figure. I propose to do you *and* Mr. Burwell."

Jackson blushed and ducked his head.

"He can hold up Madame Shaw while you're about it, to get the muscles right."

Annie protested that she weighed a good deal more than Tallie, but the girl thought it a splendid idea. "Perhaps Pauline—Miss Cooper, my flat mate—will want in on this."

"I long to see Sarah's face, assuming she walks in here while you're place-holding!" Julia said gleefully.

"I'll wear at least a nightshift if I'm to do this at all," Annie told Bertrand. "How quickly can you sketch, Tallie?"

"Bertrand will help, won't you?"

"I shall instruct and supplement. This will be something like those Renaissance dances where the ladies leap in and out of the gentlemen's arms, and are held firmly by their bottoms. Only you must hold the poses longer. And assume an attitude of extreme distress."

"That will come naturally enough. We must make the place look decadently occupied," Annie said. "Glasses with wine dregs—"

"Plates with pastry crumbs," Julia put in, "and absinthe spoons—"

"Oh, a nice touch, Madame Greene!" Bertrand beamed approval.

"You don't suppose there's a chance she'll find all this—intriguing?" Tallie wondered.

"Even if she did, which I doubt, she'll see this as her territory, and be outraged at the invasion. But it's not, so she's hardly in a position to order you out, since I am official guardian of my sister's premises."

Annie had re-sealed Sarah's letter carefully, explaining the situation to Monsieur le Poste, who was horrified on her behalf and happy to help. He would "deliver" it as soon as possible after Mother Shaw's arrival or, if circumstances favored, immediately thereupon. Bertrand and his acolytes scattered to procure canvas, paints, and scenic elements. They had, she estimated, three days to set everything up and get the poses sketched out. The concierge was enlisted to inform of any unusual arrivals. Annie removed the contents of the Crafts' wine cellar to her own apartments, and brought in a supply of such vulgar food and drink as her companions assured her would be the staples of Bohemian revelry. She encouraged the young people to leave the elements in whatever state of disarray suited them.

Julia, who had assured Annie that she was in no hurry to re-encounter her sister-in-law, had left her own letter from Sarah unopened pending Mother Shaw's arrival, and kept mostly to her own apartments on the rue Bassano. Sarah did not need to know about their now firmly established intimacy. Lest the victim of their subterfuge think to flee to her for refuge, Julia had encouraged a party of visiting English friends to decamp from their hotel on the rue de Rivoli and lodge in her spare bedrooms.

Annie had moved into her mother's larger bedroom a few weeks after Elizabeth's burial in Lenox. It only remained to set up her own old room, which faced north, as a painting studio—which she had been considering in any event—to festoon it with paint-spotted floor cloths and brushes in pots, and to load the bed with a few amateurish works in progress provided by

Bertrand from an introductory class he taught at Julian's. She set up a bowl of fruit and a decanter of wine on a small table and dabbled the outlines of a still-life.

Chapter 11

Annie sat in her accustomed spot in the nave of the American Cathedral, wondering on this sultry morning why St. Paul should be so obsessed with sins of the flesh. To listen to his Epistles, you'd think at times there weren't any other sins to be concerned about. And today's Gospel spoke of Jesus reproaching a potential follower for wanting to bury his dead father before he signed on. Well, who else was supposed to do it? There were times when Christ seemed oblivious to the necessities of everyday existence. The Martha and Mary story, for instance: He and his disciples land in on their little household and expect to be fed, so Martha gets down to it while Mary sits at Jesus' feet listening to him dispense wisdom. And he rebukes Martha when she tries to get Mary to help...

...so engrossed was she as she left her pew that she nearly didn't register the lady standing in her path until she almost ran bodily into her.

"Mrs. Kernochan!" Jackson's relative, a full-bodied woman who reminded Annie of a ship in full sail, put out a hand to steady her. "I'm so sorry, I was woolgathering over the readings."

"Entirely proper, Mrs. Shaw—that's what we come to church for, isn't it?" the lady said kindly. "I'm glad to see you looking so well. Will you come into the fellowship parlor and have coffee? There's a small matter I'd like to chat with you about."

Annie's heart sank. It must be about Jackson. In the parlor, the affable Reverend Morgan was greeting parishioners, and ladies of the Dorcas Society were handing round cups of coffee which, if past experience were any guide, were best avoided.

"Well, now," said Mrs. Kernochan cheerfully as they settled into armchairs in a quiet corner, "Jackson tells me you've been making quite a pet of him since he arrived."

"His father did ask me to give him what support I could," Annie said, "and he's certainly a pleasant and polite young man."

"That he is." Mrs. Kernochan leaned toward Annie as though to impart a secret. "I wonder if his father, or his brother, confided to you the, ah, circumstances under which he left for Paris."

Annie felt her color rising but did her best to keep her countenance. "I had the letter you know of, from Roland, but I've heard nothing from—Edgar, was it?"

"About the time Jackson embarked, I received a letter from Edgar. It seems the young fellow got himself into an entanglement that greatly concerned his family—"

"Goodness! Of what nature?"

Mrs. Kernochan scrutinized Annie, forcing her to maintain an expression of innocent inquiry with some difficulty. "A romantic one, naturally." She dropped her voice and Annie had to lean forward in the noisy room to catch her words. "With, I'm told, a young colored woman."

"That's surprising," Annie said, adding slowly, "Though perhaps not entirely so, in that part of the world?"

"The odd dalliance is not uncommon, as was the case even before the War between the States. This, I'm told, was more serious. His family hoped by sending him to Paris to put an end to whatever attachment had arisen. Edgar has asked me to keep an eye out for any signs of its having continued. Or resumed."

"How very awkward for you," Annie said, her tone all sympathy. "How were you supposed to obtain such information? Surely that's not the sort of thing a young man would discuss with a relative—particularly a female relative."

"And an older one at that. That's why I wanted to talk with you, my dear. Jackson, no doubt, will have told you of losing his mother at an early age. But it's not uncommon for a young man to seek an *unrelated* older woman's motherly advice in personal matters."

Annie laughed. "You're thinking he might see me in that light?"

"And confide in you, as he might not with me. I should be greatly obliged if you would let me know if you obtain any hints as to an ongoing connection with this—young person."

"Does this young person have a name?"

"Not that Edgar has mentioned. But you'll understand how concerned he is about the family's honor and reputation, and how he would feel obliged to take steps should anything untoward come to light. Fortunately, he has control over Jackson's allowance until he comes of age. At twenty-five."

"And is prepared to use that control—"

"In the interest of the family honor, naturally. As any head of the family would."

"I will certainly bear this in mind in my dealings with Jackson. We must make sure his prospects are not jeopardized by ill-advised entanglements." Annie gathered her reticule and rose, as did Mrs. Kernochan.

"I know I can count on your good judgment in this," said that lady, "and I will be grateful for any intelligence you share with me."

"I certainly will." *When Hell freezes over*, Annie did not add, smiling and taking her leave.

Two days later, Annie and Julia strolled on the former Expositiom grounds beneath the Tour Eiffel, with rain clouds threatenihis above and the leaves whipping back and forth on the plane tre: to After another excruciating session of Swedish exercises, Ann found herself pleased to be promenading without a cane.

"I'm feeling a bit guilty about all this."

"You're an independent woman who gives encouragement and support to young artists," Julia said, "particularly yo Americans. They needed a sizable space for their mytholo subject; your sister's grand salon was standing idle. Why and have put it to good use?"

Annie's gaze wandered up the dark girders of the tow ey It had become a landmark for orienteering and a symbol civic progress; the wide avenues beneath it, already favorab l" for promenades, would be more so when their sapling bordepr grew to maturity. Despite the Arabian Nights excess of th o Palais de Trocadèro, the dreamlike prospect from the tower's base always gave her a little rush of pleasure. She had looked forward to long walks—solitary, or with some companion as agreeable as Julia had proved—as she took possession of Paris on her own terms.

Trask, had a son ill from a fever, a few days before the 54th was to parade through Boston and ship south. She had persuaded Rob to let the man go to his family, somewhere around Waltham. It had been the soldier's last look at his child. The poor little chap died the day after the regiment left. The father had survived Fort Wagner, returned minus half a leg to his life as a blacksmith, and had two more children—not that anything could replace the lost one.

Corporal Trask, and his comrades with whom Annie still corresponded, were the only people entitled to think of her as the Colonel's faithful widow. She doubted that Sarah Shaw even knew any of the survivors' names.

The first few drops of rain fell. "If I had remarried—" Annie began.

"That would have been a good deal of trouble to go to, only to get shot of Sarah," Julia rose and opened her parasol. "But there might have been other motives. We'd best head back before this blows up into a squall."

"I've lived longer since losing Rob than I'd lived all my life up to that point. Having been his wife has meant almost nothing to my daily existence all these years. Sarah, of course, assumes it was eternal fidelity to his memory that has kept me single. But I tell you, if Mr. Coolidge were free—!"

"I must get a look at this prodigy," Julia smiled. "If the wife is a real invalid—"

Annie dug her aunt in the ribs. "Oh, Julia, that's *wicked!*"

"It worked for Alice Mason with Morgan Senior, didn't it? And don't tell me the thought hadn't crossed your mind..." Julia's elbow dug back.

"I can hide nothing from you, it seems."

"By the way, weren't Effie and Carlotta Lowell on a Grand Tour hereabouts?"

"They skipped Paris because of the cholera. I told Effie it was confined to the neighborhoods where they drink the water right out of the Seine, but she didn't want to take chances. I should have liked to see Lotta. She was only ten when I last saw her."

"What must it have been like to grow up under the thumbs of those two?"

"If I were Lotta, I'd be looking for a chance to break loose," Annie said. "I fear Effie has her embroiled in her charitable schemes, poor thing. She's the same age I was when I married Rob, but I've heard of no suitors on the horizon."

"It would be a gloomy venue for entertaining gentleman callers," Julia furled her parasol and pointed skyward. "Look, there's a little patch of blue—it was only a passing shower."

Annie pictured some nervous young fellow perched awkwardly on a horse-hair sofa, being subjected to an in-person version of one of Effie's epistolary rhapsodies on the results of her charitable interventions. And then to the basilisk gaze of Grandmamma Shaw—it would quail the stoutest heart, Lotta's little fortune and personal graces notwithstanding.

Julia stopped and laid a hand on Annie's forearm. "You don't suppose Sarah would bring Carlotta with her? Here, I mean. If Lotta were already in Europe—"

Annie's eyes widened. "Good Lord, I hadn't thought of that."

The concierge met them at the front door, in as close to a tizzy as Annie had ever seen that phlegmatic person. "Madame!" She wrung Annie's hand in distress. "Des dames Américaines sont arrivées—the older one insisted on going upstairs—and so many bagages—"

"How long ago?"

"Half an hour, peut-être—"

Annie and Julia exchanged alarmed looks. "Go home," she told Julia. "I'll send you a message—"

"Are you sure?"

"It's best for now she doesn't know."

"Quite right!" Julia turned on her heel in the direction they had come. Annie's heart sank as she watched her go. At the top of the first-floor stairs, the hallway between her apartment and the Crafts' was chock-a-block with steamer trunks. Adèle was threading her way between them with a coffee-pot in hand, which she nearly dropped when she saw Annie.

"Madame, you have heard? They are here—" her voice was a stage whisper. "Madame votre belle-mère, and her granddaughter, and their two maids."

Annie beckoned her into a corner. "Have they gone into the Crafts' apartments?"

Adèle nodded vigorously. "It was just as you left them—the jeune mademoiselle Cooper painting the two gentlemen in their, uh, pagnes, caleçons—and Mademoiselle Tallie, with only a sheet around her waist, being held above them—"

"Jambes poilus is the phrase you're looking for—hairy legs." Tallie had enlisted her flat mate Pauline Cooper, a bespectacled Pittsburgh girl, to help paint her in the clutches of the satyrs.

"The elder lady—she was in front—she staggered back. And la petite—Tallie—she dropped to the floor and rose up with great indignation, pulling the sheet around her. She said, 'Madame Shaw promised we would not be disturbed by spectators! You must leave at once!' And Madame Shaw l'aînée and the young lady backed out of the room. Mademoiselle Tallie slammed the door behind them, and there they were standing in the hallway looking bouleversées.

"'Mesdames, I said, you are perhaps friends of Madame Shaw? She was not expecting visitors—' and at that moment Monsieur le Poste came up the stairs and handed me a bundle of letters. I could see the one from America sticking out, and the elder lady saw it also—she snatched it from my hands, saw that it was still sealed, and said to the young lady, 'Look at this! They have only now delivered my letter! What kind of a postal system do they have in this'—what was her word?—'benighted country?' Then she demanded of me when did I expect your return. I said I was not sure, but if they cared to follow me into Madame's apartments, I could provide some refreshment—alors," she gestured to the coffee pot.

"You have done well, Adèle," Annie stage-whispered back. "They're in my living room?"

"The older lady fell into an armchair comme un mort and the younger one asked for a face-cloth with some vinegar on it—I took their traveling clothes, their mantelets, and hung them in the hallway—"

"Where are their maids?"

"Mademoiselle sent them to look for hotel rooms at the Grand, on the rue de Rivoli—she and her maman were to have stayed there, on their visit, before the cholera came—"

Carlotta Lowell, then, was Mother Shaw's companion. No surprise, really; Lotta had already been traveling in Europe with her mother Effie, and Sarah Shaw's daughters wouldn't have let their mother go off to Paris alone—even if that had been her desire, which Annie doubted. Lotta's mother and her three Shaw aunts would have seen her as the ideal draftee.

Annie hurried into her own apartments and found the two seated by the fireplace. Though she had expected signs of aging, Sarah's appearance shocked her. The woman whose physical presence she had found so intimidating was shrunken, white-haired, frail. Sarah's companion rose, chestnut-haired, straight-backed and vigorous-looking.

"Aunt Annie!" She came forward smiling, with her hands outstretched.

Annie clasped them and drew the girl to her. "My dear Lotta! What a happy surprise. I wasn't expecting—"

"*That* is quite evident," said Mother Shaw, in the aggrieved contralto which chilled Annie's blood just as it used to. "We learn that you had not received my letter until today."

"What letter was that?" Annie quailed inwardly, but pressed on with her part.

"Of course," Carlotta said, "you'll not have read it yet—here it is." She retrieved it from a side-table. Annie broke the seal and perused the contents as though they were new to her, assuming an expression of innocent dismay.

"I see—but of course if I'd known I should have telegraphed immediately to tell you that the apartments had been let."

"Does your sister know of this?" Sarah pushed herself stiffly up from the armchair. Annie had not attempted to embrace her, nor did her mother-in-law initiate physical contact.

"Mrs. Crafts left the apartments in my charge, with instructions to use them as I pleased."

"Indeed!" The body might have withered, but the voice had lost none of its booming quality. "She told me it would be at my disposal for whatever time I might need it. As you will see when you read my letter—" she gave Annie a look that had a glint of suspicion in it, "she offered it to me for an indefinite period."

"I do wish she had let me know," Annie said in a tone of sorrowful reproach toward an errant younger sibling. "I would not have leased the salon to the Comte de Leiningen and his students as an atelier for his project."

"The Comte de Leiningen?"

"A professor of fine art at the Académie Julian. He has embarked on a sort of apprenticeship for Miss DeKuyper and her classmates. They're at work on a significant commission—for the spa at Enghien-les-bains, I believe...perhaps it's Neiderbronn-les-bains. I get them mixed up."

"How long might the work take?" Carlotta was concerned but respectful, as if acknowledging the primacy of artistic endeavors. "We had no idea you had become a patroness of the arts, Aunt Annie. How lovely!"

"The Comte tells me this particular commission may take two or three months."

"Months!" Sarah exclaimed. "But that would mean the apartment would not be available as your sister had—"

Annie shook her head ruefully. "If she had consulted with me first, I would certainly have let her know. I had of course intended to do so, but there seemed no urgency. As it is, we must find you a comfortable base of operations—how long had you planned to visit?"

"Had you received my letter in the timely fashion I expected," Sarah intoned, "you would have learned that I have come here with a view to making Paris my permanent home."

"Permanent?" Annie raised a hand to her bosom. "I had not

thought you were fond of France. And with all your daughters and grandchildren close by in New York, it surprises me—ah, here is Adèle." That estimable bonne rolled in a tray covered with hastily assembled edibles: a plate of cold meat sandwiches, some little quiches, a few scones left over from breakfast and cut into triangles. Lotta clapped her hands.

"Oh, I'm simply starved! This looks lovely, Aunt Annie—a fresh pot of coffee, and look, hot milk! May I pour you some, Tua?" This, Annie recalled, was the grandchildren's pet name for Mother Shaw.

"I should prefer tea," said Sarah stiffly. "At this late hour, coffee interferes with my digestion."

"But of course, Madame," Adèle said, smiling benignly. "I will return momentarily."

"Well, I'd love some coffee!" Annie gestured invitation to Lotta, who nodded assent. "Blanc ou noir?"

"Oh, café au lait, please! How I've longed to visit a real Paris café!"

"I'll be delighted to accompany you." Annie handed her the cup and offered the plate of sandwiches to Mother Shaw. "Tell me about your journey. What ship did you come in on? Did you land at Le Havre?"

"It was a dreadful voyage—"

"My train journey from Florence was quite pleasant—"

The older and younger voices overlapped. Lotta cut herself off. "Of course, I came by land and poor Tua says she had a bad bout of mal de mer—"

"I'm sorry to hear it. Nothing is more miserable."

Sarah sat back in the armchair and waved her hand. "I was somewhat accustomed to it. I was a *martyr* to sickness when I was expecting my children. But the stewards were no help at all."

"It passed off, I trust?"

"Eventually. I must say you are looking rather better than I expected, Annie. Somewhat plumper than I remember."

And you are white-haired and bony, Annie did not reply, *and your skin looks like a withered apple.* "I fear my capacity to resist French pastries is not what it should be."

"I long to try them!" Carlotta radiated energy and good spirits. With her sharp cheekbones, she resembled her heroic father Charles rather more than her mother Effie. She wore her hair in a becoming twist, though her traveling clothes did nothing to show to advantage a physique which had, no doubt, been developed on horseback and on long, healthy walks. A hearty, genial girl, and her aunt already liked the adult she had become in the years since they had last seen each other. Perhaps she had even taken to bicycles.

Adèle returned with the teapot, and Annie poured for Mother Shaw. "You take lemons rather than milk, if I recall?"

"Either will suffice," Sarah said with a long-suffering air. Annie added the remaining hot milk to the cup and handed it to her. "I suppose the post is as slow in one part of Paris as another?" She began to drink noisily.

"I suppose so," Annie almost forgot to feign puzzlement. "I hadn't given it much thought."

"I wrote also to my sister-in-law—Mrs. Greene, your aunt by marriage. I supposed you would be acquainted. She lives not far from here, I believe."

Annie shot a warning look at Adèle and nodded dismissal. She took the hint and withdrew.

"As she is not a parishioner at the American Cathedral, I

do not see her there." Annie reproached herself for Jesuitical equivocation, but Mother Shaw, as she had hoped, seemed to fall for the non sequitur.

"Perhaps she or my nephew would be able to accommodate us temporarily," Sarah's long nose traced a downward arc around Annie's apartment, "since you obviously cannot."

"Have you their addresses?" Annie radiated eagerness to help. "I can send a message round—they'll want to know you are here, and to visit you at once if they are free."

Chapter 12

arlotta returned from the hallway with a small carpetbag, from which she extracted a leather-bound notebook, wetting her finger and leafing through it. "50 rue de Bassano. Is that nearby, Aunt Annie?"

Annie knitted her brows. "I think it runs south from the Place de l'Étoile. Close to the American Cathedral, not far from the avenue de l'Alma, in the Eighth. We're in the Sixteenth here."

"Those tiresome *arrondissements*," said Mother Shaw. "I don't believe there even *was* a Sixteenth, when I was last here."

"Passy was annexed some time ago, and has grown fashionable, I'm told—though not so much as the Eighth, where one finds most of the American Colony."

"Perhaps it will prove more congenial," said Mother Shaw with ice in her voice.

"Isn't the Sixteenth where they have the horse races?" Lotta asked eagerly.

"Quite right—in the southern end, in Auteuil," Annie said. "I remember—you're fond of riding, aren't you, my dear?"

"I've missed it so! We've had Red Berold from when I was little, on Staten Island—you remember poor Papa's war-horse?

And I used to ride Aunt Anna Curtis's horses, but since we moved to Manhattan..." she gave a little sigh.

Feeling like one of Lear's wicked daughters, Annie rang for pen and paper to write to Julia. *I have denied you as Peter did the Lord. Trust you will do the same for me. She means to see if you can accommodate her—and Carlotta, for that is her young companion. You are invited to tea forthwith. Let Adèle know what you will do.* She wrote the rue Bassano address on the envelope and sent Adèle off with it.

"How does poor Anna?" she asked when the door had closed. "I understand from Effie that George is seriously ill."

"No one seems to know what ails him," said Mother Shaw. "Naturally, my daughter is distraught—and, I fear, not so well provided for by her husband as I was by mine. Fortunately, should the worst happen, her father's legacy will allow her to live in comfort."

"Uncle George is still quite young," Carlotta put in. "That makes it especially sad."

"Not so much younger than your late grandfather," said Mother Shaw, "who was generous to a fault, with *non-blood* relations. He settled a number of Mr. Curtis's accumulated debts. From what I for one viewed as an ill-conceived program of lecture tours."

Annie registered the barb: dying in 1882, Frank Shaw had left her five thousand dollars in his will. She had taken it as a small apology for how Rob's death in furtherance of his parents' ideals had destroyed her own happiness.

Sarah Shaw had outlived her son and two of her four sons-in-law, and seemed on the verge of outliving a third. Annie had a flash of worry for the fourth, Frank Barlow, a one-time suitor of hers, also widowed by the War, eventually married to Rob's youngest sister Ellen. One of Effie Lowell's letters had mentioned a kidney ailment. Proximity to Mother Shaw seemed to doom the male of the species to a shortened life span, and the female to early widowhood.

Annie thought she had already faced the worst of what Mother Shaw could do to her. But here she was, invading the new life she was coming to treasure. One was supposed to defer to elders—especially to mothers, for their self-sacrifice on behalf of offspring and husbands. But Annie had done her filial duty, nursing her own mother through a tragic and troublesome dotage. She blushed for the relief she had felt with Elizabeth's passing—not that her mother was gone, for she would always miss the sparkling, warm companion she had been, but that the dull-eyed, querulous stranger who had replaced her had finally left her in peace.

There was nothing dull-eyed about Mother Shaw, whose glance bore a Gorgonian chill, but clearly she had lost none of her habitual peevishness.

"Well, Anna—Mrs. Curtis—is certainly fortunate in her family's generosity. I'm sure you have been a great comfort in her present difficulties."

Sarah all but snorted. "She has found more comfort in her grandchildren than in anyone else," she said in the aggrieved tone which seemed her keynote.

Annie refilled Sarah's teacup and inquired about each of the Shaw daughters in turn. All of them seemed to be preoccupied with either Good Works or the concerns of their own families. Her old friend Susie Minturn, for instance, had four marriageable daughters and, since her husband's death, diminished resources to help them secure favorable alliances.

Carlotta said, "We've got photographs of everyone to show you—you'll hardly recognize your great-nieces and nephews!"

"I couldn't have failed to recognize you, my dear. Your resemblance to your father is so pronounced—" Carlotta looked chagrined, and Annie realized she must hear this constantly from her elders. "He was one of the handsomest men I ever saw," Annie added hastily, "apart from your uncle Rob, of course. The four of us occupied rooms for a time at a boarding house in Readville, before we were all married."

"I remember that venue well," Sarah put in censoriously. "The reports I received of the young people's conduct," she told Carlotta, "were not reassuring. I feared for your mother's reputation—and for your aunt's, of course—"

"How trivial all that seems now!" Annie could not resist saying.

"A woman's reputation is *always* her most precious possession." Mother Shaw bent her head toward Carlotta, seeking agreement. Carlotta's eyes danced briefly with merriment and darted to Annie's; the effort it cost her to keep a straight face was almost palpable.

"Then it is as well that Carlotta is here to chaperone you, Mother Shaw, lest the gentlemen of Paris get the wrong ideas."

Sarah's brows knit in puzzlement before her features resolved into a wintry half-smile. "I had almost forgotten your Aunt Annie's, ah, unconventional sense of humor."

"I'm not sure that a good sense of humor *could* be conventional, Tua," replied the young lady gently, but with some spirit. "We were surprised to learn from Mrs. Crafts that you had remained in Paris, Aunt Annie. Do you think you'll go back to America soon?"

Annie was not prepared for the question. If she revealed her intent to remain in Paris indefinitely, it might encourage Mother Shaw to think in the same terms. But to suggest her stay was temporary might lead Mother Shaw to propose taking over her own premises.

"I haven't decided, and won't for a while yet. It's been so short a time since my sister left."

"Mrs. Crafts," said Mother Shaw, "called on us after disembarking in the City. There are, I believe, three daughters at home, still unmarried?"

"The younger two are only schoolgirls," Annie hastened to note, but the little barb from Sarah to Carlotta had gone home. She liked the young woman already. Lotta was clearly not the sort to snare prospective suitors with feminine wiles; a man who courted her would have to be unusually insightful. Lotta reminded her of herself in youth, reluctant to mask her native intelligence and intellectual curiosity. Whatever stratagems she might employ to repel Lotta's grandmother would be tempered by a desire to do this young kinswoman some good. Might she keep Carlotta in Paris and dispatch Mother Shaw back to New York?

But here came Adèle, breathless from haste, announcing the arrival of Madame Greene. Julia sailed into Annie's parlor, having changed from her earlier heliotrope into a sober walking-costume of dark blue summer wool, and advanced at once toward her hostess. "My dear Mrs. Shaw!" she gushed. "I have only just received a letter from my sister-in-law announcing her visit—" She dropped the hand she had clasped with a small secret squeeze and turned to the new arrivals. "Sarah, how do you? What a surprise! Can this be Carlotta? We missed you and your mamma this spring, my dear—is she well, I hope?"

Carlotta had risen and come forward to step into her great-aunt's embrace. Julia was only a year or two younger than Sarah, but seemed much more so.

"Well, I must say *you're* looking well, Julia." Mother Shaw's tone held a hint of grudge.

Julia squeezed Carlotta, stepping back with her hands on the girl's shoulders. "I see an equestrienne, do I not?" Carlotta smiled and nodded. "It would be strange if you weren't. How well I remember your father—no one sat a horse like him—and your mother too." She turned to Mother Shaw. "You see how slow the posts of Paris are—but when Madame Shaw's maid came to me, just as I was opening your letter, I abandoned my house guests and came away at once."

"House guests..." Sarah Shaw's tone fell between despair and resignation.

"Friends from our Somerset days," Julia replied, "come to Paris at last for a nice long visit. And now you two! You'll stay at least a week or two, I trust?"

Even if Mother Shaw's letter had said nothing explicit about intending to remain indefinitely, this was wicked on Julia's part. And if they knew one another as little as Annie had claimed, Julia would not know that Clem had decamped to America.

Julia seemed to read her mind. "Do I recall that your sister and her family live nearby, Mrs. Shaw? I met her when Henry James was visiting and we had a little soirée for him."

"They lived across the hall," Annie replied helpfully, "until Professor Crafts was offered a post at a new university in Boston. They sailed for America in May."

"And have you new neighbors?" A neutral question, delivered with a neutral smile.

"The Crafts have kept the lease, but it is subleased at present to a group of artists who are undertaking a major commission—"

Julia's eyebrows rose with what seemed to be guarded interest. "Artists! Indeed!" There was a tinge of disapproval in her expression.

"As I was telling the ladies, I'd become aware of their difficulties in finding a suitable space to execute this, ah, tableau. Three are Americans, two of them from my old City—"

"Ah, so you knew them," Julia supplied. "Their families are old neighbors?"

"In one case. In another, he is a connection of a fellow Cathedral parishioner—"

"Then there is some assurance of respectability," Julia replied with a purse-lipped smile.

"From what I saw—" Sarah began.

"Artistic standards must vary from those of everyday life, Tua," said Carlotta with a bit of a sparkle in her eye—possibly, Annie thought, even a note of wistful envy. A generous assessment from one who had, a short time since, been summarily ousted by the artists themselves. "One hears that many young American ladies come here in search of more expert instruction than they can receive at home—"

"You're staying at the Grand, I suppose?" Julia continued. "Most Americans seem to end up there—"

"Oh, we neglected to ask," Carlotta said, "How does cousin Will? And his family?"

"Growing like weeds," Julia smiled. "He has four now, and the house is bursting at the seams—he talks of moving to something larger in Auteuil, but his business interests keep him closer in."

Annie saw Sarah's last hope of familial hospitality fade. "I suppose it must be the Grand—for now," she told Carlotta gloomily, "if *they* have room for us."

"The artists are also in *residence* next door?" Julia inquired innocently.

"The population seems to vary from one evening to the next—they entertain friends from time to time, as one would expect—I did have to ask them once to keep things quieter, and they have been more subdued since then." Annie smiled inwardly at the shock with which this narrative would be greeted by Mother Shaw's daughters when she wrote to them. *Dear Annie gone to the dogs...*she found the prospect positively liberating. Effie with her Homes of Refuge for Fallen Women— how refreshing that Carlotta seemed to relish the prospect of further contact with these louche and dissipated bohemians.

"I'll let Will and Sallie know at once of your arrival," Julia said. "They'll want to host a dinner for you, among their American friends—"

Adèle showed in Sarah's two maids, who had secured rooms at the Grand which they "hoped would be satisfactory for the present." After Mother Shaw's gloomy assent, they left with Adèle to find a coachman and porter to move the steamer-trunks and carpetbags in the hallway.

"No doubt you'll want to settle in this evening and have dinner brought up to your rooms," Annie said. "Travel is so fatiguing—you must be exhausted by now. But I hope you'll come and dine with me tomorrow, and tell me all your plans for your visit." She had resolved not to acknowledge Sarah's expressed desire to take up permanent residence in Paris. "Shall we say seven o'clock? Madame Greene, I trust you'll join us?"

Julia sniffed her glass of Sancerre appreciatively. "Do you really mean to keep Bertrand and his acolytes next door?" She had left with Mother Shaw and Carlotta, but had caught another fiacre back to Annie's when they parted company at the rue de l'Alma.

"They're amenable, until I come up with a better plan. They can work on their own projects, with periodic forays into the satyr tableau—but I fear progress on that particular work may be," she sighed theatrically, "rather slow."

"You were adamant about not throwing them out?"

"I had an unexpected ally, in Carlotta. She tells her grand-mamma that one can't interfere with creative geniuses at work."

"Bertrand would relish that description!"

"She might like to try her own hand at painting. She was asking whether Miss DeKuyper or one of the others—she seemed particularly interested in Tallie—gives lessons."

"If Lotta finds a good reason to stay, doesn't that create one for her grandmother as well?"

"As duenna? I suppose so. However, if we seemed on the verge of ridding ourselves of Mother Shaw, I'd offer my own services in that respect. How to convince Sarah, as quickly as possible, that Paris is not for her? One has only so many acquaintances willing to impersonate hairy-legged satyrs."

"She's counting on you for introductions?"

"She has a small list of her own but, yes. She may look to you as well. Being nominally a co-religionist, and with so much of the social life of older women—"

"—such as it is!—"

"Don't be disingenuous—you know what I mean. Revolving around churches and good works—"

"Well, as I told you, I haven't set foot in the American Chapel in years."

"Are there any old Abolitionists among your acquaintances? That might suit her better."

"Most of them have died off." Julia set her glass on the side-table. "Rather a tiresome lot. We all know the South won in the end, and the poor Negroes worse off than before."

"Tiresome would suit nicely. There must be a few with whom Mother Shaw would have had at least an epistolary acquaintance."

Julia sighed. "I still receive the Church bulletins—one from a while back listed charitable benefactors for the church's causes. And what of those adhesive old ladies you mentioned?"

"If I'm to fob such people off on Mother Shaw, and vice-versa, I'll have to invest a hazardous amount of time in their company. Perhaps leaving them to think I wish to pursue connections I've avoided before."

"And if they and Sarah take to one another," Julia added darkly, "she has more reason for deciding to stay. Oh, here's a thought—" her face brightened. "The pension. Where all the American ladies in genteel semi-poverty stay—"

"Madame Mercure's? But Sarah's not poor."

"She might be drawn to its respectability, though. The familiarity. Madame speaks English and cooks accordingly. You don't notice the smells of her stables unless the weather's damp, when they become unbearable, I'm told. But if we got her there during a dry spell—"

"And several of the adhesive old ladies reside there. So she could make their acquaintance without my involvement. Julia, I think this may be a promising avenue of attack!"

Adèle appeared to announce that "the Comte" wondered if Madame Shaw were at liberty to talk with him. Bertrand entered and made a perfunctory bow, bestowing one of his particularly charming smiles on Julia. "Chère Madame!"

"Has everybody got their clothes back on?" Annie inquired.

"I believe your bourgeoises were well and truly épatées," he grinned. "Though you hadn't mentioned the younger lady—her daughter?"

"Granddaughter. We didn't know she was coming."

"Striking features. Not beautiful, but a portrait I should like to paint. Have you succeeded in driving them away?"

"Too soon to tell," Julia said, pouring him a glass of wine, "but they've removed to the Grand for the present. Madame Shaw and I are scheming to settle the elder lady in a respectable pension which, unfortunately, is at times redolent of its ground floor stables."

"Ah! Madame Mercure's. A fine location for ladies without a sense of smell. You two can be quite fiendish."

"Thank you," Annie replied modestly. "Would it suit you to continue working next door until we resolve things?"

Bertrand considered. "I have projects to attend to in my own studio as well as Julian's. But my protégé and her flat mate welcome the opportunity, and I'm sure young Burwell does. I'm finding this satyr project quite amusing. One of the spas might even want it as a present."

"And the others?" Julia asked.

"Tallie's enjoying herself, and I doubt Burwell grudges any

time spent in *her* company—though her friend Miss Cooper seems a bit dubious of his presence. *That* may prove an enjoyable little drama as it unfolds." Bertrand's smile was sardonic.

Annie felt a flutter of alarm. Jackson was a married man with a child. If there were a chance that he and Tallie might become romantically entangled, it couldn't end well. He must get Lydia and little Ben across the ocean.

"Miss Cooper has concerns about Miss DeKuyper's—virtue?"

Bertrand laughed aloud. "More like designs on it. And since the young Mademoiselle has so far proved resistant to *my* blandishments, Miss Cooper may have a chance for all I know."

"I don't suppose it's occurred to you that you're simply the wrong man for her," Julia said. "But that gives me an idea—do we know any elderly Sapphists we could invite to dinner and set upon Sarah?"

"Sapphists, in my experience," Bertrand raised a forestalling hand, "like most libertines, prefer their victims a good deal younger."

"I suppose *you* would know," Julia replied. "It wouldn't have to be an attraction situation—merely an expressed desire for more intimate acquaintance, and an assumption of sympathies."

"Ah, well, then, you want Madame Eyckert. She has been—I suppose one would say widowed, but not too recently, and might welcome a chance to go about again."

"The literary lady!" Julia clapped her hands together. "She's a tolerable dinner companion, Annie, though somewhat free in expressing her proclivities—"

Bertrand helped himself to another glass of wine. "Literary! I've heard it referred to as pornography. I don't go in for that sort of thing myself."

Annie had a mental picture of a woman some years older than herself, with a yellowish complexion and a bovine cast of feature. "Didn't we meet her at Miss Reubell's, Julia?"

"You did! I've known her for some time."

"Will you invite her to join us tomorrow? I do want to give Mother Shaw as wide an exposure to Paris society as possible—"

Bertrand twirled the wine glass in his fingers. "Am I invited?"

"You are always a welcome addition to a dinner gathering," Julia said, "but as you're doing a lot to help us with this business as it is—"

"—I should at least be well fed for it, as I've no doubt I would be." He gave Annie an ingratiating smile, and she felt her color rising.

"In that case, of course you're invited. Only you must be sure to insist on the complexity of your satyr project—the frustrating delays, the indefinite nature of your occupancy—and add a few salacious details—" Annie hesitated. She was a little horrified by all she had set in motion.

"—such as the irresistible thrill of holding a naked, helpless young woman aloft in one's arms—"

"Well, you needn't overdo it," Annie said, blushing furiously, "the more you leave to our guest's imagination, the more horrifically she will conjure it, I'm sure." Where might all this lead? But with Mother Shaw in Paris, or anywhere within her sphere, she could not have the life she wanted. Drastic action was necessary.

Chapter 13

The next day's post brought a long, self-justifying apology from Clem. Mother Shaw had, as Annie suspected, maneuvered her into admitting that the Crafts' Paris apartment was still in her possession and, moreover, vacant. *I had no idea she intended to go to Paris, much less take up residence there,* Clem wrote, *or I should never have mentioned it. But she got it out of me before telling me her plans—I thought she was merely concerned about your being there on your own. I can't imagine she will feel right in staying very long, though she seemed not to have formed an idea of when she might look for a more permanent place. You won't like it, I'm sure, Annie, but surely she won't be there long, and I understand she's to bring Carlotta Lowell with her, who seems a likable young person. In any event, I couldn't think of a graceful way to refuse, though I did think it presumptuous in her to ask, and indeed to assume that you would have nothing better to do than to fall in with whatever plans she has. She thinks of you still as her son's grieving widow, as an invalid in need of companionship, and since you are part of her family still, as she said several times—*

"I'll move to Timbuktu if it comes to that," Annie said aloud, startling Adèle, who was dusting. "But why should I? Paris is my home. She shall neither take over my life nor drive me away!"

She and Clem had nursed their father through his last illness; Annie, largely alone, had cared for their mother through five or six years of a failing mind and body. Annie was not among those women who derived a saintly joy in martyring themselves in the service of their elders. The nasty details of toilets and bathing and feeding, the sight of a once vibrant human being reduced to an infantile state, revolted her. Clem had pled the obligations of a husband and children to leave Elizabeth in Annie's care—a surge of retrospective fury washed over her at the memory, at the impossible position in which her sister had now placed her. It was all of a piece with the role into which she had fallen with the Crafts—caretaker, mother's helper, chaperone, useful appendage—the thought of those fallow years was nearly unbearable now. It had never occurred to Clem to wonder whether Annie was content with her lot. In those years caring for her mother, she certainly hadn't been, though it was only after Elizabeth's death that she could admit to herself how much she had hated the role of nursemaid. It was just as well she had never had children. She might have been a terrible mother...

The thought of doing for Sarah Shaw what she had done for Elizabeth was not to be borne. She didn't for an instant credit Sarah's cant about providing "companionship" to an "invalid" daughter-in-law. Quite the reverse; Mother Shaw hoped to obtain the attention and care from Annie, who surely had nothing better to do, no longer on offer from her own daughters.

The woman Annie had been when her path and Sarah's had first crossed was gone as surely as Sarah's son and, with him, all ties of duty and kinship with the Shaws. Who had, she recalled with a fresh wave of anger, shut her out, when her husband was killed, from the decisions that were rightly hers as his next of kin—what should become of his remains and the relics of his life. There should have been a grave for her to visit, a stone to remember him by, but the Shaws forbade disturbing the sand trench into which Rob had been thrown with his black comrades.

I owe this woman nothing, she concluded.

Yet she had stayed for all these years in cordial contact with Rob's sisters and their families. Good women all, and it was her friendship with Susie that had brought Rob into her life. Effie, if tiresome in her relentless philanthropizing, was an affectionate correspondent who sent little snippets of news she thought would interest Annie, which they often did. Anna and Ellen, too, regarded her as a sister. She hoped she could get rid of Mother Shaw without alienating them.

Meanwhile, there was a young couple to whom she *had* pledged her assistance. Time to move forward, before the snares of Paris took Jackson Burwell away from his wife and child.

If Mr. Burwell will apply directly to Mr. Meriweather, my assistant chargé d'affaires, said Mr. Coolidge's letter, *he will provide him with the necessary papers to allow Mrs. Burwell and her child to join him in France, provided that he furnish evidence of a suitable domicile and confer with the Paris municipal authorities about regularizing the connection at an early date.*

He must find them a home and they must have a civil marriage, that meant. Jackson, in his present circumstances, could afford neither.

"I can advance you a loan to find a suitable place," Annie told

Jackson after summoning him across the hall to tea, "or lease it until you have the means to take it over. And I will pay the passage for Lydia and Ben."

Jackson seemed nonplussed, even a trifle embarrassed, which Annie attributed to his disheveled state—a paint-spattered smock hastily thrown over his furry satyr-trousers.

"I shall have to write to her at once—"

"You hadn't broached the possibility with her?"

"I feared to raise her hopes, and have them dashed," Jackson dropped his eyes sheepishly. "I should have realized that when Mrs. Annie Shaw says she will do a thing, it is bound to come about. I thank you heartily."

Annie handed over Coolidge's letter. "She will need time—to prepare for the journey, break the news to her aunt. Mrs. Kernochan, of course, must hear nothing of this, until Mrs. Burwell has arrived and you have—"

Jackson looked up smiling from the letter. "—regularized the connection."

"And found yourselves a little home to start out in."

"I'm loath to be in such debt—even to so gracious a lady as yourself."

Annie handed him a plate of galettes. "But it can't happen otherwise, can it? Repay me when you have the means. For now, the important thing is reuniting your family."

Jackson's smile was happy, but his eyes looked troubled. Perhaps he was having misgivings about whether a country girl from the South could adapt to life in an exotic metropolis like Paris.

"You needn't fear that we would treat other arriving Americans as we plan to do Mother Shaw. Madame Greene and I and other friends will do all we can to help Lydia and Ben settle in and feel at home. Off you go, back to your licentious tableau, and write to her this evening."

Jackson stood as Annie rose. Something vulnerable in his stance made her go to him, ignoring the paint spatters and the silly, hairy hooves, and fold him in a maternal embrace. "I'm so looking forward to meeting your wife and son!"

It would be months before that meeting would happen. He would have ample time to find a place for them and get under way with his studies at the Beaux-Arts, from which he expected to hear his examination results any day. She had no doubt they would admit him.

"Escargot, ris de veau, sardines à la sauce moutarde, pieds de cochon, fromage Roquefort, prunes—? This is an unusually *French* menu for you, Madame." Adèle looked skeptical. "I myself have never eaten pieds de cochon."

"Nor have I," Annie said. "I find the prospect repulsive. But we must convince Belle-Mère Shaw that if she wishes to live in Paris, she should dine in the true Parisian fashion."

"I do not know of—"

"—any Parisian who eats in this way. Nor Scots who eat haggis, for that matter. But Mother Shaw doesn't know that."

"The cook fears that you have taken leave of your senses. And what is haggis?"

"Tell her that we intend for our guest of honor an immersion in French culture, from which we hope her digestion will be a long time recovering."

"Oh-la-la! You yourself are blessed with a good stomach,

Madame, but there may be a limit even to that."

"Have the bicarbonate of soda to hand, will you?" Annie felt a wicked smile blossoming at the thought of tonight's guest list; Bertrand had agreed to invite along one Aloysius O'Connor, an Irish artist making a name for himself in bohemian circles as a prodigious drinker and brawler, and in artistic circles as a daring and superb colorist.

"He's a bit—rough-hewn," Bertrand warned, "and I wouldn't trust him around a decanter. But a thoroughly charming fellow at his best, if somewhat contentious in conversation—and his work impresses me. He has a place in Pont-Aven, but happens to be in Paris."

"I look forward to meeting him!"

For all their advocacy of the Negro, the Shaws had been openly prejudiced against the Irish. Annie often wondered how Rob had summoned the courage to tell his parents he was courting a young lady named Haggerty. O'Connor sounded like one who would confirm Mother Shaw's worst fears about the race, and Annie was prepared to make a favorite of him for the evening.

Ten at her table would be a strain on the small dining room, but manageable. Julia had secured an acceptance from Madame Eyckert; Bertrand would arrive from across the hall, full of details about his latest exercise in artistic sensuality. Retta Reubell had gleefully assented. By way of pièces de résistance, Annie had secured the presence of both the dreaded Dr. Finkelmann of the École des Mines, whom she planned to seat at Mother Shaw's right hand, and on her other side Capitaine LeBoeuf, the putative hero of Sedan. Bertrand was cued to press upon Mother Shaw the more repulsive of the assembled French delicacies; if all went as hoped, she would take to her bed for a week with an attack of dyspepsia.

Cook had engaged a sous-chef for the evening. Falling in with the spirit of the occasion, she had wickedly suggested "une assiète de tripes," but Annie drew the line at pigs' trotters. Julia had cued Retta about the aims of the occasion; she and Annie reasoned that leaving Madame Eyckert, the artist O'Connor, Dr. Finkelmann and Capitaine LeBoeuf to their natural proclivities would combine to stoke Mother Shaw's misgivings about her resettlement project. But well aware of the tendencies of best-laid plans to miscarry, Annie and Julia remained on the alert. Neither was eager to alienate Carlotta, to whom both had taken a liking, and whom they hoped to cut out of the familial herd and keep in Paris if her grandmother left.

Capitaine LeBoeuf clicked his heels together and bowed to Sarah Shaw, who was in her usual black ruffled silk and white lace cap. "Ah, madame! Such an honor to meet the mother of a fallen hero of the late American war—I was myself blessé— wounded—at Sedan, as Madame Annie Shaw may have told you—"

"I thought you could tell Madame Shaw yourself," Annie interposed sweetly, "and I'm sure she'll be glad to tell you more about my poor husband's heroism." Mother Shaw gave her a dubious look, but murmured, "Delighted, I'm sure, mon, ah, Capitaine," no doubt thinking that Rob had outranked LeBoeuf considerably. Madame Eyckert, true to Bertrand's prediction, had advanced on Carlotta and appeared to be appraising her face and figure. Lotta's maroon silk set off the reddish highlights in her hair and displayed a modest amount of neck and throat, where gleamed a jeweled locket Annie remembered being given by her father to her mother.

"I am always so happy to meet new arrivals from America!" gushed Madame Eyckert. "Your country exerts a strange fascination—so raw, so vigorous, so—shall I say, violent in its young history?" Perhaps not the most tactful thing to have said to a young woman orphaned by war, but Carlotta took it smilingly.

"Oh, we're not so violent as all that in the East. You must go out to the Wild West for the Indians and the cavalry. We lead very quiet lives in New York, don't we, Grandmother? May I introduce to you Madame Eyckert—the famous Parisian authoress, I believe?"

Madame Eyckert, pleased, raised a deprecatory hand. "Really, my dear, I scribble a bit, and some of my work has merited print—"

"I am happy to meet you, Madame," said Mother Shaw in a tone that suggested otherwise, "though I fear I am not as familiar with your, ah, oovreh as my granddaughter."

"We can correct that in time," Julia said brightly. "I have several volumes of Madame's work I'll be happy to lend you— but how silly of me! Authors would rather sell their work than have it lent about, wouldn't they?"

"I am glad to be read under any circumstances. My late friend Miss Ethel McCaslin—" there was a momentary and seemingly genuine catch in Madame Eyckert's voice, "who was a countrywoman of yours, my dear—" this addressed to Carlotta, on whom she seemed to have fixed her attentions, "always said that the dialogue between the writer and her reader was like the intimacy of *lovers*, and as sacred!" She cast her eyes to heaven in exaltation. The new arrivals looked alarmed.

"Come," Annie said, "You must meet Dr. Finkelmann, a revered colleague of my brother-in-law's from the École des Mines." Mother Shaw extended a hesitant hand, which the professor seized and kissed with a wet smack.

"A great honor to meet you, Madame! I have been, in my hours of leisure, a student of your American Civil War. To converse with someone who was *there*—so intimately involved—I am sure that my friend Herr Doktor Crafts always regretted that he had been abroad for the duration of that stirring conflict. I am told that your son led a regiment of *Negroes*, is that not a most remarkable thing?"

The door to Annie's salon burst open and Adèle entered, followed by a grinning, balding, red-bearded giant. "Madame, ici Monsieur O'Connor—"

"A pleasant good evening to all!" the giant boomed. "There you are, de Leiningen. What distinguished company you've brought me amongst!" He looked around and his huge hands opened, seeming to embrace the room. "And this would be our charming hostess, am I right?"

Annie gave him her hand and he bent to kiss it, straightening back up with a flirtatious wink. She liked him already.

"Madame Shaw, Dr. Finkelmann," said Bertrand, "allow me to introduce Mr. Aloysius O'Connor, visiting us from his studio at Pont-Aven." Mother Shaw looked dubious, but gave him her hand.

"Pleased to meet you. I am not familiar with—Pont Aven, was it?"

"As fine a locale as any painter could wish, ma'am," said

O'Connor heartily. "There's quite the colony out there, on the ocean's edge—Finistère. The ends of the earth. That rogue Gauguin, a troublemaker if I ever met one, talked me into renting a place—"

"And what brings you to Paris?" Annie said.

"The company, ma'am, the company. It gets lonesome sometimes, on the edge of the sea. I get a dose of the City for a couple a' weeks and then return, fed up with my Paris companions, ready to get back on the wrestling-mat with the Muse."

"I have never met a Muse," said Sarah with the glimmer of a smile. *Give her credit,* thought Annie, *she's trying to be gracious.*

"Right enough, she's an awful elusive little baggage," said O'Connor, looking around, Annie realized, for a drink. Adèle handed him a glass of Côtes de Provence, which he drank off in one swallow and handed back to her startled maid. "Ah, that's lovely!" At Annie's nod, Adèle hurried off to bring a fresh glass.

"Wrestling with the Muse. What an interesting idea!" said Carlotta from behind her. Annie waved her forward.

"This is my niece, Miss Lowell. She's looking forward to exploring the Parisian art world."

"I doubt I have artistic talent myself—so far as I know," said Carlotta, a note of hope in her voice. "But I long to see the wonderful art that is happening here—only think, Mr. O'Connor, we thought we were going to stay in Mrs. Crafts' apartments," she gestured toward the hallway, "but the Comte de Leiningen is there, with a group of real artists, working on a composition—"

Seeing from O'Connor's arched eyebrows that Bertrand had not enlightened him on that point, Annie explained. "The

Comte and his atelier are at work on—a classical theme, isn't it, Monsieur?"

Bertrand, smiling, stepped forward and gave O'Connor his hand. "Glad to see you again, mon vieux." Sarah Shaw was eyeing Bertrand with disapproval, perhaps understandable given the hairy-hooved, half-naked state in which she had first encountered him.

He turned to Sarah, and Annie picked up her cue. "Madame Shaw, may I present Bertrand, Comte de Leiningen, who is to have the misfortune of being my painting instructor."

Mother Shaw nodded, graciously enough, but did not extend her hand.

"Enchanté, Madame—and this, I take it, is your lovely daughter?" He turned back to Carlotta with a salacious leer. Annie covered her mouth to keep from breaking out in laughter.

"Granddaughter," she managed. "Monsieur le Comte de Leiningen, my niece, Miss Lowell."

"Mademoiselle!" Bertrand turned toward Carlotta, who gave him her hand. He kissed it with the lightest brush of the lips, which would have sent shivers down Annie had the hand been hers, and nearly did so in any event. Lotta looked mildly amused; her grandmother appeared scandalized.

"How do you do?" Carlotta said. "I'm so sorry we interrupted your work."

"De rien, de rien! You did take Miss DeKuyper by surprise, however, and I fear her manners were not the most cordial—"

"Oh, we quite understand," Carlotta said eagerly, though Mother Shaw was giving him a look that could have drilled through plate-iron. "Our letters had not reached my aunts—"

"You know Madame Greene, I take it," Annie smiled

innocently in Julia's direction. "She received her letter when the ladies arrived, as did I. The Paris posts are very slow, aren't they."

"I have often found them so." Bertrand's eyebrow raised slightly. "Madame Shaw, how comes your life-drawing of Miss DeKuyper? I see no evidence of its progress—"

"Goodness, Monsieur, you can hardly think I would have it out where my dinner guests could see it—"

Carlotta's eyes widened. "Aunt Annie, you're working on a..." she dropped her voice. "*nude?*"

"It's barely begun," Annie said with a cheerful little shrug. "Just the pencil-sketches so far, and Miss DeKuyper is so taken up with your tableau, between painting it and modeling for it—"

"A nude, is it!" Aloysius O'Connor clapped his hands together. "Startin' right in on the deep end—good for you, Missus Shaw!"

"Modeling—!" Mother Shaw had turned even paler than usual.

"What would be the point in satyrs if they weren't abducting a water-nymph?" said Bertrand.

"Water-nymph..." Sarah sank slowly onto a divan.

"Hence my study," Annie said brightly. "The Comte thought it would be a splendid opportunity for me to try life-drawing, what with their effort under way across the hall—"

"Oh, it will be far more than a mere effort," Bertrand said. "I expect it will be at eye-level in the next Salon, and the critics all of a twitter in its praise."

Julia steered Dr. Finkelmann over to Mother Shaw, handing each a wine glass. "Dr. Finkelmann longs to talk with you about his Civil War researches, Sarah!" She beamed at them both. "He has made a study of the colored regiments after the War, haven't you, Professor?"

Dr. Finkelmann puffed up slightly, even as he modestly lowered his eyes. "A hobby of mine, Madame—though I could never seem to interest my young former colleague—or indeed Madame Annie Shaw herself—but I am sure that you, Madame, must take a great interest in such matters—now, for example, the so-called Buffalo Soldiers—" He was off and running, edging closer to Sarah, whose brows were contracting in what looked like the beginning of a sick-headache. Annie left him to it and took Carlotta to meet Retta Reubell, who was talking with Aloysius O'Connor about his landscapes.

Retta took Lotta by both hands. "I've heard from Madame Greene that you're interested in art, my dear. Will you be taking lessons while you're in Paris?"

Carlotta cast a sideways glance at Mother Shaw. "I should certainly like to—I haven't drawn since I was a child, but I used to enjoy it greatly."

"You should come to our workshop in Montmartre and we'll give you a lesson or two," said O'Connor, twinkling benignly at her. "I've a young friend name of Bernard—Émile Bernard—about your age he'll be, Miss Lowell—who'll make a name for himself one of these days. I'm more or less subsidizing him in the studio, but I don't mind that—you've got to have that wee pied-à-terre in the City, don't you, and we have a grand time of an evening in the café-concerts. I could persuade him to show you a bit about composition and so forth."

"Uh—I think—that would be—" Carlotta blushed, eyes bright with hope. Annie suppressed a rising chaperone instinct. As if reading her thoughts, Retta Reubell said, "I haven't seen your Paris digs, Aloysius—why don't I bring Miss Lowell for a visit? What day would suit you?"

"I'd better ask my grandmother," Carlotta said, visibly drooping. "We haven't found her a suitable place yet, and she'll need my help with that—"

Really, it was too bad. For every impulse she was following to drive Mother Shaw away, Annie had developed an urge to enfold Carlotta in the Paris milieu, to break her away from the suffocating atmosphere of East Thirtieth Street. Getting rid of Mother Shaw was a matter of soul-survival; if the price of that was depriving Carlotta of an opportunity to blossom, she wondered if she were prepared to pay it.

Herr Finkelmann was still bending Sarah's ear when dinner was announced. She looked pained when he took her arm to escort her to the dining room, exulting about the honor his hostess had done him in pairing them, and seating her at the foot of the table opposite Annie. Capitaine LeBoeuf was already standing on Sarah's left, with Madame Eyckert next to him.

Chapter 14

other Shaw's reaction to the escargot was all Annie could have wished. Perhaps the combination of Herr Finkelmann's halitosis and the powerful garlic aroma of the buttery snails was too much to expect anyone to bear. Sarah picked at one shell with her little two-tined fork, made a feint of raising the morsel to her lips, and discreetly dropped it on the edge of her Haviland escargot plate. Annie's other guests, including Carlotta, seemed to be enjoying the rich entrée and the accompanying Chablis.

Perhaps the oily, salty sardines in mustard sauce had been a bit excessive for the fish course which followed; this time, Carlotta was less than enthusiastic in finishing hers, though the others except Mother Shaw addressed them with relish.

"Such—interesting flavors, Aunt Annie," Carlotta said as the sardine course was cleared. "How lovely to introduce us to so many authentically French things!"

"I resolved to, my dear, when you said you hoped to immerse yourselves in Paris life. The next course is more delicate in flavor," Annie told Carlotta, "but no less authentic." Adèle and her assistant for the evening brought in plates of ris de veau, an item whose texture Annie herself found repellent. Bertrand shot a glance toward her, but she merely smiled and kept resolutely to her conversation with Carlotta and Retta Reubell on the subject of autumn millinery. She was beginning to feel a little sorry for Sarah, still entrapped in Doktor Finkelmann's unending historical monologues. Sarah took a few bites of the sweetbreads, clearly not relishing the experience but seeming determined to extract what nourishment she could from a dish that, unlike the prior two, did not repel her outright. It remained for the pieds de cochon to cement what Annie expected would be a lifelong aversion to indigenous French dishes. Their appearance alone was revolting enough.

But not for Capitaine LeBoeuf, who exclaimed with delight when a pair of trotters was set before him. "Madame Shaw, you have surpassed yourself! The most authentic cuisine du pays I have had since before the War!" He turned to Sarah. "They were once considered fit only for les paysans—the peasants—but when the Siege came, and everyone had to survive as best he could, they became a great delicacy—alors, I will show you how to eat them." He impaled one of the pig's feet on his fork and began stabbing it with his knife with commendable bellicosity. The hideous thing, which had been simmering for many hours, fell apart and looked, if possible, more grotesque than before. "Allow me," he said, "it is perhaps hard for a lady to penetrate the skin." With that, he leaned over Mother Shaw's plate and repeated his ministrations on her serving. "The meat from between the toes is the sweetest. Any true Frenchman will tell you that, Madame!" Sarah met his beaming satisfaction with one of her wintry smiles, but gamely forked a morsel and nodded graciously as it passed her lips.

"We will make a Frenchwoman of you yet, Sarah!" said Julia from the middle of the table.

"They are," Sarah grimaced, "quite flavorful. Really, Annie, you need not have gone to all this trouble—I am sure we should have been satisfied with a plain American dish or two."

"Never in life!" said Annie. "Whatever would be the point of coming all the way to Paris to eat what you can get anywhere at home? Paris is a cornucopia of culinary offerings—I shouldn't dream of subjecting my dinner-guests to something bland and insipid."

"Well said, Madame!" Capitaine LeBoeuf hoisted his claret glass, which he was emptying, Annie noted, at a rate competitive with Mr. O'Connor.

"Hear, hear!" cried the Irishman, and his tablemates raised their glasses.

"But we must make allowances, surely," said Madame Eyckert, who had been trying with little success to get a word in past Sarah's gentlemen companions. "The ladies are newly arrived, and it will take them some time to become used to our ways of eating—indeed, ladies, I hope you will do me the honor of dining with me next week. I shall plan a menu à l'Américaine." She gazed rapturously on Carlotta, who looked dubious, but Mother Shaw pre-empted a reply.

"The honor would be ours," she said in a tone that combined gratitude for the offer with reproach of Annie's culinary selections. Julia and Retta Reubell exchanged knowing smirks.

"Well!" said Annie brightly, "perhaps we may do better with coffee and dessert—if the ladies will join me in the library?" She rose and led the women off, having hinted to Bertrand to join them quickly to bring the evening to an early close. She doubted he and O'Connor would have much in common with Herr Finkelmann or Capitaine LeBoeuf.

In the library, she offered Sauternes, Roquefort, and an aged and more than usually redolent chèvre, along with coffee, melon slices, strawberries, and early pears.

"I had not thought French food quite so, ah, aromatic," Sarah told Julia as they entered.

Julia arranged her violet skirts around her on the divan. "I dare say we have gone quite native after all this time, haven't we, Mrs. Shaw?"

"Oh, please, tante Greene," her hostess simpered, "now that we are reacquainted, you must call me Annie, as you used to in America."

"I thought it was all very—interesting," Carlotta said, "though certainly richer than what Grandmamma and I are used to. And such fine pears!"

"What *is* this cheese, exactly?" Mother Shaw was staring at the wedge of chèvre Annie had cut for her.

"It's a goat's cheese—from the Savoy region, coated in cypress ash. They say it's very healthful."

"I don't believe I have ever eaten anything from a goat before."

"But you traveled in Europe for a time, when your children were young, didn't you?" Julia cut herself a slice of Roquefort. "You must have been exposed to quite a variety—"

"We kept a very *simple* diet then," said Mother Shaw, "for the children's sake. One could not expect them to appreciate, let alone tolerate, such *exotic* flavors."

"What a beautiful Sauternes this is," said Carlotta, handing forward her glass for Annie to refill from the demi-bouteille. "We don't get anything like this at home, do we, Tua?"

"Indeed, our style of life continues to be quite modest," replied Sarah in a repressive tone, "as befits our circumstances." Now *she* was being disingenuous; Frank Shaw had left his family amply provided for. If she lived in Puritanical style, that was from choice rather than necessity. Her daughter Effie Lowell, who had worn nothing but widow's black for decades, would likely be of Sarah's mind. Annie shuddered to think of the dinner meetings of charitable confederations in New York and Boston—shoe-leather beef and rubbery chicken, most likely. Carlotta was clearly welcoming the change.

"Mamma is so often away from home," Lotta was telling Retta Reubell, "that my grandmother and I generally content ourselves with the simplest of meals. But I must say I find that already Paris lives up to its reputation as a Mecca for the epicure." She sent Annie a smile that seemed to mingle amusement and gratitude.

"It's a Mecca for a great many things," said Miss Reubell. "Whatever one's *tastes*—" she gave Sarah a significant smile, "there's someone, or some place, to accommodate them for the right price." She took a silver cigarette-case from her reticule. "Annie, dear, if you don't object, I'll go out on your balcony and smoke." Annie nodded graciously, and Mother Shaw's eyes widened in horror.

"If you ladies would accompany me to one or two of our fine restaurants," said Madame Eyckert in a seductive tone, "I would gladly introduce you to the most cosmopolitan cuisines. I think you would be delighted with the North African tagines, Miss Lowell." From what Annie had heard of the lady, she would persuade them to foot the bill as well.

"I might like to join you for such an expedition," said Julia, inserting herself easily into the conversation and, Annie suspected, serving as a buffer between Carlotta and Madame Eyckert, who seemed to be setting her cap for the younger woman. "We widowed ladies don't get out as much as we might like, and I for one have always longed to dine at Lapérouse."

"Oh, Lapérouse!" said Madame Eyckert with a deprecatory wave. "I was thinking of a charming little spot on the Boulevard Raspail, known thus far to only a select few—"

The district was one which Annie had heard was a hotbed of Sapphism; no doubt the authoress would prefer to take Carlotta there without any chaperone, let alone two.

"It is, ah, somewhat early for us to be making social commitments," said Mother Shaw, having conveniently forgotten her acceptance of the invitation to dine chez Eyckert, "since we have not yet determined where we are to live, the contemplated premises," she aimed a dark glance at Annie, "not being available as we had been told."

"Oh, don't let that get in your way, Sarah!" said Julia. "I meant to tell you of Madame Mercure's—a fine little pension in the Eighth, very popular with respectable American ladies. One of them informs me that a suite has come vacant, on account of the demise of its occupant."

"In the Eighth? And are meals provided?"

"She is a lady of English birth, and I'm told her cuisine is plain and healthful."

Carlotta looked chagrined at the prospect, but Sarah had brightened considerably.

"Perhaps, Julia, you would accompany us, so that we might inspect it—and make an introduction?"

"Gladly—it might do very well. I'll meet you at the Grand

in the afternoon—will that suit? The weather promises fine tomorrow." Which meant that the emanations from the ground-floor stables would be less apparent than in damp conditions. Carlotta, for her part, might welcome the proximity of horse flesh, having inherited the Shaw girls' delight in riding. But if they took the suite and the weather turned wet, they would soon discover the disadvantages of the new location. And then—? Anything that fueled Mother Shaw's doubts as to the wisdom of her Paris venture could only aid the campaign to be rid of her. There remained the question of what she proposed to do as a long-term Parisian, and how long Carlotta might be part of her ménage. The danger to Annie's tranquility could only heighten if Carlotta returned to America alone.

The gentlemen entered from the dining room, engaged in a friendly and loud disputation on the subject, it seemed, of what constituted justification for warfare. "I'm inclined to side with the rebels of any sort," O'Connor was saying, his face glowing scarlet from, Annie guessed, both drink and enthusiasm. Mother Shaw looked scandalized. "But I suppose that's natural enough, coming from oppressed people as I do."

"Surely, monsieur, you would not consider the Southerners in the late American War so oppressed?" Capitaine LeBoeuf sounded scandalized himself.

"I've no doubt they saw themselves so," said O'Connor cheerfully. "Beggin' your pardon, ladies, we've been debatin' the merits of the Paris Commune, which your man here—" he cocked a thumb at the Capitaine, "seems to take a wee bit personally."

"If you had been there, Monsieur," LeBoeuf replied stiffly, "I doubt you could view it in so favorable a light—"

Bertrand stepped between the two and raised his hands, smiling. "Now that we have joined the ladies, I think we had best turn to more—amiable subjects—perhaps the forthcoming racing-season at Longchamp? What do you think of Verveine's chances for a repeat of the Prix Vanteaux, Madame Greene?"

"Not my favorite," Julia said. "I've got my eye on that new filly out of the Rothschilds' stables—"

"My money's on Fantasia," said Retta Reubell. "Verveine's getting long in the tooth. But my young friend Francine swears by Floride, and she," she let out a happy sigh, "could persuade me to almost anything, if the mood struck her."

Mother Shaw's eyes widened. "Do ladies gamble on *horse races* here?"

Annie took Julia aside as the gathering broke up. "Sound her out about her aims for living here, when you go to Madame Mercure's. It would be a natural query from you—what led her to choose this course? An incident with one of her daughters? Clem may have abetted her by worrying about my living in Paris alone—she'd harped at me on that point before they left."

"—and what could be better for our poor invalid than a loving in loco parentis to keep an eye on her?! If I had your sister here, I could not guarantee civility! Aren't you glad I sent you for the Swedish gymnastics? It's clear that you're fully able-bodied and—"

"—therefore available to look after an invalid myself. She'll construe it as best fits her aim. Which is, I believe, to secure an unpaid nurse and companion."

"She has four daughters for that—"

"—who relish the prospect no more than I do, I'm sure. Effie may be domiciled next door, but she's rarely at home these days. Ellen has her committees too, Anna her poor sick George, and Susie her four eligible daughters—a full-time obligation, I imagine. Whereas I, having neither parent nor child to look after, must be at a loss for a useful occupation."

"I'll sound her out. I fear you may be right. But I mustn't forget that you and I have only just become re-acquainted, and I'm thus ignorant of your plans and circumstances."

"While you're at it," Annie said with a wicked smile, "see what she thought of Mr. O'Connor. I'm hoping he horrified her."

"And you?"

"I'd like to see more of him. I found him a delightful addition— even if he *was* stumbling a bit on the stairs on the way out."

Annie woke in the night with her heart racing, which happened occasionally if she had drunk unwisely. But last evening she'd been temperate, to stay sharp while navigating the complications—and the cuisine—of the dinner. It was the gut-roiling realization that she and Carlotta Lowell were seeking the same thing: a life of her own, on her own terms, and only one of them would get it. One or the other was expected to serve as Sarah Shaw's Paris companion and nursemaid. If Annie declined or evaded the role, it would fall to Carlotta, since her mother and aunts had already washed their hands of Sarah. Carlotta, raised to be dutiful above all, would not abandon Sarah unless Annie took her over, the one thing Annie was determined not to do. Carlotta had one escape route which might override her sense of duty: marriage and children.

But marriage, at least, seemed the last thing Lotta wanted.

What Annie herself had barely begun was a journey of self-discovery. She might yet make of herself a salonnière, an artist or musician—though she had no illusions of being exceptional or even particularly good in either case—a party to friendships of mutual enjoyment and enrichment. That was developing nicely with Julia, who had come into her life providentially, and had already expanded to a circle of interesting minds; Mother Shaw's arrival, on the other hand, felt like some cruel jest of fate.

If it came to that, she would have to tell Mother Shaw the truth: that she considered her plans to move in next door an invasion and an imposition. That Sarah was free to live in Paris on whatever terms she chose, except those that involved Annie's serving as companion. Was Mother Shaw not satisfied with having wrecked her own son's future? She might see his death as a glorious martyrdom, even an apotheosis; to Annie it had been the waste of a beautiful young life, the loss of hope for a family of her own, an aching emptiness under her heart even now. To her own surprise she began to weep, tears that she had thought long shed coursing out again uncontrollably, heaving sobs of grief and of rage. Sarah Shaw had ruined her happiness once. She would not allow her to do it again.

Chapter 15

mbrellas aloft against wind and rain, Annie and Julia strolled along the Quai Debilly beside a sullen, choppy Seine.

"As you suspected," Julia said, "she confided that her daughters seem to care nothing for her, being too taken up with their own affairs, and that she might as well live on the moon for all she sees of them."

"They're not so far flung, surely—"

"I think her expectations are unrealistically high. Although Will and his family live close by, we dine together perhaps twice a month. It seems the right frequency for continuing to enjoy one another's company. Four small children demand a great deal from a household, even one with competent help—"

"I should think so. Sarah's grandchildren are getting on with their own lives, I suppose."

"The ones who are allowed to," Julia said grimly. "Not our poor Lotta. In any event, the notion of moving to Paris was impulsive on Sarah's part—perhaps, indeed, announced in the hope that one or another of her children would beg her to stay."

"And then Clem, for Lord knows what reason, went to call

on her when they disembarked at New York—"

"As Sarah reports the visit, it seemed providential. A lovely home already furnished, hers for as long as she cared to occupy it—"

The umbrella nearly slid from Annie's hand. "Is that what Clem said to her?"

"It's what she took from whatever Clem actually said to her. Along with her sense that Clem worried about your staying in Paris alone."

"It would not follow that I needed looking after by Mother Shaw." Annie furled her umbrella, scowling.

"Seems to have stopped for the present." Julia glanced skyward and furled her own umbrella. "It's certainly what she decided after her talk with your sister. Now she's even more convinced of it."

"Why? I'm obviously quite well, and—"

"Under the sway of irregular companions, who no doubt mean to compromise your morals and siphon off your fortune. She aims to enlist me in the project of rescuing you from these corrupting influences—"

Annie's incredulous laugh startled a passer-by. "You're the one who introduced us."

"She doesn't know that. I affected concern, naturally. Bertrand, she assumes, is a charlatan who intends to separate you from your money, no doubt by flattering you that you are a sound judge of art and that he and his cohorts are worthy of your patronage." Julia paused for breath. "She proposes to buy out their lease and relocate them elsewhere."

"How *dare* she!"

"She considers herself to have arrived just in time to rescue you from ruin," Julia continued with grim humor. "She's sure that your sister would endorse and indeed be grateful for the intervention."

"Of all the—" Annie sputtered. "She mightn't even be so far off in her assessment of Clem."

"—who doesn't know of your arrangements with Bertrand?"

"Naturally not. I hadn't time to inform her, and hoped I wouldn't have to. I doubt she'd approve. When she told me to make free with the place, I think she pictured me wandering in there and fiddling about on the grand piano."

"Nonetheless—she knows your feelings about Sarah."

"Of course she does. Clem is of a somewhat—placatory nature, has been from childhood. Always anxious to please, to say the right thing, to avoid unpleasantness."

"—and she counts on your doing the same, I fear."

"That's what's so infuriating." Annie skirted a puddle. "Her letter says she's sure I won't like it, but assumes I'll raise no objections. I've a good mind to send her a telegram—"

Julia raised a hand. "That won't solve your immediate problem. We must keep Sarah from occupying the flat." They reached a café, warmly lit and inviting, attached to a modest hotel, and seated themselves at a table in the rear near a clanking radiator. The day was so unseasonably cold and damp that the warmth was welcome, along with the place's red velveteen furniture and gilded cupids.

"A pot of coffee, I think." Annie said. "And have you enlisted in Sarah's 'rescue' attempt?"

"Naturally not, though since I'm not supposed to have been in your company, I couldn't gainsay her altogether. I did say that a couple of the guests were mutual acquaintances, and that if she aimed to live in Paris she must expect encounters with people of an artistic way of life."

"I lacked such opportunities for twenty years. I'm happy to be making up for the lost time."

"I mentioned, for example, that Retta Reubell was a well-regarded benefactress of the American Cathedral, and that I understood she and Mrs. Crafts to have been on friendly terms. 'Not *too* friendly, I trust,' says Sarah, 'That lady did not strike me as any kind of moral exemplar.' She heard Retta say something at dinner about Henry James mooning over some younger fellow for years, and that it was time he declared himself and got on with it. Unfortunately the fellow in question is," Julia grinned, "one of Sarah's nephews."

Annie howled. "The Sturgises are ubiquitous. You daren't throw a stone at random for fear of hitting one." Steaming pots of coffee and milk arrived, and the waiter poured them cafés au lait. "You said yourself Retta was a misleader of youth."

"Just the ticket for such a miserable day." Julia sipped blissfully, waving away the sugar-bowl. "In any event, Sarah clearly feels it her duty to take action—"

"She didn't like Madame Mercure's?"

"She pronounced it acceptable for the present, though with no great enthusiasm. Thank goodness the weather was dry and the stables were not, ah, announcing themselves. Nor, happily, was Monsieur in evidence. He can be vociferous in his political views, particularly after hitting the brandy, which I understand he does frequently. She took the empty suite for herself and Lotta on a month-to-month basis. The Grand's prices are unconscionable, she says. But she plans to deal with 'this so-called Comte and his cohorts' sooner rather than later. She intends to engage an estate agent to find studio space somewhere in the vicinity and buttonhole Bertrand about buying out his supposed lease with you."

Annie's nostrils flared. "Bertrand already has a studio. But of course she doesn't know that. I suppose she'll read him a lecture about taking advantage of a lonely widow's good nature while she's at it. I must write to Clem. She had no business fouling my life like this, and I won't have it. How long will Carlotta stay, do you think?"

"Carlotta? She talked of a month or six weeks. The *Wieland* out of Bremen calls at Le Havre toward the end of August. She'd rather leave before hurricane season gets too far along—last year was a nasty one, you'll remember. She belongs to a young ladies' literary society—though I wonder—"

"Go on—what were you going to say?"

"I'm probably just being my gossipy self, but—she seems to have taken a shine to Tallie."

"She certainly admires her—she's hoping Tallie will take her on as a pupil—" Annie sat back and contemplated her friend. "You mean, you think she's—she has—"

"Tallie seems to have a wide circle of admirers. Miss Cooper among them," Julia added, "though that one at least seems unrequited."

"As opposed to—?"

"I'll let you form your own surmises, based on your own observations." Julia smiled complacently. "It's always helpful to have unbiased eyes in these matters." Julia flagged down the waiter. "L'addition, s'il vous plaît."

*   *   *

Annie re-read her letter to Clem with satisfaction and reflected that under other circumstances she might have gone in for the law.

I am in no need of looking after from anyone, especially not from Sarah Shaw, nor have I any wish to look after her as an unpaid companion, and I have no intentions of allowing her to disrupt an arrangement I have made with friends and which I am enjoying immensely. Our father was a great supporter of rising artists, and I feel sure he would applaud my belated discovery that I take after him in that regard. I cannot conceive what would have led you to think either of us a suitable companion for the other, or that I could countenance having her as a daily and near neighbor. She plans to tell you, I learn, that I have fallen among bad companions and must be rescued from prospective exploitation. The only exploitation of which I am in danger is having my peaceful and pleasant life here in Paris disrupted by a woman who, as you well know, was responsible for wounds of grief and misery in my past which have never completely healed—which, indeed, this unfortunate and unlooked-for episode has reopened. You will therefore, I am sure, tell her, when you receive her letter, that you wished me to make free with your apartments, that I do so with your full concurrence, that she has no authority whatever to change arrangements I have made, that you were unaware of these when she proposed her occupation of the apartments, and that whatever she construed as an offer from you to occupy the apartments cannot therefore take effect.

She dropped a blob of hot red wax on the envelope, slammed her seal on it as if smashing a cockroach, and rang the bell for Adèle. "Will you see that this goes by the next possible mail-packet?" She related her conversation with Julia about Sarah's intentions.

"Mon Dieu, madame, we must prevent this!" said Adèle. "To think of evicting the gracious Comte and the young Tallie, who is so agréable—they have allowed me to see their painting as it progresses and it will be une merveille, I am sure! I have not until now had a chance to see les artistes at work—it is a delight." She took the letter and read the address.

Annie in turn scanned her maid's sculpted features. Why had she so rarely acknowledged what a remarkably handsome woman Adèle was? Indeed, she had little sense at all of what kind of life this individual, an expatriate like herself, led in her private time away from the avenue Henri Martin. Who were her friends? Was there family? Others who had come from the French West Indies? Surely there were sweethearts, suitors…

"You should be in their painting—if you liked."

Adèle's brow furrowed. "Moi, Madame?"

"You'd be an excellent subject for an artist. Indeed, since I propose to take up painting again myself, I wonder if you'd consider sitting to me for a portrait—" Adèle was shaking her head, "—only when I've improved enough to justify your time and patience. In the meantime, I heard both Bertrand and Henry Tanner say that they would relish an opportunity to paint you. They would pay you as a model, of course—"

Adèle put a hand to her cheek. "Monsieur Tanner! That would be an honor—he is très gentil, and has such a beautiful voice—" She looked away.

Annie recognized a budding tendre. And why not? She thought of the discussion in Retta Reubell's salon about the connections between artists and their models. Tanner was known for bringing out the dignity in the humblest of subjects. Who knew?

"Ah, but Madame, here is Monsieur le Poste!" Adèle turned and all but ran from the room, returning with the smiling postman in his blue uniform.

"I have also some letters for the elder Madame Shaw," he said apologetically. "Evidemment she has given the address of Madame Crafts to her friends." He handed Annie a bundle. "Madame votre belle-mère is not staying there, I see. It did not seem that the lady's arrival was an agreeable development?"

Annie smiled. "Far from it, monsieur—"

"Ah, oui, I understand! My own mother-in-law is something of a—I think you would say a dragon?"

"In this case I might say a Gorgon, but they have much in common."

"I cannot think that Paris would be agreeable to such a lady. She seems to expect things to be done in the American fashion." At his back, Adèle nodded and sighed.

"You have a gift for understatement, Monsieur. Perhaps she will find a comfortable situation within the American Colony, where one may live quite insulated from one's surroundings."

"—but surely we may hope not!" he said before turning to descend the stairs.

He looked so earnest that Annie could not suppress a laugh. She glanced at the bundle of letters in her hand. From the American Ministry came a confirmation that the documents which Lydia Burwell would need for her Atlantic crossing had been sent to Jackson's lodging. And as though the letter had conjured him, the young man was coming up the stairs, carrying a wooden paint box, as the postman went down.

"Bonjour, Madame Shaw!" Jackson swept off another imaginary plumed hat and made a bow. "We're going to work on Tallie today—she has us roughed in on her own painting—"

"I'm glad to see you, Jackson! I have a note here from the American Ministry—the papers are en route to you—"

He stopped in mid-climb.

"For Lydia and Benjamin," Annie whispered. "A passport, and the visas—"

"Oh!" He took the letter. "I thought it would take a good deal longer. I can't say how much I'm obliged to you. I'll write to her tonight."

"They'll need the passage money. I'll secure a draft from the bank in the morning, and you can include it with the letter."

He bit his lip and bowed his head. "I'm so much in your debt, Mrs. Shaw—"

"Enough of that, young man. We've settled this long since. Write your letter, and give you joy of the results! Oh, one thing I should mention—" Annie recounted her meeting with Mrs. Kernochan at the Cathedral. "You indeed have cause for concern. She all but asked me to spy on you and report back with any evidence of a continuing attachment."

Jackson's eyebrows rose. "I can't say I'm surprised. But it's troubling all the same."

"I told her I would, of course." Annie watched his expression turn to dismay. "She didn't hear me add 'When Hell freezes over.'" The boy's face cleared.

The door of Clem's apartments opened and Tallie stood there, slight and shivering in what looked like a nightshift for a Grecian deity. "There you are at last, Jackson! It's getting cold in there. Madame Shaw, Bertrand has brought us the strangest assortment of leftovers, and says that they came from you—" She smiled up at Jackson and stood aside to let him pass into the flat.

"Come and dine with me tomorrow. You and Miss Cooper. We'll feed you something more agreeable than pig's feet."

"They're not so bad, if one's really hungry. Was your mother-in-law properly horrified? I do hope so! Pauline—Miss Cooper—is engaged tomorrow evening—"

Annie resisted the urge to throw her silk shawl over the girl's shoulders. "Then it will be just us two. I hope all this silliness is not detracting too much from your own work?"

"Au contraire!" Tallie beamed. "I'm learning a great deal. They've each had a go at dropping the satyr-legs and giving us a chance to do some muscle studies. They're both well-built—Jackson more than Bertrand, of course—it's only natural, he being taller." She almost simpered. "The situation is more agreeable than I expected." She turned back toward the Crafts' door. Annie had a frisson of foreboding.

Good heavens, she thought, *is everybody falling in love?*

Chapter 16

"Pauline and I visited Mr. Tanner in his studio," said Tallie over an aperitif. "Such a dank, poky little space—but his work simply *glows*. And the way he does hands—I could learn a great deal from him. If only he weren't so preoccupied with Biblical themes— it's terribly old-fashioned of him, and I worry he won't sell anything."

Annie poured them more sherry. "They'll do well in America, I'm sure."

"I hope you're right, Mrs. Shaw. If he weren't a Negro, he'd have been a wild success in America long since. It's such a shame that people still can't see past that. It's the same with being a woman."

"There are always churches, I suppose," Annie mused, "as places that would welcome religious art like Mr. Tanner's. Are you indeed profiting from the satyr exercise? Have you and Miss Cooper been modeling as well?"

"Pauline refuses to model. I can't blame her. The students and even the instructors aren't always respectful—and one's supposed to think being asked to be someone's mistress is the height of flattery. It's not as if any of them has money! Oh, dear—have I shocked you?"

"Indeed, no—I drank too fast," Annie spluttered; her sherry had gone down the wrong way. "Surely the whole point of being someone's mistress is that he supports you financially? I understand the French have legal contracts for that. The ladies I've heard of in such arrangements—" Annie was sure she had met one or two of them at Retta Reubell's salon—"seem to have more enjoyable lives than their protectors' wives."

"And if he wants to be rid of her, when she gets old and frumpy?"

"One may get old without becoming frumpy—Madame Greene is surely a case in point! Under the contracts, they must continue the support, unless she takes up with another."

"How enlightened!"

"The old kings set the standards. The King's official mistress occupied a position of honor and privilege. Power in some cases—Madame de Pompadour, for one."

"Lovers are a different matter. It seems much the best way, for people like us—artists, I mean—we're not out to set up domestic establishments, but companionships of hearts and minds..." Tallie looked wistful.

"I had a friend, my husband's cousin, who lived for many years with another lady. When poor Loulie died at twenty-five, Anna, her companion, was heartbroken. She took to wearing black, just as if she were a widow." Annie had been in Nice with the pair in 1874 when Loulie died from consumption.

"Surely men enjoy such companionship too—but it seems only female friendships can escape being judged improper!" Tallie rose and paced the little parlor. "And many such connections are far from platonic."

Annie smiled. "I've never thought it my business to inquire. I had an uncle who lived single his whole life, but left a great deal of money to a gentleman with whom we'd thought him only casually acquainted. Mr. Collison, a near neighbor—by design, it seemed."

"Did the family object to the will?"

"We thought Mr. Collison a decent and courteous fellow. And I for one had pitied Uncle John for what seemed a lonely life. Clem and I fantasized that he'd been thwarted of some true love in his youth—it may even have been so, only not as we supposed. So I was glad to think he might have been happy after all."

"What a decent woman you are, Mrs. Shaw! So few Christians actually live by the principle of 'Judge not, lest ye be judged.'"

Annie shrugged off the praise. "Who could live in Paris on other terms? At least, in the Paris I want to live in? It seems enough to me to strive for one's own goodness and let everybody else take care of themselves—unless they hurt or harm others one cares about. In which case I can be quite merciless." The little ménage next door, she realized, now fell into the category of those she would protect, along with Carlotta, whom she had so recently come to know. "My antipathy toward la vieille Madame Shaw, for instance, arose from the harm I saw her doing to her son—but that affected me too—"

"You have a gift for understatement!"

"What frustrated me," Annie wondered what was moving her to open her heart so, "was his inability to see it for himself—that she was making him a sacrificial victim to her cause. She had convinced him that her life had been one long sacrifice on her children's behalf."

"It's hard to imagine someone that driven by ideals. I've grown up in a far more grasping and cynical age. Sometimes art feels like the only truth there is."

"Oh, I hope not! Surely loving one's neighbor can always be a cardinal principle—treating others with decency and charity—"

"There! I've shocked you a little at last."

"Was that an aim of yours?"

"No—but I find the lack of moralizing in a lady of your—ah, generation—unusual."

"It's because I never had children, I suppose." Annie went to the window to watch the evening light turn gold. "Mothers have the duty to endow the young with the proper attitudes and virtues, so that daughters will do so in their turn, and sons will expect the same of their wives—"

"—enabling them to feel at ease about being off cavorting with their mistresses!"

"Tallie, you're even more cynical than I."

Tallie joined her at the window. "I have so many opportunities for first-hand observation. It's going to be a nice sunset, isn't it?"

"Have your instructors so reliably made improper suggestions?"

"It's the rare one who hasn't—and only, I think, because their inclinations lay elsewhere."

"Perhaps the moralists are right, about the threat to female virtue from the artistic milieu."

"Female virtue is threatened," replied Tallie with an expression grown grave, "when the male has something the female needs—a hot meal, a place to lay her head, the power to decide her future—"

"—to offer her the security of marriage?"

"I was thinking of admission to art school. But in the artists' world, no one thinks the worse of a girl because she's lost her so-called virtue. It's an aspect of Paris life that Mr. Burwell's having trouble getting used to."

"Well, he comes from that old world of preux chevaliers and lily-handed ladies, where the ladies' pedestals are a foot taller than ours—"

"—except that the noble cavaliers kept their ladies lily-pure by debauching their Negro slave girls," Tallie said. "I doubt that's changed much since the days of Honest Abe."

"Goodness, have you shared such observations with Jackson?" Annie wondered momentarily whether her old suitor Roland, who'd seemed the soul of gentility, had relieved any frustrated desires on the bodies of his father's slaves. Hard to imagine Roland doing deeds of darkness with women helpless to resist him, but her parents' friend Fanny Kemble had brought back shocking tales from her brief marriage to a Georgia plantation master. That entire civilization had been built on hypocrisy. Else how to explain Lydia Burwell, so far from being a full-blooded African?

"Jackson has got away from all that," Tallihe said, "by coming to Paris. Black and white can mingle freely here, without harm. It's sweet to see how friendly he and Mr. Tanner have become already, how much he feels he can learn from him—about technique, and light effects, and so on. Isn't it funny that he's had to come abroad for that?"

Jackson, Annie surmised, was hoping to learn more from Tanner than painting techniques, such as how he might help a Negro wife adjust to Paris.

"I think for both of them the attraction is the chance to study at the Beaux-Arts—and with the eminent instructors who teach there." she added, recalling that the Beaux-Arts, free to its attendees, was barred to females.

"It's so unfair!" said Tallie, swerving onto the secondary topic as Annie had hoped. "Bad enough they don't admit women, but the places that do, like Julian's, charge us more than the men. Because, they claim, it costs more to set up the all-female ateliers."

"And here you were claiming that the art world lacks hypocrisy in such matters!"

"Especially when you think of the lives of its female models," Tallie said, lifting her head and sniffing. "What is that heavenly smell?"

Adèle summoned them to the dining room, where a savory coq au vin awaited. "Hypocrisy in that instance is profitable," Tallie added with a touch of bitterness. "Hence the modeling— and other threats to female virtue—to earn enough to pay our fees, and keep body and soul together. Oh, look at this. I should like to paint it if I weren't going to devour every last morsel. Your china's so elegant, Mrs. Shaw—Limoges?" Adèle poured claret into their cut-crystal goblets.

"Haviland, yes. I'm very fond of the matte gold, and the curves. What do you think of the Art Nouveau style?"

"You're thinking of redecorating?" Tallie said eagerly. "Oh, I don't mean—"

"The place needs it, don't you think? Mamma was a true Victorian—everything covered and overstuffed, like the old Queen herself. And the colors are entirely too dark. Mamma's been gone four years—it's time to lighten things up in here."

"I'm surprised you waited so long."

"My sister wanted to hold on to her memories of our mother—

it might have been a desecration in her eyes, if I'd made changes."

"But it's your flat!"

"True. And now that Mamma's gone—and Clem too, in a different way—"

"It was sweet of you to wait, when you longed to put your own stamp on the place."

"I didn't have a stamp to put on it—I've only begun to think of it seriously since the Crafts left."

"Then you must let your artistic protégés show their appreciation by helping you think about color schemes and so forth. Do you miss the Crafts?"

"Not as much as I'd have thought. I love them dearly and we've had many treasured times together, but—"

"You were a bit stifled, weren't you?"

"It's about time I grew up, I've been thinking. Odd, isn't it? Most women my age are striving to seem younger."

"And here's your mother-in-law come to reduce you once more to a state of younger-generational servitude. Mrs. Shaw, do you find Jackson Burwell as charming as I do?"

As conversational volte-faces went, this equaled anything Annie was capable of. "It's part of their breeding, I suppose," she said. "When his father came visiting as a young man, our Northern boys seemed ill-mannered louts by comparison—which didn't prevent me from rejecting Mr. Burwell and marrying a New Englander. Manners aren't everything…"

Tallie smiled. "What are you thinking about?"

"I was wondering whether Roland's mother—Jackson's grandmother—she was the Mrs. Saint Clare straight out of *Uncle Tom's Cabin*—might have been an even worse mother-in-law than the one I got. Who, despite the brevity of the formal connection, assumes that I'm as much to be imposed upon as any blood relative."

"Is Jackson's mother living?"

Was Tallie thinking of a possible mother-in-law? "Ten years gone. She was a gentle soul, it seems, and he misses her greatly."

"So you're a bit of a substitute mother to him!"

"I hope not. I thought I was done with all that when my nieces left."

"He speaks of you in reverential tones. I sometimes think he's a bit homesick."

You have no idea. Erotic-classical tableaux or not, two healthy young people in daily proximity would naturally develop an attachment. But perhaps Tallie was merely curious. There might have been dalliances with other young women in her past; Annie recalled Bertrand's acerbic comments about her and Miss Cooper. "He could be. Were you homesick at first?"

"Heavens, no—I got away as soon as I had the chance. And Jackson seems to be planning on a long stay. He told Bertrand he's looking for a better living situation. D'you think he'll settle here? In Paris?"

"Too soon to tell, I think."

"Because, you see, there's a flat on the floor below us, coming vacant soon—and I wondered if I should mention it to him—"

"How large is it?"

"One big room to serve for living room and bedroom, a little kitchen—the toilet's out on the stairs. I should've thought you'd ask how much it cost."

That wouldn't suit a young couple with an infant, who could afford something with an ensuite lavatory once Lydia arrived. "Perhaps you should mention it to him," Annie said, afraid that hesitancy was evident in her tone. "If it's not too expensive."

"Do you think he'd see it as—improper in some way?"

Annie resolved to make sure Jackson had booked passage for Lydia and Ben. "I don't see how, but I'll mention it to him as well."

Adèle arrived with pots de crème infused with almond and laced with tangerines and orange liqueur. A pair of allongés, dark and aromatic, steamed in little round cups. Annie began peeling a tangerine. "We have the North African colonies to thank for these—"

"Wouldn't it be wonderful to visit Morocco? I've longed to see it ever since that Sargent painting with the votary all in white over the ambergris burner. Can you imagine—riding into the Sahara on a camel—what could be more romantic! In the moonlight—a full moon—"

Perhaps it was only age and inertia that conjured in Annie visions of overcrowded bazaars, hordes of importunate beggars, and bad-tempered, foul-smelling beasts who spit at you.

"You couldn't wear corsets," Tallie went on. "We'd have to wear something more like trousers and shirts."

Annie laughed. The notion of herself in trousers no longer seemed as ludicrous as it would have before the still-dreaded Swedish exercises. "You could carry those off splendidly."

"A painting expedition! If we ever had the money—Jackson and Bertrand and I—" Tallie waved her custard-spoon, rapt in her vision. "You too, Mrs. Shaw—just think of the colors, the costumes, the mysterious alleys—"

"What a terrifying prospect. Isn't that the land of the drug-crazed murderers, from whom we have the term 'assassin'?"

"You're laughing at me! Hashish merely renders one giggly

and sleepy—well, a little amorous too, perhaps—maybe I should try it on Jackson—"

Annie gulped. "If you mean to play the vampire, surely you'd find a more ready victim in Bertrand? His interest in you seems not entirely artistic."

"Indeed it isn't," Tallie sounded shocked, "and I'm thankful that Jackson's been there to serve as a buffer. I prefer not to be alone with Bertrand if I can help it!"

Comprehension dawned. "You spoke earlier of improper suggestions—"

"Who did you think I was talking about? Isn't it obvious he considers me his bespoke property?"

"Then I should never have set things up next door—" Annie felt her cheeks flushing.

"Don't think that, Mrs. Shaw! These are occupational hazards for women, artists or models. I'm grateful for Jackson's presence—his gentlemanly nature puts Bertrand to shame—and I've learned to deflect Bertrand's more unwelcome, ah, overtures."

"But why would you—"

"He's a great artist and instructor, in spite of his belittling comments. That portrait I did of him that's sitting in his studio—that was a real breakthrough, and I owe it to him."

Annie recalled the supposed self-portrait which had so impressed her. "The one in the red cravat, that I assumed was an example of his own best work."

"Did you really?" Tallie's face lit up. "I suppose he must have liked it too, since he keeps it there. Perhaps he shows it off to other prospective students?"

"I would, if I were he. Do you think him a good teacher for Jackson?"

"Certainly—at least until Jackson gets into the École. Bertrand teaches there too, you know."

"What a shame they exclude women! How can they justify—"

"Because women may receive free art instruction in Paris, at the École des Arts Décoratifs. They teach you how to paint flowers on teacups!" Tallie shuddered.

"I suppose it's expecting a lot from a man," Annie mused, "to remain disinterested when painting a female nude—"

"No more than we expect from doctors, who are daily confronted by females in a state of undress. The problem's more when it's an unclothed male being painted by females. He feels—defenseless, I think—in a way that we don't in such circumstances—and must assume that the woman who's depicting him is attracted to him. They can't bear to be thought of as mere objects of artistic study." This to Annie was a rather subtle insight; Tallie seemed to have surprised even herself with it.

"Ah, there's an element of vanity to it!"

"Or there's something about being looked at in that way, that arouses certain feelings in the male, since he *has* let his defenses down. Like the excitement men feel when they pay girls to tie them up and abuse them, I suppose—oh, now I *have* shocked you, Mrs. Shaw—"

Annie took a hasty sip of Sauternes. One knew, of course, that Paris was a mecca for all varieties of erotic experience, and that some of the houses catered to specialized tastes, but…

"One of my classmates at Julian's paid her way in that fashion," Tallie continued. "She's quite in demand at our Friday gatherings, for the entertainment value of her stories."

"I *have* led a sheltered life. Still, I don't suppose people can ask their wives for that sort of treatment—"

Tallie laughed. "There's plenty of cruelty in marriage, surely—but not of the sort such men find entertaining. Danielle hints that some of her clients are in positions of great responsibility in real life, and find being ordered about relaxing."

"There are more things in heaven and earth, Horatio—'

"—than are dreamt of in your philosophy. I'm very fond of Shakespeare too. Jackson was quoting him the other day—something about a rich jewel in an Ethiop's ear."

"I wonder who he was referring to."

"Well, Juliet, of course—" A deep flush crept up Tallie's throat and face. "D'you suppose there's been a Juliet in his life?"

Knowing Jackson to have a rich jewel of an Ethiop in his present life, Annie was at a loss for a reply. She settled for deflection. "And has there been a Romeo in yours?"

"Romeos and a lot of other things. I fear Jackson's a babe in the woods by comparison."

"Speaking of such—it seems my niece by marriage, Miss Lowell, has been infected by the artistic miasmas of Paris—"

"She showed me sketches of people she did on the voyage. I think she has an eye for the essence of character—"

"Here's my dilemma. I'd like Carlotta to stay and explore her interests—and if you discern some talent there, I think she'd benefit from a guiding hand. I'm not sure how to get rid of Madame Shaw the Elder without also losing Carlotta, but in the meantime, would you consider taking her on as a pupil? She's well able to pay you what you're worth."

"Why not Bertrand, or even Jackson? I'm not the most experienced instructor—"

"Bertrand has plenty of pupils already, and it's obvious to me you're a good deal farther along than Jackson."

"It's kind of you to suggest it—I'll be glad to talk with Miss Lowell and see if we're a good match as teacher and pupil." Tallie's words were slow and hesitant, which Annie attributed to doubts about her instructional skills.

"I'm delighted to hear it. However long it takes Mother Shaw to realize that Paris is not for her, my niece may at least profit by it."

"Jackson told me that you had thought of going to Cannes, to your house there?"

"Indeed, and you're all invited to join me. I have a notion to be painted in my garden there—perhaps with Madame Greene, if that doesn't sound too Impressionist—"

"Do you really mean it? That would be—oh, I hardly dare think of it!"

"I'd go once the weather turns cooler. But I have to scheme how to get us all there without leaving the field to Mother Shaw and finding her installed in my sister's apartments when I return. Or, worse, having her follow me there." Annie had looked forward to being the sole chatelaine of Les Anthémis, and felt renewed anger at the thought of having to make her own plans around another's. If one weren't to experience the joys of a husband and children, couldn't one at least have the satisfaction of making her own plans on her own schedule?

"Never fear, Mrs. Shaw—we will occupy the apartments until there isn't a tube of paint left in all of Paris!" Tallie raised her arm like Delacroix's Liberty leading the sans-culottes.

"I hope it won't come to that—but it won't be overnight either, I fear. Sarah is a single-minded woman. Perhaps we should take her to the Chat Noir, or one of the absinthe dens in Montmartre—"

"Get Madame Eyckert to do that," said Tallie. "She clearly has designs on Miss Lowell, and there are certain, ah, clubs there which would give Madame la Belle-Mère Shaw more than she bargained for."

"Madame mentioned a place on the Boulevard Raspail—"

"Not the Palome Salée?" Tallie's eyes widened.

"I believe that was the name—you know it?"

"I barely escaped unmolested," Tallie shuddered, "by the predatory crew that frequents the place. If I'd found any of them attractive, it would've been one thing. But even by my standards, it's a den of iniquity."

"Just as well, then, that Madame Greene offered to accompany the party. Perhaps if Mother Shaw fears for her granddaughter's virtue at the hands of these vampires, it will accelerate her return to America."

"What if Carlotta likes it?" Tallie had the air of one asking a painful but necessary question.

"Of course she—goodness, is that why you suggested one of the men as an art instructor?"

"After a while in Paris, one develops intuitions."

Could Carlotta be an unwitting Sapphist? It would explain a good deal. Annie had heard of Boston marriages, indeed counted several parties to them as close friends. But she couldn't quite envision the mechanics of it. Easier to assume that the affection and attachment displayed by such couples was a sublime and refined thing. But her own brief time with Rob had told her that, once fixated on the object of its passion, the body would not be denied.

"Are there—houses in Paris, like the one you were describing where your friend Danielle works? But for female clients?"

"This is Paris," Tallie said. "If you can conceive of it, and have the money, there's nothing you could wish for that isn't for sale."

Annie couldn't catch her breath for a moment. "Children?"

"Boys and girls both. There, the clients are all male, though the procuresses aren't, of course. Among women, the interactions are less—imbalanced, it's fair to say. Like the traditional whorehouse, they've probably rendered many a marriage tolerable."

Odd to be hearing all this from a girl barely past twenty. "So, you think Carlotta's attracted to other women."

"It's only a hunch," Tallie raised a hand. "But a strong one. If I were her teacher, I'd know soon enough. It's not that I find her repulsive—she's pleasant and intelligent, and I'd like to be friends with her. But if those are her feelings, I couldn't reciprocate them. It could be awkward."

"How would she convey such feelings to you, if she did harbor them?"

"As I might convey mine to her, or anyone else, if I had them—a look, an accidental touch here and there, a book left open to some suggestive passage—"

Annie wondered what had inspired Jackson's quote from *Romeo and Juliet.* Had Tallie left a book open?

Chapter 17

nnie and Bertrand headed away from the patisseries of Passy's main retail district. The ghastly sessions with Fröken Johansson were bearing fruit; she was walking easily, more upright, her stride noticeably longer even in the mid-July swelter. Temperance in the pastry department might justify a new dress in the slim-fronted style coming into fashion.

"What progress have you made in displacing Madame Gorgon?"

"Very little—she's evidently finding the company at Madame Mercure's more agreeable than I'd have thought. Madame Greene describes their discourse as 'competitive organ recitals,' in which my erstwhile belle-mère can more than hold her own. Is there anything more tiresome than an elderly valetudinarian female?"

"Happily, I don't know any. Nor do I intend to—even for a prodigious portrait commission—" Bertrand gave Annie his arm to cross the avenue de la Muette, dodging carriages with practiced skill. "Well, perhaps if it were sufficiently prodigious." The sky seemed stuffed with mattress ticking and a wind sprang up, rattling the leaves on the plane trees and providing slight relief from the sultry afternoon.

"My niece-in-law has taken a great interest in art since her arrival—"

"Or perhaps in artists." Bertrand's eyebrows waggled. They reached the entrance to the Jardin du Ranelagh. "She appears quite taken with young Tallie; she's to have some lessons from her. I shall try not to be offended that you proposed her instead of me. Perhaps an aunt can be forgiven for a spot of matchmaking." He laughed aloud at Annie's horrified expression.

"Bertrand, I assure you I had no idea until Tallie suggested it that Miss Lowell's interests might run that way—"

"Whereas Tallie's do not—at present, anyway. She's smitten with that puppy Burwell, who seems blissfully unaware of her capabilities as a femme fatale."

Annie's heart contracted. "You, on the other hand, are—?"

"Not directly. God knows I've tried, but she deflects me at every turn. To the point where I think of trying my chances with more mature specimens of the fair sex." Bertrand pressed Annie's hand for emphasis and gave her an ingratiating leer. Something in his tone—perhaps only in her absurd imaginings—went beyond the jocular.

"You think to turn fortune-hunter?"

"Only if the fortune accompanies a lady sufficiently agreeable. I'd content myself with the role of 'kept man'—I've no need to be anyone's lord and master." This time, his look was direct.

"Indeed!" Annie composed herself with difficulty. Though she was his senior by a dozen or more years, the idea of Bertrand's thinking of her in such terms was producing a not unwelcome thrill. She must take care; her improved physical state was engendering romantic fantasies.

"I require only good food and wine, pleasant looks and sparkling conversation."

"And a blind eye turned to your other dalliances."

This time his smile was dimpled and accompanied by a tiny shrug. "Discretion is the cardinal virtue in Paris, isn't it?"

"One certainly hopes so, for the ladies' sake." Annie hastened to turn the conversation before Bertrand could confirm that he was merely being playful. "But, truly, do you think Tallie has designs on our young chevalier?"

"The designing may be mutual," Bertrand said, "not that he's said anything openly—but, gentleman that he is, he wouldn't."

Annie waved them both onto a shady park bench under a plane tree. The sticky heat had left the park thinly populated. "Does he see you as a rival?"

"Perhaps. In any event, they're quite wrong for each other. He may think he wants a bohèmienne, but I think he's the sort to put a woman on a pedestal and expect her to stay there. He'd want a Dulcinea, and Tallie—" he spread his hands.

"—is more of an Aldonza." By Tallie's own account, this was accurate enough, but it offended Annie to hear a man perceive her so.

"She's not fond of pedestals, in any event. Still, if he stays in Paris long enough, his standards may change."

Annie rummaged in her reticule for a handful of francs. "Your first test as a potential kept man is to buy us a pair of iced lemonades from that kiosk." Bertrand rose, bowed, and went off to carry out the commission.

"So, Carlotta wants Tallie," said Annie as he handed her a

paper cup. "Tallie wants Jackson, you think Jackson wants Tallie, and so do you. What a tangle!"

"Not I," Bertrand said, sipping his lemonade through a straw and smiling above it. "I have in mind the sleeve of quite another lady to carry into the joust."

"What nonsense you talk!" Annie laughed, but felt herself coloring. "Will you go to the Comtesse Greffulhe's musicale this evening?"

Bertrand sighed. "She expects me. I'm becoming one of her pet artists. You, however, secured her approval purely on your personal charm—shall I call for you at eight?"

"People will begin to talk."

"I certainly hope so." Bertrand rose and took Annie's hand to help her up.

It was her own fault, Annie reflected, for setting up such a compromising situation as the satyr-tableau in the Crafts' apartments. She hadn't thought that a married man, a father, would succumb to an improper connection. Tallie was blameless; for all she knew, Jackson was unattached. Jackson must put things right, and soon.

Whoops were coming from the Crafts' apartments when Annie gained her own floor. She found Tallie, Carlotta, and Miss Cooper dancing Jackson around the grand salon.

"Jackson has just had good news!" Tallie grabbed Annie by the arm and pulled her into their circle. Could Lydia have made her arrangements so soon? But this tableau did not have the air of friends congratulating a young husband on an imminent reunion.

"Do tell!" Annie managed, out of breath with the whirling.

"I've been admitted," said Jackson, his eyes lowered, "to the École des Beaux Arts. I'm so happy they think my work is good enough—"

"Enough of this false modesty, Mr. Burwell," said Miss Cooper, who was in an expansive frame of mind, for her. "When I first saw your work, I said you have an excellent eye for color."

Annie caught Jackson's eye; he was blushing deeply. She almost laughed aloud that they had both caught the unintended double entendre.

"Congratulations! I hadn't a doubt they'd take you," she said, "When do you start?"

"Next month," he beamed.

Jackson would be rid of his fees at Julian's. Though Annie rejoiced, the injustice of the school's refusal to admit his companions, who were as talented as he, if not more so, rankled.

"We must celebrate," she said. "Tomorrow evening, let's all dine together. I'll speak to the Comte and Madame Greene— she'll be delighted to hear your news." She had planned to take Jackson aside after stopping in her own apartments, but Adèle met her at the door.

"You have a visitor, Madame," she whispered. "I told her you were out, but she said she would wait." Annie's stomach fell.

"Madame Shaw l'Américaine?" Adèle nodded.

There was no reason for surprise; relatives were entitled to call upon one another without prior notice, but Annie's gut was telling her this would not be a pleasant encounter.

Chapter 18

ou'll have brought her tea. Thank you, Adèle. I might have known when I found Miss Lowell next door that she was here." Annie dropped her hat on the hall table and reluctantly entered the parlor.

"Mother Shaw! What a pleasant surprise. How are you getting on at Madame Mercure's?"

The equine nostrils flared. "Frankly, it leaves a good deal to be desired. I am surprised that it was recommended to me."

Annie squared her shoulders. "Indeed! I was not familiar with it myself until Mrs. Greene mentioned it, though I have since learned that some Cathedral ladies live there. Are your rooms uncomfortable? It is an older property—"

"The rooms themselves are unexceptionable, though shabbier than I might have expected for the price. The food likewise, though I am not fond of the so-called 'family style' of service among unrelated persons. One or two of the ladies are entirely too aggressive at mealtimes. But the odor from the stables is not to be borne by anyone with a functioning sense of smell. Had I realized that the place was in part a stable-yard, I should never have consented to live there." Sarah paused for breath. "And the proprietor!"

Annie adopted a look of astonishment and put down her teacup. "Madame Mercure? But Mrs. Greene said that she was the most amiable woman in existence."

"That is a great wonder, given her husband. It is he of whom I speak. A foul-mouthed drunkard and, moreover, an overbearing boor when in his cups. He considers himself an expert in politics—"

"A universal trait among a certain class of male Parisians," Annie said, as though Mother Shaw had made an amusing observation.

"He has ruined several dinners. I should be embarrassed to invite any acquaintance to join me at that table. And it is not right for my granddaughter to be exposed to such vulgarities."

"Carlotta is surely capable of looking after herself." Annie pushed her cup and saucer away, despising herself for the tremor in her hands.

Mother Shaw fixed Annie in a reproachful gaze. "You have obviously never been a mother, otherwise you could never take such a view."

And whose doing was that, Annie bit back. "I am sorry you have found the situation so unsatisfactory. Perhaps a discreet word with the landlady—"

Sarah's expression hardened. "The situation is intolerable. And I think it high time to put an end to the little *misunderstanding* which has thus far prevented me from occupying the place that was promised to me. I learned from a functionary at Munroe Brothers this morning that there is an atelier—that is what they call a studio, I believe—at a reasonable price only two or three streets from here. From what he tells me, it should be more than adequate to meet the requirements of your Comte de— what was it again? And his, ah, *artistic* undertaking. I will pay his relocation costs and any difference between what he pays you and the lease rate in the new location. That, I should think, would satisfy everyone involved."

"Indeed it will not!" Annie sprang to her feet, her body flooding with heat. "It is not for you to dispose of my sister's property on her behalf."

"It was promised to me!" Mother Shaw's heavy features grew, if possible, paler.

"It was left in my charge." Annie's fists tightened with the effort of controlling her trembling. "My sister told me nothing of lending it to you or anyone else. I made an arrangement with a group of people with whom I am on friendly terms—"

"Just how friendly *are* your terms with this Comte de Leinergen or whatever his name is?"

"And what concern would that be of yours?" Annie found herself nearly shouting now.

"As a member of your family I have a natural concern for your good name, your reputation. The irregularity of this arrangement—"

Annie closed her eyes and drew in a deep breath. It did little to calm her, but her voice came out quieter and more controlled. "You ceased to be a member of my family—and I of yours— thirty years ago when my husband of less than three months was killed. When you and *your* husband decided not to retrieve his body for decent burial, despite the fact that I was his legal next of kin and that decision was mine by right. You have no standing to comment upon, much less criticize, my domestic arrangements now." Her voice was pitching upward again; despite Sarah's years and frailty, her Gorgon gaze still made Annie's guts roil.

"If you have felt that way all this time," Sarah said icily, "why did you accept the legacy my husband left you? You who need never want for anything, coming from wealth as you did?"

"I viewed it as a small degree of reparation," Annie retorted, "for depriving me of a happy home and family. He, at least, seemed to regret what he had done."

"My son chose his own path—"

"With a good deal of pressure from his parents. The boy you reared in the belief that you had martyred yourself for him could not resist your calling in that spurious debt." Annie wondered where the words were coming from. It was as though a boiler had exploded inside her.

Sarah, who had risen slightly, fell back in her chair as if stabbed. "You hold me responsible for my son's death."

"He might have died elsewhere and in other circumstances. But those particular circumstances came about on your account. Can you deny it?"

"I did not come here to be subjected to this!" Sarah's lips were trembling.

"Then why you *did* come here? And what did you expect of me?"

In the ensuing silence, Sarah seemed visibly to deflate.

"Kindness," she said at length. "Sympathy. Understanding, at least." Her eyes had filled with tears, her voice cracking with the strain of holding them back.

"None of which were on offer from your own family?"

"I had begun," Sarah sighed and bit her lip, "to feel like King Lear. Welcomed and loved nowhere. No outright hostility, merely preoccupation. Anna has her grandchildren, Susie her daughters to see married, Ellen her husband's career—"

"—and Effie her committees," Annie finished.

Sarah nodded. "To find oneself viewed as surplus property, rather than—an honored elder. Old women are only a nuisance these days, it seems. Perhaps it has always been so…everyone wishes us out of the way." Annie thought of Julia Greene, whom no one would wish out of the way. "One's friends dead or decrepit, the causes to which one devoted oneself forgotten. So I thought—my son would never have been indifferent to me; perhaps in his wife I would find—"

Sympathy at least, but she left it unspoken. She was speaking simple truth now, and Annie felt a stab of pity—she herself had clung to Paris life in part because of her family's manifest indifference, the sense of herself as the appendage she would have been if she returned to America with the Crafts.

Something else bound her and Sarah: the demise of all their hopes for the race for whom Rob had died. The Shaws had worked tirelessly in the cause of the freedmen for many years after the War, only to see all their gains undone when the white men of the South took back what they considered their patrimony and their racial prerogative. With the full concurrence, Annie thought bitterly, of many Union men who had fought, or so she thought, to free the slaves. The Negroes, and those like Rob who had sacrificed for them, had been betrayed. They would never be accepted as equals in America. In Paris, at least, people like Henry Tanner and, she hoped, Lydia Burwell could lead the lives to which their talents and character should entitle them. Like the life Annie herself now hoped to live.

She sank slowly back onto her chair. "I am his widow. In some ways I never was his wife. Twenty-six days—*days*—were all we had as man and wife before he went to his death, and he fixed by then in his duty to the exclusion of everything else—as *you* wished. We never had a married life together. And you expected that, only because I have borne his name for thirty years, I would feel the affections and obligations of a daughter toward you?"

"You should never have married him," Sarah said, as offhandedly as one might say, *You should never have bought that carpet.*

"You opposed it at the time. So did my parents. I myself was reluctant, fearing the worst that in fact came. He wanted our marriage badly enough that I could not find it in my heart to deny him. 'Give me this happiness,' he said. 'I want to have tasted this joy at least.'"

A flicker of pain crossed Sarah's face. Annie went on, "But why even talk of this? It's ancient history now."

"Why did you never marry again?" There was genuine curiosity in Sarah's tone.

"I had offers, a number of them. But the men I *would* have accepted made other plans. Did you think it was undying devotion to your son's memory that held me back?"

"I assumed so," Sarah said slowly. "Perhaps it was unfair to expect that." The self-righteousness had crept back into her voice; it seemed reflexive with her.

"It was," Annie said, settling back in her chair, "If we clung to those who widowed us, we would lose out on a great deal of living. Your son-in-law Frank Barlow is a case in point—by all accounts he worshipped his first wife, but I think he and Ellen have made each other happy."

Sarah smiled. "As a husband, Barlow is something of a trial

at times. Preoccupied with his crusades as he has been—" she stopped, as if realizing what she had admitted to.

"Don't they say daughters tend to marry their fathers?"

"A fair point!" Sarah laughed aloud then, and to Annie's surprise did not add, *though you certainly did not.*

"If I ever had married again, I could have done worse than a man like my father." Ogden's genial face rose in Annie's mind; he had been a fond, if not indulgent parent.

"I liked your father immensely."

"Did you? I didn't know that." Annie could have sworn she saw Sarah blush.

"I found him—quite attractive, to be truthful. His great good humor, his love of art—" Sarah gestured around the room at Annie's walls, as if in appreciation of the modest paintings that hung there, most of them once Ogden's. "Dear Frank was all I could wish in a husband, but your father made me laugh, which is something I've had little enough of in my life. New England is not known for its rich stores of humor, whereas the Irish…" she opened her hands.

"There's more to love than shared ideals, I've found," Annie said over her teacup. "There must have been in my parents' case—no one ever accused either of them of rampant idealism." It was the apparent absence of that inconvenient quality, she recalled, that had initially attracted her to Rob, in his aimless days as a young clerk in his uncle's office. That, and the wicked humor he had not inherited from either parent, shared though it was with his aunt Julia. And then the humor vanishing in the tidal surge of hereditary zealotry that returned when he took the Negro regiment.

"Your mother's last years were—painful ones for her, your

sister says." Sarah sipped her tea and set the cup down; it must long since have gone cold.

"For all of us—for myself most of all, and Clem would not deny it. I became her nurse and keeper as she grew more and more lost to us. Clem had her husband and children—"

"She was a difficult patient? Your mother always seemed so amiable."

"Difficult enough." Annie had no wish to share the visceral details. "We had to take precautions to keep her from injuring herself—someone had to be with her constantly, even sleep in her room. She would scream that we were imprisoning her. She would get up in the night, thinking it was day, put on her coat over her nightdress, and go out into the street—she was nearly killed when she stepped in front of a horse-cab. After that, we had to lock her in—" Annie stopped, seeing on Sarah's face a shadow of fear, as if picturing herself in a similar condition.

"She was one of the most lively and agreeable ladies I ever met. It is hard to imagine her brought so low."

Annie rose and looked at her mother's portrait which still hung over the fireplace, feeling momentary guilt over her plans to take it down. "We endured it by thinking of what she became as someone other than who she had been—in whose memory we owed our devoted care to the creature she *had* become."

"It must have been a relief, when she passed on at last."

Annie bristled, despite the element of truth in Sarah's words. She would not give her the satisfaction of thinking she could read her thoughts. "In part—but the greater feeling was sorrow at the loss of all she had been to us."

"I wonder what my daughters will feel, when I am gone." There was a tinge of self-pity in Sarah's voice, though she seemed to be trying for a smile.

"Surely no one can view the loss of a mother with indifference." There could be many feelings—relief, bereavement, satisfaction in substantial legacies, remorse—but Annie doubted that Mother Shaw's demise would be met with indifference. She did not even wish that for her.

"That leaves a lot of room," Sarah said, and this time she had indeed read Annie's thoughts.

"People will feel what they feel. I've never seen any point in trying to change them." Annie knew from her own history how futile that would have been. She had loved her doomed cousin George, though it made no sense, and could not choose to love Roland Burwell instead, though it would have. Briefly, after the War, she could have loved Schuyler Colfax, the Indiana Senator, but he was smitten with Alice Hooper Sumner, whom no one could outshine. Why did the poets so often paint love as mutual, when so often it was one-sided?

"I was wrong, then," Sarah interrupted her musings, "to believe that you must feel some vestige of affection for me, if only for my son's sake." The tone was full-blown self-pity now. *I felt none from the first*, Annie was tempted to reply.

"You were wrong to expect that the sense of obligation which you thought would compel me to care for you would so long survive the end of our familial connection," she replied instead, gentling her tone to soften the words. If Rob had lived, if they had built a life and raised a family together, Sarah would always have been a wedge between them. From the beginning she had viewed Annie as a rival, not the fifth daughter that Frank Shaw had seen in her. To have decamped to Paris in the hope that Annie would become the Cordelia she sought spoke to a state of desperation and desolation Annie could barely imagine. How hideous, to be loved by no one.

"You are not the Annie Haggerty I once knew." Sarah's tone was more wondering than reproachful. "That young woman was gentleness and respect personified."

"Indeed I am not, and I rejoice in it. I am sorry that what I have become is not to your liking, Mother Shaw—"

"Oh, for God's sake, stop calling me that!" Sarah snapped. "You have no daughterly feelings for me. You said so yourself."

"But I must call you something," Annie shot back, "and for better or worse we share a surname neither of us was born with."

Sarah Shaw seemed to withdraw into thoughts of her own. "What a fool I was to think of spending my last days here. To think I found New York cold and unfeeling—it is *tropical* compared to Paris."

"Perhaps you should return to Boston," Annie said more gently, "where you have so many blood-ties and the surroundings are familiar. I have not found Paris as you describe. It is how one approaches a place, and what one expects from it, that determine one's experience of it. For many years I lived in the insularity of the American Colony—I might just as well have been in Boston or New York. I am only now beginning to live in Paris."

"—and the last thing you need, then," Mother Shaw could not keep the injury from her tone, "is another elderly American to put a spoke in your wheel."

Indignant on Elizabeth's behalf, Annie replied, "Mamma never did that until she was too sick for it to be otherwise." And Julia Greene, she did not add, would never narrow anyone's horizons; she was too busy expanding her own.

Mother Shaw rose and smoothed her skirts. "I must think

about what to do." Picking up her reticule with the remnants of her dignity, she said, "For the present, you must keep to your, ah, arrangements with your artist friends. I will not be requiring your sister's apartments after all, I find. But I cannot think to stay much longer where I am situated."

The resulting wave of guilt almost led Annie to contemplate clearing out Bertrand's party from the Crafts' apartments, but she bit her tongue and nodded her assent. "Carlotta—" she began, rising in her turn.

"—has grown fond of Paris. She will not wish to leave, if it comes to that." Sarah turned in the doorway.

"Should you object to her staying?"

"Her mother left her in my charge—"

"She is an adult woman of means and mature judgment," Annie said, "and she may be experiencing the City quite differently from—from either of us," she finished diplomatically.

"That," said Carlotta's grandmother grimly, "is what I am afraid of."

Chapter 19

nnie watched Sarah make her slow way down the stairs without having called for Carlotta from Clem's apartments. As her mother-in-law's back disappeared, a wave of weakness washed over her, as if after a bout of influenza. When she turned, Adèle was standing in the kitchen door with a cut-glass stem on a tray and raised eyebrows.

"I thought you might like a little Poire Williams, Madame." A smile flooded Annie's face.

She took the glass and returned to the parlor, dropping onto the divan Sarah had vacated. Sipping from the exquisite little glass, she felt the sweet fire of late summer bathe her throat. "Tu es toujours une merveille, Adèle. Merçi."

Carlotta stood framed in the doorway, tall and slim and strong-looking. "Is all well, Aunt Annie? I came over while you and Tua were talking, but Adèle suggested I wait—"

"Have a seat, my dear." Annie waved her to her own vacated chair; Adèle had already handed Lotta a tiny glass. "Your grandmother has not found the welcome in Paris she hoped for. I fear she assumed that I would be lonely, and thought to provide company which she now realizes I did not—"

"—either wish or care for," Carlotta finished. "I thought it might be so, though I couldn't bring myself to say so to her. Oh, dear," she bit her lip, "I should have, shouldn't I? I brought it up with Mamma, but she was occupied with some organizational crisis or other and said she was sure it would all work out for the best. I thought Tua should sound you out before making plans, but Mamma said she had always done as she pleased and no one could persuade her otherwise."

Effie Lowell's response had been predictable in one to whom her mother's presence had likely become a chronic irritant. She'd had no motive to dissuade Mother Shaw from her impulsive course.

"No doubt," Annie said mildly, "your grandmother always does what she thinks she *ought* to do, but I expect it's the same thing most of the time. Have I been cruel?"

Carlotta considered, sipping her eau-de-vie. "I've lived with her so long it never occurred to me I'd have a choice in the matter. She's always been a fact of my existence, like the Staten Island Ferry, or Trinity Church. We've always agreed pretty well—I suppose I think of myself as her favorite grandchild, though perhaps that's only a matter of proximity."

"A neat avoidance of my question." Annie drained her glass and reached for the decanter.

"This is sublime." Carlotta held out her own glass for a refill. "As if they'd captured the soul of the pear. How did you leave things with her?"

"She no longer plans to install herself next door. As to whether or how long she'll stay in Paris—"

Carlotta rose and stood by the fireplace, her arm on the mantel. "Last night's excursion probably didn't help. Madame

Eyckert, from your dinner?" Annie nodded. "You may recall her mentioning, that evening, a place on the Boulevard Raspail."

"The Palome Salée?"

"I wouldn't have thought you'd have heard of it. Tua was reluctant, but I thought it would be fun, and Aunt Greene came along, only—"

"Not more escargots and pieds de cochon?"

"The food was the least of it—unexceptionable by our standards. And the décor, though a bit—voluptuous, was respectable-looking enough. It was the, ah, company. Which was more foreign to us than the difference in nationality and language.

"I began to notice ladies," Carlotta went on, "in trousers, dining in some cases with another similarly attired, in others playing the gentleman to her dining partner, ordering the food, lighting her cigarette—and then *dancing*—"

"Goodness! No real gentlemen in sight?"

"Not a male in the place. Even the sommelier was a woman. It was like finding oneself among the Amazons. And everyone seemed to know Madame Eyckert, who by her own telling was a habituée of the place and on the jolliest of terms with the owners."

Annie contrived to look rueful. "Perhaps I should have inferred so much from her writing—what I've heard of it."

"She is, it seems, the most enthusiastic of Sapphists. And I realized, belatedly, that—oh dear, I don't even know how to say this—" Carlotta turned several shades of scarlet.

"That she had taken a fancy to you?"

A tight nod from Carlotta.

"Oh, dear, indeed. What of Aunt Greene?" Relishing the

scene most wickedly, no doubt.

"She was listening to Tua talking about Mamma's plans for the Brooklyn Refuge for Fallen Women, about which I have heard as much as I care to. They both seemed oblivious—"

"And meanwhile, Madame Eyckert?"

"Was finding every opportunity to take my hand, pat me on the arm—I got up to evade her by going to the lavatory, and as I passed the bar there were all these women in trousers and weskits, and it was like walking through a gauntlet of leering eyes—really, Aunt Annie, I felt like a sheep among wolves—"

"Goodness, I had no idea ladies of that persuasion could be so—"

"—so much like ungentlemanly men. Indeed! And when I reached the lavatory, I opened the door—which wasn't locked— only to find two ladies embracing in a corner, and—" Carlotta stopped and swallowed, her flush deepening.

"No need to go on. What did you do?"

"Well, I decided I didn't need to use the lavatory after all. I went back to the table. Madame Eyckert was dancing with another lady—one of the trousered ones. Aunt Greene and Tua looked up—I must have looked rather pale—and they began looking around. Finally, it seems, realizing what sort of place we were in. Tua looked at Aunt Greene in horror and said, 'We must leave here at once.'"

"Had Mrs. Greene noticed, do you think—"

"I can't say—but when Tua said that, she looked around, and it was as if comprehension dawned. 'Of course, dear Sarah, you're quite right,' she said. The dance had stopped and Madame Eyckert—who really does bear a strong resemblance to a starved Holstein, by the way—broke away from her partner and came over as if to take *me* out onto the floor. I said, 'Grandmamma is unwell. We must get her home right away.' Aunt Greene called the waitress over, and Tua was emptying her reticule to pay the bill. I asked the girl to fetch us a fiacre, and we said a hasty good night to Madame Eyckert and came away."

Carlotta's distress was genuine, but it was all Annie could do to keep a straight face. "Then you've been exposed to an aspect of Paris life that I've managed to miss these past twenty years."

"Goodness, Aunt Annie, you don't think there are such places in New York, do you?"

Whatever Carlotta's proclivities, the experience had clearly distressed her, and Annie felt a stab of guilt. "Mamma told me that when we lived on Warren Street—when I was very small— there was a, ah, house of assignation just down the street. Quite well known, apparently. Later on, I confirmed her story by other means. Ever since then I have suspended disbelief about anything I hear about New York."

"I've led a sheltered life, it seems," Carlotta said, resuming her seat. "Poor Tua even more so. I thought she might have a cardiac crisis."

"She seemed well earlier—if certainly not happy." Annie paused and resolved to proceed. "If she *were* to return to America, what would you want to do?"

Carlotta's troubled look deepened. "I should be obliged to accompany her, of course—but I must confess that, in spite of last night, I feel I could be at home here, Aunt Annie. Except—I fear we have intruded on your life, yours and Aunt Greene's, quite enough as it is."

"Dear Lotta! I will tell you all—I was indeed troubled by your grandmother's arrival, and particularly by her plans to install herself across the way and make a companion of me—for which I had neither desire nor inclination. We have a complicated history, she and I, and it has not grown any less so since she came to Paris.

"But as for you, my dear—we'd met only once or twice when you were a little girl, and I was pleased that you were with her. That pleasure has only grown since we've begun to know each other. I think you could do very well here, and be happy—in spite of last night's debacle."

Carlotta's smile held a tinge of gratitude. "I do like it here—very much. If I can steer clear of the likes of Madame Eyckert, I might be very content. May I ask you something, though?" Annie nodded.

"The guests. At your dinner. The older ones—"

"Herr Doktor Finkelmann and Capitaine Leboeuf?"

"And Madame Eyckert—"

"Chosen with your grandmother in mind. The Professor was a colleague of my brother-in-law's—I wouldn't typically have included him in my own gatherings—and the Capitaine was an acquaintance through a doctor friend. I thought that being a military man he would enjoy talking with your grandmamma about the War—and Madame Eyckert had been represented to me as a literary lady. I recalled that Mother Shaw, in her Miss Sturgis days, had been a devotee of Margaret Fuller's, and so thought there might be common ground there." Annie was being disingenuous, but why burden the girl with the truth of her wicked plotting with Julia?

"Your own circle of friends, then—"

"—is substantially more Parisian. But they're used to being addressed in their own tongue."

Carlotta's brow furrowed. "We'd been told it was quite possible to live in Paris without knowing French—"

"So it is, if you confine yourself to the American Colony. Which is more or less what my family did for years. Other than the fact that it's cheaper to live well here than in New York or Boston, one might as well have stayed at home."

"I should love to meet some of your real Paris friends, Aunt Annie." Carlotta's tone was timorous, but hopeful. "I've been working hard on my French—"

"I'm fairly new at this Paris society myself," Annie confessed. "Between caring for Papa when he was dying, and traveling with Mamma, and then I was ill for so long. Once that was done, there were my nieces to be chaperoned, and Mamma declining, and Clem preoccupied with husband and daughters and charitable works—"

"We're not given much choice in these matters, are we?" Carlotta mused. "Only expectations. And assumptions. That one will become 'the Consolation of the Household.'"

"Is this the voice of sad experience? You're much too young for that."

"An unmarried woman is never too young—once it's clear she'll never marry. Something must give her a purpose in life. "Carlotta's voice held a tinge of bitterness. "I've never wanted to marry, Aunt Annie—but I don't want to be Tua's companion either. I wish I could stay here!"

"I wish you would. No one should have to live out a derivative existence."

"I'll have to take Tua back, if that's what she decides to do."

"Perhaps. But you can come back on your own, surely? Or with—a friend?" Her niece-in-law must have funds from her grandfather Shaw's estate, and her father's.

"My inheritance is in trust till I turn thirty," Carlotta said. She paced back and forth in front of the fireplace. "But that's only two years away now—perhaps it's not out of the question—"

"Why leave Paris at all? There must be some suitable lady we could engage to be your grandmother's companion for her voyage home. I can clear out my old bedroom for you—and once Bertrand's finished with his tableau—"

Carlotta's face was a mixture of hope and distress, her hands clasped tightly. "Oh, Aunt Annie, don't even say it! You're finally getting your chance to live as a free woman, and we've nearly ruined it for you. I could never dream of putting you in such a position! Besides, how would Tua…"

…feel about being rejected so utterly while her granddaughter was welcomed, Annie realized with a flash of misgiving. She had come to like Carlotta so quickly, to see in her the hopeful girl she herself had been at the same age. But to move her into one's house, to make a daughter of her, was not the answer. If she grew to rely on Carlotta's presence, Annie might eventually make the same demands on her that she now deplored on the part of Mother Shaw and Effie Lowell. Better to go back to the Crafts and Boston before it came to that.

"It would only be temporary. To help you launch on your own here—I should derive much pleasure from seeing you build a life in Paris while you're young and healthy enough to take advantage of it."

Carlotta paced the room as though to work off the feverish emotion Annie's offer had produced. "I have friends in New York who've talked about going on a long excursion together— perhaps one of them would return with me. I've had little to spend my allowance on. What I've saved could tide me over until I'm thirty—and I should so like to continue my studies with dear Tal—with Miss DeKuyper. She is an inspiration. Though I fear the time she takes away from her own work—"

"Until she becomes well known and her work sells well, she must earn a living. Teaching you must be more agreeable than modeling in a life-studies class in a cold and smoky studio."

"Is that how she's lived?" Carlotta's eyes widened.

"She has often done so, she tells me. But as you've learned already by being with her and the others, the female reputation is of little concern among the Bohemians."

Carlotta laughed. "I begin to think I'm approaching the age at which a virtuous reputation gives way to being viewed by the world as a dried-up old maid."

Annie glanced at her mother's portrait. "Mamma threatened me with that when I refused a couple of proposals after the War."

"Oh, Aunt Annie—" Carlotta came to her and seized her hands. "I don't think I ever want to marry. I shouldn't mind children, but I don't want a husband—isn't that too dreadful?"

Carlotta might be a candidate for a Boston marriage. Whether Carlotta could acknowledge that to herself was another matter. "Medieval ladies who felt as you do had the convent to turn to," Annie said. "And many took in foundlings, so they needn't have been deprived of children. The world is changing. Your generation of women will have many more choices than mine. I know ladies, for instance, who set up housekeeping together. They could adopt orphans, if they had the means to provide for them."

Carlotta retreated to her armchair. "I can just picture Mamma's and Tua's faces if I walked in the door with an 'orflink' in tow!

Mamma cares about them in the aggregate, but to keep one at home—I'd have to live on my own for that."

"There are offices now, I'm told, where the secretaries are all women—nurses, too, in the great hospitals. We'll have lady doctors before long—" Annie stopped, thinking of Julia's lost daughter and her companion. "Did you ever meet your mamma's cousin Bessie Greene?"

"Is she Aunt Greene's daughter?"

"Was. She drowned in a shipwreck seventeen years ago, at just about your age. She had a beloved friend—a doctor, Susan Dimock, who died in the wreck too."

"I've heard that name. They were like sisters, Tua said, though in a tone that suggested she didn't altogether approve."

Annie refrained from observing that disapproval was Sarah's reflexive tone. "They were closer than that, I'm told. Poor Bessie's body was never recovered. But the Greenes buried Dr. Dimock in their family plot, as if she'd been their own child."

"Aunt Greene's a jolly decent sort. She seems so much younger than Tua, for all the sorrow she's had. I'd enjoy getting to know her better."

"She repays acquaintance. Do you think your grandmother will return to New York?"

Carlotta thought for a moment. "She's not one to give up on a project once she undertakes it. But you know that—she'd been an abolitionist since she was very young, and kept trying to help the freedmen, until Grandpapa died and she finally lost heart. And *he* was one of the last who still seemed to care about the Negroes in the old Confederacy."

"Perhaps she should take up the cause of the Negro again," Annie said. "From what I hear, the South has all but re-instituted slavery. It's a crime to be a black man on a public street, and then they ship the poor fellows off to prison farms where they're rented out to plantations and worked to death. At least when they were slaves, they had to be fed properly and cared for." She grew warm with indignation.

"The North gave up its power to compel decent treatment for the Negroes a long time ago. My poor father must be rolling in his grave—uncle Rob too—to see what's come of their sacrifice. Oh, I'm sorry, Aunt Annie, what a distressing thing to say—"

Annie shook her head. "I've thought the same thing many times. Slavery brought down a curse on America—one I fear will never be lifted. Lincoln was wrong—our country wasn't conceived in liberty. Slavery was its germ-cell. 'Liberty' was for white men only."

"You sound like Tua!"

"At least we agree on something." Annie gave Carlotta a wry smile. *I wish you would stay*, she almost added. How odd; all those years of disconnection from the Shaws, then Julia appearing in her life, and now Carlotta. They would go about Paris like the Three Musketeers. Could she endure Sarah for Carlotta's sake? A month ago, there would not have been a question. Now, the thought of losing Carlotta was more painful than her regrets at the departure of her own nieces. And worse: to send her back into that stifling household where Duty reigned supreme, where nothing might happen to her for the rest of her life.

"You must get back to painting, Lotta, for as long as you're here at least."

"I should go and see to Tua." Carlotta rose slowly and retrieved her reticule.

"I'm sorry to have caused her pain. I'd hoped she would

conclude on her own that Paris was not the refuge she's seeking. I hadn't meant to be cruel, but—well, there it is." Annie turned to read her niece's face.

"She forced your hand, it seems. She does that."

Where would Sarah Shaw go, if she decided to leave Paris? Back to New York at first, certainly, but—could she really be as unwelcome in her own daughters' households as she was in Annie's? She found herself hoping not. Surely gentle Anna Curtis or the ever-obliging Ellen Barlow could make her at home, if Effie could not.

"Lotta—for however long you remain—please come and see me any time you can. Any time you'd like to, I mean."

Carlotta bridged the distance between them and enveloped Annie in a hug. "I will, Aunt Annie. And I'm going to take as many lessons with Tallie—Miss DeKuyper—as I can."

Mother Shaw had seen the silly satyr-abduction project for the canard it was. How could Annie have expected otherwise? Her refusal to accede to Sarah's plan to move the artists out was evidence enough of that. She should tell Bertrand and the others to abandon it. It had been a great deal to ask of them, to interrupt their own work on her behalf.

She sat a long while after Carlotta's departure. Her home territory was safe now; she could let Bertrand and his students clear out of Clem's apartments and ready them for the literary and artistic salon she hoped to establish there with Julia. Sarah Shaw seemed on the way to viewing her Paris foray as ill-conceived, but if she persisted long enough to give it a thorough trial, at least it no longer posed a threat to Annie's domestic tranquility. If she had alienated Sarah outright, she could not wish it undone, though she had hoped to rid herself of the woman without overt hurt to her feelings. But Sarah had, after all, forced the issue.

Chapter 20

eturning from another session of Swedish exercises, Annie found the opportunity to force an issue of her own. Adèle had accompanied her, watching her make the rounds of Fröken Johansson's torture machines, with hands to her face and "Oh-la-la's" escaping her at intervals when Annie let out a groan from one wrenching or another.

"This is what has been making you better, Madame?" The fiacre bumped across cobblestones, and Annie winced. "C'est incroyable—it looked like what one has heard of the Spanish Inquisition. Ah, oui, even in Martinique we heard the stories. You look as if you will not be able to walk for a week."

"That willow-bark extract in your tisane will put me right in no time. It's amazing how much better I feel by the next day—oof!" Annie's eyes closed in pain over another bump, "It's quite miserable in the meantime."

The fiacre clattered to a stop. Adèle paid the driver and helped Annie lower herself stiffly from the carriage. "Et voilà Monsieur Burwell!"

Jackson, coming down the walkway, rushed to help Adèle with the heavy iron gate.

"I'm glad to see you," Annie said, after assuring Jackson there was no cause for alarm. "How go the plans to reunite the family?" Adèle gave her a nod and went upstairs.

Seeing Jackson's hesitancy to respond, she gestured him to a bench in the building's small front garden. "Has there been some change?"

"A change? No, of course not. Well, I mean, I've been admitted to the École—"

"—so now you won't have Julian's fees to worry about, which can only help..." Annie fluffed out her skirts, still overheated from the Swedish gymnastics; her petticoats clung unpleasantly to the backs of her legs. "You've written to Lydia, to begin making preparations?"

He reddened and bowed his head. "I have. I confess I was surprised by her response. She seems—more hesitant than I'd have expected."

"Some degree of hesitancy is understandable—" and then, looking at Jackson's face, Annie added, "That's not it, is it?"

"It's not surprising she'd find it hard to believe in such good fortune, so soon after my arrival here." His blush deepened. "She doesn't know you as I do, and, well—"

Light dawned. "She doesn't trust my intentions in helping you. I must have some hidden motive that will create difficulties in the future, like monopolizing your artistic output, or wanting you to focus on portraits when you should be doing landscapes, or requiring your firstborn son in exchange—"

"Something like that." Jackson smiled and his shoulders sagged with the relief of seeing that Annie wasn't immediately horrified or furious. "I've written back, assuring her your intentions are benign, telling her about your father's history as an artists' patron, but—"

"She has learned, with good reason, to distrust white ladies."

"I'm afraid so. I'm sorry, Mrs. Shaw."

"I'll confess to chagrin that my motives are being so misinterpreted, but it's understandable. How can we reassure her?"

"She gives me more credit for my art than it deserves, and assumes that anyone interested in it must hope to exploit my imminent fame." He smiled ruefully. "If only that were something to worry about! I've told her that I'll keep the strictest accounting of your gifts and repay them as soon as we can, and that when she knows you she'll see her concerns are unfounded."

"What if she's right?" The corners of Annie's mouth twitched. "How do you know I'm as disinterested as you think?"

He looked momentarily horrified, then smiled. "You struck me from the first as trustworthy. You could have told Aunt Kernochan everything, but you've kept our confidence."

"Well, let's hope your letter convinces Lydia. I'll write to her myself, if it comes to that. And speaking of confidences—" Annie lowered her voice, "Tallie—Miss DeKuyper—came to dinner the other evening. She talked of you a great deal, in glowing terms."

Jackson fidgeted with the hem of his jacket, but said nothing.

"I fear she's conceived an attachment to you—perhaps inevitable in the circumstances—for which I must bear a good deal of responsibility—"

Jackson held up a hand. "Mrs. Shaw, you mustn't think that! Artists must learn to separate our natural responses—that is, to subordinate them to our artistic purposes—"

"That can't be easy," Annie said, "since they celebrate the

beauty of the human form, and must surely be moved by it to induce that feeling in the viewer."

"How well you understand!"

"Perhaps," Annie was thinking of the discussion at Retta Reubell's about the portrait of Madame X, "it's more difficult for a woman to detach her feelings from the object of her gaze. In any case, I think it would be well if you confided your own attachments to Miss DeKuyper."

Jackson flushed. "Tell her about Lydia, you mean?"

"And Benjamin. God willing, they'll be here soon, and I'd hate to think Tallie would have proceeded upon false assumptions and got herself into—well, a fool's paradise."

Jackson's flush deepened and he turned his head away. "I hadn't mentioned my circumstances to her or to de Leiningen—I've told no one but you—and I fear that to raise the matter now..." he stopped and took a deep breath. *Would lead her to think I had been trifling with her affections,* he did not add. Annie waited.

"—would be premature, until I hear back from Lydia."

"You think she might decline to join you?"

"It will be hard for her."

"Harder if she arrives and meets someone who seems to have an emotional claim on you—"

"She has none!" He rose, his tone indignant.

"What would you do, Jackson, "Annie stood and brushed down her skirts, "if Lydia can't bring herself to leave Georgia?"

He seemed to consider the possibility for the first time. "I—I should have to return, I suppose."

"That would be difficult in many ways, so I hope she'll see the wisdom of joining you here. I don't know her, but you are her family now, and you told me her parents are gone—"

"I could never force her to do something she didn't wish!" Annie saw the beginning of tears in Jackson's eyes. She sat down again slowly, and he followed.

"Of course not. Not all husbands feel as you do, I'm sorry to say. But if you prepare your friends, as you have me, surely they will accord her the warmest welcome you could wish."

Jackson's look was pure plea. "I can't let Aunt Kernochan find out about this, Mrs. Shaw—you must understand that."

Annie rose from the bench, fully this time, and Jackson sprang up to offer his arm. "I agree it would be dangerous now, given what she feels to be her familial duty. She'll have to know eventually, surely. I take her for a kind-hearted, if conventional woman—and I'll be your ally with her when the time comes. Lydia sounds like someone who inspires affection."

"That she does." Jackson smiled. "She's already done so in you, I see, and you haven't even met her."

"Not yet—but I'm looking forward to it." Annie's gaze swept the small garden. "Look how beautifully the briar roses are coming along. It was I who suggested those plantings."

"I'll write to her again this evening."

"Here's a thought—as a man of color, Mr. Tanner could help Lydia adjust to Paris life. If he knew of your plans, I'm sure he'd sympathize, perhaps make some introductions among the gens de couleur he's come to know since arriving in Paris. I could arrange a dinner—"

"You've done so much already, Mrs. Shaw—"

"Nonsense! You haven't even called yet on the loan for your new apartments and your family's passage-money. I enjoy Mr. Tanner's company, and what could be more natural? Now, if you'll help me upstairs, I'll let you get off to wherever you were headed."

Despite Jackson's denial—indeed, because of its vehemence—
Annie worried about the impact of his news on Tallie. She
might present herself as a hard-bitten, worldly bohèmienne, but
she had clearly opened her heart to him. By Jackson's account,
matters had gone no further. Perhaps Bertrand's obvious interest
in his protégée had created a sort of useful chaperonage—insofar
as Bertrand had any qualifications in that line.

Jackson departed amid a flurry of promises to write
immediately to Lydia, to call on the Minister's man at the
Consulate, to consult the sailing-tables, and to search in earnest
for new accommodations for both family and studio. It was
not until after he had gone, and Annie was sipping gratefully
at Adèle's pain-relieving tisane, that she realized the promises
had not included acquainting Tallie with his domestic situation.
Perhaps he had thought it went without saying.

Mother Shaw, Annie learned a week later, was going to Nice to
escape the stagnant heat of Paris. She had given up the attempt
to occupy Clem's apartments but had evidently not ruled out
remaining in France. Thank goodness Sarah hadn't learned of the
seasonal home in Cannes and prevailed upon her complaisant
sister to lend her that as well. At least the title to Les Anthémis
was in her own name. Annie herself was contemplating a visit
to les Anthémis, as she'd thought of doing in prior summers
instead of deferring to the Crafts' routines. Cannes and Nice
were uncomfortably close, Mother Shaw not entirely avoidable,
but Annie planned to fill the house with her own guests: Julia,
Bertrand, Tallie, Retta Reubell, Henry Tanner, perhaps even
Jackson with his wife and child. Carlotta could take the train

over from Nice for painting lessons with Tallie, and Annie supposed she might even invite Sarah for a dinner or two.

Though Cannes summers were warm, the Mediterranean breeze kept the air fresh and healthy. There would be willing subjects for portraits. Her gardens afforded lovely settings for informal figure studies and impressions, and of course there was the sea. What painter could resist the blues of the Mediterranean and the reds of the rugged cliffs east of the town? She felt a wave of joy at the thought of the artistic opportunities for her young friends; even Bertrand could hardly be indifferent to the charms of the place. Adèle would be ecstatic at returning to a locale that always reminded her of her island birthplace.

When she broached the subject to Tallie in the hallway, however, she was met with a cold look and "Thank you, but I sha'n't be able to go. I've made other plans."

"But I thought—" Annie found herself speaking to a closed door. The group was close to completing their magnum opus, and would, she thought, have seen the chance to join her in Cannes as thanks for their effort. Puzzled and chagrined, she returned to her own apartment.

"Adèle!" Her maid appeared from the bedroom she had been tidying.

"Do you know what might be troubling Mademoiselle Tallie? I just saw her in the hallway—she won't come to Cannes with us, she says."

"Vraiment? I have not seen her in a few days—and then she was talking of it with great eagerness—how she looked forward to the light on the sea—she told you nothing of why?"

"My impression was that she's angry—that I had done something to offend her. I can't think what it might be."

"Alors," said Adèle, "I told them I would bring them tea this morning. I will see if I can find out anything."

"Who is there now?"

"I saw the Comte earlier, but I am not sure if the jeune monsieur came in. But, Madame, are you not to meet Madame Greene for the theatre?"

"Goodness, yes, I must change." Annie had had a royal blue silk of her mother's, barely worn, altered into a more modern silhouette. She and Julia were going to the Théatre des Fleurs in the Bois de Boulogne for an al fresco performance, in French, of Shakespeare's *As You Like It*. Neither was sure how the Bard's exquisite language would survive translation, but it was a lovely warm evening with only a few scattered clouds, and promised well.

Julia was in emerald-green, which offset her snowy hair and the Shaw blue eyes. "Don't we look fancy!" she said with good cheer as they arrived at the entrance to the Pré-Catelan under a nearly full moon. "That blue is lovely on you, Annie, and you look taller than you used. I'm certain of it."

Annie smiled, happy she had noticed. "The torture-chamber is responsible for that, I dare say—*for as I am, I live upon the rack*."

"That's from *The Merchant*, isn't it? Don't tease—it has done you good, hasn't it?"

They entered the great hedged oval of the Théatre and made their way down its center aisle to their seats. A soft breeze wafted the scents of roses from the woods and gardens west of the stage, which seemed an outgrowth of the sylvan landscape itself. Happily, the stage-lighting came from the warmer, softer gas lanterns rather than the more modern electrics, and the huge moon's cheery, pockmarked peasant face provided nearly enough light to read their programs by.

Settling in her little folding chair, Annie found her mind drifting back to a night in Stockbridge, the moon as bright as this one, when the great Christine Nilsson—she had become a family friend—had sung for the Haggertys and a dozen friends on an outcropping at Echo Lake. That Berkshires summer had been soft and cool, perfect for promenades in muslins and parasols, and Annie at thirty-six had not given up hope of a romance…she rolled her bare shoulders now without difficulty, and it felt easier than it had in years. Maybe fifty-six wasn't too old for a new romance either…

"Are you cold?" Julia whispered as Orlando hung his dreadful poems—even more dreadful in French—on the hapless stage-trees.

"Just making sure my neck still works."

"I'm going to weave you a wrap to go with that dress," Julia told her as they shared a table at the interval, consuming airy slices of chocolate mousse cake and sipping champagne.

"I had no idea you were a weaver."

"I'm a regular Arachne now." Julia waved her glass airily. "Took it up by way of distraction—after we lost Bessie. What I have in mind for you will be light—a blue and silver gossamer—but it will protect your shoulders from drafts, and set off that dress nicely."

"What a lovely thing to do," Annie sighed. "I'm hopeless at all forms of needlework. I was more or less disinvited from a Sanitary sewing circle during the war—apparently my struggles were distracting the other ladies. I got quite good at rolling bandages, though."

Julia accepted a refill from a passing waiter. "Look, isn't that one of your Cathedral ladies, in that wretchedly overstuffed brocade? She looks like a mobile davenport."

"It's Mrs. Kernochan, Jackson's second cousin or whatever she is. Look, she's seen us—let me introduce you."

Julia's sartorial assessment was harsh; Mrs. Kernochan's ample proportions were more architectural than adipose, and she carried off the peach-and-gold gown with Junoesque dignity.

"Mrs. Shaw!" she smiled and came forward. "I thought that was you in the orchestra—how lovely you look in that blue!"

Annie thanked her and presented Julia. "Mrs. Greene and I had each been living in Paris for years, but met only a short time ago, despite being related through marriage." Mrs. Kernochan beamed as Annie explained the connection.

"How lovely for you, when your own family has gone— such fortuitous timing! What do you hear from your sister? We greatly miss her guiding hand at the helm of the Dorcas Society."

"I believe she means to replicate her Paris successes in Boston. Professor Crafts' family connections in that area will afford her ready entrée to its social circles."

"Dear Mrs. Crafts would make her own way in any event, I'm sure." Mrs. Kernochan seized Annie's hand. Julia saw a couple she knew and excused herself to greet them. "Jackson came to tea last week," she said in a lowered voice. "I took the opportunity to inquire about how his, ah, social life was progressing."

"Well, I hope?" said Annie innocently.

"He told me about the painting project he's engaged in with the artist—Leiningen, is it?"

"Yes, it's been rather fun having a group of artists next door."

"I was surprised to hear of him embarked on a group project, when I thought he was coming to Paris to pursue his own artistic development."

"But he tells me he's learning so much from Comte Bertrand and the others—"

"I understand that the others are ladies—though perhaps that's overstating it a bit—"

"They seem very capable artists. I'm sure Jackson can learn from them."

"I thought of coming by to visit," Mrs. Kernochan said. "It would be most interesting to see artwork in progress, and I admit "m curious about these young—ladies—he's associating with."

Annie quailed at the thought of Mrs. Kernochan coming upon Bertrand's group in its habitual state of deshabillé. "The work is almost complete, I understand, and they're a bit sensitive about visitors at this stage. Did you have a time in mind?"

"Couldn't I just drop by, say, to call on you, and then pop across the hall for a quick look? Frankly, I was wondering whether Jackson might be forming an attachment to one of the young ladies, and if so, it might reassure his brother regarding—ah, the other matter we spoke of."

Annie laughed. "Most American relatives might react to such an attachment with dismay, given what one hears of the bohemian ladies hereabouts."

Mrs. Kernochan looked troubled for a moment, then her brow cleared. "Well, those are likely to be transitory, aren't they? Young men being what they are. It would certainly be preferable to a liaison with—the young person I spoke of. You haven't heard anything of that from him, have you?"

"I told you I would let you know if I did." Annie said.

As she hoped, Mrs. Kernochan took this for a denial. A silvery bell signaled the end of the interval. Jackson's caution in keeping his marriage secret for the present was clearly well justified.

Chapter 21

dèle brought Annie's morning café noir and sat down. "Alors, Madame—something has happened between the jeune monsieur and Mademoiselle Tallie. They spoke yesterday only as needed for the painting. She chatted with the Comte and Miss Cooper much as usual, but she avoided the other."

"Miss Cooper was there?"

"Ah, oui—I was with her in the kitchen and said, 'Mademoiselle Tallie seems not herself—does something trouble her?' She said that Tallie and Monsieur Jackson had quarreled when she told him of the apartment in their building. The rent is cheap, Mademoiselle Tallie said, and it would be much more convenable. But he said he did not think it advisable, and in a most—comment dit-on?—distant fashion. Mademoiselle Cooper herself was puzzled by his tone. She had thought the two had some sort of understanding, but Jackson said it could give the wrong impression if he were to install himself so near to friends who were unmarried ladies."

"Oh, dear—"

"And Mlle. DeKuyper said, 'I see we are not suitable company for you after all—I'm sorry we don't meet your elevated moral standards!' and walked out. They have not spoken since— Monsieur Jackson began to go after her, but evidently his courage failed him. He sat down on the divan, Mademoiselle Cooper says, and put his head in his hands, then got up and went away."

Annie had confided Jackson's family situation to Adèle, since she would need her help arranging passage-tickets and gathering household goods for the new arrivals. "So, he still hasn't told Tallie about his wife and child?"

"I think not, Madame. The young ladies think that now he has been admitted to the École, he wishes to build a more respectable set of connections. Oh, and—Mademoiselle Tallie said to Jackson that 'Mrs. Shaw must have been poisoning your mind against me.'" Adèle delivered the blow reluctantly.

Annie's heart sank. Surely Jackson hadn't thought Tallie would breach his confidence if he told her of his marriage. More likely he feared, having let things between them go too far, to tell her the truth. Tallie now held Annie responsible for Jackson's withdrawn affection—which was true, in a fashion— but she mistakenly thought she had judged her unworthy of a respectable young gentleman, and warned him away from such a compromised young woman.

"How horribly unfair!"

"Vraiment, Madame—if I had been there, I would have set her to rights. I know you would never slander Tallie—anyone can see how fond you are of her."

"I meant Jackson. Had I been Tallie, I might have reached the same conclusion from his behavior. He's been cowardly and unchivalrous to both of us. How could he have behaved so?"

Adèle shook her head. "He is afraid to tell the truth. Afraid and ashamed—"

"—of his wife and child?"

"Of having let things go so far, I think. Of letting Mademoiselle Tallie think he had conceived a tendre for her—"

"Apparently he had! And he had no business doing so."

Adèle shrugged. "It is not so strange. He is young, far from home and from his family, and in Paris, things are different, especially for the artists."

"He is a married man, Adèle!"

"Entendu, but his wife is a colored lady—perhaps it is not considered a real marriage—"

Annie nearly upset the coffee in her indignation. "A vow is a vow—a promise is a promise—and there is the child—"

"In Martinique," Adèle said, "it is common for the married men to have one or two—maîtresses. And children with them too. As here in France as well, I believe. Mademoiselle Tallie is so pretty, and so lively—it would be easy for a man to fall in love with her. The Comte already had, je crois."

That shattering of her private fantasies did nothing for Annie's disposition. "Bertrand, at least, is unmarried—"

"—perhaps not unattached, Madame," Adèle said gently.

"Well, that's neither here nor there." Annie found Adèle's speculation about Bertrand oddly wounding. "Mr. Burwell should have told Miss DeKuyper of his true circumstances. He has compounded one round of ungentlemanly behavior with another, and left her to feel she had something to be ashamed of, when it is he—"

She thanked Adèle and left her to her day's tasks. What had she expected? She had set up a situation in which the breaking of a heart, or of vows, was all but inevitable. Jackson was surely to blame, but perhaps she herself was too, for having set it all in motion.

She was clear, at least, about two things: she wanted Tallie to have the joy of working in Cannes, and she wanted her artist friends to work there together in honest harmony. But perhaps she was wishing for the impossible. Feeling overwhelmed, she sipped at her coffee, which had gone penitentially cold.

It was all so awkward—Jackson was in her debt, but she had no right thereby to judge or control his behavior. But if he were bent on reunion with his family as he seemed now to be, and if he had created expectations on Tallie's part, he must undo the harm he had done. Tallie's interpretation of his hurtful behavior was understandable; wasn't it natural that a woman who had taken the near-maternal attitude toward him that Annie had, should feel compelled to warn him against involvement with an adventuress?

Yet she might have hoped that Tallie, who could have found nothing of judgment or disapproval in Annie's demeanor toward herself, would not jump to the conclusion that Annie had betrayed her to Jackson. Perhaps she simply assumed that given Annie's age and background, she could not stop herself from moralistic meddling. And of course that was true—but not in the fashion Tallie had surmised.

"I could task you with naïveté, I suppose," Julia said. "That hem should go up another inch, Mademoiselle—"

Annie was at Laferrière's, being fitted for a next-season's wardrobe and thankful the day was cool for midsummer. The dress was a wool and cashmere challis, which promised warmth despite its light weight, in a Paisley pattern of maroons, soft grays, pinks, and blue-greens. A slimmer cut than she was accustomed to, but as the couturière turned her this way and that, she found herself pleased with the silhouette in the mirror, particularly with the progress she had made in reducing what had nearly become a dowager's hump. Fröken Johansson's stern warnings had troubled her; the mid-fifties were too young to be taken for an old lady, especially as she looked forward to a new life governed by her own wishes rather than someone else's.

"What about the neckline?"

"In your case, Mademoiselle is right to give it a more rounded contour. Square is more a la mode at present, but fashion must compromise with what flatters the particular form. Besides, the lace panel will camouflage any décolleté—we'll address that in the fitting for the evening gown."

Annie regarded the bolt of fabric. "It's a bit—fussier than I'm used to. I don't wear patterns as a rule."

"Paisley is fashionable this season—you must have at least one if you aim to be au courant." Julia tweaked a fold out of the fabric.

"A bit more courant than I have been, I suppose," Annie said dubiously. The couturière finished re-pinning the hem and gestured her toward the dressing alcove, where she slipped out of the paisley and into a walking costume of Guardsman's red trimmed in dark navy. "I'll be downright conspicuous in this one!" She pirouetted in the three-way mirror. A high-necked muslin chemise under the skirt and jacket would soften the costume's lines.

Julia beamed approval. "What point in wearing red otherwise?

I can't wear it myself—it makes me look too pale, and I refuse to rouge my cheeks. But you have the complexion for it."

Although Annie expected to spend much of the winter in Cannes, she was intrigued at the thought of making an entrance at one of the musical salons to which Julia had introduced her.

"I suppose I *was* naïve," she told Julia while Mademoiselle made adjustments to the jacket. "Jackson professed so much devotion to Lydia it hadn't occurred to me he could be tempted."

"Naturally," said Julia, walking around her to appraise the jacket's drape, "the young fellow was lonely—and to be in daily proximity with a bright-spirited and charming girl like Tallie, who was completely unaware of his circumstances—"

Annie shrugged, drawing a reproving "Madame!" from the couturière, who was pinning a shoulder. "Why didn't he confide in her and make it clear his heart was already engaged? And more, that he is a father?"

"I wonder," Julia said, "whether his Southern gallantry was aroused at the jeopardy he perceived in Bertrand's attentions to her."

"That was none of his concern—"

"My dear, the fastest way to engage a man's interest in a woman is a perilous situation."

"Ah—the damsel in distress. Tallie doesn't seem obviously distressed by Bertrand's attentions."

The dressmaker tugged lightly at the jacket and stood back to assess her handiwork. "Ça fait mieux!"

"A salacious remark or two from Bertrand could have turned Jackson into Tallie's champion. It's a short step from that to infatuation, surely."

Annie blew out a sigh, and the couturière looked alarmed.

"Madame does not care for the costume?"

"Au contraire," Annie said hastily, "je la pense une merveille, and I can't wait to promenade it on the Champs-Elysées."

"Ah, bon! Then you will step into the dressing room for the evening gown?"

The gown was elegance itself, ivory silk with a pink satin rose at the bodice, a swath of écru voile around the shoulders to compensate for a lower cut than Annie had dared to wear in some time, and a light swag of celadon at the hips.

"How lovely that will look with pearls!" Julia said.

"You don't think the swags are too bulky?"

"Indeed, no. The line is slimmer than it's been in several seasons. I *am* sorry that Tallie has decided that you're responsible for Jackson's turning so suddenly cold. And even more so that he lacked the manhood to explain himself."

"I was tempted to blurt out the truth to her. But I had promised—"

"You're better at keeping promises than Jackson himself, it seems."

"I can understand his fear," Annie sighed. "Mrs. Kernochan's been doing a fair imitation of a bloodhound in trying to find out whether he still has the 'entanglement' that so concerned the family." She turned slowly at the dressmaker's direction, and saw her mirrored face nodding its satisfaction. "You have done well, Mademoiselle."

The lady gave a sharp nod as if to say, "Of *course* I did."

Julia straightened a crease in the gown's skirt. "We may hope at least to heal the breach between you and Tallie. As for the two of them, I hope he will realize that he owes her the truth along with a profound apology, and that a friendship may be salvaged on honest terms."

"It may be too late for that."

"We'll do what we can. But you sha'n't be denied the friendship of that delightful young woman because of a misunderstanding you had no part in creating."

"He owes her so much!" Annie's indignation was rising again. "Between her and Miss Cooper and Bertrand, the Montparnassians have taken him into their fold. He would never have got so far on his own."

"I wonder," Julia said as they sat at their favorite table at the Café de la Paix, "whether he's having misgivings about how his wife will adjust to Paris life. Her race aside, she's a country girl, isn't she? And she must be concerned about her child growing up so far away from any of her connections—"

"She did question the plan at first. I got it out of Jackson that she mistrusted my motivation in offering them assistance. I think he's reassured her on that."

Annie sipped at an iced café noir, glancing wistfully at the pastries arrayed in their glass case like edible jewels. It would be too bad if her new frocks were too tight before she even took possession of them. "Her parents are dead, and she's an only child. There are aunts and cousins, though, and I'm sure it will be hard for her to come away. Poor girl!"

"Jackson's coldness toward Tallie was clumsy and cruel, but at least indicates his renewed commitment to his original course." Julia eyed the pastry-case. "If I indulge in a millefeuille, will you have some?"

"A bite or two, perhaps." Annie would eat half or more, as

they both knew.

"I shall tell Jackson," Julia said with determination, "that if he doesn't disabuse Tallie of the notion that you are responsible for the estrangement between them, I'll do so myself—though without betraying his confidence."

"You are a good friend. I've no wish to entangle him in guilt; he feels obligated to me as it is. That only leads to resentment and further estrangement."

"It would serve him right. But it's true, it wouldn't accomplish anything. Switching to an even less pleasant topic, what do you hear of Sarah?"

"She'll be en route to Nice in a week or two. Mr. Barrett from Munroe Brothers has business there and has offered to escort her, so Tallie will have time to work on Carlotta's portrait—"

"Ah, the portrait!"

"Indeed. I'd forgotten about that. Will Tallie reject the commission now, since I'm the one who instigated it? That would be a shame—"

Julia ran a pinky over the plate, retrieving a smear of cream and pastry-flakes. "Perhaps Lotta can help. If we were to tell her of the misunderstanding, and she were willing to probe Tallie as to the source of her current animus—"

"That might only entangle matters further." Annie recounted Tallie's observation that Carlotta seemed romantically interested in women, wondering whether enlisting her as a messenger of peace might only disturb Tallie.

"I'd wondered about that myself. Carlotta reminds me so much at times of Bessie—so, any intervention from her might be perceived as—not disinterested?"

"I fear so. And if we are able to resolve things, and get everyone down to Cannes, I'd like Tallie to be comfortable in Lotta's company."

"Then I'll pursue the thing directly." Julia rose.

Annie realized with horror that she had consumed two-thirds of the millefeuille. "May I walk you home? I've made a pig of myself with your patisserie, and I'd best exercise away as much of it as possible. I'll take the omnibus from there if I'm not up to the full walk."

"Wasn't your hat going to be ready soon at Raymond's? And mine should be done long since. Let's stop there on the way. I always feel buoyed when walking the streets of Paris with a hatbox in hand."

"It occurs to me," Annie said, "that the velvet and wool extravagance I ordered will match the new walking-costume. At least one thing's going right at present."

"Two. You're getting rid of Sarah."

"She could always change her mind, if she finds Nice agreeable."

"She won't be moving in across the hall, at any rate. Perhaps Paris could be big enough for both of you, under the right conditions."

"—and if she did stay, Carlotta could stay as well."

"She may do so without Sarah, surely." Julia paid the waiter and they set out for the modiste's. "It's time we were past all this foolishness about chaperonage—Carlotta's twenty-eight, and I doubt has any interest in marriage. Besides, any man these days who's so nice about a girl's reputation is deeply suspect as a potential husband and likely to prove the worst sort of domestic tyrant."

The black hat with the red velvet ribbon was as dashing as Annie had imagined. Julia, turning to admire her own reflection in a new maroon chapeau, nodded approval. "What about one in deep purple, with a black band? That would set off the new paisley well, and have a bit of dash to it."

The milliner, who was standing aside deferentially waiting for their verdicts, brightened and clapped her hands. "Ah, oui, the aubergine would look lovely on Madame! Perhaps a softer silhouette on the brim, not so sharp of an angle on that one. Comme celui-ci—" She snatched up a hat in bright yellow from a mannequin head. "Not this color, of course, but what does Madame think of the style?"

"I like it. And…what would you say to a black plume?"

"That's the spirit!" Julia replied. The modiste beamed approval.

"Bertrand," Annie said suddenly, startling her friend. "Could he have started this trouble between Jackson and Tallie, out of possessiveness? Ah, sorry, Madame—" she removed the hat, which was indeed an egregious yellow, "May I see something in the aubergine? Purple is a color for which the shade is everything—"

"Entendu!" Madame bustled off to the back of the shop. "Un moment, s'il vous plaît."

"She's pretty and vivacious," Julia said after a moment, "and a good deal more intelligent than most. He values intelligence. I like to think that's why he attached himself to me—it certainly wasn't for the largesse. I'm in no position to be a patron to him."

"I am, though—" Annie said, her heart sinking again.

"If he'd been after that, you'd never have seen it coming. I've watched him charm more than one wealthy dowager over the years, to her cost—though I think most of them felt well enough recompensed. I think he considers you and me friends, insofar as friendship is in his repertoire."

"But he might have wanted to drive a wedge between Tallie and Jackson?"

"I'd have been surprised if he didn't. In an odd way, he's protective of her."

The milliner returned with a swatch of purple velvet so dark it seemed almost black, but when looked at in the daylight of the window it gave off an agreeably royal glow. Julia fingered the soft nap lovingly.

"Purple is *your* color, though," Annie said.

"I'm willing to share it with a friend. If you had a dress in that, I'd be insanely jealous."

Annie ordered the hat in purple, and Madame packed the hats they were wearing in the shop's bandboxes so that they could wear the new ones home. Along their route to Julia's, the women they passed darted glances at the milliner's name on the hatboxes and then to the pair's heads. Wearing one's new hat home was something of a tradition, and a triumphal progress. Annie resolved to do it more often.

Chapter 22

n the side-street bordering Julia's apartment, a fashionably dressed man detached himself from the pedestrians and crossed the street to intercept them.

"Mesdames! How charming to find you together!" Bertrand cried. "And what is this—new hats from Raymond?" He stopped them and circled around, appraising. He folded his arms and nodded. "I approve in both instances. Madame Shaw, the red and black is splendid on you!"

"After such flattery, you must come up for tea." Julia's tone was sardonic, but her smile was pleased. "While I'd question your judgment in matters of principle, mon ami, I've always found you quite sound in matters of taste."

Bertrand tipped his own hat. "One must specialize in these complex times. I was just coming to visit you. I don't suppose you have a supply of those macarons on hand?"

Julia shot Annie a knowing look. "As it happens, I'd laid in a supply in anticipation of Madame Shaw's joining me after our expédition de mode."

Julia's apartments were on the fourth floor of a wedge-shaped building, her small salon the apex of a rough triangle. The walls were papered in a deep green and gold Jacobean pattern, which rendered the space rich and elegant rather than shrinking it. Annie had come to feel particularly at home there.

"I'll miss that grand studio space across from Madame Shaw," Bertrand said, "My own atelier feels bare and echoing by comparison."

"And what has become of the satyrs and nymphs?" Julia poured the tea, a passionfruit and rose white tea blend from Damman Frères in the Place des Vosges. It smelled like a summer day in heaven.

"Not quite finished, I'm afraid—"

"Oh, you needn't," Annie said hastily. "It was only my foolish little scheme—"

"You insult me, Madame," said Bertrand with mock severity. "Whatever its origin, I wouldn't dream of leaving it unfinished. Only, the nymph seems to have done a disappearing act, and I wasn't quite done with her. Have you seen her?"

"Tallie? Last I knew, she was starting a portrait of Miss Lowell." Annie slapped Bertrand on the fingers as he reached for a raspberry macaron. "That is my favorite, and the only one left."

Bertrand's hands flew up. "Far be it from me to deprive a lady—the Gorgon's gone south, I take it?"

"The dowager Mrs. Shaw is about to decamp for Nice, and I trust she'll feel no need to venture over to Cannes while we are ensconced there."

"We?" Bertrand's eyes held a hopeful light.

"I propose to remove you and your atelier for a few refreshing weeks in the sea air. Miss Lowell may visit us. I'm sure she'd love to join your little band intermittently, if you're willing."

"I'm not sure there will be much of one. Young Burwell thinks he needs to stay in Paris—though the autumn term at the École doesn't start till October. He's taking fancier lodgings, I'm told. Can't imagine how he can afford it."

So, Jackson was finally taking steps to provide a Paris home for his family. Annie had arranged for him to draw on an account at Munroe Brothers. That meant Lydia and Ben would be embarking soon.

"Do you think that's got something to do with Tallie's disappearance?" Bertrand said. "A lover's quarrel or some such?"

"I certainly hope not!" said Julia.

"Why do you say that? I don't think they're at all suited either, but I doubt he'd seen a girl with her clothes off before—it often turns a young fellow's head. And I think she finds the Southern cavalier aspect appealing. There aren't many gentlemen in the bohème."

"Tallie didn't strike me as setting store by such things," Annie said.

"What Tallie says she 'sets store by' and what she feels aren't always the same thing. Otherwise—" Bertrand grinned, "how could she have resisted my attentions all this time?"

"Perhaps," said Julia, "because they weren't confined to her?"

"Touché, Madame. And here I was thinking it was because she preferred other ladies. Which has been true from time to time."

"Tallie thinks I conveyed something of that sort to Jackson—which I certainly didn't, having no personal knowledge of her, ah—interests." Annie could feel a flush rising.

"But she confides in you, does she not?"

"When I am confided in, Monsieur, I do not break the confidence."

"C'est juste. My apologies—of course not. I myself have been unusually gallant and discreet, having forgone several opportunities to bandy the lady's name in response to Burwell's evident fascination with her."

The fault, then, must lie with Jackson's clumsy attempt to pull back from what had become an improper connection. He must tell Tallie the truth, and soon. It was probably too late to mend matters and retain a friendship, which saddened Annie, but if it was that or his marriage, the choice was clear. And he owed Annie herself the repair of her relations with Tallie.

"How far had things gone, do you think?" Julia posed the question Annie hadn't dared ask.

Bertrand shrugged. "Hard to say with these gentlemanly sorts. They often lose their hearts before their actual virtue—if that term even applies to the male."

"It should," Julia said tartly. "My late spouse had advanced views on the equality of women. Indeed, on social organization in general. Some of the current crop of anarchists have been known to cite his writings on communitarian syndicalism in their propaganda sheets."

"You'd best not let that get about, or the authorities will be knocking your door down and hunting for bomb-throwers in your wardrobe. The current hysteria on the subject has encompassed the ranks of harmless bohemians and demimondaines—I've had several friends hauled away for questioning, for nothing more sinister than a subscription to *La Revue Blanche*."

"There's no chance of Tallie's having been caught up in

anything like that?" Annie's hands twisted in her lap.

Bertrand considered. "She's never shown any interest in politics in my hearing. I wondered if she might be up at Chéret's—the poster artist, you know, in Saint-Ouen."

"The fellow I met at Saint-Marceaux's salon?"

"She often models for him. Haven't you noticed her in some of the Folies posters?"

"Goodness, now that you mention it—" Posters for the cabarets and café-concerts of Montmartre, though uncommon on the streets of Passy, were abundant on the kiosks of the Champs-Elysées and in the older neighborhoods. And the light-haired young ladies cavorting at the center of Chéret's scenes did indeed resemble Tallie at her most effervescent.

"But there does seem to have been a breach between her and Burwell, and she's an impulsive little thing at times—"

"Have you applied to Miss Cooper? How do you know she's not just at her lodgings, or going to her other classes at Julian's?" Julia said.

"I haven't been round. I don't much care for La Cooper in isolation, and don't relish being turned away by the angel with the flaming sword—"

"—but Tallie hasn't quarreled with *you*, surely?"

"Perhaps," said Bertrand with palpable reluctance, "I should go and inquire. I worry about her a bit, though she wouldn't thank me for it, I'm sure—but I can't expect you ladies to venture into the wilds of Belleville to seek her out. I do want to get that painting finished. It's terribly Academic by my standards, and thereby has a good chance of a favorable notice at the Salon." He rose and retrieved his ebony walking-stick.

"You'll let us know how you fare?"

"Bien sûr, Madame Shaw—and should I find her, I'll convey your greetings."

Annie rose. "Perhaps, since I must be heading home, you'll accompany me to the omnibus stop? One doesn't have a new hat from Raymond's every day, and I intend to show it off."

Bertrand tucked his stick under his arm and picked up the hatbox while Annie adjusted the new headgear in Julia's hall mirror.

"I shall be pleased to escort you there—that line in the other direction will take me where I'm going, and in the meantime I may be thought an indulgent paramour—" he swung the hatbox suggestively, "—whose lady has extravagant tastes."

Annie flushed again. She seemed to have been turning pink all afternoon. "What nonsense you talk! I'll make my own way—"

"Please! I do but jest—unless," he gave Annie a shrewd look, "you'd rather I were serious."

Julia sat on the sofa, smiling wickedly. "You see? I warned you what would happen if you shed your dowdy plumage, my dear—you'll have would-be admirers trailing you off the omnibus—"

"Oh, now you're *both* making fun of me!"

"Never in life!" Julia rose and clasped Annie by the hands. "Let us know what you find out, Bertrand."

Annie swung her apartment door open gently, stopping when she heard singing—the "Habanera" from *Carmen*, in a rich mezzo-soprano which, she realized, must be coming from Adèle.

> L'oiseau que tu croyais surprendre
> Battit de l'aile et s'envola;
> L'amour est loin, tu peux l'attendre;
> Tu ne l'attend plus, il est là!...

As the words took their sensuous course, Annie marveled at her maid's command of the melody, cadences, lyrics. Why had she never recognized the talent there? She closed the door gently behind her and set the hatbox on the hallway table as quietly as she could. But the noise and movement brought the beautiful song to an abrupt halt. Adèle, who was dusting Annie's paperweights, gingerly replaced the one she was holding, a favorite with a spray of white callas. "Oh, Madame! I am sorry, I didn't hear you come in. A letter for you—" she held it out, and Annie recognized Jackson's hand.

I wish I hadn't disturbed you, she wanted to say, but she was afraid of making her so self-conscious she would never sing again. Adèle sang often, in little snatches in the kitchen, while changing the bed linens, emptying the ashes from the fireplace in the colder seasons, but never for very long and never full-throated as she had just done. They were mostly folk songs from her native isle, Annie had supposed. She hadn't heard her at this level, superb and unconstrained. The lines rose in her mind from Gray's *Elegy*:

> Full many a gem of purest ray serene
> The dark unfathom'd caves of ocean bear:
> Full many a flower is born to blush unseen,
> And waste its sweetness on the desert air.

And here was a woman with a rich gift whose sweetness should not be wasted on the desert air. How to encourage her, how to help her let it out into the world? Adèle stood expectantly, now only an attentive maid. Annie let the moment pass, vowing to find a more opportune one once there was no chance of immediate embarrassment.

"Do we have any of that Evian water, Adèle? I need a little digestif." Annie settled herself by a window with the letter.

My dear Mrs. Shaw, it began.

I am writing to beg your forgiveness for my recent ungentlemanly conduct, with regard both to yourself and to a lady we hold in mutual esteem. Regarding my interactions with Miss DeKuyper, I am forced to conclude that I allowed my own loneliness and trepidation of my new life among strangers to combine with the appreciation that any man must have of that lady's vivacity, talent, and charm, and to grow into feelings which were thoroughly improper in light of the domestic situation which I confided to you.

How charmingly Southern he was! And how like his father.

I should, of course, have removed myself long since from such a compromising situation—for both myself and the lady in question— and I wish to be quite clear that there were no overtures on the lady's part which induced me to distract myself from the commitment of love and care I have made to my wife and child. It was my own weakness which led the lady to conclude that I was in a position to reciprocate the warm feelings of friendship and affection she had begun to display toward me. I will never forgive myself for the insult I have offered to one whose regard has become important to me on both an artistic and a personal level. Nor can I excuse my failure to correct at once the lady's mistaken impression that it was some communication of yours, dear Mrs. Shaw, which led me to take an adverse view of the budding connection. That, at least, I trust my letter to her will have accomplished.

I am making what amends I can in a letter to Miss DeKuyper, confiding the details of my personal circumstances and the need I felt to withhold that information from my Paris friends until I could be sure that Mrs. Burwell would assent to the difficult request I made of her—to come with our young son to a place where she has never been and knows no one, to abandon her prior connections in favor of an uncertain future with one whose capacities may fall short of supplying her needs. Had she declined, I should have returned and somehow found a way for us to make a life together in America.

To my great joy, Lydia has agreed to set out with Benjamin very soon, and I have booked passage for them on the La Bretagne, which is to sail from New York to Le Havre on the twenty-first of this month. She has a cousin, a Mr. Mathis, who will accompany her and little Ben by rail as far as that port, and see them safely aboard. I will meet them in Le Havre on the thirtieth.

I can never thank you enough, nor repay your many kindnesses, Mrs. Shaw, and it grieves me deeply that ingratitude and implicit slander have been added to the list of my wrongs to my friends. I beg you will advise me as to how I might begin to make it up to Miss DeKuyper for my cruel and humiliating deceptions. You and she are two of my dearest Parisian friends, and I should wish above all things that my wife and child would be welcome in your company. Perhaps my injuries to Miss DeKuyper are past mending—and perhaps to you too. But I beg you will allow me to call on you and make my apologies in person...

Annie's eyes brimmed and she felt a smile forming. She looked up from the letter and found Adèle paused in her dusting, gazing at her with avid curiosity. She offered the letter to Adèle, who held up her hand.

"Oh, no, Madame, it would not be right! Only—what does he say?"

"That he has wronged both me and Miss DeKuyper, and that he is anxious to make amends. And that his wife and child are to embark shortly for Le Havre."

"Oh-la-la! La négresse?"

"Indeed, Mrs. Burwell is a lady of color. I am looking forward to meeting her."

"But what of la petite Tallie? She does not know—"

"Jackson has also written to her. Whether she can forgive him, I don't know. I hope so—"

"Why did he not just tell her in the first place, Madame?"

Annie sipped the mineral water. "He was very concerned that Mrs. Kernochan would find out, and tell his brother, who would have cut off his financial support. And I suppose it's difficult to find a way to introduce such a topic to a lady in whom one suspects an attraction for oneself, without seeming presumptuous and humiliating her."

"But it is far worse now, is it not?"

"I fear so—but if he can express himself as humbly and decently to her as he has to me, perhaps all may yet be well. I am going to reply, and ask him to tea tomorrow—will you see it delivered for me?"

Chapter 23

nnie was working on a street-scene of the mansions across the avenue, with their tricolor flags still waving a fortnight after Bastille Day. She had been harboring a perverse desire to visit the Chapelle Expiatoire, the shrine commemorating Louis XVI and Marie Antoinette on the site of their first burials. While contemplating whether to look for a fiacre or walk there, she wandered across the hall to the Crafts' apartments, where the classical canvas stood unfinished on its easel.

What a shame it all was. For a project conceived in so shallow and silly a fashion, it had a seriousness of content and execution that gave it a sort of integrity. The two satyrs strode through a rugged, wooded landscape not unlike some of the scenes Asher Durand had painted for her father so long ago: Miss Cooper, who specialized in landscape, knew her way around foliage and topography. And there was dynamism in the musculature of all three main figures, the horns and hairy legs of the men detracting little from the seriousness of the renderings. The faces were a miniaturized wonder, deftly detailed, recognizable as their originals but with a timelessness of expression—outrage and fear on the nymph's delicate features, salacious but not overdone leers on the men's—that captured the drama of myth. It seemed all but finished.

"It's coming out quite well, isn't it?"

Startled, Annie turned to find Tallie leaning in the doorway. "No surprise," she said, "given your collective talent." She went to the girl and folded her in her arms. Tallie returned the embrace with energy, burying her face in Annie's breast.

"Mrs. Shaw, I am so, so sorry! How could I have—"

Annie pulled away and scrutinized her at arms' length. Tallie's face was stained with tears. "What were you supposed to think, when he'd told you nothing of his situation?"

"I should have known better than to think badly of one who's shown me nothing but kindness and friendship. Oh, Mrs. Shaw, how could I have been so stupid? After all the time I've spent among the men of Paris—"

Annie closed Clem's door on the painting and led Tallie back across the hall. "I don't think he's like them," she said, "but he was lonely and afraid, and this bright light came into his life when he was at his lowest. And here I was—talk of stupidity!—bringing you together in the most compromising circumstances—"

"You mustn't say that! Artists are supposed to be professional about these things—to regard the body as an object of study, not a—"

Annie held up a hand. "Supposed is one thing, and natural human impulses another. He was certainly in the wrong, to let you think he was in a position to return your feelings."

Tallie flopped down in an armchair. "And he has said so—indeed, he didn't deny that he did return my feelings, but admitted that he had no right to do so. I'm finding that part very hard to forgive. I fear he took me for—a coquette, a diversion."

Adèle, looking concerned, appeared in the doorway and Annie sent her off for tisanes and cakes with a smile that told her things were on the mend.

"I shouldn't defend him, since he wronged me too. But I don't think he's capable of such shallow regard. He had no right to any attentions toward you—but I don't think he ever felt anything but respect and admiration for you, as a person and an artist, beyond those tender feelings."

Tallie bowed her head and struggled in vain to hold back tears.

"That must make it even worse, thinking of what could have been, if he had been free."

The girl looked up and nodded. "I'm not a Jezebel, Mrs. Shaw, however it may appear. When I love, I do so without reserve. And I'm very clear to distinguish between a casual dalliance, mutually agreed as such, and a true bond of affection."

Adèle returned with the tea tray, darted a look of inquiry at Tallie, and withdrew.

"Had there been a declaration, on either part?"

"Would you regard a kiss as a declaration?"

"It depends on how it was given, and how received."

"I gave it as a pledge. He returned it, I thought, in the same spirit. But just after that he grew cold and distant." Tallie took up the teacup, but set it down again untasted.

"Being concerned for you, but bound by his confidences, I urged him to tell you the truth. I knew, of course, that that could only be hurtful."

"It was cowardly of him!" said Tallie indignantly. "He admits as much in his letter. And unfair both to you and me."

"Not to excuse him, but there could be consequences fatal

to his life in Paris if it came out. But he should have known he could trust you as a friend." Annie paused, scrutinizing Tallie's face. "What will you do?"

Tallie shrugged and gave a small, brittle smile. "He wishes for my friendship and my artistic camaraderie, but he's sure that's too much to ask for. He's right."

"I understand. In the circumstances I should feel as you do, but—"

Tallie's smile faded. "Should I forgive him?"

"I was thinking of Lydia. His wife. And the child—how lonely it will be for them at first. How badly, in such a situation, I should need friends. Did he tell you she's a colored lady?"

"You could hardly expect me—" Tallie stopped as Annie's words registered. "He didn't mention that."

"That's why the brother's so determined to put an end to it. Does it make a difference?"

"Honestly—I don't know. I didn't think they allowed that, down South."

"It's hardly allowed anywhere in the States. In Georgia, a couple like that is putting their lives at risk. That's why they've never been able to live together as man and wife. And why he's been so chary about keeping the information from the Colony. His brother had asked Mrs. Kernochan—a relative and a Cathedral lady—to report any evidence of the connection's continuing, with the threat of cutting off his financial support."

"But they *could* be married in France," Tallie said, her face concealed for the moment behind the teacup. "How old is the child?"

"A year younger than the marriage, I believe," Annie answered the unasked question. "Jackson has a small allowance—by no means enough to support the three of them living apart—and he's gambling everything on succeeding as an artist. Perhaps that's wrong of him—"

"No! I mean—you can't look at it that way. It's a calling—it mustn't be ignored."

"*...and that one Talent which is death to hide...*"

"That's Milton, isn't it? Yes—that's it exactly." Tallie leaned forward, hands pressed together as if in prayer.

"You sympathize with him, then."

"In that respect only."

"You're right. I can't expect you to accept the situation. But— oh, it's terribly selfish of me, but I was so looking forward to having you all in Cannes!"

"That's impossible now, surely—" It came out almost as a question.

"For him perhaps, until he gets them settled in Paris. But we still have a few weeks of sticky Paris summer to avoid, and I don't see why you and Bertrand and Madame Greene shouldn't join me at les Anthémis—"

"Oh, Bertrand!" Tallie went red and turned her head away.

"He was going to look for you—we talked about not having seen you. He didn't want to admit it, but I could see he was worried—"

"I'd gone off and hid at Julian's, getting lost in a still-life I'd been working on. Slept on a cot in a vestibule. But I came home, and then he was on my doorstep. He did seem glad to see me. I'd just read Jackson's letter—" Again, there was a blush and a turn of the head. "I was glad to see him, since I was feeling bouleversée at that point. He's an old friend, after all."

Something in her tone made Annie uneasy, but she let it pass.

"I'm sure Carlotta's looking forward to having you paint her. She and her grandmother go to Nice in a few days, but it's an easy train ride—she could come for a sitting, or you could—"

"—venture into the Gorgon's lair?" Tallie laughed. "I'm exactly the sort of young person of whom she'd most strongly disapprove. And of course, the circumstances of our meeting—"

Annie laughed in her turn. "I'd have paid good money to see that. Carlotta can come to Cannes if you need her for sittings. She'll probably enjoy it too."

"I've never been to Cannes," Tallie said, wistful.

"I'm going to give you Tinta's old bedroom, with a sea view—that's my namesake niece Anna Kneeland Crafts—Codman, now. The eldest."

"It has a view of the sea? The Mediterranean?" Tallie was clasping her hands, like a child who couldn't quite believe a promise of good fortune.

"Unless you'd rather have a garden view—there's a ground-floor one, with its own little terrace—"

"Oh, no, the sea view, please!"

"It's all blue and white, with French doors and a little balcony—she often sat out there in the mornings, with her coffee and a book—she's as much of a bookworm as I, though I don't suppose she'll have much time for it now that she's going to be a mother."

For Annie, it would have been a hardship to give up her reading for the constant distractions children would have brought into her life. Selfishly, she felt she had lost something when Clem had her babies; they had been great companions in the world of books, and James Crafts as a new husband had often joined in their talk. But particularly when Marian, the second child, came along, Clem seemed to lose all span of attention. "Milk-brain," she had called it, good-humoredly, but Annie had missed the give-and-take of their literary discussions. Her niece Tinta, once grown, had loved books as much as she did, but Annie wondered whether she, too, would be lost to motherhood and its obligations. She felt a little lonely at the thought. But here was Tallie, restored to her as if she had been an errant niece.

"I wonder if it compensates," Tallie was saying. "Motherhood, I mean. I can't think of anything I'd be willing to give up painting for—nor my freedom, to go about with friends and talk for hours in cafés."

"We'll have to see what Jackson makes of it—and Lydia herself. She's a skilled seamstress, I'm told—one can do that at home, while caring for a child."

"What's she like? It's odd to think of having been in competition for a man's affections—"

"I only know what he's told me, and what I saw in his portrait of her and their little boy. If it's true to life, she's tall and slender and quite lovely. There was a secret ceremony, with a colored preacher," Annie added. "They're not yet legally married, but certainly married in the eyes of God."

Tallie's mouth set in a grim line. "He had evidently forgotten that."

"The circumstances were certainly difficult." Annie laid a hand on hers. "He set out here, partly at the urging of his family who wanted to separate them—they knew of the attachment, though not the marriage or the child—partly in hope of developing his skills to be able to support Lydia and Ben in the north somewhere. But it was all so uncertain."

"And he took comfort where it was offered."

"Are we sure that in similar circumstances, we mightn't do likewise?"

Tallie rose and went to the window, her gaze unfocused on the lush greens of the courtyard's trees and shrubs. "I don't need comfort, Mrs. Shaw. I'm content with freedom."

"I don't see why we can't have a bit of both. Though I've had too many years of the comfort, and I mean to find out more about the freedom. You can help me with that, if you're willing—I'm new at all this, despite my advanced years."

Tallie's look suggested that Annie might be making fun of her.

"No, truly—I've heard of la vie bohèmienne, but I've been living la vie bourgeoise, and worse, Américaine, all these years. I long, for instance, to see a shadow-play at Le Chat Noir."

"Do you really?" Tallie laughed. "Even I haven't dared go there unaccompanied. But the two of us might manage it, if you don't mind being thought of as my—ah—"

"—Sapphic patroness? That would be amusing. We might muddy the waters further by asking Madame Greene along."

"A lovely idea!" Tallie's face clouded. "Does she know about Jackson, and his family?"

"I've shared the news with her, now that he has—ah—" This was equivocation. Julia had known of Jackson's circumstances shortly after Annie herself did, but she couldn't bear for Tallie to know that she was among the last to be undeceived. "She's concerned for you."

"Was it so obvious as all that?"

"I suppose one looks for such things, when a pair of attractive young people are in such circumstances as yours. Like seeing the lead actors in *Romeo and Juliet* and wondering whether offstage they, you know—" It was Annie's turn to blush. "My father was a notable patron of the arts, but there weren't many ladies in painting circles in his day."

"And you never found some dashing protégé of your father's to fall in love with? Or were you too taken up with the eligibles?"

Annie started to laugh until a memory turned her serious. "Just after I married Colonel Shaw and he'd gone south, I thought I'd fallen in love with an artist who kept a studio on a rocky little island in Penobscot Bay. A Mr. Brown, with a wife—"

"Goodness! You didn't model for him? On his island?"

"No—he gave me and my sister a couple of lessons. I converted my attraction to him into a love for painting. And he paid me a compliment or two about my artistic potential. In all that came after, though, I let the painting drop until now—what are you smiling at?"

Tallie was struggling to control her features. "It's just that— would it have been so awful to have fallen in love with both? This Mr. Brown *and* painting? I suppose, being a good and sensible young married lady, you put the thought of Mr. Brown out of your heart—"

Annie hadn't thought of Mr. Brown in decades. She felt a catch in her throat. There *had* been something there, too, the way he looked at her…the way she'd felt when he checked her dance card and claimed the last dance…a hot flush crept over her cheeks.

Tallie took her hand. "Sorry, I'm teasing you. I couldn't resist. You shall have lessons when we go to Cannes. From me and from Bertrand. I'm sure he's looking forward to it."

"He came to find you—"

"—and he did. He even said he had been worried. I didn't mean to cause alarm—I just needed a spell of solitude."

"An admirable impulse." Annie stacked their dishes on the tea tray. "Did you tell him about Jackson's letter?"

"I took him quite aback. When I opened the door and saw him, I blurted out, 'Did you know that Mr. Burwell is married and a father?' And he said, 'Well, that explains everything, doesn't it?' And then I couldn't help it—I started to cry. And he said, 'He's nothing to you as an artist, though I've no doubt he'll develop—but you might have held yourself back, so as not to intimidate him, and that would have been a shameful waste of talent.' D'you know, that's the nicest thing Bertrand has ever said to me."

"And the most sincere, I'll wager. I'd give much to know what has made that man as sardonic as he poses. He wears irony like a suit of armor."

"Oh, he really *is* the most dreadful cynic! I don't think it's a pose at all."

"You see no warm but broken heart, then, beneath the exterior?"

Tallie laughed. "I think those only happen in three-volume novels written by frustrated spinsters." She stopped, and ruminated briefly. "Broken, perhaps. Whether it was ever warm, I'd give much to know. I'm a bit afraid of what I might conclude—"

From the doorway, Adèle cleared her throat, startling them both. "Pardon, Madame, but Monsieur Burwell is here—"

Annie bolted out of her chair. "Oh, Lord, I'd completely forgotten—I'd invited him to tea." She saw her own alarm mirrored on Tallie's face. There was no way for the girl to leave without encountering him. Tallie stood up, and nodded as if at a question Annie had voiced directly.

"I was never going to avoid him indefinitely."

Chapter 24

he door reopened and there stood Jackson, tall, fair, a lad any woman might fall in love with. Adèle had obviously warned him of Tallie's presence.

He stopped on the threshold, uncertain of his welcome. "Mrs. Shaw. Miss DeKuyper. How fortunate to find you together. I may at least hope that the misunderstanding I was responsible for creating between you has been amended?"

"I have apologized to Mrs. Shaw for my misjudgment," Tallie said stiffly. "I was never justified in leaping to the conclusion that it was she who had wronged me. That fault is my responsibility alone. I should have known better."

"I have been cowardly and dishonest beyond forgiving," said Jackson. "Nonetheless, Mrs. Shaw, in her generosity—"

"You have not had *my* reply in that regard," said Tallie, with as much dignity as so slight a figure could muster.

"I deceived you, Miss DeKuyper—not with cold deliberation, but only because I am a dam—an utter fool, and it took me too long to recognize that the warm feelings of friendship I felt— toward and from you—had crossed into forbidden territory. In my clumsiness and fear, I insulted you and Miss Cooper with my cold response to your friendly efforts regarding the apartment. I couldn't yet bring myself to tell you that I needed room for three."

"—which I take it you have now secured?" Tallie's tone was neutral. "And—Mrs. Burwell is to join you soon?"

He nodded, blushing. "I have been fortunate. On the Square St-Romain, three rooms, a little kitchen and bath. A clerk at the École knew of the vacancy. His aunt is the landlady."

"That will be a step up from your Montparnasse rat-warren," said Annie, trying to lighten the atmosphere. Jackson gave her a grateful look; Annie's response to his letter had included a draft on Munroe Brothers to cover Lydia's passage as well as the first few months' rent.

"Is it furnished?" Tallie asked. "We have a pair of small tables we got at St-Ouen, but there really isn't room for them—"

Jackson's eyes filled with tears. "How good of you. I have no right to expect any kindness from you—" Tallie's upheld hand stopped him.

"You're quite right, Mr. Burwell. Nonetheless, it is on offer."

"You…are willing to forgive me, then?"

"Provisionally—if in all our future dealings you will be candor itself. To include any critiques I request for works in progress. As for any future misleading overtures to young ladies, I shall have a word with Mrs. Burwell, who I assume will see to that in times hereafter." She was trying, Annie could see, to suppress a laugh at the horrified look on Jackson's face, and ultimately gave it up. Annie silently cheered the exaction of a small revenge.

"I deserved that."

Tallie slapped his hand. "You certainly did. Look, here's Adèle back with a fresh plate of—are those currant-buns?" Warm from the oven, they gave off a heavenly sweet smell.

"Better than that," Annie said. "Raisin brioches." A tall, bearlike figure followed Adèle through the doorway.

"Sorry not to announce myself," said Bertrand de Leiningen airily, "but I followed a tantalizing aroma of baking up the stairs."

Tallie startled like a frightened deer. "What are you doing here?"

Bertrand's smile was playful and proprietary. "Only to report to Madame Shaw that I had found you well, with hopes for the reward to which a bringer of good news is entitled. And—" he took a long, appreciative sniff at the plate of brioches, "I see I'm just in time."

Adèle went to find china and cutlery for the latest arrival, who fluffed the tails of his frockcoat behind him, settled into an armchair, and accepted Annie's offer of jasmine tea. Tallie and Jackson eyed him with apprehension, the latter perhaps wondering how much of the history he knew, and Tallie, Annie surmised, embarrassed by her little romance and its sad aftermath.

She would not, Annie thought, care to entrust Bertrand with revelations of a potentially embarrassing nature. It was currency in his various salons, though she had observed that the objects of his scorn courted notoriety and should not have been surprised when it materialized.

Bertrand, however, was at his most suave, reacting to Jackson's news about the arrival of his wife and child with neither surprise nor any indication of prior knowledge—a delicate balance. But Annie caught occasional veiled glances toward Tallie as if to gauge her reactions. Tallie was treating the matter like a revelation between casual but kindly inclined acquaintances, inquiring about the baby's age and stage of development, murmuring sympathetically at the idea of a father's missing his son's first steps or earliest words. In similar circumstances, Annie doubted that she herself could have summoned such reserves of courage and dignity.

"How you must have missed them!" Tallie said in a perfect imitation of the tones of an American Colony matron commiserating with one whom business has unavoidably separated from his family. "We must have a little gathering, don't you think, Mrs. Shaw? After they've had a few days to recover from their journey?"

"Presumably after Burwell's Aunt Kernochan has done so?" Bertrand interjected easily. "She's your closest connection in Paris, isn't she?"

Jackson darted Bertrand a look that bordered on outright hostility, but he mastered his features. "I haven't yet acquainted my cousin—my mother's cousin—with the details of my domestic situation. It may be some time before I do so. I trust I may rely on your discretion." *For reasons I don't care to explain to you at present,* he did not add.

"Of course," Bertrand said, looking suitably chastened.

Annie interposed. "When do they arrive?"

"They are due at Le Havre on the *La Bretagne* at the end of the month."

"May I recommend," said Annie, "a few days at the Hotel de la Manche, to get her land-legs back? We often stopped there after a crossing—"

"I'm fond of the Manche myself," Jackson said. "We stayed there when I was a child, when I first came to France. I wonder if it's still there."

So, Jackson's parents had come to France, but Roland had made no attempt to contact her. He did well; it would have been nothing but awkward for all of them, especially his poor wife. Still, it was bittersweet to be reminded of a time when one had been considered desirable, when being in attractive male company was entirely at one's own option. Annie smiled to think of it—here were two attractive young men in her parlor, one of whom regarded her as a beneficent aunt, or even a fairy godmother, the other—well, what did Bertrand de Leiningen see in her?

Not what he would have seen in her twenty-five-year-old self, certainly. One heard, from time to time, of scandalous marriages between rich Parisian widows and handsome, younger men of dubious occupation and prospects. Bertrand surely harbored no such ambitions toward herself; there had been no concerted campaign of ingratiation. Indeed, the most flattering aspect of his approach to her seemed to be his assumption that she was too intelligent for that sort of thing. But her health and looks were much improved in the last months, and the thought arose that perhaps, after all, she might not be impervious to a campaign of seduction.

"If it is, the hotel will have a telephone," Bertrand was saying. "Nasty things, but I suppose one can't run a business these days without them. We'd have found you much quicker, ma chèrie," he turned a luminous smile on Tallie, "if you and Miss Cooper had one in your garret."

"Don't be absurd, Bertrand—we can barely afford the rent."

"Burwell, I'm looking forward to the sight of you as a doting papa. And to meeting Madame, who no doubt must be exceptionally lovely. I've never known a handsome man to marry a plain-looking woman unless there were a great deal of money involved—"

"Which means," said Tallie with forced brightness, "that the little fellow will be uncommonly handsome. I shall have to paint him—if his mamma will allow it. I haven't had much exposure to babies as portrait possibilities, but it could be a profitable side-venture, as Miss Cassatt has demonstrated."

"He was easy to paint when I last saw him," Jackson said wistfully. "Only a few months old, and slept through it like a cherub. And now he's—" his voice caught. "What I've missed."

"We must see him, then," said Tallie, "as you last saw him."

"You will show them, won't you, Jackson?" Annie said. "The Madonna and Child?"

"Oh, it's not—"

"I think it's exquisite. If you think it's not a good likeness, however—"

Jackson flushed. "It's only that she's so much lovelier in real life."

"*Paint/ Must never hope to reproduce the faint/ Half-flush that dies along her throat.*" This, to Annie's surprise, from Bertrand, whose English was accomplished but whom she had not imagined as a Browning aficionado.

"Well, I'm no Fra Pandolf, as you well know," said Jackson. "But you may see it if you like, and when you meet the original, I'll hope for a critique."

"Of the lady?" Bertrand teased.

Tallie slapped him on the arm. "Really, Bertrand! He does you the honor of asking you to help him with his work—"

Bertrand threw up his hands. "A poor jest indeed. I will count myself fortunate to be introduced to her. Is she also an artist?"

"She's an accomplished needlewoman. A dressmaker, in fact, much in demand among the fine ladies of our little town, such as they are. She can hone her skills here, if she's taken on as an assistant somewhere—she's eager to see what the ladies of Paris are wearing. They're always a year or two ahead of us, she tells me."

Annie handed him the plate of brioches. "We must enlist Madame Greene. She's gone completely native in the couture department. She'll have some good ideas, possibly an introduction or two. As to furnishing your apartments, I'm planning to redecorate. I'll have a few pieces that might suit you for a stopgap. I'm going to finish turning this room into a proper library. My books have been scattered among Clem's and in boxes for too long. And I'm expecting a few things from America, now that our summer place has been sold."

It had stabbed her to the heart to sell Vent Fort, but she hadn't set foot in her Lenox home in nearly twenty years. The dear old house had been moved across Walker Street and renamed Bel Air—Annie refused to sell the property unless the house was preserved—and the Morgans were building something huge in red sandstone that the architects had labeled "Jacobean Revival." But it was Vent Fort's grounds that held the memories, of walks in the pine grove with George, and then with Rob; of their cruelly curtailed honeymoon, of hilltop picnics and al fresco music—Nilsson singing "Casta Diva" on the outcropping at Echo Lake, the full moon's light shining in her blonde curls and making a silver path across the lake's mirror-still waters. The lush greens of the Berkshire Hills had soothed Annie's shattered heart in the first days of widowhood. Just as well she hadn't been there to see it all go.

"You don't sound too happy about that, Mrs. Shaw," Tallie said gently.

"Oh, I haven't seen the place in forever. I'm sure it's much changed—it's been rented out over and over. It's not as if I plan on going back to live there. It's far too big for one person."

The three pairs of eyes on her seemed to be probing for some evidence of vulnerability, of sadness. As friends would, she realized with a little spurt of contentment.

"Have you seen Miss Lowell lately?" she asked. If Tallie were due to paint her portrait, she had lost a few days over the imbroglio with Jackson.

"I sent her a note this morning, though there may not be time now to do much on the portrait before she leaves for Nice."

"It's not so far from Cannes. I dare say Mother Shaw can spare her occasionally. Apropos of which, there's a nice old carriage house on the property—I think it might convert easily and quickly into studio spaces—"

"You wouldn't do that on our account, surely—"Tallie began. Bertrand darted her a repressive look.

"The two younger Crafts girls are probably dabbling in art by now. I'm thinking of movable partitions that could easily be disassembled if some future occupants owned a carriage."

"That sounds splendid," Bertrand said. "Burwell, you've painted your wife's portrait?"

"Several times," Jackson admitted, "though the one Mrs. Shaw has seen is the only one that remotely does her justice. After I'd introduced myself when I saw her reading to a group of children, I'd see her on the street from time to time—how striking she was—and eventually I worked up the courage to ask if she would allow me to paint her. She was naturally, and rightly, suspicious of such an overture from a white man—"

Bertrand's eyebrows shot up. "Your wife is a colored lady?" Jackson nodded. "That *was* audacious of you, and courageous of her to agree."

Jackson's eyes shone. "Nothing to the courage it took for her to accept my marriage proposal. For me, the mouth is the most challenging feature, and regrettably my first few tries—"

Tallie's mouth, Annie saw, had begun to droop at the edges. The wound was still too raw for this sort of talk. "Well, we'll have to compare your portrait to the original in due time," she said. "For now, I must chase you all away, since I'm due to dine at Miss Reubell's and can't go out for an evening looking like this."

The ivory and celadon gown wasn't ready for Annie to show off at the Reubell mansion, but she felt confident enough in the royal blue silk to wear it again, and was greeted with an approving look from her hostess.

"Henry James is contemplating another Paris novel," Retta said, handing her a flute of champagne as a footman took the silk shawl Julia had woven for her. "He's threatening to include me as a character, and I'm not sure what to think about that."

The Reubell salon, as usual, was a mix of the haute monde and the bohemian, the former, Annie suspected, enjoying the frisson of mingling with disreputable people. The signature turquoise of her reception rooms made a pleasing backdrop to the pastel rainbow of ladies' summer gowns set off by the smart black-and-white of the men's evening suits—a Béraud social commentary come to life. That ingratiating artist was ringed by a circle of admirers, retailing some nugget of gossip he had picked up from one of his subjects.

"What's become of that charming young artist of yours?" Retta asked, handing her a flute of champagne. "The little blonde girl, I mean."

"She's coming with me to Cannes. Oh, you should know—my mother-in-law and niece by marriage are bound for Nice shortly. In case you planned to visit your house there."

Miss Reubell clapped a hand to her bodice. "Thank you for the warning, as regards—what did you call her, the Gorgon? I doubt she has any interest in crossing paths with the likes of me. But Carlotta strikes me as a young person with potential."

Annie took a salmon canapé from a passing waiter. "Miss DeKuyper thinks her art may develop in promising directions."

Retta slapped her playfully with her fan. "You know that's not what I meant."

"Far be it from me to conspire in leading an innocent astray, especially a relative. But you'd mentioned coming over from Nice to les Anthémis. You may find her there, sitting to Miss DeKuyper. Tallie's a little nervous about it, having the impression that Carlotta has conceived a tendre for her."

Retta Reubell smiled wickedly. "Perhaps I should attempt to distract her."

"I was thinking more in terms of chaperonage."

"Annie Shaw, I've never known you for a killjoy."

Annie spotted Bertrand coming toward them. "I gave up the role when my nieces left for America. It never suited me."

"Then how could you even think of *me* in that light? What do you think, Bertrand—would I make a good chaperone?"

Bertrand gave Retta a wolfish grin. "It would depend on the parties involved. I shouldn't take kindly to any of that where my attentions to the charmante Madame Shaw are concerned."

"Talk is cheap, Monsieur, as they say—" Annie began. Bertrand took her arm, pushed up the lace-edged sleeve of her dress, and planted a kiss on the inside of her wrist. Annie's heart raced madly, her body suffused with sensations she had rarely felt since her time with Rob Shaw.

"But not without backing, chère madame. What a lovely perfume," he straightened up and gently let go of her arm. "Chypre with a top note of star jasmine, is it?"

Annie realized too late that she hadn't pulled her hand away when he took it, and felt herself turning scarlet. Retta Reubell was giving them both a sharp, speculative look, as if gauging how seriously to take Bertrand's overture.

"It seems to me, Annie," said Retta, allowing Bertrand to light her cigarette, "you don't need my chaperonage, but my offices as a friend—to keep you from falling into a pit compared to which the circumstances of Henry James' Isabel Archer would seem paradisical."

"Oh, really, now!" said Bertrand, with indignation that seemed not altogether feigned. "You compare me unfavorably to one of the most disagreeable villains ever written. However mixed my motives, the happiness of the lady to whom I should offer my hand would always be paramount—"

"—Insofar as ignorance is bliss?" Retta spurted a jet of smoke toward the ceiling.

"This is Paris, dear lady—it's well known how things are done, and as I recall the rest of the verse, 'Where ignorance is bliss, 'tis folly to be wise.' That runs both ways, for that matter."

Annie felt her heart rate slowing sufficiently for speech. "Then I'd need not worry about my little adventures with younger gentlemen, since you're prepared to turn a blind eye to them." She spotted Henry Tanner across the room and rose to greet him.

"Speaking of gentlemen, Annie," Retta said, "I had a letter from Alice Mason. She tells me there's a new man in her life—an American painter who's come to live in London. A New Englander—Maine, was it? In any event, someone who knew you long ago and asked to be remembered to you. Brown—that was it. Harrison Bird Brown."

Annie stopped, and felt her heart speed up again. "He took me oil-painting, on an island in Casco Bay. After I was married, and not long before—well, a long time ago." She felt herself blushing under Retta's gaze. "He's taken up with Alice? He was married when I knew him."

"Widowed for some time, she tells me. Just came to live with his daughter and her new husband in London. He's planning an excursion to Paris, and she wants me to invite him to one of my Sundays. Should you like to see him again?"

"If I haven't gone off to Cannes by then, I'd be happy to," Annie said, more casually than she felt. "I haven't seen him in nearly thirty years. I suppose he'll have changed a great deal."

"Have"t we all?"

Chapter 25

week later, when Lydia and Jackson Burwell were shown into Annie's drawing room, Lydia's face seemed to mingle anxiety and curiosity. Annie rose and took her hands. "Mrs. Burwell, I've so looked forward to this! And here is Benjamin—" the little boy, with his old-gold mop of curls and a wary expression, sat uneasily in his father's arms. So much of his life had already passed in Jackson's absence, and the young man's smile at his son was bittersweet. Annie felt a wave of tenderness and worry over the little family's adjustment to life in a strange land. Even Parisians were capable of provincialism and xenophobia, and young Mrs. Burwell might well be anxious about fitting in.

"He's a mite fussy this mornin', Ma'am." She took him from Jackson and nestled him in the curve of her neck, which her husband had captured well in his Madonna portrait.

"If you call me Ma'am I'll feel a hundred years old," Annie said. "Call me Mrs. Shaw if you wish to be formal, though I hope Benjamin might think of me in time as Aunt Annie. Is the little one eating solids as yet? We've got a tomato bisque soup—"

Lydia looked at Jackson in that wordless conference Annie

had seen so often between spouses, and sometimes envied. "That sounds real nice, Mrs. Shaw—I think he could manage a little soup, if we let it cool in a saucer first."

They got the baby settled in a highchair rummaged from the Crafts' storage area in the building's cellar. Adèle put down the soup tureen and stared in unabashed delight at the little boy. Her hands were twitching to hold him. He crowed at her, and her smile widened to a beam.

"Mrs. Burwell, may I introduce Mademoiselle Adèle Fourget, who runs my household. Miss Fourget is an expatriate like us, a native of Martinique—"

"Oui, Madame, from Fort-de-France." Adèle turned to Lydia. "Perhaps the little one will eat some mashed potato with milk?" Lydia smiled and nodded.

"Tell me about your voyage."

"Well, ma'am—" Lydia caught herself, "It was right rough for the first couple days, and I got pretty sick. A kind French lady in the next cabin kept looking in on us. She took Ben when I was at my worst. It sure helped till I got back on my feet." Her voice was rich and low, the cadences Southern, the diction crystalline. Jackson's painting hadn't flattered her; her nose was long and straight, with a slight uptilt of the delicate nostrils, the eyes large and dark, the mouth a soft new-blown rosebud against olive skin. The lovely long neck enhanced her straight, slim build. She had taken great care with her appearance—a buff-colored costume trimmed in dark blue, with frog closings on the jacket. Her gold-bronze hair was tucked into a tidy chignon.

"But after the seasickness, you were comfortable enough?"

"The cabin was so big! I thought everything on a ship would be—you know—poky and tight. But we had a nice li'l sitting room as well as the stateroom, and Ben could sit and play on the floor. And the meals were real good, once I was fit to eat again."

Annie smiled approval at Jackson and he nodded shyly.

"D'you know, Ben and I saw dolphins leaping one day, when it was sunny and we could go out on deck? I'd never thought to see anything like that—" Lydia stopped, as if fearing she had been talking too long, and turned to spoon a little soup into the baby. He crowed and banged his hands on the tray of the highchair, a smear of orange around his mouth.

"I always thought dolphins were magical, like something from a fairy-tale. How I'd love to see one again!" Annie had never been fond of ocean voyages, and had been quite ill on several of them, but those sparkling days when the dolphins danced alongside the ship had almost been worth the discomforts.

"Jackson's found us such a pretty place," Lydia said. "I didn't think we'd have so much room—I figured Paris would be expensive—"

"Not if you know where to look," Jackson smiled. "I'll show you the little hole in the wall I started in. Like a real starving artist."

"I can hardly believe we're here." Lydia looked shyly around, taking in all the room's little luxuries—Annie's collection of glass paperweights, the Turkey carpet, the delicate Alençon lace curtains. "When I was a li'l girl, I was going to run away to Paris and be a ballerina."

Annie wondered how much of a barrier Lydia's race would have been, had she tried to fulfill that childhood dream. Her skin tones were more Levantine than Negro, her features exotic but not beyond the limits of European; they looked somehow familiar. This was what generations of plantation rape produced, but whatever its origins, it was beauty. No wonder Jackson had fallen for her. She might have passed for European in some large northern city like New York or Philadelphia, though the Southern cadences might have given her away. Best, then, with all the American laws and customs hostile to their union, to make a life in a totally foreign place.

"I have a friend I'd like you to meet," Annie said, "who's very attached to the ballet. She's my late husband's aunt—"

"Mrs. Greene! Jackson has told me so much of her—and of you. You must know that your husband's name is revered among our race." Lydia looked shyly at Jackson, "Where we come from isn't far from Charleston and the Sea Islands. When Jackson told me he'd made a friend named Mrs. Shaw, I wondered if there could be a connection—and then I learn you were the noble colonel's wife!"

For seventy-seven days, Annie did not say, pleased at Lydia's praise of what Rob and his men had accomplished. If she must wear his name forever without him, it was a comfort to know he was revered. "We had only three weeks together as husband and wife, before he was sent South. Sometimes it feels as if the marriage was just a dream." She saw Lydia take Jackson's hand and squeeze it hard, as if to say, *don't you let that happen to us.*

"We hadn't too long ourselves, before I was sent away," said Jackson with a wistful look at his wife, "but I aim to make it up to Lyd—Mrs. Burwell, even if I am going back to school. And it's high time Ben got to know his daddy." His own cadences had softened in his wife's presence. She had brought a bit of rural Georgia with her like a soft, warm breeze.

Adèle brought in a golden roast chicken surrounded by carrots, potatoes, and some leafy green stuff imported from her native islands to obscure corners of Les Halles, appraising the table with a satisfied nod, chucking the baby under the chin, and departing with their thanks.

"Jackson, will you carve?" In the Haggertys' home Ogden had delighted in "doing the honors," especially on holidays. The young man looked pleased and surprised, serving Lydia first after Annie rebuffed his attempt to put the favored skin-slice on her own plate. "That's for our guest of honor."

"These look like collards," said Lydia as the greens landed on her plate. "I wouldn't have thought y'all would have these in France."

"Adèle calls them 'callaloo,'" Annie said, "and nags Cook to get them when she sees them at the market. They come from the French West Indies, she says. How do they taste?"

Lydia finished a mouthful and set down her fork. "Right close, but not as bitter, and more tender. You'd have to cook collards for hours to get them like this."

Adèle came in as they were finishing an excellent lemon tart, carefully closing the dining room door behind her. "Pardon, Madame, there is a lady to see you—a Madame Ker-no-kan. Are you at home?"

The mouthful of tart stuck in Annie's throat. She and Jackson exchanged glances of alarm. "Oh, Lord," he said, "of all the bad times—"

Annie managed to swallow. "Please let Mrs. Kernochan know that I have a sick-headache and am indisposed, but thank her kindly for her visit, which I will return as soon as I may."

Adèle cocked an eyebrow and gave her a sideways smile. "Bon, Madame."

"She's Mama's cousin," Jackson told Lydia in a whisper. "I

called on her when I got here, and a couple times since. She's the one Edgar talked to—"

"I remember you told me about her." Lydia turned to Annie with a fleeting look of suspicion. "She's a friend of yours, Miz Shaw?"

"A parishioner at the American Cathedral. I forgot she told me she might 'drop by' to see the great painting in progress next door. She's been trying to enlist me as a spy, to report any evidence of a continuing connection," Annie said. "Naturally, I've denied all knowledge of your existence."

Lydia let out a breath.

"She seems kindly disposed, but family loyalty comes first with her. You'd be well advised if the legality of your union is beyond question by the time she does meet Lydia."

Lydia twisted her napkin in her lap. "A *fait accompli*, is that the expression?"

"Jackson, you don't inherit till you're twenty-five—" Annie said.

"Three years from now—and she'd have to let Edgar know that I'd defied the family's wishes in reuniting with my wife. And you *are* my wife, no matter what anyone says!" He took her hand in both of his and gripped it tightly.

Lydia's brow furrowed. "I think Miz Shaw is right, Jackson. Might be we should get married like we talked about, in front of a French judge. Or whatever they call them here. Since there's no law against it like back home."

"Honey, I wouldn't put it past Edgar to tell me to divorce you, or desert you, on pain of stopping my allowance. Do any of the white Burwells know you've up and left?"

"Not from anything I or mine would've told them. If anyone

asks for my sewing services, they'll say I'm on an extended visit to family up north. Paris is north of Georgia, isn't it?"

"And we are family," Jackson smiled. "Mrs. Shaw, how do we have a civil marriage here?"

"You go to the Mairie of your arrondissement—you're in the Sixth now, aren't you?—apply for a license, and set a date for the ceremony. It can be done on the same day, I believe."

"Let's do it tomorrow," Jackson said.

Lydia looked alarmed and laid her hand on his arm. "Honey, Ben and I just got here. We're not even all unpacked yet. I'd like a little while to get us settled in—"

"Well, if you think it best—" Jackson's expression mingled concern and surprise.

"You'll want to avoid Mrs. Kernochan in the meantime," Annie said.

The young woman's demeanor suggested to her that there was more to it than getting unpacked. Had Lydia sensed Jackson's hesitancy in the months before he sent for her? Perhaps they had talked about Tallie and his other new friends since coming to Paris; maybe Lydia wanted to learn a little more about what had transpired during her husband's time alone.

Annie could sympathize. She remembered with a squeeze of the heart the letters that had come from Rob to his mother, though not to her, in the weeks after the regiment's departure from Boston, his praise of Lottie Forten, a young colored woman in the corps of teachers sent to help the newly freed slaves of the Sea Islands. Forten's diary of her time there, published a year after Rob's death, did nothing to quiet Annie's suspicions that their relations had gone beyond casual friendship. The young teacher had been just Rob's age, cultured, poetic, passionate about the Union cause. Mingled with the grief of his loss was anger toward him and toward the woman who had evidently shared whatever joys he had in the weeks before his death. If he had come home to her, there would have been a reckoning over that...

In the small hours, Annie awoke from a dream whose details dissolved like sea foam before she was fully awake. Whatever it was, though, it had triggered a troubling memory. There had been something oddly familiar to her about Lydia Burwell. It seemed to Annie they had met before, though she couldn't imagine how. And now, in the dark with only the dim glow of a nightlamp coming from her sitting room, it came to her.

Chapter 26

April 27, 1851

It's one of those soft spring nights that only the South can offer, magnolias and jasmine scenting the warm breeze. The French doors of the Edgar Burwells' dining room stand open to the indigo sky, and though studious Annie has complained of missing school and her friends on the long train ride to Georgia, she's charmed by the garden's ambrosial scents, the candlelight on the room's primrose walls, the winking crystal and the gentle solicitude of the Haggertys' host.

She's telling Roland's father Edgar about the elephant they saw at Mr. Barnum's museum, throwing out her arms to describe the immensity of the creature, when her left arm collides with that of the serving-maid, a diffident young colored woman ladling turtle soup into Annie's bowl. The ladle's thick brown contents go flying, splattering onto Annie's pink muslin. "Oh, I'm so sorry!" Annie cries, but the young woman is unnerved—her eyes grow wide, the ladle clatters back into the tureen, and she hastily deposits it on the buffet.

Roland's mother, at the far end of the table, comes halfway out of her chair, tight-lipped and furious, nodding the girl into the kitchen and following her there. Roland's sister escorts Annie to a nearby water-closet, and another house-slave is summoned to attend to the stains. Annie hears Mrs. Burwell in the kitchen, her voice a serpentine hiss, words like "clumsy" and "shiftless" and "good for nothing but the fields." And then she hears a slap.

"It wasn't her fault at all—I was waving my arm!"

Her helper darts a fearful look toward the kitchen. "It don't matter, miss, she shoulda seen you—hold still, I think we can get this out with a li'l baking soda—"

"No, really, it was my fault—" *Annie feels herself turning scarlet,* "she had no warning—don't worry, Mamma's maid will take care of it. I'll go back now, thank you—"

"Lily ain't been the same since she got back—" *her helper starts to say, almost visibly bites her tongue and shakes her head.* "Mmph, mmph, mmph."

"Got back from where?"

"Nothin', miss, you go on back now and tell your mama's maid to come get me later, and we'll fix that dress up—tell her to ask for Sally Ann."

When Annie returns to the dining room, Mrs. Burwell settles herself back in her place with a rustle of plum silk, gives her guests a bright smile. "Now what were you telling me about that musicale you went to, Elizabeth?"

As they dress for bed, Annie asks Mamma's lady's maid Elsie, who's helping her unlace her corset, what Sally Ann meant about poor Lily not being the same since she got back. Elsie, a hefty Irish girl, looks around to make sure Elizabeth is still in her bath. She and Annie have a conspiracy to share below-stairs gossip, a useful delight to Annie; she owes the girl much of her education as to the facts of life.

"Well, Miss Annie, this poor Lily was indisposed for some time—

havin' a baby—"Annie gasps and covers her mouth, "—and just now got back to work. She's not usually a dinin' room maid, sez Sally Ann, but there's another one of 'em out—she's havin' a baby too—and 'tis said 'tis by the Master's brother, Mr. Crawford Burwell—"

"Oh, I met him! Rather charming, I thought, in a roguish way—"

Elsie's brows knit. "That he may be with white ladies, but they say no pretty colored girl hereabouts is safe from him, and the plantation's littered with his by-blows—"

"So this Lily, she just had a baby to him?"

"Not that anyone'll admit to," Elsie looks around again and drops her voice. "Mrs. Burwell's at her wit's end with him, they say, but the Master won't hear a word against his dear little brother, so he keeps at it, waylaying the slave-girls on their way back to the quarters of an evening. And that overseer—"

"Stockton? The wolf in a frock coat?"

"He is that," Elsie nods grimly. "Another one they're not safe from—" Elsie darts a look over her shoulder again. "Well, I've said enough."

"So she takes it out on the poor girls themselves," Annie feels the angry heat rising in her face. "How can they bear it?"

Elsie laughs ruefully. "Bear it, Miss? They're slaves. The Missus might fuss and beat them, but every babe is a new set of hands for the plantation someday."

"But these children are half-white—their own children…"

"So they might end up as house servants. Though if this fella keeps at it, they'll have more than they can use, and it'll be out to the cotton with them like the rest. They don't ask too many questions hereabouts, as to who's the father of the slave-girls' babies. Just put them down for a pack of immoral sluts—"

The bathroom door opens and Elizabeth emerges in her nightdress,

*damp tendrils trailing from the edge of her bathing-cap, and Annie is
left to wonder at the life of these poor colored girls, about her own age,
with no say whatever about what happens to them, and punished for
it to boot. She sees no more of the unfortunate Lily for the rest of their
stay, but her delicate frame, long neck and mournful prettiness stay
in a painful corner of her mind. And as years pass and Roland presses
his courtship, the way her prospective mother-in-law treats Lily and
other innocent victims of a white man's lust becomes another reason
to refuse him.*

Coming back to the present and half-awake among her feather
pillows, Annie realized that the enslaved Lily of her youth,
of whom Lydia was the very image, must have been Lydia's
grandmother—so her grandfather was Jackson's great-uncle
Crawford, the plantation libertine. Either or both might still be
alive, though Crawford would be an old man now.

After that spilled soup incident, Annie had avoided the man
and responded glacially to his pleasantries, leading Elizabeth
to accuse her of incivility. Reluctant to get her mother's maid
Elsie into trouble for sharing gossip, Annie hadn't explained her
antipathy. That was the way of it, back then: white men with
power over helpless slave women used them at their pleasure;
the men's wives and families turned a collective blind eye. As she
might have been expected to do had she become the mistress
of Elm Hall. And while she couldn't imagine the chivalrous
Roland forcing himself on anyone, she recalled Elsie's gossip
that young men of his ilk routinely went to "the quarters" for
sexual initiation, as though for a necessary rite of passage.

She resolved to ask Lydia about her family, to confirm her

surmises. If they were correct, what then? Perhaps her deep wish to do well by the young woman had arisen in an equally deep, though forgotten, guilt about the part Annie herself had played in the suffering of Lydia's ancestor. But she wouldn't distress Lydia with unwelcome reminiscences. She must find out what Jackson had told Lydia about the Haggerty family and its connections to his own.

Annie had lost a husband in the cause of the Negro. Perhaps that counted for something—against what? Her own and her family's complicity in slavery? Her fortune and her sister's were built upon it. Perhaps it was no accident that she'd chosen to love a man doomed to fall and mingle his bones with the Negro's, as those vile men of the South had once mingled their seed. But here was a young man of the South taking a colored woman in the honorable estate of marriage; there was a gentler justice in that.

She wondered if the lot of Negro women in the South had improved since slavery ended. For such a woman to marry a white man who treasured and revered her was still beyond most Americans' imagining. Not so in France; the renowned Dumas père, for one, was the child of a black Haitian general—a war hero—and his white French wife, and no one made much of it.

Perhaps it was best for Lydia and Jackson to take a little time before legalizing their union, having been a long time apart. Lydia was distressed about her lack of French; a hopeful look had passed between her and Adèle, who had instantly volunteered to help her. If nothing else was familiar to Lydia in the great strange city, the friendly presence of another lady of color seemed to reassure her, along with Adèle's obvious delight in little Ben.

*   *   *

A week later, the young Américaine with the cherubic baby on her hip entered the hallway at 30 avenue Henri Martin and was shown upstairs by the concierge, who ruffled little Ben's curls and told la jeune dame that Adèle awaited her in the kitchen of the apartment of Madame Crafts. Or so Lydia understood her to say.

"I thought this would be better. La cuisinère m'a interdit la cuisine là-bas," Adèle jerked a thumb toward Annie's apartments, smiling at Lydia's fearful look. "Elle fait quelque chose de compliqué pour ce soir."

"Someone's in the…kitchen?" Lydia ventured, setting the baby in the highchair. "Mrs. Shaw's kitchen?"

"Ah oui, vous faîtes déja bien!" Adèle laughed. "The cook is making something complicated for tonight, so we are forbidden the kitchen. Aimerez-vous du café?"

"Mais oui, I would love some coffee, and I've brought something for you that I made myself." Lydia reached into her handbag and withdrew a white paper sack, which she laid shyly on the table. Adèle peered in and her smile widened. "Des pralines, oui? Fait à main?"

"Main. That's hand, isn't it? Yes! I mean—oui. It's the only French thing I know how to make. So far," Lydia added.

Adèle poured them both coffee and added cream to her own, noting that Lydia had taken nothing in hers. "Please—use up that cream." She laid the pale gold pralines on a white plate.

"Oh, I'm used to it this way." Lydia's eyes lingered on the little jug, however, and after a moment she pulled it toward her and poured a sizable dollop into her coffee.

"You are still nursing, *oui?*"

Lydia blushed and nodded.

"It is good for the mother to have milky things. It will make the p'tit stronger."

"I'll take that as my excuse, then, Mademoiselle."

"Please call me Adèle—I hope we will be friends?" It was Adèle's turn to hesitate.

"Of course!" Lydia's face brightened. "Bien sûr?—and please, it's Lydia."

"Très bien! For today, we take a little time to know each other, yes? I will send you home with a little French, certainement. I come from Martinique, in the Mer des Caraïbes—the Caribbean—you have heard of it?"

"A beautiful island, isn't it? The Island of Flowers?"

"L'île des Fleurs, oui!"

Lydia repeated the phrases, Adèle correcting her pronunciation. "How did you come all the way from there to Paris?"

"Ah, that is a long story." Adèle leaned over with the pot and warmed up Lydia's coffee. "My mother, on the island, she was a blanchisseuse—a laundress—"

Lydia's eyes widened. "So was mine!"

"Vraiment? Is she still alive, *ta maman?*"

"She died five years ago, from a fever. I still miss her. I went to her grave to say goodbye, and felt as if I were abandoning her."

"Five years is not so long ago. I lost my maman when I was eight—"

"Oh, how awful!"

"Our blanchisseuses would take their washing to a big stream on the mountainside—the Rivière Roxelane. There had been heavy rains, though that day was sunny, and there was an inondation subite—a flash flood, you'd say? It came up so quickly, and swept her away as well as some of her friends. They tell me she was the best, so careful with the linens—it was the trousseau from a wedding that day, the bedsheets and table-linens—so fine and light. She tried to save them, but she got tangled up in them and couldn't escape. The rich people in St-Pierre knew how good she was, so she had as much business as she liked—"

"My mother did her washing in a wooden tub with a washboard," Lydia remembered, "outdoors over a fire. She made her own soap—"

"Mine did too! She taught me how. But now, about you, ma petite. What do you think of Paris so far?" Adèle helped herself to another praline.

"Everyone's so kind. I'm a little scared, though—I know so little French—"

"Alors, we will fix that! And you have your husband again, that's good?"

"Yes," Lydia said slowly, "of course…"

Adèle scrutinized the younger woman's face. "Your little one, he's doing well? He looks very healthy."

"Yes, thank goodness! Just think—he can learn French at the same time as English, maybe easier—perhaps you can speak to him directly, Mam'zelle—"

"Please—it's Adèle!"

"Bien sûr. Adèle." Lydia said, looking proud of herself.

"Très bien! Now tell me, when you were a little girl, did you dream of going to strange places? I wanted to go to Paris—"

"So did I! It sounded so elegant, so exotic—and here I am." Lydia shook her head.

"Is it what you expected?" Adèle pushed the plate of pralines toward her guest. Little Ben grabbed one as it went by, stuffing it in his mouth and crowing with wicked glee. His mother jumped up and tried to extricate it.

"He shouldn't eat sweet things—his teeth won't come in right!" Lydia retrieved the remnants of the treat and wiped her hands on a napkin. "I'm sorry—you asked me a question. About Paris—it's a lot bigger than I thought it would be. We went to New York to get on the ship, so we passed through many cities on the train—Richmond and Washington and Philadelphia—but Paris is the only one I've really seen. This neighborhood, now, so pretty and green, not how I thought of a city—"

Adèle smiled. "What Madame Annie calls the 'real city' is across the river. Passy was—what do they say in English? A suburb? A satellite village—until it was made part of Paris."

"I love to look at the Tower," Lydia said. "What a marvel! How do you say that in French?"

"La Tour Eiffel, quelle merveille! That's mer-vay. I love to see it all lit up at night. At first, many people thought it was ugly. But now everyone likes it."

Lydia cleared her throat. "You don't live here in Passy, do you?"

"Mais non! I have rooms in my cousin's house, near the Hôpital Saint-Louis and the Canal St-Martin. I come here on the omnibus. It's a long way—sometimes I spend the night, if Madame hosts a dinner. She has not done that often, but more so since her sister and family moved back to America. Since she met Monsieur Jackson, in fact."

"She's been so kind to him—and to me."

Adèle leaned toward Lydia confidentially. "It has been good for her—after so many years with her sister and nieces, she begins to have a life of her own at last. To make her own friends."

"Jackson says her mother-in-law tried to move in here—"

"Oh la la! What an affaire that was. Madame la belle-mère Shaw had plans to make her home here. She had persuaded Madame Crafts—Madame Shaw's sister—to let her use this apartment, and she planned for Madame Annie to care for her in her old age. Madame Annie was beside herself! She never liked the lady, you see."

"But she's not here now, the older Mrs. Shaw?"

"Voilà how they got rid of her. Madame Annie gave the apartment to Jackson and Monsieur le Comte de Leiningen and Mam'zelle Tallie—" Adèle broke off, as if uncertain whether to go on. "Have you met them yet? And Mam'zelle Cooper?"

Lydia shook her head. "Jackson's told me about them—we'll meet them soon, he says. And Mr. Tanner."

"Ah, oui, le jeune homme si gentil. Madame Annie commissioned a painting, and they took turns doing pieces of it—a huge thing—and modeling for it too."

Lydia looked around. "Where is it now?"

"Monsieur le Comte took it to his own studio. But not till long after Madame Sarah Shaw and her granddaughter arrived and walked in while they were working on it—Mam'zelle Tallie ordered her out and said they weren't to be disturbed—she was half-naked at the time too!" Adèle laughed at the memory.

Lydia's brow creased. "She was their model?"

"And they hers. And Mam'zelle Cooper's. It was—comment dit-on—a mythological scene. 'Nymph abducted by satyrs.' Jackson was one satyr and the Comte the other."

"That doesn't sound like Jackson's style of painting. But then he's in Paris now—"

"The idea was to horrify the new arrival and drive her away. But Madame Sarah Shaw insisted she had the right to the place. She tried to make them move to another studio. So finally, Madame Annie had to tell her the truth—that she did not want her here."

Lydia looked troubled. "Why did Miz Shaw hate her mother-in-law so much? I never even met mine—she died a long time ago. Not that she'd have liked *me*."

"Enfin, she blames her for her husband's death. If he had not taken that regiment, Madame Annie thinks, he would have survived the war. She believes his mother made him do it. The elder Madame is—une femme authoritaire—a bossy woman?"

Lydia's face fell. Adèle realized she must have thought of Madame Annie's husband as a true hero for their race. But if he'd only done it because of his bossy mother, was it still heroic?

"This Monsieur Comte," Lydia said. "He teaches art?"

"And is himself an artist, bien sûr. Tallie studies with him at the Académie Julian—"

"Jackson's been studying there—"

"Oui, until he was admitted to the École."

"What kind of an artist is she—Mam'zelle Tallie?"

"A good one! Portraits are her forté, says Madame Annie." Adèle recalled something and clapped her hands. "Monsieur showed them his painting of you and le p'tit." She patted the baby's head. "And Monsieur le Comte wants to paint you too. But I warn you—he is un séduiseur—a flirt, you would say. He thought you were very beautiful."

Lydia flushed. "He's never even met me!"

"Perhaps it was to annoy Monsieur Jackson. I think Monsieur

le Comte is a little jealous of him—" This time, Adèle's self-censorship was unmistakable.

Lydia frowned. "Jealous—of what?"

Adèle recovered herself. "Because he is younger and more handsome, bien sûr. And perhaps because he is American. The French find certain Americans fascinating, if they are as—agréable as Monsieur Jackson."

"The École des Beaux Arts—am I saying that right?" Adèle nodded encouragement. "Do they allow ladies to study there?"

"Hélas, no. Mam'zelle Tallie and Mam'zelle Cooper long to go there. They do not charge as Julian's does, and it is the premier school of art in Europe. But it is only for the men. The only ladies there are the models."

"I don't think we'd call them ladies in America," Lydia said wryly. "Do either of the artist ladies model there?"

"Mam'zelle Tallie, oui. She needs the money. Mam'zelle Cooper has money from her family. Alors, shall we speak a little French?"

Jackson and Lydia's courtship had come as a surprise to both of them, but he, having inherited his father's chivalrous ways, quickly made his honorable intentions clear. Lydia was skeptical in the early days; Jackson was not the first man, nor even the first white man, who had shown interest in her. He proved the first who was sincere in his aims, and won in turn her affections and her hand.

But since they had had so little time together as man and wife before their sad and necessary parting, Jackson's long absence created ample room for doubt. So many men she knew or had heard tales of weren't to be trusted—her own father, who'd quickly found other women to comfort him even before her young mother left him and the little farm for life in town. Jackson's great-uncle Crawford Burwell who, local gossip said, was her own grandfather, having forced himself on her grandmother Lily, and on other young women in the quarters. The men, colored and white, who had buzzed around her mother, and started buzzing around Lydia herself as soon as she became a woman. She'd had to fend them off even after she'd had Ben— nothing unusual for a "colored girl" and no one thinking much of it, least of all imagining her as the honored and cherished wife of the white man who had fathered him.

In the lonely nights in the two-room cottage whose living room doubled as her sewing studio, she had wondered about Jackson's doings among the notoriously wanton females of Paris. Even if he resisted their attentions, they would surely find him a target. Might loneliness have made him susceptible to the wiles of some bohèmienne?

Chapter 27

loysius O'Connor arrived at Annie's welcoming dinner with Henry Tanner and Jackson's former flat mate James Haverford.

"Tanner and I are just back in town, and delighted by your kind invitation. We've been having a grand time at Pont-Aven, haven't we?" the Irish giant boomed, clapping the slight Tanner on the back. "I don't know if you'll have met Mr. Haverford—" the pale, neatly dressed young man turned a soft blue gaze on his hostess and bowed, black hair flopping into his eyes and dashed aside in what was clearly a characteristic gesture.

"Enchanté, Mr. Haverford." Annie gave him her hand. "Weren't you and Mr. Burwell garret-mates until recently?"

The lad grinned crookedly. "We were, ma'am, and it's awfully quiet around the place now. But I'm told he'd got a better offer—"

"I did indeed, Jimmy," said Jackson, coming in behind him with Lydia on his arm. "My dear, may I present James Haverford. My wife, Lydia Burwell."

The momentary glint of surprise in Haverford's eyes quickly gave way to warmth. Lydia extended a slender hand and he took it as if afraid of breaking it. "I guess you did at that! She's much better looking than her picture, Burwell—well, that's why we're in art school, to improve. An honor to meet you, ma'am. And who's this?"

Behind them, Adèle entered, carrying little Ben and smiling as if she had won a lottery.

"My son and heir, Master Benjamin Burwell." Jackson's arm swept over the pair. Benjamin twisted in Adèle's arms and reached for his father's neck.

With Jackson momentarily distracted, Henry Tanner emerged from behind Haverford into Lydia's line of sight. Something like surprised recognition passed between them, though Annie was sure they had never met. "Mrs. Burwell, have you met Mr. Henry Tanner? Perhaps Jackson has mentioned him—another of our young American artists—"

"I'm delighted, Mr. Tanner," Lydia said, extending her hand. "Jackson's been telling me how much he admires your work—"

But not that you were a colored man, Annie surmised. She saw the shoulders of Lydia and the young artist drop slightly, as if the other's presence had allowed each to relax a sort of vigilance that must prevail in other company.

"He's very kind," Tanner said, "but here's a gentleman who can teach both of us a few things." He turned to allow Annie to introduce Aloysius O'Connor, who beamed unabashed admiration in Lydia's direction but was, for once, vocally subdued.

A bustle in the hallway announced the other ladies of the dinner-party, Julia Greene and Retta Reubell in brilliant silks and, finally, Tallie DeKuyper in a blue muslin summer frock which had belonged to Annie's niece Marian. Her gaze took in the assembly, stopping on Lydia and on the golden-curled child Jackson was holding. She let out a silent little "Oh!" and fingered a cameo at her collar. After introductions were made to the senior ladies, Annie took Tallie by the arm and brought her forward.

"Mrs. Burwell, allow me to present my friend Miss DeKuyper, who's an artist and a student at the Académie Julian."

Lydia looked at Annie and bobbed her head toward Tallie in a little bow, her smile tentative. "I'm delighted, Miss DeKuyper. I've heard so much about you from Jackson."

Tallie's eyebrows shot up. "He's told us very little about *you*, Mrs. Burwell," And then, giving Lydia her warmest smile, "which I hope to remedy by our friendly acquaintance. And I've so looked forward to meeting your little one!"

Really, for all her bohemian airs, the girl was remarkably well-bred. Mention of her son put Lydia at ease. She turned to Adèle, who handed over the baby. "Here he is—Ben, this is Miss DeKuyper." The baby chuckled and hid his head in the crook of his mother's arm. "I don't reckon he'll remember names for a while yet."

"Might he remember 'Tallie'? That's what everyone calls me." Tallie reached out a finger with a look of inquiry. Lydia nodded and Tallie chucked the little boy under his chin. "Hello, Ben, I'm Tallie. What a pretty boy you are." Her voice caught slightly on the last words and she turned aside, darting a glance at Jackson that made him flush. "Mrs. Shaw, Miss Cooper—Pauline— asked me to tell you how sorry she is to miss your dinner. She hopes to meet Mrs. Burwell very soon." Her composure restored, she turned to Aloysius O'Connor and took his arm. "I do hope you'll be taking me in to dinner," she said, just as Bertrand de Leiningen entered.

"That pleasure will be a younger man's this evening, alannah."

the Irish giant waved a hand toward James Haverford. "I've been asked to accompany Mrs. Burwell meself."

Tallie smiled brightly, braced her shoulders and set off to intercept Jackson's friend, darting a brief look at Bertrand as he made an admiring bow and took Lydia Burwell's hand to kiss.

"Perhaps inviting Tallie last night was a mistake," Annie said over a tisane in Julia's parlor.

"Things were a bit uneasy when the ladies withdrew," Julia said, "but it was bound to be awkward. D'you think Jackson has 'fessed up' about his little dalliance?"

Annie put down her teacup. "I doubt it. But it's natural to wonder what one's handsome husband has been up to during a lengthy absence…do you remember the young colored woman who published her Sea Island diaries in the *Atlantic*, a year after Rob's—?" She bit her lip, the painful memory sharpening again.

Julia, a quick study as usual, laid a hand on hers. "And this must seem to you like the other side of that coin. A wife would naturally be on the alert, and it mightn't take more than a casual mention or two—and then they meet, and no denying young Tallie's attractive—"

"Even as subdued as she was. I thought the baby might break the ice. But she seemed, if anything, hesitant about holding Ben when he was offered."

Julia brushed powdered sugar from her dress. "They're a convincing demonstration of the wife's bond with the husband, aren't they? Tallie might have accepted the situation on a rational level, but hadn't yet done so with her feelings. They don't have to be friends, you know. Your home is probably the only place they'd meet."

"I suppose—"

"You needn't always make everybody happy. It's not what you set out to do. Becoming a real Parisienne, isn't that what you said? Mingling with artists and scholars, painting, perhaps a little collecting—and what are you doing instead? The same thing you did with your nieces—"

Annie looked stricken. "I'm being the foster mother again?"

"In Jackson's case, I don't suppose you could have refused a dying request from your erstwhile chevalier. And Jackson is a charming young fellow. His situation was, if not pitiable, likely to invite womanly sympathy. With Tallie, though—"

"She's the first friend I've made independently, after yourself. It's only natural—"

"Friend—or niece? It strikes me that your interest has been more than a little—maternal." Julia watched Annie's lips tighten.

"No! I admire her—her independence, her dedication. She's working against the odds, given her sex—having forgone a ladylike reputation and prospects for an advantageous marriage."

"You consider that admirable?" Julia's cheek twitched.

"I do! If the price of a life and vocation of one's own is a lost reputation, there are other ways to love and be loved, and to thrive in the world—and…"

"Go on," Julia said gently.

Annie took a deep breath. "I want to help her with that. Picturing myself, born thirty or forty years later than I was, setting out on a similar course."

Julia went to the window, gazing out on the rainy street. "It's not too late, you know—if you know what you want."

"I suppose…" Annie said, a note of wonder in her voice, "that I've never really known what I *want*. Until the family left, there was only what I *ought*. So I haven't really asked, much less answered the question of—my purpose in life. That sounds so pretentious, doesn't it?"

"Could it be that in Tallie you see someone who's doing something that would bring *you* joy if *you* were doing it?"

"You mean—art? Painting?"

"It could be anything—playing the piano, composing music, decorating. Writing poetry or, heaven forfend, a three-volume novel. Designing dresses—I don't know. We know what *isn't* for you—good works, needlework, charity committees, superficial socializing. I watched you at that first salon of Retta's, unfolding a petal at a time. How they listened to you, took your words seriously. You belonged there, didn't you?"

Annie twisted her rings. "I felt that way."

"You love music, and books, and art. You're knowledgeable, and not in a superficial way."

"I started learning to paint once—really paint, not just girlish dabbling. A long time ago. Just after the wedding, actually. And you know how much I've been enjoying it since I took it up again."

"I have a suggestion," Julia said, returning to her armchair. "Postpone your trip to Cannes. Take some lessons here—but not with your protégés."

"But I already—"

"Buy some of their work, if you like it, so they can spend more time making art. It's what they most want to do, after all. You wanted to redecorate, didn't you? A few nice pieces of your own would get you started. Sell the ones from your parents' collection that you don't care for—or store them, if sentiment forbids. Turn the Crafts' apartments into your personal art gallery."

Annie's face brightened, then clouded. "Jackson and Lydia."

"What of them?"

"They aren't legally married yet."

"What more could you have done to bring that about? Or are you waiting for an invitation?"

"I fear the matter's in doubt now," Annie said, a wave of sadness washing over her. "The way she and Tallie kept apart from each other—when the ladies withdrew—as though she knows. And I tried so hard to..." Her eyes filled.

Julia put a hand on her arm. "Why do you feel so responsible for Lydia too?"

"Because I owe her—and her family—a great debt." Annie told Julia of the Haggertys' long friendship with the Burwells, the plantation visits, the memory of the young slave-woman, Lydia's grandmother, unjustly punished for her younger self's carelessness.

"And the blood-sacrifice of a husband wasn't enough to pay that debt? If indeed it was one?"

Annie reached for a book from Julia's shelf, opening it at a page tabbed by a ribbon. "What was it Mr. Lincoln said? ... *until all the wealth piled by the bondsman's two hundred and fifty years of unrequited toil shall be sunk, and until every drop of blood drawn by the lash shall be paid by another drawn with the sword...* Our wealth—my wealth—hasn't been sunk, Julia. It came from that unrequited toil as surely as the Burwells' did. And it wasn't I who offered Rob's life as a sacrifice, or a reparation. It was his parents."

"But it was you who bore the sharpest loss. Your future, your happiness, the children you might have had. The Shaws and the Sturgises, God knows, had a lot to atone for—not slavery," she said in answer to Annie's puzzled look, "but the China trade, which enslaved men with opium as surely as with shackles. We're all soiled by ill-gotten gains. No getting around that."

"One way or another, I feel an obligation to Lydia."

"She and Jackson must work things out for themselves," Julia said, more sharply now. Either they'll reconcile, or they will part. In the latter case, you can help her and the little boy with their living situation. In the former, for which we may hope, you may dance at their wedding and get on with your life."

"What a ridiculous position," Annie shook her head. "Fifty-six years old and still wondering what one should be when one grows up."

"Better late than never, don't you think? Most women never even ask themselves that question. Wife, mother, grandmamma—the world answers it for us. You're lucky, in a way. And fifty-six isn't so old. You've still got time."

"There may be something in what you say." Annie rose and reached for her reticule. "Meanwhile, I'm due at Retta Reubell's."

Miss Reubell's windows were flung open to capture the few light breezes wafting from the Elysée Palace gardens and the Place Marigny. Despite the day's sticky warmth, her guests were dressed impeccably or eccentrically as usual, with only a few loosened cravats and an energetic fluttering of fans betraying discomfort.

Retta handed Annie a glass of chilled wine. "You just missed a fascinating discussion that I feared might end in fisticuffs.

Between M. Aldrophe—"

"Rothschild's pet architect, who did the Hotel de Marigny?" Annie waved her arm toward the famous mansion.

"The same. And a young upstart named Guimard, who insists that there's no distinction between the fine arts and the decorative. All that matters is the creation of beauty, he says."

"That seems unobjectionable."

"Aldrophe felt Guimard was being dismissive of the architect's technical skills—plumbing, load bearing, that sort of thing. He pled an appointment and left in rather a huff, from the looks of it." Retta seemed amused.

"M. Guimard sounds interesting. Can you introduce us? I may have some work for him."

"You're going to redecorate? What fun! Guimard goes in for what the Belgians are calling "Art Nouveau"—if you go with him, you'll be very avant-garde. He lives in the Sixteenth too. Aloysius O'Connor's here, and was asking after you. But here comes Bertrand, with someone I don't know yet."

The Comte was in the doorway, accompanied by a tall, solidly built man with a lost expression and an unfashionably long gray beard. There was something familiar about him. As Bertrand towed him over to where she and Retta stood, Annie broke into a smile.

"Mr. Brown, is it not?"

The tall man beamed in return. "Mrs. Annie Shaw! After all this time—I was hoping our paths might cross in Paris, and here you are!"

"You know each other?" said Bertrand, who had evidently been looking forward to introducing them. He turned to Retta. "Miss Reubell, may I present Mr. Harrison Bird Brown?"

Retta stepped forward and offered her hand. "Mr. Brown, I'm delighted to meet you at last. I've heard much about you from Mrs. Mason." Was it wishful thinking, or had Annie caught a look of chagrin crossing the artist's face at the mention of Alice Mason?

She turned to Bertrand. "Mr. Brown was my first—so far my only—serious painting instructor, a great many years ago. I hear that you've forsaken Maine for London?"

The corners of the artist's fine mouth drooped. "I had begun to find my native places cold and empty, having lost both my sons and finally my wife. My daughter Nellie and her new husband Mr. Seaverns, a Bostonian, asked me to come and live with them in London. I had no good reason to refuse."

"I hope you'll find Dr. Johnson's famous dictum about London to be true. And if you ever do find yourself tiring of the place, you have only to visit Paris to find refreshment and renewal, as I have been doing these last months. But how rude I am—you haven't even a glass of wine yet—" Annie turned and found Bertrand beaming at them with a wineglass in each hand.

"You must retire to the divan and regale each other with your doings since your last meeting," he said with faint irony. Mr. Brown was old enough to be Bertrand's father, and Annie had a flash of regret that her younger friend might be seeing her in that generational light. She flushed at the recollection of their flirtations, and at her delusion that there might be something serious in Bertrand's attentions.

Here was a man with whom she had once felt herself falling in love. And, she blushed to remember, not yet two months married at the time…was he really Alice Mason's new paramour? He didn't seem her type. But, then, neither had Senator Sumner.

Chapter 28

June 23, 1863

Strolling along the bluestone wharves of Portland with her father, Annie's surprised to find herself glad to be away for a few days, although temporarily out of reach of Rob's letters. One doesn't have to dress up for society here as in Lenox, which the Haggertys fear is being taken over by the smart set. She delights in the salt air, with undercurrents of fish from the warehouses and burnt caramel from their host's sugar refinery, and the bustle of a growing industrial port.

Ogden takes in a great sniff. "Ah! The sweet smell of money!" He's trying to teach Little Mac, not yet grown into his huge paws, to walk on a leash; the Irish wolfhound sits and regards him with inquiring intelligence, as if his words foretell a treat.

They've accepted the invitation of his old friend John Bundy Brown (not being a diehard abolitionist, he insists on the middle name), whom Annie and Clem refer to as "Papa's friend the sugar baron," to visit his new mansion and art gallery. He and Ogden have been friends since the amicable and, Annie guesses, brandy-soaked resolution of a tussle over a Powers bust at an auction in

'45 that, her father reports, came within a hair's breadth of becoming unseemly. The families have visited one another regularly.

She's glad to be married, she realizes. She has only now, at twenty-eight, become an adult in the eyes of the world, and she's relieved to have escaped the vigilance of New York's duennas, the old crows, of which there are always a surfeit at festive gatherings. Tonight she's going to dance to her heart's content at the ball Mr. Brown's hosting in their honor, and no one will have anything to say about it. As a married lady she may give her dances out where she pleases and accept bouquets from admirers.

Rob might not care for that. But Rob's been writing home with chatty news of teas and receptions given in the regiment's honor, of plantation belles who seem happy enough to betray brothers and sweethearts, off fighting these Northern invaders. She will write to him of the fine time she's had. A little jealousy may add motivation to keep himself safe to come back to her.

Perhaps it's not such a bad thing that he left the Second Massachusetts. His old comrades were in some dirty business at Chancellorsville, the very week of her all-too-brief honeymoon with Rob at Lenox. The white heat of the war is now in northern Virginia, the Confederates rumored to be planning an invasion of the North itself. The Sea Islands are a relative backwater, long since pacified. It's safe for a few days to dance among old friends and good-looking strangers—those not already in the field. Where any man worth the name has already gone.

As they sit out an overly energetic polka that evening at the ball, Clem hisses in Annie's ear, "who is that Byronic-looking fellow dancing with Mrs. Phil?" Annie squints across the ballroom, following her sister's gaze. "Hmm—the forehead is Byronic. He's one of Mr. Brown's pet artists—we met him once—but his name escapes me."

The music crashes to a stop and the dancers disperse to chairs along the walls and to supper tables in the room beyond. Fanny Brown, pink and panting in sunny yellow brocade, tows the gentleman in question over to their spot beside a huge potted palm. His forehead is high and noble-looking, his nose long and Roman, his brown eyes bright.

"Ladies, may I present Mr. Harrison Bird Brown? Mr. Brown— Mrs. Shaw and her sister Miss Haggerty. Mr. Brown returned recently from a long artistic sojourn in the West. *"*

Annie tries not to smile at Fanny's provincial awe and gives the man her hand. Brown towers over her even more than he does Fanny, and his dark, penetrating eyes—stormy, intelligent eyes—are fixed on her in a most disconcerting fashion, his hold on her hand firm. She glances down at her gown, to see if she's spilled something, but the new garnet silk with its looped overlay of purple lace and beading is unsullied, her décolletage within acceptable limits.

"You don't remember me, Miss Hagg—uh, Mrs. Shaw," he smiles. "But I recall a most entertaining afternoon in Mr. Brown's library, perhaps twelve years ago, and a lively discussion of the works of Mr. Cropsey."

Annie feels a warmth passing between them, a field or bubble that's shutting out the other two. Fanny Brown's smile thins and she says, "Annie, Mr. Brown—no relation, as Papa's always saying—is a renowned artist these days! His seascapes have been exhibited at—"

"—the National Academy!" Annie interrupts. "I didn't make the connection at the time, but I saw them back in, '58, was it? Clem, you remember?"

Clem smiles politely and inclines her head. It's a sorrow of Ogden's life that she has no interest in art other than for its decorative potential in a drawing-room.

"I long to see Monhegan Island. Who can imagine a more romantic landscape—seascape, I should say—such passion in those crashing waves!" Annie stops. Her mind has been drawing correspondences between the action of a stormy tide and the act of love. Which, having tasted and enjoyed, she's dismayed to find herself missing.

"I should love to show you Monhegan. I won't be going back there for a month or so—but perhaps you'd like to come and see my studio? On Cushing Island, in the bay—an hour by boat." Belatedly, Brown widens his glance to encompass all three ladies, but it swings back to Annie.

"I should like that very much," Annie says promptly. "Clem, we're not engaged for Friday, are we? Would that suit you, Mr. Brown?"

"Excellently. I must only confer with my wife and make sure we haven't other plans for the day." Brown looks out over the couples forming up for the Lancers. "There was something about taking Baby to the doctor, but I think that's next week. Let me find her and I'll let you know at once—"

Annie abruptly turns away from him to greet her partner for the quadrille. It was duplicitous of Mr. Harrison Bird Brown not to mention a wife until she had committed herself to his invitation; she feels vaguely betrayed, though there was nothing overtly improper in either the invitation or its acceptance.

But she can't resist the opportunity. Wild surf against jagged rocks, an artist's solitary retreat, redolent of linseed oil, salt spray and starched canvases—she wants to see how he's set it up, in case some day she furnishes a studio for herself. She's told no one how much painting matters to her. The family praises her watercolor landscapes and oil portraits, but not, even in her father's case, with any degree of discrimination; they tell her what they think she wants to hear.

This trip to Cushing Island is merely an artistic exploration, she *reasons. But she has an empty slot on her dance card, before the last waltz, and she's wondering how to get Harrison Bird Brown's name on that line.*

She whirls herself dizzy in the quadrille, but she won't sit down; she doesn't want questions from her mother about whether she's "feeling quite well." If she has a secret to share, it will be Rob who hears it first... so why am I standing by the punch bowl, craning my neck to find the man who wants to take me to his artist's island hideaway? Which he shares, apparently, with a wife and child?

The artist comes up on her blind side and touches her gently under the elbow. "Shall I fetch you a glass of punch?" He picks up the scrolled ladle and deftly fills a silver cup with pink liquid. "Sarah—Mrs. Brown—is engaged in town on Friday," he says, handing her the cup, "but she insists that I should host you all without her. You will come, won't you?"

Annie's about to say that she'll have to make sure her mother is available, but remembers that it will be perfectly all right to go with Clem, for whom Annie herself, being duly married, now constitutes a proper chaperone. Perhaps Ogden will come too; she'd like him to take an interest in Harrison Bird Brown.

"I believe we can manage it. Perhaps Mr.-Brown-no-relation can arrange a boat for us."

Harrison Brown breaks into another broad smile. "I shall book you space on—shall we say the ten o'clock ferry? And speaking of space, Mrs. Shaw, is that a blank spot I see on your dance card? The next-to-last waltz?"

Annie blushes, having been dangling the card from her wrist on its silky pink cord to display its inside surface. "Oh, is it?" She picks it up and glances at it. "I suppose it is."

"I have been dancing all night with ladies named Mrs. Brown. Half the people in Portland are named Brown, you know. It will make a nice change."

Whirling in his arms, Annie's troubled by the electric effect his touch is having on her. She's a newly married woman, deeply in love with a man who's serving his country in its hour of crisis, with more depth and dedication than most of his peers. A man who's reawakened her senses and her appetites, who may already have given her a child. And still she wants this great dark-bearded man to hold her close in his strong arms, let her sink her head into his chest and carry her off to his salt-scented island where the waves crash and foam...

By Friday evening, Annie has managed to convince herself that she's in love with the artist's life, not with the artist himself—with the sea-girt island's sheer cliffs, the waves loud and spectacular as fireworks, the simple, cozy studio—warmed by the sun this time of year—and the abundance of canvases in various stages of completion, the paint-splattered pots and their little forests of brushes, the scents of paint and oil and turpentine.

Dear Rob, *she writes,* between Staten Island and Casco Bay, the seawater is getting into my blood. Mr. Brown, the artist I mentioned, was so kind to show us around his island, and I thought how much I should like to live in such a place—at least in fine weather—and have a little studio where I could dabble in my landscapes. Mr. Brown gave me and Clem a short lesson, and he generously praised my 'eye for line and color.' Do you think we might have a home by the sea some day? A modest little cottage...

She's not telling him the whole of it—how Brown took her and Clem down a path to a small sandy cove, with a cliff looming to the west, on a calm day, warm and slightly overcast but with an occasional breeze riffling the hair on her neck. Sailboats dancing in the bay, and just as she'd imagined, the passionate surf against those sheer walls of stone.

"Plein air is the thing these days, ladies—I shall set you to little oil-sketches, or impressions as they're calling them in France." Brown had gone off to see to something in the studio after giving them a few pointers for an impression of the sea at the base of the cliff, and came back to stop behind her. When she turned, his face wore a look of astonished pleasure.

"Forgive me, Mrs. Shaw—how long have you been painting? You have a deft hand with a brush—indeed, a striking eye for line and color. This could sell as a miniature, if you wished."

She blushed at the praise, and he went on. "It is not merely the composition, though that is notable. It is—how should I put it?—the feeling you have captured. The emotion of the thing."

"You see, Annie?" Clem said, beaming at them both. "We've been telling you right along that you have talent. Truly, we all have," she assured Brown. "But it means so much more, coming from a real artist."

"As to that," Brown said quickly, "your father has as discerning an eye for art as anyone. You should take praise from him at face value."

"It's just my little hobby," Annie shrugged. "I've mostly done watercolors—the hills and dales around Lenox—but there's something I like about these oils. They're so much more forgiving, for one thing. I think I'll get some."

"Pray, do! I am only sorry you're here for such a short time—I should enjoy working with you on some real canvases. But I have colleagues in New York who summer at Lenox. I shall write to them about giving you lessons, if you'd like. You ought not to waste such a gift."

She would like that very much, she'd assured him. She's done little painting since things grew more serious with Rob: so much to attend to, the daily letters, the wedding preparations, the distractions of his physical presence—so brief, now, it seems. Rob knows little about this aspect of her—that she sketches as a well-bred girl would do embroidery, or play the piano, as a pastime and to entertain at family gatherings.

Until now, Annie herself has never viewed painting as anything but her pastime. And while it's agreeable to be told that one should not be wasting one's gift, she wonders if Mr. Harrison Bird Brown was entirely disinterested. She is, after all, the daughter of one of New York's more notable art patrons, and Brown may wish to enlarge his marketplace beyond the provincial environs of Portland, Maine.

In a house by the sea, she could escape the numbing social rounds of the City, feel the wind in her loosened hair on a fine sparkling morning, enjoy the sight of children digging with little spades in the sand and bringing her starfish to admire. Rob would grow permanently tanned, go fishing with friends and bring them home dinner...

She wonders, as she often does, where he is right this minute. Somewhere on that humid, moss-hung coast, perhaps developing a taste for seaside life himself. But the lowlands of South Carolina surely can't compare with this wild, rocky, island-dotted bay, the sort of place where another Emily Brontë might spin savage tales of fiery women and their pirate lovers. Perhaps she'll write such a tale herself, publish it under a man's name and shock everyone when she reveals herself. She loved to write adventure stories as a child, and still has her juvenile embarrassments tied up in ribbons on a wardrobe shelf. She can't bear to throw them away. Perhaps because she remembers reading them to her brother Oggie, who sat cross-legged and wide-

eyed in the nursery and wouldn't let her stop till the story was done.

She'll read them to their son. It's going to be a boy; she's sure of it. He won't care how silly or old-fashioned they are. She'll make sure Rob's out of earshot; she can't bear the thought of him laughing at them. Odd how protective one feels of one's own frail creations.

But she is proud of this little painting of the Cushing Island cliffs, and she longs to stay in Portland and explore the bay with a few canvases and a box of paints. There's really no reason to go back, either to Lenox or New York, other than that the family is expected in one place or another. Well, she and Rob have formed a new family now, and surely that should give her some right to set her own itinerary. But still, a woman, even a married woman, can't really go about alone. It just isn't done.

If she's right about the changes she's sensing in her body, she wouldn't be alone in any case; a new being will be growing within. But she won't tell anyone yet, not even Rob, until she's sure.

Chapter 29

ulia and Annie were drinking chilled Alsatian pils at an outdoor table of the Brasserie Lipp, on a steamy August afternoon with a hint of thunder in the air.

Julia's right eyebrow rose. "Bertrand tells me he has a rival for your affections."

"That suggests he thought himself in competition for them." Annie wiped a trace of foam from her lip. "I see no evidence of lovesick swainhood on his part."

Julia grinned. "You're avoiding me again. Who's this Mr. Black I've heard so little about? Bertrand says the two of you blathered away, and were only reluctantly parted when most of Retta's guests had left."

Annie was annoyed to find herself blushing. "Mr. *Brown* is an old acquaintance from my Haggerty days." In fact, their closest interaction had come when they met again in the month after Annie's marriage. "Clem and I had a painting lesson from him. He had a studio then, on an island in Casco Bay."

"How romantic!" Julia's smile widened. "Why haven't I heard of this before?"

"I'd forgotten all about him. Besides, he was married."

"—then. I understand he's a widower now?"

"Living in London with his daughter. According to Retta, he and Alice Mason are a twosome. Or so Alice told her in a letter."

"And what did you think?"

"Well, he never mentioned her—and before you ask, neither did I." Indeed, their conversation ended with Mr. Brown in an animated state, assuring Annie that he intended to visit Paris frequently "to revisit my numerous old friends here." They had exchanged addresses and promises to correspond. She was thinking of inviting him for a winter sojourn in Cannes, and resuming the long-interrupted painting lessons.

"I wonder if Alice's charms may be fading at last," Julia said with cheerful malice. "Perhaps this gentleman has more sense than Senator Sumner did."

"Age brings wisdom, they say." Annie decided not to mention that, besides Bertrand's barely concealed expression of chagrin, which she put down to his territoriality when his lady friends were paying attention to other males, she'd caught Aloysius O'Connor watching her and Mr. Brown with rather a glum look. She had found the Irish giant's company engaging; it hadn't occurred to her that his interest might be shading beyond friendship. Such intriguing possibilities all of a sudden...*how conceited I'm becoming*, she thought, with a tiny shake of her head.

"What are you grinning at?" said Julia.

"When will the Burwells have their—ah, formal wedding?" Tallie asked. She and Annie had picked up Julia and Carlotta from Julia's flat on the rue Bassano and were rattling along the boulevard de Clichy, en route to the Cabaret du Chat Noir in Montmartre.

Annie and Julia exchanged glances over Tallie's head. "I don't believe they've confirmed a date." Annie aimed for an off-handed tone. "I think Mrs. Burwell was tired by the journey, and wanted to give herself time to acclimate herself and Ben to Paris." The delay had her concerned. She suspected that Lydia had confronted Jackson about his relations with Tallie; the young women's tension had been apparent in the drawing-room after her welcoming dinner.

She was also concerned for Tallie. The girl was looking both worldly and ethereal in steel-gray silk with ruffled apron panels and a rosette at the bodice—a *pourboire*, she said, from a recent portrait-sitter, perhaps a little heavy and warm for the late-summer night—but she seemed paler and thinner, more subdued than on prior outings. Annie had helped her sweep up her gold hair with tortoiseshell combs and lent her a pair of fingerless black net gloves, to which Tallie had added a little black hat, tilted at a fetching angle. Julia was in silk moiré, in a hue Annie had teasingly labeled "eponymous Greene," trimmed in black lace and jet beads, and Annie herself in sparkling black trimmed with jet and silver bugle beads, another reworked gown of her mother's to suit their destination in the Parisian bohème. She had a private fancy that the costume resembled that of Berthe Morisot in Manet's famous painting.

Carlotta in her new bronze silk, her thick auburn hair piled high in a pompadour, sat across from Tallie and darted concerned glances toward her; Tallie's unaccustomed pallor had evidently registered with her as well. Lotta and Mother Shaw were to depart for Nice in two days. Annie and Julia had persuaded her to come for what was most likely her last fling in the demimonde. Bertrand, finishing a commission due the following day, would meet them later but had asked his friend Rivière, the artist whose shadow-play they were going to see, to reserve them a table. The ombres chinoises, as Rivière called them, would begin at ten, later than Annie was used to being abroad except for the odd consular reception or Colony charity ball, but a postprandial coffee had given her a second wind.

The carriage clattered to a halt and they emerged into soft, moist air, the afternoon's rain having cleared and a few stars beginning to show through ragged remnants of cloud. At a narrow, gabled doorway stood a fantastically attired Swiss Guard, complete with halberd, who waved them into the medieval-looking building. The cabaret seemed left over from an earlier time, nearly packed with couples and small groups of men on tiered benches, gazing enviously at Annie's party as it was seated at a table nearest the lantern-screen. A silver bucket containing a bottle of Pommery appeared, the cork silently extracted, the wine poured for the ladies and an extra flute left for "Monsieur le Comte," who arrived out of breath just as the lights were dimming, declining the champagne and requesting an absinthe and water. Tallie and Carlotta exchanged raised eyebrows.

"What have I done," Bertrand marveled, "to merit the company of four such lovely women in one evening? Miss Lowell, I must paint you in that gown." The waiter arrived with the little set, the slotted silver spoon with its tiny sugar-cube, the Green Fairy of which Annie had heard so much glimmering in its glass like a great emerald, and a little pitcher of ice-water, twinkling in the light of the magic lantern. Bertrand carefully let a few drops of water drip from the pitcher onto the sugar cube and into the thistle-shaped glass. The glassy green liquid turned a milky white. He sipped, grimaced, and added a few more drops.

"Are you seeing any visions, Comte Bertrand?" Carlotta was in a festive mood. "May I try?"

Bertrand smiled and pushed the glass toward her. She raised it, took a sip, and hastily set it down. "Licorice! Oh dear—it reminds me of a cough elixir I was forced to swallow as a child."

Annie's curiosity got the better of her. She took the glass and almost drained it with a healthy mouthful, instantly regretted. Licorice indeed, but mouth-numbing, astringent, unnatural. She tried to wash away the taste with Pommery, flagging down the waiter and ordering another absinthe for Monsieur, who was enjoying her discomfiture immensely. She passed the glass to Julia and Tallie, who finished it off between them just as the waiter placed a new glass before Bertrand. He covered the glass with his palm in mock alarm.

"We're cured of our morbid curiosity, Bertrand," said Julia. "I for one will stick to Champagne henceforth."

"Your costume suits the experiment, Madame Greene. Were you and Tallie to exchange dresses, she could pass for La Fée Verte from Muchas' poster." Tallie looked pleased.

"And has the Green Fairy ever visited you?" Annie inquired, her tongue still numb, and a curious dreamy sensation stealing over her.

"On one or two memorable occasions, which I recorded on canvas in a couple of my more fantastical works. Redonesque, if you like that sort of thing."

"—all blurry and luminous and impenetrable? Redon has never made much sense to me." Annie wished for a chunk of buttered baguette to get the licorice taste out of her mouth. She took a few more sips of the champagne, but it tasted peculiar now.

The house lights dimmed, the magic lantern glowed, and a marvelous series of silhouettes began to flow across the screen. *Les Métamorphoses d'Ovide* proved to be a languid journey through the great Roman's fantastical tales—here a beautiful nymph pursued by an amorous god, transformed into a tree of lacy, intricate delicacy; there the hapless hunter, spying the naked beauty of the virginal Artemis, turned into a stag and torn to pieces by his own hounds. Every image exquisitely detailed, more eloquent, more suggestive, in its concealments than a fully realized image could be. The naked goddess was voluptuously lingered over, the detail of a taut nipple and a rounded flank faithfully rendered, the damp curls at the neckline. Then the ravishing of the innocent Philomela, the details truly obscene, her attacker's huge phallus erect as he stalked menacingly toward her, the horrid detail of her tongue cut out, the relief in her transformation into a beautiful nightingale. All this accompanied by an invisible piano trio. Annie felt as if she were floating away—a pleasant, slightly frightening sensation. Perhaps she could grow accustomed to the taste of licorice.

There had been a mania for silhouettes during the War. Rob had insisted on her sitting for one and sending it to his winter encampment. So much more romantic than photographs, he said; instead of the wooden stare of a tintype, you could imagine the play of expressions across your love's face—amorous, flirtatious, ironic, laughing, pensive. He had sent Annie one in turn. She had treasured it, still had it somewhere, though for a panicked moment she couldn't think where. But she hadn't been able to imagine Rob's expressions; his silhouette was an enigmatic blank. If she could find it, and consume a little more of this curious green potion, perhaps she would see now what she had missed then...

Now the silhouettes on the screen were enacting her favorite of the Metamorphoses, the sweet, poignant tale of the humble old couple Baucis and Philemon, who gave food and shelter to gods disguised as beggars and so were allowed to die together and transform into an exquisite pair of trees: he an oak, she a linden, their leaves and branches intertwined forever over the little temple their home had become. What loving pair could not wish for such an eternity? Annie's throat closed, her eyes brimming at the thought of what had been taken from her and never found again. But it was George she saw, not Rob, the dark curls, the lean cheek, beloved cousin, husband that should have been, the one she would have chosen to share whatever senseless or thoughtless eternity might succeed their mortal existence. She resolved that when her time was over she would join him in Lenox, in the green burying yard of the Church on the Hill. Perhaps his dust and hers would eventually mingle. The thought comforted her. She came out of the reverie, thankful that the others were too intent on the elegant beauty of the shadow-figures to have noticed the momentary shaking of her depths.

The piano and violin began a frenetic duet, pursuing one another up and down the scales with infernal intensity. There was a new shadow-play, *Les Bacchae et le châtiment*—" downfall? punishment? *de Pentheus*. Dozens of naked women, some grossly fat, some slender but voluptuous, rolling like a wave across a hillside, encountering a band of shaggy, horned satyrs, hoisting great flagons from which wavy streams flowed—a depiction in motion, it seemed, of the frieze in a Grecian vase, lingering on a dance that devolved into mass copulation, drawing gasps from the rapt audience, a stifled start of revulsion from poor sheltered Carlotta. At length the Bacchantes encircling the hapless heretic king, an inchoate crowding, an arm emerging with a severed head, still crowned...a solitary bowed figure returning to stand devastated in the middle of the screen—Pentheus' mother, Agave, with her son's heart dripping from a stick, who in her god-drunk rage had led the wild women to tear her son limb from limb like a pack of beasts. The music dying away into something like a funeral dirge.

The screen went dark, the house lights flickered to life, and the audience erupted in applause. Carlotta sat stunned; Tallie looked thoughtful and clapped lightly.

"Well," said Julia, "there's something you don't see every day—are you all right, my dear?" She was looking anxiously at her grand-niece.

"I'm fine, dear aunt—these are the stories rendered truly, after all—most of the time they leave out the, ah, sensational details the ancients supplied. Strange, isn't it," Carlotta turned to Annie, "that the more advanced the civilization, the more it feels the need to hide these elemental aspects of human nature? I admit I was shocked at first—but how much healthier to let us see ourselves as we truly are!"

"Well said, Miss Lowell," said Tallie. "You have a true Parisienne sensibility!"

Annie watched Carlotta's face fall. It burst on her like a lightning-flash how grieved the girl must be at leaving a place that had so awakened and stirred her imaginative faculties—and, it seemed, her romantic sensibilities, which had no scope for expression in the company of Mother Shaw. It was so unfair, this enslavement of younger women to old ones...

"The lady's grand-mère would give you no thanks for that," observed Bertrand. His pupils were dilated, his gaze bright, a rather sensuous softness in the set of his limbs. As if he had caught her looking at him, he gazed directly into Annie's eyes—only for an instant, but what a wealth of sensation in that gaze! She felt a semi-familiar tingling in her nether parts, along with a feeling of having slid into a warm, rose-scented bath. Had she imagined it? Wished it? She dropped her own eyes and when she raised them again, he was looking at her with a quizzical smile, as if wondering himself whether something had just happened or merely been imagined.

Carlotta was weeping, Tallie's arm around her shoulder. "I shall miss Paris, indeed I shall." She was rifling her reticule for a handkerchief. She raised her eyes and looked around her in an unfocused way, a look that punched Annie in the gut. Remorse for her part in Carlotta's imminent departure washed over her in a hot wave. In her urgency to be rid of Mother Shaw, she had closed off for this poor child the one avenue that might have led her to freedom, to follow her own desires and inclinations...the life Annie had wished for herself, and was at last beginning to lead. But how selfish—she'd had so many chances of her own over the years, and had foolishly forgone them; should she not take this burden from this young woman and allow her, with all these years ahead of her, to pursue her dreams? Carlotta was too good and dutiful to abandon her tiresome charge, who hadn't the slightest idea of, nor interest in, her granddaughter's quest for soul-nourishment. Why were so many women imprisoned in familial duty? What good did it do anyone?

Because someone had to do it, and no man was going to. It was the woman's sphere, this taking care of anyone in need, or want, of caretaking, for which women were naturally equipped. Or that's what they told you. After thirty years of practice with her mother and her nieces, Annie felt no better equipped for looking after people than she had as a girl, certainly felt no inclination for the role. Yet poor Carlotta... Lotta's mother Effie Lowell had an iron-clad rationale for escaping her mother's clutches, even living under the same roof: who could criticize a life devoted to philanthropy? Devolving the caretaking onto her daughter, Effie was free to roam the country, pursuing ideals that had driven her since youth. But what about Carlotta's passions? Were artistic, creative pursuits more selfish, less worthy, than charitable ones?

"I suppose they must be," she told herself, only realizing she had spoken aloud when Julia stared at her and said, "Beg pardon?"

"Sorry! I was wool-gathering," Annie said. "It must be the green stuff—Julia, it's not right. She should stay. She has her whole life ahead of her—"

Julia slowly shook her head. "Who'll look after Sarah? Effie's not going to, and she *will* be looked after, one way or another. It's not right, but—"

"Couldn't Effie hire her a companion..." Annie trailed off. Sarah would make sure never to find anyone who would suit her. Nor, having fixed upon this grandchild as her duty-bound caretaker, would it occur to her that Lotta might want and deserve a future freely chosen. Carlotta herself, fated to love her own kind while absorbing the lessons of her Puritan forebears that such things were wicked, might feel herself preserved from a life of sinfulness. What *stuff* it was! A kind-hearted young woman who couldn't harm anybody—her conscientious nature played upon, taken advantage of for the convenience of others. A tragic waste, of talent and of the potential for individuality.

The piano that had accompanied the shadow-play was still tinkling on the edge of Annie's hearing, its melodies having shifted into minor-key adagios, barely audible above the murmurs and occasional cries of conversation, but falling now on her ears like some profound declaration, something of great significance just beyond her grasp. A river plunging to a crash at the base of a falls, the end of a series of rapids, broadening and calming as the turbulent stretches passed, a peaceful setting for a boat-bound reverie on a warm afternoon…she let herself drift with it. Someone had opened a window to the mild darkness to let the fug of tobacco-smoke escape. She felt a breeze on her cheek like a lover's caress. How heavenly everything was here— the beauties with their white shoulders, their winking diamonds, the demigods whose white shirts glowed against their raven-black jackets, the sonata—was it Liszt?—rippling under the piano keys, the vase of dahlias and scented lilies on a shelf, the smiles of her dear companions—they *were* dear to her, each of them, and how sad, how unutterably tragic, to think of any one of them having to die, or to have to die herself and leave them all, and this magical city with its tower of light…

She rose and clasped her reticule.

"Are you well, Aunt Annie?" Through the faint mist that seemed now to pervade the place, she saw the concerned white face of her niece-in-law.

"Oh, my dear!" Annie's heart broke to think that she had caused this sweet girl a moment's worry. "We must go and look at the Tour Eiffel with all its lights on. From here, it should be magical."

"The sight-lines are quite wrong—" Bertrand began, but Tallie glared at him and laid a repressive hand on his forearm.

"What a lovely idea," she said. "We need the fresh air too. We can walk a bit to the west, toward the Cemetery—"

"—and climb to the top of the walls. Of course! How clever you are—" Annie beamed at her, Tallie shooting her a look to see if she were making fun, laughed at the naïve earnestness of her expression.

An officious guard at the Cimetière de Montmartre made to turn them away, but Julia gave him a Gorgonly stare, nodded toward Annie and said, "Madame doit rendre visite à son mari." The others assumed a funereal aspect and the intimidated fellow bowed them in, advising only to watch their footing. Annie thanked him gravely. They ascended the stairs and she made sure they were out of earshot before allowing her entourage to dissolve into unseemly laughter. They made their way north and west along the dim gravel paths, a fingernail of moon and the distant glow of streetlamps all there was for light. Something furry darted in front of Annie's feet and she stifled a shriek—a gray cat—and then as her eyes adjusted, more soft hulks hunched atop the marble and granite slabs, pairs of luminous green and amber eyes watching their progress with impassive vigilance.

"Et voilà!" Tallie's arm swept over the top of the wall and the vista below: to the south and west, Eiffel's grand, ingenious folly, a beam of light sweeping circles around it as if from an earthbound lighthouse for a race of giants. Its beauty struck them mute.

"Oh! How can I go!"

Annie turned and found Carlotta weeping in Bertrand's arms. The light beam at that moment swung toward them and she felt it strike her brain.

"You sha'n't," she heard herself say. "I shall ask her to come to Clem's after all. I should have been kind to her. I should have welcomed her." She felt a surge of exaltation, her chest filling with a golden glow that went all the way to her ears, her own eyes prickling with tears. "She's only a poor lonely old woman that nobody loves. I'll look after her and you must find a place of your own—in Paris—and start a new life here." At that moment, Annie felt she could do anything—even climb the wall of the cemetery and fly all the way to the Eiffel Tower.

Carlotta left off weeping and stared at her, mouth half-open. "You can't, Aunt Annie."

Carried forward on a tide of irrefutable logic, Annie said, "My dear, you were never meant to be your grandmother's caretaker. You and your mamma were traveling in Europe, so it was convenient that you meet her and get her to Paris while your mother went back to America, to her committees and such. Sarah's plan was for me to take things from there." She flung her arms open like a lawyer resting his case.

"That was never *your* plan, Aunt Annie." Carlotta's voice was small and hesitant.

"No reason you should inherit a responsibility because I didn't want it." Annie failed to notice Julia, Bertrand, and Tallie staring at her as if she had gone mad.

Julia was the first to speak. "Annie dear, I can't think your idea would benefit either yourself or Sarah. Perhaps not even Carlotta. Sarah wouldn't let her go off on her own into la bohème."

"How would she stop her? She's an adult."

Julia and Bertrand exchanged dubious looks and head-shakes. "More to the point," Julia went on, "you and Sarah can't abide each other. It couldn't possibly end well."

The glow infusing Annie's breast reddened into a martyr's fire. "I shall just have to work hard at it. There are debts that we owe to the old—and the young."

"Debts you never agreed to! Annie, what have you been about these last few months?"

Carlotta swallowed visibly and said, "Let's talk about this tomorrow. It's late now and everyone must be tired—"

The mere suggestion seemed to take the air out of Annie's body. She rallied long enough to agree and allow Bertrand to shepherd them back to the street and hail them a pair of fiacres.

Chapter 30

"Aunt Julia, I can't let her do this." Carlotta wrung her hands. "Neither of us was quite—sensible last night. She can't have meant it. If she did, I'm sure she regrets it already."

Julia Greene contemplated her great-niece. "But you'd like to stay in Paris, wouldn't you?"

"Of course I would! I've never been in a place where everyone's free to do what makes them happy—where no one speaks of duty and propriety—"

Julia sighed. "The young friends you've met have turned their backs on claims that have been made on them. No doubt rightly so. You'd be quite justified to do so with your grandmother."

Carlotta covered her eyes with her hands. "But she needs me—or somebody, surely." She straightened up. "It would be wrong for Aunt Annie to take it on. She's not even a blood relation. And they dislike each other."

"Sarah's particular combination of the despotic and the dependent would turn any Christian martyr to a heathen. I wonder how you've tolerated it, even as sweet-natured as you are."

Carlotta went to the open window, drawing in a deep breath of the warm, moist air. It was raining and the trees on the rue Bassano below dripped slow water from their leaves. "She's always been kind to me. Teaching me to read, buying me little presents, taking my side when Mamma scolded me. That's bound me to her—"

"—along with your inbred Puritan sense of duty."

Carlotta smiled ruefully. "If we hadn't come here, perhaps I'd have been content to remain her companion until she dies. But now—"

"She blames Annie for exposing you to corrupting influences. What do you imagine will happen if she occupies the Crafts' apartments as she originally planned, with you yourself free to make a home elsewhere in Paris?"

Carlotta's brows knitted. "She won't approve. She's always been a fiend for propriety with the girls in our family. It must come from having grown up when marriageability was everything, and a young lady's 'purity' her greatest asset in the marriage market."

"A young lady's greatest asset in the marriage market has always been her fortune. Purity's secondary—and measured by reputation, which isn't the same thing. I expect Sarah feels responsible for you—someone's got to guard your virtue, and she wouldn't trust Annie with that. If she moves into the Crafts' apartment, she'll expect you to join her there if you stay in Paris. And submit to her, ah, guidance as you always have."

"Then I might as well take her back to New York," said Carlotta bitterly. "I'll tell Aunt Annie so."

"Annie will think you're merely being self-sacrificing. And she'd be right. The only thing that would make *her* self-sacrifice worthwhile would be your defying Grandmamma to live in Paris on your own terms. Could you do that?"

"As long as Tua was in Paris, I should feel constrained, even living elsewhere."

Julia rose and put her hand on Carlotta's arm. "Then surely the thing to do is get Sarah back to New York. I could accompany her on the return voyage."

"You, Aunt Julia? Why would you do that?"

"I haven't been back since I buried William. It's been years since I saw my brother Quincy—he's the only other one of us left. And there are so many people I should visit."

"You didn't say should *like* to visit. You don't want to leave Paris any more than Aunt Annie or I do."

"It would only be a month or two, and then I'd be back. What good times you and I and Annie might have together! When you aren't among your younger friends, that is."

Carlotta's wistful look made Julia's heart clench. "I doubt she'll go back without me. She told Aunt Annie that no one there cares about her—that's why she thought to make a new life here, with Aunt Annie as her companion."

"She might have inquired as to Annie's feelings on that first, or indeed have anticipated them based on past experience. It's never been her habit to do so, which is one reason she finds herself bereft of agreeable company—" Julia broke off.

"You were going to say something else."

"Only that Sarah is good at sensing people's instinctual guilt. She exploited it to full effect with your uncle—I doubt he'd have taken that regiment if not for feeling he owed it to her for her supposed sacrifices on his behalf."

"You think she sensed that in Aunt Annie as well?"

"And in you, my dear. If Sarah can't get her way by fair means, she's quite capable of using others' feelings against themselves."

"You make her sound like a monster, Aunt Julia."

Julia's laugh held a rueful note. "We've all done it to some degree, especially if we're mothers trying to get our children to behave. Indeed, I don't think we're directly aware of it."

In the shabby little parlor of Madame Mercure's pension, Annie sat across from Sarah Shaw, a crapulous headache worsening her unease about what she had come to do. "I wished to see you to tell you I am sorry I made your life difficult when you arrived in Paris. I was wrong to disregard my sister's wishes—and yours. I've come to ask if we may begin again, as you had hoped when you first came here."

Sarah squinted at Annie over her demilunes. "What has occasioned this change?"

"I've had time to—reflect on the situation. I let long-ago feelings of anger and grief intrude upon circumstances that called for the kindness and understanding I should wish for myself."

"Carlotta and I leave for Nice tomorrow—"

"—and I am sorry I delayed so long in broaching this. As I understand, you hadn't yet determined what course to take after your sojourn in Nice."

Sarah Shaw's stare felt like a hot arrow above Annie's left eye. "I am surprised to hear this from you, Annie. You propose that I occupy your sister's apartments on our return to Paris?"

Annie nodded, her throat too dry for speech.

"And Carlotta will return to New York." It was not a question.

"If she wishes. My impression is that she'd prefer to stay in Paris."

Sarah frowned. "She seems infatuated with the place. Indeed, I have been concerned. I do not consider the circles in which she has been moving to be wholesome company for a young woman in her circumstances."

Annie half-rose. "Surely that is for Carlotta to decide."

"She is an unmarried young woman with a considerable fortune, and altogether too trusting of strangers. Were she to stay in Paris, I would consider it my duty to continue as her chaperone, and to make a home for her—in your sister's apartments with me, if your offer is genuine."

"It is genuine." Annie felt a lead weight plummeting down her gut. She snatched a breath. "It is, however, conditional."

Sarah Shaw's eyebrows lifted. "Conditional?"

"On Carlotta's being free to choose her living situation, in Paris or elsewhere. And unless I hear it from her own lips, I shall not consider any decision of hers to live with and be chaperoned by you as being undertaken freely."

"I see you are up to your old tricks, Annie." Sarah's eyes bulged. "Once more you seek to drive a wedge between me and my family. To alienate their affections as you did with my son."

It was a punch to the solar plexus. Annie felt it along with a flush of rage that swept up to her face. "Is that what you thought?" Her throat tightened with the strain of trying to sound reasonable. "When your son, at a fully mature age, fell in love with me and only after his persistent pleas, overcame my reluctance to marry him?"

"Oh, you played the reluctant bride very well," Sarah hissed between her teeth, "It must have been quite an effort for someone so close to being on the shelf. Knowing how helpless he would be to resist such a challenge—lonely as he was away from his family, which only devotion to his country could have compelled."

"If missing his family was what saddened him," Annie retorted, "how could any attempts by me to alienate him from them—from you!—have succeeded? Did it occur to you that what he really wanted, as a young man in the prime of his life, was a family of his own? I was a reluctant bride, as you put it, only because I foresaw how the war would shatter that dream for both of us. As it did but three months after."

"That war deprived my daughter of a husband and Carlotta of a father," Sarah bit off the consonants. "My husband and I felt it our duty to supply the parental love and guidance she would otherwise have missed. Until she is settled with, as you put it, a family of her own."

"By that I suppose you mean a husband."

"Naturally," Sarah snapped.

"What if the family Carlotta wishes to form were simply her own household? Herself, a servant or two, perhaps a companion?"

"That is hardly the natural propensity of a young and healthy woman. If she did not wish to marry—I realize that some women do not—then her place is with her family of birth."

"She has no brothers or sisters, therefore no household in which to play the role of maiden aunt, as I did. If she does not marry, how do you think she should live after you—and her mother—have passed on?"

"I, of course, may be taken at any time." Sarah raised a pious gaze heavenward. "Her mother enjoys good health and is not yet fifty. She can expect to live for some time longer, and therefore be in a position to provide a home for her only child."

"She may live with her mother, then, or she may live with a husband. You see for her no other alternative?"

"What other could there be?"

"A home of her own—as I have."

"I hardly think that your choices in life may be regarded as a model for a respectable young woman of good family."

Annie stood up. "In that case, you are hardly likely to want me as a neighbor." The small room had grown stifling. She went to the window and pulled down its upper sash.

Sarah appeared to be cogitating. "It would not be an insuperable barrier, if you were willing to make some changes," she said at length.

"Of what nature?"

"You are still a parishioner in good standing of the American Cathedral. That community, I am told, offers a wholesome range of activities for ladies, whether married or single. Charitable undertakings, and the like. You may also know that my nephew is attached to the American Ministry, which affords a range of social and cultural activities to its expatriate community."

Annie perched on the edge of her chair. "You propose that I confine my activities and engagements to the American Colony." *I'd rather die*, she did not add.

"Certainly I should feel more reassured of a respectable environment for Carlotta. In addition, it would mean that you and I could share the burden of chaperonage."

"And if Carlotta does not wish to be chaperoned?"

"That is not," Sarah's mouth tightened, "a matter in which a young woman typically has a great deal of say."

"Nonetheless, I should like to ascertain her views in the matter."

Sarah rose. The interview was over. "If she will not agree to abide by reasonable standards of conduct—if she were to contemplate, for instance, living elsewhere in Paris, thus forgoing her reputation and her future, I shall insist on her return to New York with me. If you will excuse me, I have our packing for Nice to oversee."

By the time she got home after a more than usually jarring cab ride, Annie's headache was nearly blinding, and her stomach was heaving. Adèle came into the hallway, started to say something, and stopped. "Madame! You look terrible."

"A bromide powder and some water, please." Annie took off her bonnet and dropped it limply on the hall table. "I'm going to bed and I'm not at home to anyone."

"Oh-la-la! But your appointment at Dr. Kellgren's—"

Annie waved an impatient, suffering hand. "Send a note to Fröken Johansson."

Adèle returned with the patent remedy and helped Annie into an old summer nightgown.

"Close the curtains, please," Annie croaked. She gulped the fizzy, salty medicine and chased it with fresh water. Adèle helped her crawl into bed, and blessed oblivion took hold.

ry-mouthed, groggy, but otherwise feeling human after the worst dyspeptic episode she could remember, Annie awoke with no sense of the time of day. She had made two or three semi-conscious forays to the toilet, but whether it had been day or night she couldn't remember.

Hearing her stir, Adèle knocked gently on the bedroom door and entered, appraising her critically. "Your color is better, Madame. How do you feel?"

"I think I'll live." Annie sat on the edge of the bed and shakily poured water into a tumbler. She took small sips, thankful that the nausea seemed to be gone. "What time is it?"

"Half past eleven—of the morning, Madame."

"That can't be—"

"Mais oui, it is Sunday. You have slept for nearly a full day."

Annie shook her head slowly. "Good heavens, I'll have missed church—"

"C'est vrai, and the gathering of last evening with Mademoiselle Reubell."

"Oh, no! I had been looking forward to that—Fauré's new piece—" Annie winced as the ghost of the headache momentarily returned. She drank more water.

"I sent her your regrets, Madame. You were so deeply asleep and you had been so unwell I thought it wrong to wake you." Adèle looked worried.

Annie smiled. "You did right. I was in no condition to go out."

"Your encounter with Madame la belle-mère?"

"—even worse than I expected." What a terrible idea it had been, to think of having Mother Shaw next door. She should have known better. She doubted now—hoped fervently—that it would not come about, but she had promised Carlotta she would take her place as Sarah's companion if Lotta could summon the courage to strike out on her own in Paris. Everything depended on that. If Lotta agreed to stay in the Crafts' apartments under Sarah's gimlet eye, it would be the worst possible outcome for both her and Annie.

"I must get hold of Carlotta," she told Adèle.

"Ah, oui, Mademoiselle Lowell! She came by yesterday, but insisted I not disturb you."

Annie felt a rising panic. "She leaves for Nice tomorrow. I must talk with her."

"She said the same thing. I told her I would send her a message when you are ready. The same with Madame Greene, and Monsieur le Comte. And Monsieur Jackson."

Annie shook her head a little. "What can they all want at once?"

"Forgive me, Madame, I do not think you should concern yourself until we put something in your stomach. The cook has made a nice light chicken soup, and I will run you a bath—"

Annie gave her maid a look of bleary gratitude. "A thoroughly wise course of action."

*   *   *

"We're not going to Nice, Aunt Annie." Carlotta stood in her aunt's parlor, pale and older-looking than when Annie had last seen her. "We're going back to New York. There was a telegram from Mamma last evening—"

"She's unwell?"

"It's Uncle George Curtis. He hasn't long to live, and Aunt Anna has been asking for her mother. We're embarking on the *City of Paris* on Tuesday."

That, thought Annie, was woefully ironic. "I had heard George was poorly, but it didn't sound critical. Do they know what's wrong?"

Carlotta shook her head. "He's been ill for three months now. It may be cancer. Whatever it is, it's clearly killing him. Aunt Julia offered to take Tua back, but it wouldn't be right, and besides, Tua and I are already packed—"

"Oh, Lotta." Annie enfolded her niece in her arms. "I so want you to stay in Paris."

Carlotta's eyes brimmed. "So do I, Aunt Annie. I think you know how badly I want that."

"You'll come back—"

"Perhaps. We'll have to see how things go. If Tua feels needed, wanted after all, perhaps she'll stay on in New York. At any rate, my obligation as traveling companion will be over. I hope we get there in time—it's the fastest ship on the Atlantic, they say."

In time for a funeral, at least. "Can I help? Get you anything to take back with you?"

Carlotta gave her a wintry smile. "Croissants and café au lait don't travel well. But perhaps you'd ask Miss DeKuyper—oh, no, it's silly—"

"About her sketch-portrait of you?"

"Perhaps she'd sell it to me and send it on. It was only partly done but she was capturing—something about me that I liked."

"I'll speak to her, and I hope she'll want to do that."

"The cost doesn't matter. She won't ask for enough, but I can always send her some extra. But I don't want her thinking it's charity on my part."

"She'll be honored that you want it, I hope." And perhaps a little relieved, Annie thought. "You must come back and resume your painting lessons. You were barely getting started and I could see you loved it so."

"That goes for you too, Aunt Annie. It's nice that you're such a help to us young ones but you mustn't neglect your own talents." Carlotta held Annie's hands in hers. "I shall miss you dreadfully." The tears that spilled over triggered Annie's.

"Then you'll just have to come back," Annie said, her voice breaking. "Go with God, and may your journey bring comfort to all of them." One last hug, and Carlotta turned to go. "Wish your grandmamma a good passage from me. And a peaceful outcome when you arrive."

So, there, it was done. She had her life back, her freedom back. At the cost of this young woman's happiness. She dropped into her armchair and quietly wept.

"Tallie is enceinte." Bertrand de Leiningen slammed the parlor door behind him, stood on Annie's Turkey carpet and hurled his declaration across the room. "By me."

Annie turned from the courtyard window. "Are you sure?"

"That it's mine, or that she's pregnant? I am. On both counts. She has faults, God knows, but dishonesty isn't one of them."

"Sit down. Why do you come to tell me this?"

Bertrand ran a hand through his hair, defiance fading to anguish. "I want you to help me convince her to marry me."

"Me? How long have you and she—"

"Oh, it was just the once. That day you sent me to look for her. When she opened the door she propelled herself into my arms. One thing led to another and…" he sighed, "here we are."

"But how could you have—"

"Let that happen? I'm a human being, Madame Shaw. I'm a man. And I've been in love with her since I met her."

Annie dropped into her armchair. "That wasn't the impression you gave—"

"Of course not." He gave a short, sardonic laugh. "One must have one's defenses. I was her teacher, and she's a good deal younger than I—"

"Then how could you have taken advantage of her so?"

"That's not how I would characterize our encounter."

"She told you what she'd learned about Jackson's marriage, didn't she? She was badly hurt, and felt he'd abused her friendship, as indeed he had."

"So I should have pushed her away when she wanted comfort? The world she and I live in doesn't recognize your rules of propriety, Madame."

Annie's throat was dry again. "Does she have any interest in marrying you?" She reached for a water-carafe.

"Au contraire. She wants an abortion and my help in getting it. Nothing is more important than her art. She said."

"Do you doubt her?"

"I'm not sure what to think. She seems to mean it, but…"

"Did you tell her—how you feel toward her? Besides asking her to marry you."

Bertrand's laugh was bitter. "After I abased myself even to that degree, she said she was fond of me but had no intention of marrying anybody."

Annie tried and failed to picture the tiny, vivacious young woman in an advanced state of pregnancy. "She's so young," she said feebly.

"*Younger than she are happy mothers made.*"

"Your command of Shakespeare is impressive for a Frenchman." Annie smiled. "So you must remember Father Capulet's riposte."

He blew out a sigh. "I do. But I could make her happy, if she'd let me."

"If this hadn't happened…?"

"I knew I didn't have a chance with her. You know what she is—free with her affections, but wishes no deep ties."

"One had the impression you were the same way, Bertrand."

"That's why I know her so well. We're birds of a feather. But something in me has changed, with this news. I'm as surprised as anyone, I admit."

Annie rose and went to him. His face had turned vulnerable, boyish-looking. That softness she'd noticed at the jawline. She put a hand over his, which was gripping the arm of his chair.

"Unless *her* feelings have altered," she said slowly, "surely it would be unwise—"

His nostrils flared and he half-rose from the chair. She drew back, startled. "Women aren't the only ones who want children," he said gruffly. "I never thought it would matter to me—to have a son, or any child, of my own—but I find, after all, that it does. But she wants—"

"Wants...?"

"She wants me to give her the money for the—avortement. I can get it, of course, but it's the last thing I want—"

"In these circumstances, I'm afraid, it's what she wants that matters."

Bertrand looked up at her sharply. "You don't want me marrying her, do you? You thought—" he shook his head, laughed quietly. "You thought I was interested in you."

Annie recoiled as if he'd struck her. "What a terrible thing to say." Terrible, and true enough to carve a dark hollow in her gut.

"Then why are you blushing?" Bertrand was out of his chair and heading for the door. "I should have known. You've hardly been out of the American Colony. You don't understand how things are done here."

"If I had been," Annie said, her temper rising, "interested in you, and vice-versa, what would have been so absurd about that? The gap in our ages is less than the one between you and Tallie. Don't flatter yourself, Monsieur le Comte. I'm well aware of 'how things are done here,' as you so churlishly put it, and I assure you I had no expectations of anything serious between you and me. I'm capable of shallow flirtation myself— or did *you* think there was more to it?"

He had turned from the door and stood staring at her, a half-smile on his face. "Do you know, Madame Shaw, you look quite fetching when you're angry? I should love to capture that expression in paint. I am sorry," he went on in a more sincere tone. "Truly I am. That was churlish indeed. Forgive me—I'm not in control of my feelings at present. And I feel rather helpless. I came to you because you have been a real friend since I've known you, and I threw that friendship in your face."

Mollified, though still wounded, Annie gestured him back to his armchair and took her own. "I'll help you both as much as I can. But I can't pressure her into accepting your proposal. Young as she is, she has been an exemplar to me. She's making a life based on her soul's passions and her talents, which is hard to do coming from her background. I'd be loath to see her freedom curtailed by a child and a marriage she didn't want. But perhaps she hasn't fully taken stock of her feelings and wishes. I know from my own experience that a child can come to be a compelling desire—"

"But you have no—"

"I lost that heart's desire—under distressing circumstances," Annie smiled sadly. "Though in my case, it was something I wanted from the start. I will help Tallie sort out her feelings, but we must all abide by them, however it turns out. Can you live with that?"

The look on Bertrand's face was heartbreaking. "I do love her. I couldn't force her to do anything she truly didn't want. But it will be so hard if it comes to that."

"I understand," Annie said gently. "Can you imagine what it would be like? If she wished to force you into marrying and giving up your art to raise a child?"

"I'm a man. Women are made for that, aren't they? What woman doesn't want children?"

"My friend, you have no idea," Annie said. "The stories I could tell you—!"

He gave her a twisted smile. "I'm the one guilty of naïveté, I suppose."

"I'll let you know when I've talked with her," Annie walked him to the door. "That's all I can promise." She shut it behind him and leaned back on it, closing her eyes and feeling her temples pounding so hard that the wood seemed to vibrate with them.

Chapter 32

ydia Burwell entered Annie's sitting-room, wearing the ivory day-costume she had on when they first met. She fidgeted on a loveseat while Annie poured tea.

"I'm sorry I was indisposed when Jackson came by." Annie gestured invitation to a plate of strawberry galettes.

"We both hope you're feeling better, ma'am—" Lydia caught herself, "Miz Shaw. We decided it would be better if I came to tell you our news."

Annie's eyebrows arched. A wedding date, finally? Another child on the way? Lydia gave a little shake of her head.

"I've been taken on at Maison Rouff," the words tumbled out, "as a seamstress. I wore this when I applied, and the head of the *atelier* asked me about it. When I told her I'd made it all myself, she said, 'Well, let's start you in bodices'—*corsages*, she called them—'and if you do well there, we'll try you out as a *tailleur*'— that's a tailor, I believe—'and maybe have you sketch a design or two.' It's a great opportunity, Miz Shaw—I'm so excited—"

"That's wonderful that they recognize talent when they see it, Lydia. Jackson must be very happy for you—"

Lydia's hand came up. "That's the other thing, Miz Shaw. I'm moving to my own place. Me and Ben, with the girl who got me the interview. She has a little girl, and they live with her mama, who takes care of little Francine. She'll look after Ben too."

Annie's throat closed. "What happened? Between you and Jackson?"

Lydia went to pick up her teacup, but her hands were trembling.

"After that night here, that dinner, when I met Tallie—well, I wondered. So I asked Jackson about her. I could tell he didn't want to talk about it—"

Annie began to interrupt, but thought better of it.

"I told him what Adèle had told me. About the painting—" She gestured toward the Crafts' apartments. "And them all working on it together. I asked him, had he fallen in love with her. He said no, but I just kept looking at him. Finally he said, she hadn't known he was married, he hadn't told anyone except you, for safety's sake, and she took a liking to him, and they trifled with each other a little. He said he was sorry, I was the only one he loved, but he'd been lonesome ..." she opened her hands, her eyes brimming.

Annie cleared her throat. "From what I saw, that was a truthful account of the situation."

"Miz Shaw, I can't go through with it just now—the legal marrying. I still love him, and I think he loves me, but I want us both to be sure." The tears spilled over. Annie went to the girl and wrapped her in her arms. So young, in a strange place with a strange language, no one to comfort her. Thank goodness for a clean handkerchief in one's pocket. She handed it to Lydia, who tried discreetly to wipe her nose, gave up, and blew into it with vigor.

"It'll be a test, you see, for both of us," she said when she resurfaced. "He'll go off to that art school, and I'll work at my new job, and Madame Theriault—my friend's mama—says he can come see Ben whenever he wants. We'll walk out together on my days off. And next year we'll see how things stand."

"Are you angry with him?"

"I was, at first. I was lonesome too, back home. And I wouldn't have lacked for male attention if I'd wanted it—" she grinned for a moment, "some of them came buzzing around my house like blueflies, wanting to help me out with this and that. They didn't know I was married, and with colored folks, you know, it doesn't matter so much if you've had a baby. But I kept them at bay. Some of them were nice sincere fellas too."

"Things are more—permissive, I suppose, in Paris. Especially among the artists and younger people. They assume a newcomer will fall in with their ways. I'm not excusing anything," Annie added, seeing Lydia's stormy look. "An attractive, talented young woman—"

"—like Tallie—"

"No, I was about to say like you—might find temptations in your own path. I wonder how Jackson would react to that," Annie smiled at the thought, and saw that Lydia was smiling too.

"Well, now! I may have to find out. I love Paris already, Miz Shaw. I've met some of Adèle's colored friends, and that makes me less homesick. Rouff's pays pretty well—enough to afford the lodging and the care for Ben while I'm working. This way Jackson will have enough to live on too."

Annie scrutinized the young woman's face. Lydia's news meant the collapse of another of her schemes to help a young friend. But there was good sense, even courage, in the decision. Lydia's face showed determination and wisdom, if tinged by sadness.

"How will you do, with your French—"

Lydia broke into a wide smile. "Adèle's been helping me so much. I'm a pretty fast learner, Miz Shaw, and Jeannette—my new house-mate—taught me the words you need to know as a dressmaker. Maybe I could—"

Annie took her by both hands. "Come by and we can speak French together? I'd enjoy that. I think Mrs. Greene would too."

"I thought you'd be upset with me."

Annie sighed and smiled. "I don't blame you a bit. Jackson loves you and little Ben dearly—I'm sure he'll do whatever it takes to earn your love back." Another thought came to her. "Do the people at Rouff's know your situation?"

Lydia shook her head vigorously. "No, ma'am, they don't. If they did, they'd never have hired me. They don't hire married ladies, much less mothers. Girls have to leave if they get married. Jeannette had to pretend—she couldn't tell them about her little girl. We'll keep each other's secret. Her mama's a lovely woman. She'll help with my French too, 'cause she doesn't speak a word of English. And Ben will be a li'l Frenchman before we know it."

"You and Jackson were very young when you met," Annie said. "And as long as Benjamin gets the love and care he needs, from both of you, I think you've made a wise decision. But I confess I'm a little sad about it." Even as she said it, Annie was surprised by another feeling: relief. No need, for now, to worry about Mrs. Kernochan, that pillar of the American Colony, finding out that her young kinsman was married to a colored woman and had a child by her.

"So am I, Miz Shaw. But it feels right. Jackson will be free to decide what he wants—and who he wants to be with."

"Not that you asked, but I think whatever feelings Tallie had for him are in the past now. I've come to know her well these last few months, and she'd never have set out to seduce a man she knew was married. Oh, I did so hope you could all be friends!"

Lydia's smile was rueful. "I don't think we dislike each other at all. But it's so awkward now…perhaps in time, things will get easier."

"You're alike in one way. You're both very good at what you do, and I should rejoice to see the world reward your talents with success."

"I hope that for all three of us." Lydia rose, her tea and pastries untouched. "Thank you, Miz Shaw. For all the help you've given us, and your understanding. Jackson and I will pay you back as soon as we can."

Annie held up her hand. "I told him what I'll tell you. If some day you care to present me with a piece of your work, I'll feel fully recompensed. Design me a gown, when your circumstances permit—I'll get you the fabric—and I'll boast of it to all my friends."

"I'd sure enjoy doing that. Miz Shaw—" Lydia was clearly hesitant to go on. Annie nodded encouragement.

"I wondered—you've done so much for Jackson and me. Was there—a particular reason?"

"Well, I'm sure Jackson told you about his father being a suitor of mine. I couldn't return his love, but we remained friendly. He wrote to me, just before he died, asking me to help Jackson when he got to Paris—"

"I do know about that. But I wondered—when we first met, you looked at me—as if we'd met before."

"You *are* a perceptive young woman." Annie took a breath. "You reminded me of someone I met on the Burwells' plantation, when I visited with my family. Long before you were born. Thinking back, I'm sure it must have been your grandmother. Her name was Lily, I think?"

Lydia's eyes widened. "You knew my grandma?"

"She was a servant, in the big house. A sweet and shy young lady, very lovely." Annie had been on the verge of telling Lydia how Lily had suffered on her account, and that in helping Lydia and her family, she hoped to make amends. But she held back. The guilt of that occasion was hers to bear; she had no right to ask for pardon from poor Lily's descendant. "What became of her? After the war?"

"What I heard—not from Mama, she wouldn't talk about it—" Lydia looked down and then directly into Annie's face, "is that she had my mama to a brother of Jackson's grandfather. Not by her own choice."

I cannot wish the fault undone, the issue of it being so proper. What was that from? *King Lear?* Annie pictured Lily's miserable face, felt rage and sorrow rising. "If that War were good for anything, it would be for putting a stop to that. No doubt it still happens—" she caught the challenging look from Lydia, "but at least the victims aren't completely in the power of the villains, nor are their children enslaved by them now…it's not much, is it?" What must it be like, to know your grandfather was a rapist?

"It's something, I guess," Lydia's smile was rueful. "Grandmama

Lily died before I was born. She'd come to live in town, with my mama—and daddy, before they split—but she was always sickly, Mama said."

Annie felt her eyes fill. "I'd hoped she'd have lived to enjoy her freedom."

"Doesn't matter how sickly you are. Being free's better than being a slave, any ol' day."

Lydia took her leave. How little in life, Annie mused, turned out as planned, especially when young people were involved. If she had borne Rob's child—a boy, she knew—he'd be twenty-eight now, like poor Carlotta. What if he married a colored woman? Or preferred the company of his own sex? It was easy to accept the choices of others' children. Would she have been as forbearing with a child of her own? She hoped so. As she hoped that Jackson would in time prove himself worthy of Lydia.

She thought of Tallie. There had been enough truth in Bertrand's accusation of Annie's own romantic interest in him to trigger her angry, defensive response; it had been a pretty delusion for a while, like any good flirtation. But it was over, and now Annie was charged with being, in Herr Bismarck's phrase, an honest broker in helping Tallie face a momentous dilemma. She believed in Bertrand's love for Tallie, his desire for a child; his reluctant acknowledgement, proud and guarded as he was, was evidence of that. Was it enough for them to build a life together?

What of Tallie's art? Annie recalled the quote from Milton: *that one Talent which is death to hide…* Women weren't supposed to have those. She'd seen Tallie's portraits, revealing but compassionate; her lovely candid nudes, her evocative interiors. She had an eye that couldn't be classified, neither academic nor impressionist nor neo-classical. Anyone—almost anyone—could have a child. But only Tallie DeKuyper could put that vision of hers on canvas.

She would visit her, try to help her past the fear and panic that must attend a situation like this, to a thoughtful decision about her future—if help were even welcome. Whatever Annie's own longings and losses concerning children, Tallie's was the life to be led; the decision must be hers alone. It was Annie who had unwittingly set all this in motion by enlisting her young friends in the scheme to thwart Mother Shaw. There was no end to reasons for guilt today.

She went to her desk to write Tallie a note.

Chapter 33

he old grist mill of the Cimetière Montparnasse, the Moulin de la Charité, was an odd place for a rendezvous, but on a clear afternoon with a cool hint of autumn in the air, an agreeable one. Tallie had suggested it for privacy; the few other strollers and occasional mourners took no notice of the women embracing at the tower's massive oak doors.

"Do you feel all right to walk—" each began to ask, and their laughter broke an awkward moment.

"I'm fit as a fiddle, thanks to my Swedish torture chamber."

Tallie looked Annie over. "You're taller than when we first met. Your tormentress has done wonders."

"And you?" Annie was struck, as on their last encounter, by Tallie's pallor, the absence of her characteristic vivacity.

"The mornings have been quite unpleasant."

They paced slowly in the tree-lined shade of the Avenue Transversele, too absorbed to notice the ornate monuments to the obscure dead. "Bertrand came to see me," Annie began.

"He wants to marry me. He wants me to have the child."

"What do you want?" Annie asked gently.

Tallie turned toward her. "I want my future back, Mrs. Shaw. I'm not cut out for motherhood—"

Annie waved her to a marble bench in the shade of an old lime and they sat. She saw Tallie shiver. "I told him I'd talk with you. What I meant was, I'd listen, hear what you're thinking."

"Do you know what I've endured, even to begin being taken seriously as an artist?" A thrum of nerves tightened to breaking in Tallie's voice. "Especially when I've had to model to make ends meet. When you take your clothes off for a nude study, these so-called artists assume it's an invitation. Which I've resisted since I came to Paris. And now—"

"There are women here, I've heard," Annie ventured, "artists, who are mothers but manage to make arrangements—" She broke off, seeing Tallie's eyes flash.

"Let me tell you about my friend Marie. A better painter than I'll ever be—" she waved an impatient hand as Annie began to demur. "She had a child nine years ago. A country girl—she didn't know she had a choice. She never knew who her own father was. Her mother's a drunk and a whore, but loving as far as she can be. Marie's choice was to go on making art, hope for success, let her mother care for her child, or give up art and care for him herself.

"She chose her art. Her mother weaned her son on cheap sweet wine, the same swill she drinks herself. Nine years old and he's an alcoholic. He has fits of rage—tears up furniture, throws his food around, runs down the street howling and has to be brought back by the police. Marie's sold some paintings, and she's hoping to have one in the Salon, but she still has to model to pay the bills. The men still harass her, treat her like a convenience. A few years back, she tried to kill herself. That's the kind of life I can hope for."

"But Bertrand says he wants to marry you—"

"Bertrand's a genius at wanting what he can't have. Now he thinks he wants a child. And a wife! A man like him! Even if I loved him—and I don't—do you think I could trust him to see me through eighteen years of rearing a child? To support me and my work? I don't."

In Tallie's position, Annie would have the same misgivings. "He sounded as sincere as I've ever heard him." She heard the weakness in her own voice.

"That may be, Mrs. Shaw. But I can't stake my future on that. I have to end it. Soon. Will you help me?"

Annie reached for Tallie's hands and held them. "How far along are you?"

"Not too far. I knew right away—when I missed my first monthly. And started feeling ill in the mornings. The sooner I'm done with this, the better."

"What if you—" Annie stopped. She had been about to suggest that Tallie move in with her, that she and Adèle could care for the infant while Tallie pursued her art. There it was again—that urge to save someone, to make all well for a friend. Her conversation with Julia came back to her. *I'm playing foster-mother again, aren't I?*

"I can't imagine *any* circumstances in which I'd want to have a child. Not even with a mansion full of nursemaids. Perhaps that will change some day. Not now."

Annie nodded, resigned. "How can I help you?"

"I need a small loan. The procedure at this stage is simple and cheap, but I don't have the money. And I can't take it from Bertrand when he doesn't want me to do it."

It was out before Annie could stop it. "Why did you even tell him? If you were so sure, and it's so early on?"

Tallie rose from the bench and walked a few paces. "I was feeling helpless and frightened, I suppose, and I wanted him to—make it all right for me. I thought he'd say, *I'll help you find the place and the money*, that would be the decent thing. And then he starts talking of marriage, for God's sake! I was taken aback, I must say."

"There are laws—who can you safely consult? You know where to go?"

"It's one of the first things you learn. The sages-femmes do a roaring trade among artists' models—" Tallie's crooked smile faded and her eyes filled, triggering a sympathetic response in Annie's. "I never meant for this to happen. I feel such a fool!"

This was the situation Annie had feared for her niece Marian. What would she have done? Marian would have come to her, not to Clem; aunts were made for this sort of thing. And of course she would have helped her.

"My main concern is your health and safety," she said. "Whatever the legalities, there must be—providers with better reputations than others. Find the one who's best respected, who puts her clients' health first. The cost won't be a concern."

Tallie looked at her as if afraid to see judgment in her face. Annie opened her arms and the girl walked into them. For several moments, neither of them moved.

"Come to Cannes, when it's all over," Annie said at length. "There's much to paint there, and you'll want to get started on a submission to the Salon."

Tallie's eyes brimmed. "Only if I can paint you. I'm chiefly a portraitist, you know."

"Madame Greene will be there as well, and you know what a great subject she'll be."

"You, Madame Shaw, will be a much more gratifying challenge."

Julia and Annie, in summer muslins, were promenading the grand terrace of the Jardin du Luxembourg on the hot, breezy afternoon following the American Minister's soirée at the elegant Hôtel Gramont. Annie had reconnected with Fred Sears, her cousin by marriage and Julia's nephew by blood; Fred's wife Eleanora, Coolidge's daughter and hostess; and the Minister himself. Mrs. Hetty Coolidge had not appeared.

"The Ambassador's Residence is a lovely space for smaller receptions," Julia said.

"The Ministry building itself is ghastly, Thomas tells me."

"So it's 'Thomas' already! You've made a conquest."

Annie twiddled her parasol. "We're practically related, after all. But he is married—"

"For better or worse," Julia grimaced. "In Hetty Appleton's case, the latter. The poor man needs stimulating female company. And you looked particularly fetching in the new ivory silk."

"I'm glad I wore the pearls. Young Fred's a dear, isn't he?"

Julia looked wistful. "He reminded me of my baby sister Marian, gone so young. She was the loveliest of us, and so sweet-natured."

"Just Rob's age when she died, wasn't she?"

"Give Sarah her due," Julia said, "she and Frank made Fred one of the family till he went off to school. That's why he was so eager to see you—you're almost a sister-in-law."

"The Americans last evening were the most intelligent and agreeable I've met. I wouldn't mind seeing most of them again. He mixed things up nicely with the local Parisians too, as if he'd been living here for years. Wasn't Retta Reubell looking well?"

"I enjoy Retta immensely. I wish she'd invite your Thomas to one of her salons and proceed to scandalize him—"

"Oh, stop! He's not 'my Thomas,' he's your nephew's father-in-law. I may invite him to a salon of my own, though I can't think he'd accept. Look at that adorable little blond fellow with the sailboat."

The cherubic tot in question was eagerly pointing out his floating prize to his nanny, who had rented him the vendor's largest boat. The fountain paths were filling up with nursemaids and their charges.

"Let's walk over to the Medici Fountain," Annie said. "It'll be quieter over there, and I want to talk to you about our young friends."

The great oblong pool glimmered dark green under its canopy of arching plane trees, the bronze giant at the fountainhead looming over a pair of entwined marble lovers. Except for a soft breeze whispering through the leaves, it was deserted. Annie felt the relief of the dim grotto after the sun's glare and inhaled the mossy, loamy smell that wafted from the fountain's basin. She trailed her hand in the water. "I wonder if I'll see Bertrand again."

"You think he blames you for Tallie's decision?"

Annie sighed. "I've written and told him how it went—I'm sure he'll think I could have done more. Or he may associate me with one of the more painful episodes in his life, and keep his distance. I believe he really loves her, and at least at the time, he'd convinced himself he wanted to be a husband and father."

"These things happen all the time in their world," Julia said, "One wouldn't last long there if one took matters too much to heart."

"Have you heard from him?"

"Not in the last week. So he let you see him in a moment of weakness?"

"A defenseless moment, I'd say," Annie replied after a pause. "No evidence of the cheerful cynic. It's so hard. If he were sincere, if she's wrong about him—if she and a child are his heart's abiding desire—it's a tragedy, isn't it?"

"For him, certainly. And not his first, I fear, which is why he's always been so guarded. That façade of devil-may-care…"

"Those stray cats Tallie mentioned," Annie dipped her hand again in the dark pool. "Sensitive people, I've found, let themselves lose their hearts to animals, but not other people."

Julia studied her for a long moment. "You can't make it all right for him. And you mustn't feel responsible."

"I suppose not, but—"

"Artists are luckier than the rest of us in some ways," Julia said. "They have their work to escape into. A place to vent their griefs. Sometimes that makes the most powerful art there is."

"I hope he'll understand some day. I couldn't make her change her mind. If there had been any room for that—"

Julia shook her head. "What he asked of you wasn't right. He hoped you would play the moralizing mamma and tell her it was her duty to go through with it, or tug at her heartstrings on behalf of this as-yet-all-but-hypothetical child."

"—so that she'd feel guilt-ridden enough to keep it, and accept him? What a terrible way to begin a life. We've all known girls this happened to, and—"

"Nary a happy one among 'em, is there?"

"It rarely ends well." Annie shook the water drops from her hand. "D'you know what I briefly contemplated—"

"Let me guess." Julia leaned an arm on the edge of the balustrade. "Moving her in with you and becoming the child's nursemaid. So that she could go on with her art and Bertrand would get at least a piece of his heart's desire—the child part."

Annie laughed softly and shook her head. "How well you've come to know me."

"Well, I knew you a little, all those years ago. There are patterns and tendencies one observes. Concede, for instance, that part of your feeling for Rob was maternal."

Annie opened her mouth to protest, then closed it. "Not so much that," she said. "But he reminded me sometimes of Oggie—"

"The brother you lost when he was, what, eight?"

"Seven. And all those years afterwards, of being a deputy mother, so to speak. It's ingrained, I suppose."

"You'd have been a good mother," Julia gave Annie her hands and helped her up. "It's too bad you didn't have the chance."

"I had the chance, Julia. I lost it. The child, I mean."

Julia's fingers went to her mouth. "I didn't know."

"No one did, not even Rob. We had been—ah, intimate before we married—after we were engaged. I wanted that, because I knew we'd have to part and that I might lose him. And I thought, well, should the worst happen, perhaps there would be a child—to remember him by."

"Tell me."

"I'd been at Lenox since Rob went south, but in mid-July I went to visit our doctor, in Manhattan. Who confirmed the pregnancy. I was going back to Bond Street, to write to Rob and tell him. I got caught up and nearly killed by the rioters. The draft riots, you remember?"

"Could anyone forget?"

"That night," Annie said, "I lost the baby." There was more she couldn't bear to tell Julia—the Irish mob accosting her, almost surrounding her, the well-dressed Negro man who had intervened, saved her. *Get out now. Get away from here.* He'd been swept away in her stead and, she later learned, hanged from a lamp-post and set afire. Terrified, she had run home to Bond Street. The debt she could never repay, the reason she'd often felt there was a cruel kind of justice in Rob's death at the head of his black troops. A life for a life.

But not for two lives.

"Oh, Annie." Julia's eyes were wet.

"Your own sorrows were worse—two gone as babies, then Bessie—"

"One thing I learned, with the two who survived to adulthood—they're all going to write their own stories. You can't do it for them. And the endings won't always be happy."

"Can any of us do that, really? Write our own story?"

"Those of us lucky enough to have funds to live on have a chance—but even that's not enough. Luck plays a part, certainly. But the courage to defy expectations—social, familial—"

"—like Tallie—"

"And even Jackson. In his feudal world, I suppose, it's easier if you're a younger brother. But, still, there's no guarantee of a happy ending."

"—and Rob's men," Annie said, "of the 54th, and the others. They wouldn't let the white world write their story—even if it cost them their lives. What courage that took."

They walked in silence back into the sunshine and across the front of the Sénat to the Orangerie museum. "Shall we see what Orientalist exotica Monsieur le Conservateur Bénédite has on offer?" Julia said. "There was talk of a Gérôme retrospective."

"Ugh! Slaves and gladiators—oh, all right, just a quick look if that's who it is."

Annie woke the next morning to the celestial scent of Adèle's coffee, idly wondering what that excellent woman would have found in the marché for breakfast. She found Adèle closing the hallway door, her arms full of flowers wrapped in green paper.

"Madame! These just came for you—shall I find a vase?" No smile at such a pleasant surprise; Adèle's look spoke of a troubled heart.

"Who are they from?" Annie took the little card tucked into the bouquet: *Avec les compliments de Bertrand, Comte de Leiningen.* Spicy and sweet scents, a lovely but unusual mix of colors and textures: carnations, both deep red and striped, blue anemones, perfumed pink stock, white tulips—where did he find those?— deep purple scabiosa, blue verbena, white bellflowers, yellow chrysanthemums.

Annie searched her brain for the flowers' meanings: a broken heart, rejection and regret, a forsaken lover, an unfortunate attachment, abiding affection, apology, a wish for the recipient's happiness. She smiled. A gallant gesture of friendship in the language of flowers.

"From Bertrand. I must write to him after breakfast." Adèle still stood there with the flowers in her arms. "Adèle—is something wrong?"

"I must get you a vase, Madame." Adèle headed for the pantry, Annie following.

"Please, what is it?"

Adèle let the bouquet fall onto the zinc counter. "Oh, madame, I must tell you—I am leaving your employment."

A dark hole opened in Annie's gut. "Please—come into the kitchen. What has happened?" She poured coffee for them both.

"I am going to study music—singing." Adèle's words came out in a rush. "I have been saving—you and your family have been so generous—I have enough for lessons with Madame Artôt-Padilla. A Belgian lady. She studied with Madame Viardot—"

"Oh, Adèle!" Annie dropped into a chair, her chest tight from trying not to weep. "That's—that is wonderful. I wish I had said something to you—I've come in sometimes when you were singing and it was so beautiful—especially that last time, when you were doing the *Habanera*. I thought, 'her gifts are wasted here'—"

Adèle smiled, shaking her head. "Only now have I stopped being so afraid—no, I am still afraid, but more afraid of missing my chance to do something with my voice. To make something in my life. I am over thirty, I must delay no longer." She dropped into the chair opposite and sipped her coffee.

Annie's mind was racing, the dear dark familiar face in front of her blurring. How would she manage her life without Adèle? She had taken this supremely competent woman for granted; that she would always be there, as a housekeeper—and just as importantly, as a friend and confidante. Nerissa to her Portia. That wasn't supposed to happen; one was supposed to keep one's distance with servants. She opened her mouth to protest that as far as she and the family were concerned, Adèle had accomplished miracles, but realized how fatuous it would sound.

"How did it come about?" she said instead, hoping it didn't sound like accusation, merely friendly curiosity. She had half-expected, always dreaded that Adèle would come to her some day to tell her she was getting married, starting a family. She wondered now if there was a man involved, making promises about how he could help Adèle to a singing career. Someone who would deceive, exploit her...

"I sing in my church's choir—Saint-Martin-des-Champs— near the Canal and the Saint-Louis hospital. The director, Madame Beaulieu, herself studied at the Conservatoire and had a little career at the Opéra-Comique before she married. She began asking me to sing solos—I did the *Kyrie*, from the Mozart Mass, you know it?"

Annie nodded, her throat tight. "It's lovely."

"And a great challenge," Adèle smiled. "We did it at Easter, to raise money for the new organ. I sang well—le bon Dieu was with me, I prayed so hard to do it right—afterwards she came to me, and introduced me to Madame Padilla, who she had invited to come and listen. 'This is the young singer I was telling you about,' she said. Madame was so lovely—she took my hand—and she said, 'Would you like to study with me?' Such a famous woman! I could not speak at first, but then I said yes, it would be an honor. She will prepare me for the Conservatoire auditions—I do not know if they have ever admitted a black lady—"

Adèle's excitement infected Annie. "If they haven't, they couldn't do better with you as their first!"

"You're so kind, Madame," Adèle's eyes brimmed and tears spilled over. "But to leave you—this house—"

Annie shook her head. "I haven't the slightest idea what I'll do without you. I don't know the first thing about running a household—" her voice cracked.

"I will stay for a month," Adèle said. "To work for you would be an enviable situation for any housekeeper. There are a few I can bring for you to meet, with good references—"

"Are there any from Martinique?" Briefly recovered, Annie rose and took a pair of still-fragrant croissants from their paper bag, placed one on a plate before Adèle. "We were so lucky to find you. If we hadn't had you when Mamma was ill, I can't think how we'd have managed."

"I did what anyone would have, Madame. What a hard time that was for your family—you especially. So sad—your maman was always so sweet, even at the worst times."

"That she was," Annie smiled. "It was hard to remember that, in those last bad days. You were a model of patience with her. I'll always be grateful for that—and so much else." She tried to keep down the flutter of panic in her chest. Adèle had glided in and out of her days, nearly invisible, inaudible much of the time. But her solid presence always there when she needed a tisane, a glass of wine, help with a shopping trip, solace when she felt troubled. Especially these last few months, when the family had left her alone—or she had decided to be left alone—there was always Adèle to help her manage things. How inadequate the terms were. Femme de ménage. Housekeeper. La bonne. None of them began to describe the difference Adèle had made in Annie's life, the impossibility of replacing her.

"You'll be all right? Financially, I mean?"

Adèle gathered croissant flakes into her apron and brushed them onto her plate, smiling. "Madame Beaulieu has thought of everything. Our curé's housekeeper was very old and has gone to live with her son in Picardy. There's a lady who cooks for him, but he needs someone to take care of the presbytère. It is not too large, and he is a tidy man—a kind man…it won't take much time, but the pay is quite good. Ça me détendra jusq'a ce que… it will tide me over—until I see what I can do."

Annie rose abruptly. "Come next door with me." She took the Crafts' keys from the rack, tripped across the hall, threw the door open and made for the great black piano in the salon. Riffling through the sheet music in the stool, she found what she was looking for, opened the piano, sat and began to play, waving Adèle over to stand beside her. Her maid's features opened into a smile at the introduction to 'Porgi, amor,' the forsaken Countess's aria from *Figaro*. Adèle began to sing. The glorious notes filled the rooms and wafted into the hallway. Annie could barely read the music for her tears. Monsieur le Poste, arriving with the day's mail, halted at the top of the stairs and tiptoed into the doorway. Unseen by either woman, he stood rapt until the song ended and tactfully stole away again.

Chapter 34

r. John Morgan, Rector of the American Cathedral, entered his church from the deanery early in the afternoon to check on the progress of the workmen installing new stained-glass windows in the south clerestory.

The Rector moved quietly to avoid disturbing any parishioners in private devotion. By one of the front pillars on the side from which he had entered sat a familiar-looking lady, head bent in prayer, or perhaps merely thought. He quietly crossed the chancel and walked down the opposite aisle to the porch.

Annie barely registered his footfalls. Adèle's news had shaken her to the roots. She had come to think things over in comforting solitude. Self-reproach warred with a wave of bereavement that puzzled her with its intensity. No one who mattered to her had died; no one—except her sister and family, now months gone—had left Paris even for the summer. Yet with Adèle's news, everything came into sharp and troubling focus.

Her maid's words echoed. *Afraid of missing my chance to make something in my life. In* my life. Not *of* my life. All these months, she had been trying to help her circle of young artists do that— with money, food and wine, a listening ear, encouragement—

overlooking, meanwhile, her companion of long standing, perhaps the most talented of them all—and what had it come to?

Heartbreak, pain, the little circle torn apart. Carlotta gone back to her imprisoned life in a New York brownstone. Jackson's youthful folly losing him a wife and son. Bertrand, shedding his armor of cynicism at just the wrong time, loving a woman who couldn't love him back. Tallie forced to choose between her life's work and a motherhood she'd never wanted. Lydia alone with her son in a strange land.

But what they all still had, the ones who stayed in Paris, was a determination to make something, to follow their passions, use their gifts, show the world something it had never seen—or never as they envisioned it. What mattered most was their soul's work, and if it came to a choice between soul and heart, the heart must be allowed to break.

In the clerestory level above the nave, she heard voices, humorous, rough, and irreverent, the sounds of hammers tapping and chisels scraping—the workmen resuming their installation, removing a clear glass panel and replacing it with one of the new, colorful offerings. Curious, she rose and found herself a vantage point to see what they were doing. She was startled by an echoing clatter, a tool dropped from the scaffolding above her head, followed by a most un-ecclesiastical curse—in English. A workman scrambled down the scaffolding to retrieve it. On impulse, Annie went to intercept him before he could ascend again.

"Monsieur—pardonnez-moi—excuse me—"

The burly chap with a dark shadow of beard and rolled-up shirtsleeves stood expectant.

"Will it disturb you if I watch a little?"

The man's face split in a wide grin. "Nah, Missus, we're used to it, like. A lotta folk have been in and aht, seein' what we're up to—"

"You're a Londoner!"

"Cockney born and bred, within the sound of Bow Bells," he said proudly.

"Is your whole—ah, team, English?"

"Lor' love yer, yes! Well, nearly. Couple a Welshmen too, mebby. Mr. Beckham wouldn't trust no foreigners messin' abaht wif his glass. Most of our work's in England, 'course, but this is the biggest they've ever done, and—" his chest swelled slightly, "'e wanted 'is best men on it. Mind you, can't say it's been bad bein' stuck in Paris. Nice town, Paris is. Miss the trouble-an'-strife an' the nippers, but we get switched out every three months, like."

"Alf!" came a shout from high above. "Wotcher doin' dahn there?" A face appeared at the edge of the scaffolding. "Ooh, sorry. Chattin' up the ladies again, 'e is," he said to someone on the platform behind him.

"Goodness, I'm sorry—I must let you get back to work," Annie said. "Just a question—what's the versicle on that panel your friend's carrying?"

"Ted, wot's written on that there?" Alf called up to his mate.

Ted's brow contracted. "*Day by day we magnify Thee.* Nearly done with the bloody thing, we are—savin' yer presence, ma'am."

Annie smiled and waved a deprecatory hand. She thanked Alf, who was already climbing the scaffolding. "What beautiful work it is."

After six years of labor, James Beckham's illustrated *Te Deum*—no other like it in the world—was almost complete;

of the forty-two windows, only the half-dozen of the Petition verses remained to be installed.

And what of herself? What had she ever made? A painting or two…quite a few actually, in her youth; that brief flirtation with oils and landscape in Maine, just before the news about Rob. With oils and, she blushed to recall, with Mr. Harrison Bird Brown, who had praised her talent and potential…now within arm's reach across the Channel and a frequent visitor to Paris…

…*we magnify Thee.* That was the artist's work, wasn't it? To carry forward Creation, use God-given gifts to add to the beauty of the world. She thought of the Parable of the Talents, of the servant who buried the one talent the Master had given him. Because *I was afraid*, he told the Master. The fear was understandable—given only the one talent, the servant hadn't trusted himself to do something pleasing with it, thus earning the Master's reproof for doing nothing. He had missed the point. It wasn't about pleasing someone else, but about making the effort. Some were given more than others—but whatever one was given, one must make something of or, in Adèle's words, *to make something in my life.* What had she been, Annie Shaw, but that faithless servant, too fearful to do something with her one little talent?

She spotted the Reverend Dr. Morgan who, seeing her reverie broken, approached her by the center aisle and warmly took her hand.

"Mrs. Shaw, I'm glad to see you! You're looking well. I'd meant to inquire about the Crafts—we miss your sister greatly, as you can imagine—"

"Dr. Morgan, I wanted to ask you—that window they're putting in. Does it have a sponsor?"

The Rector's brows rose. "A sponsor? You mean a donor? I'm not sure—there were one or two still going a-begging, as it were. Come into the Deanery office and I'll check our records."

The "We Magnify Thee" window was one of only two remaining which had not attracted a donor. "I fear it's because of the north light," Morgan said. "People like to see sunshine streaming through a stained-glass window, but of course we can't have that there. Silly, isn't it," he allowed himself a little smile, "by tradition we have to call it the south clerestory, when by the compass it's due north?"

North light—artists' light. Because it kept steady through the day and kept your colors true. The light by which *we magnify Thee*. "What," said Annie, "would be a useful sum to the Cathedral, from a donor of that window?"

The Rector named a significant sum, but well within Annie's means.

"Will you put me down for that one, please? That one in particular."

The Rector beamed. "I'd be honored. Shall it say, 'Gift of Mrs. Robert Gould Shaw'? The attributions can easily be painted on, as you'll see on the ones already installed—"

"Can it just say 'In Memoriam' and the donor remain anonymous? I'd prefer that."

"That thine alms may be in secret: and thy Father which seeth in secret Himself shall reward thee openly." The Rector smiled. "A laudable sentiment, Mrs. Shaw. And quite characteristic, I might add. But 'In Memoriam' to whom?"

"Oh—too many to name, Mr. Morgan," Annie smiled. *Oggie, and George, and Rob, and the brave men of the 54th, and Ogden and Elizabeth, and William Greene, Bessie Greene and Susan Dimock, and Roland Burwell…* "May we leave it at that?"

Day by day, we magnify Thee. Clem, and Julia, and most other women she knew, had made lively and beautiful children. James Crafts made new compounds—useful ones, Annie supposed— from the elements of God's earth. Bertrand and Tallie, Jackson and Aloysius O'Connor, Henry Tanner and Harrison Bird Brown brought the transient beauty of faces and of earth and sea to life in paint and on canvas. Lydia Burwell turned shapeless fabric into lovely garments created with skill and imagination. Monsieur Debussy and his friends—and now Adèle—made beauty from raw, meaningless notes, beauty that could be shared across the world.

It was long past time for Annie to try to make something herself. That's what Paris could give you—the room to create, in ways that might be frowned upon elsewhere, to take chances, to risk failure and even ridicule. That's what made you a true Parisian, one worthy of a place in the great city—taking those risks. She had held back, cocooned in her family and in the American Colony, in part from distraction, in part from duties assumed as an all-but-maiden aunt, as a widowed daughter without progeny of her own—in part, too, she could now admit, from fear. She might have no talent to speak of, but in her heart she felt a flicker of hope—what little art she had made had drawn praise, perhaps not disinterested, perhaps merely polite— but it would serve as a small hand-hold to begin her climb.

*   *   *

Her mother's old bedroom smelled now of linseed oil and turpentine and ashy charcoal from Annie's sketchbook. She let her glance fall with shy fondness on the half-done canvases propped against the wall, the little flower studies, oil-sketches of a street-view from the Crafts' balcony, of Adèle—oh, Adèle!—from the back, working in the pantry. Begun when Sarah Shaw was arriving in Paris to threaten her peace and her hopes for the future, as a ruse to occupy the one free room in her apartments—and yet there had been pleasure and absorption in them.

A good-sized canvas, blank, snow-white, sat in a corner. She put it on her easel and went to the parlor to retrieve the bouquet Bertrand had sent. As good a place as any to start. She must send Adèle to Père Tanguy's for fresh paints and brushes—no, not Adèle. She would go and choose for herself—she must learn to do things for herself.

In her belly she felt a flutter of delight at war with a trough of panic. It bubbled up into her throat and she cried out a little, a small whimper, a child's noise. Her brush-work would be hesitant at first—someday, perhaps, she would know the freedom she saw in her friends' paintings, the facile sweeps of the brush, the light feathering as the stroke was truncated for just the right effect. Fluency—as she had achieved with the piano, but only after long hours and days of tedious practice. She was a beginner at painting, as her nieces had been beginners on the piano, and she would learn again to tolerate frustration and tedium in the hope of mastery. She would need teachers, too. And before Adèle vanished from her life, she would ask to paint her portrait—her face this time, in full-throated song, not her laboring back.

Epilogue

tanding in the Crafts' great salon, Annie wrung her hands. "I should never have done this, Julia. What was I thinking? Me of all people putting on a salon? What if nobody comes? What if everybody comes? I'm nervous as a cat."

"Nonsense!" Julia Greene, in purple brocade trimmed with black velvet and a charming little veiled hat, made a slow pirouette of the room. Dustcovers had come off the Crafts' furniture, and Annie had moved a colorful selection of newly acquired paintings into their apartments while the young designer Hector Guimard was exercising his carte blanche to redecorate and refurnish her own rooms across the hall. "You've all the essentials to encourage conversation: new artwork, an excellent piano, the best caterer on the rue de la Pompe, and a motley assortment of guests, with just enough chairs and sofas!" She nodded with approval at the bouquets of chrysanthemums, cotoneaster berries, late roses and deep red carnations spilling over from their pedestaled jardinières in each corner of the room. "And the florist has outdone himself."

"He always does," Annie smiled, her gaze rising from the

gleaming parquet floor to the gauzy windows where the pale light of a November afternoon was dwindling. "It does look nice, doesn't it? But Julia, the paintings—isn't it rather—arrogant—to have put my own work next to Mr. O'Connor's and Tallie's and Jackson's? Not to mention Bertrand's satyrs—the Cathedral ladies will find that one a bit shocking, I'm afraid—"

"We all know you're just beginning," Julia laid her hands on Annie's shoulders. "I'm rather proud of the portrait you did of me. It recaptures some of my, dare I say, ancient days of beauty. I'd like people to see me that way. Besides, Mr. Brown said it was all right—indeed, he's the one who suggested it, isn't he? A teacher won't do that if he thinks his pupil will disgrace him."

"I suppose not—but he's not a portraitist." Annie felt herself turning pink. Harrison Bird Brown's several long forays to Paris since their re-encounter had featured lessons in landscape painting in the gold and bronze autumn woods of the Bois de Boulogne, among other pleasures.

It was Tallie DeKuyper, however, who had enabled her progress with portraiture, "A fair trade, Mrs. Shaw, since you're giving me a winter fortnight in Cannes," she had said, refusing payment for lessons and critiques.

"Ah, here you are! Are we ready?" Retta Reubell bustled in, in a gown of pumpkin and black striped silk and a tiny tricorne hat that sat pertly on her red hair.

"Goodness, Retta, no turquoise?" Julia embraced her. "I'm glad you're here. Annie's having an attack of nerves."

"With Julia and me as co-hostesses? I'm dismayed by your lack of confidence!" Retta kissed Annie on both cheeks. "Besides, you look marvelous. Garnet is certainly your color. You should wear it all winter. Is that a Laferrière? Of course it is."

"Actually, no," Annie smiled. "My young friend who works at Rouff's made it. She did a lovely job on the beading too, didn't she?"

Retta stood back, considering the gown more closely. "I must meet this wonder. The cut's exquisite, and the detail is subtle but striking. She's one of their new designers?"

"All but there. She's working her way up through the ateliers. She'll be a déssineuse soon, I've no doubt. You'll meet her today, I hope."

The dining-room door swung open and a grave-faced young woman in a crisp new maid's uniform drove a wedge under it to hold it open. "All is ready in the kitchen, Madame."

"Thank you, Lilli. Retta, Julia, this is my new housekeeper, Mademoiselle Lilli Tran. Lilli, these are my friends and co-hostesses, Madame Greene and Mademoiselle Reubell. Lilli came to Paris from Saigon, in French Indochina."

The young woman, slender, high-cheeked, and ivory-skinned, bobbed her head and excused herself. "Adèle met her at church," Annie explained. "She was registered at the same domestic agency that sent Adèle to us. She'd got to know her and thought we would do well together. She's very capable, but still quite shy—won't drink morning coffee with me yet, though she makes it wonderfully."

"Give her a few months and she'll warm up," Julia said. "French father, I'd guess?"

"Raised in a Catholic orphanage," Annie said, "so that seems likely."

"Will she go to Cannes with you?"

"Certainly. I hope you're all going to Cannes with me—I'll be starting to pack soon—"

"And your London gentleman?" Retta teased. "He'll be coming too, I hope?"

Annie turned pink again. "Oh, Retta—"

The doorbell rang in the Crafts' hallway. Julia looked at her watch. "Ten past—right on time, by Paris standards! I'll take the first round of greetings. Who will be our pioneers?"

It was Tallie, accompanied by Aloysius O'Connor, she still laughing over something he'd said, no doubt outrageous. She ran to Annie and embraced her. "You've hung it up?"

"Not yet. It's in the bedroom, on an easel, with a drape over it. I thought I'd wait till everyone was here and we could unveil it together—I want everyone to see what you've accomplished with such a difficult subject."

Tallie grinned and punched her on the arm. "You're being silly. Aloysius, she's got yours up over there."

"Sure and she does, and a nice prominent spot it's in too. I'm rather fond of that one meself. Hated to part with it—grateful though I was for the sale." O'Connor beamed, wrapping Annie in a gargantuan hug. They contemplated his polychrome landscape, farm fields sloping off a hill at a riverbend, the colors unreal but somehow compelling, hallucinatory, fevered, the striped, jagged brushstrokes almost vibrating off the canvas. What a contrast, Annie thought, with Ogden's soothing Durands and Cropseys.

Julia ushered in an unlikely collection of newcomers—Mrs. Dean Morgan from the Cathedral, her friend Mrs. Newell, who with her minister husband was starting a little refuge for American lady art students, followed by the plump and wheezy poet Henri Legrand, accompanied, to Annie's delight, by that enthusiastic artist Jean Béraud. The caterer's staff, in crisp black and white, began circulating with trays of canapés and flutes of champagne. Retta Reubell made introductions, and as others filed in, the room began to buzz and hum with talk and laughter. Monsieur Legrand deflated into an armchair and gratefully accepted a bubbling flute, giving Annie a look of adoration.

"Before I forget, Annie, Mary Kernochan sends regrets," Mrs. Morgan said. "She's come down with a dreadful cold, so disappointed—but greatly hoping to come to your next soirée."

"Oh, I'm so sorry!" Annie bit her lip to avoid smiling; she hadn't been looking forward to an encounter between Mrs. Kernochan and Jackson Burwell, especially if, as seemed possible these days, he had persuaded Lydia to accompany him. "I do hope she's better soon—I'll call on her in a few days." She turned to greet the latest newcomers.

"Look who's here, Annie—my nephew and his bride!" Julia ushered in Fred and Nora Sears and, behind them, the American Minister himself, Thomas Jefferson Coolidge.

"My dear Mrs. Shaw! Fred and Nora told me they were coming, and I had a free hour, so I thought I'd—" the Minister looked almost diffident, and Annie allowed herself a broad smile as she offered her hand. The Cathedral ladies were nodding at each other with raised eyebrows.

The big room filled up—artist friends of Retta's, the poet Pierre Louis, Hector Guimard who had doffed his smock and crossed the hall to join the gathering at Annie's insistence. She was pleased to see Henry Tanner, walking in after Lydia Burwell.

"This is the lady I was telling you about," Annie told Retta.

"The one who made this glorious dress! I must speak to you later, Madame—"

"It's *Miss* Burwell," said Lydia shyly, her lovely features lighting up.

"Mr. Tanner," said Annie, "I hope you'll be happy with the placement of your *Concarneau*—it's in the dining room over the buffet for the moment—"

"A piece of mine hanging in any setting is cause for joy," the artist said. "But I take particular pleasure in knowing it's in your home."

They walked in together to view the soft Brittany seascape: low tide, dark rocks in the foreground, sunshine illuminating a sea-wall in the middle distance, a point beyond with the suggestion of a lighthouse. On the opposite wall was a nocturne, a landscape in deep blues, blacks, and golds, by Jackson Burwell. Annie saw Jackson enter, his gaze sweeping the room, stopping when he spotted Lydia. He came toward her, his face a mix of hope and sadness.

"Your sojourn in Pont-Aven was productive, Tanner. Well done." They turned to find Bertrand de Leiningen, smiling, with a tall, dusky woman on his arm—the model Sofia, Annie realized, coloring at the memory of the one time she had met the lady, with clothes off and hair down, posing sensuously in Bertrand's studio—so long ago, it seemed. Now Sofia looked like an aristocrat, her black hair piled artfully on her head, her gown of deep blue velvet. "I'm so happy to see you—both." Annie looked back over the great salon. People had formed little knots, conversation flowing, secondary introductions being made.

"I sold that piece I was working on when we met," Bertrand said, "to the newly minted Madame de Saint-Marceaux. She saw it at the Salon and wanted it for her boudoir."

"I'm delighted to hear it! I wonder if she'd show it to me, at her next musicale? I never did see the finished product—

though with such subj—such a subject," Annie smiled at Sofia, "it could only be stunning."

"You're too kind." Sofia took a champagne flute from a passing server.

In the salon, someone had sat down at the piano and begun a familiar tune—an Irish air Annie recognized, "The Meeting of the Waters," and people were gathering around the instrument. Someone else began to sing, softly, then with more confidence. The pianist was Aloysius O'Connor; the singer was Nora Sears.

She couldn't have wished for a better ice-breaker. Another guest arrived, a diabolically handsome man with Van Dyke whiskers and a scarlet cravat: with a shock she recognized Dr. Samuel Pozzi, who came forward to greet Retta Reubell, who led him to Annie.

"I'm told you two have met," said Retta with a wicked smile.

"Under less favorable circonstances than the present, Madame, I fear." Pozzi took Annie's hand and kissed it, his dark eyes smiling up at her.

"I wouldn't call saving my life less favorable circumstances," Annie smiled, "though I'm delighted to see you in other than your professional capacity. Please—have some champagne—" She handed him a flute, wondering if Pozzi reflexively registered heart rates when he got near a woman's wrist. If so, her clasp would have been more revealing than she'd have cared for.

Jean Béraud was at her elbow. "Pardonnez, Madame Shaw—Madame Greene has just shown me the portrait of her—you made it, oui?"

Annie gulped. "I'm afraid so."

"But it is quite good, truly. A few things I might suggest: the angle of the shoulder, for instance—you are new to portraiture, she tells me. But you have an excellent eye."

"Thank you—"

"And the belle négresse hanging next to her—that is yours also?"

"It is—" Annie looked up to see the portrait's original diffidently crossing the salon, accompanied—almost held up— by an older, statuesque woman. Adèle had come, as promised, with her teacher, Madame Artôt-Padilla, the Belgian opera diva whose career had taken her all over Europe and as far as Russia where, it was said, she had once been engaged to Tchaikovsky.

Béraud turned and followed Annie's gaze. "Mon Dieu, it is a very good likeness."

Annie and Adèle had made a pact: Annie would find the courage to hang the two portraits if Adèle would sing one aria, after which there would be the promised unveiling.

"Mesdames et messieurs!" Retta Reubell clapped her hands. The room fell silent. "We have a special guest with us this evening, making her first public performance." The guests took their seats, some staring in unfeigned surprise at the sight of a black woman in their midst. Annie saw Lydia Burwell catch Adèle's eye and nod encouragement, her face alight with pleasure.

"Je vous présente," Retta continued, "Mademoiselle Adèle Fourget, accompanied by her teacher, Madame Désirée Artôt-Padilla, in a short selection of songs from the opera."

After polite sprinkle of applause, Madame Padilla settled herself on the piano stool and began the introduction to Mozart's *Voi che sapete*, from *Figaro*. Adèle, in blue silk with black lace sleeves, bent her head, then drew herself up and took in air. The pure, lovely notes poured out, rich and rounded, seemingly without effort. A showpiece for the stronger mezzo end of Adèle's range, Annie thought, though once warmed up she was more than capable...

The song ending to far more enthusiastic applause, pupil and teacher moved on to the *Habanera*. Annie remembered Adèle singing it to herself in the kitchen, and shivered to think what a near thing that Adèle was finally able to follow her passion. How tragic if she'd missed it. She thought again of the Gospel story of the talents.

Madame Padilla rose from the piano. "We will do one final song together, a cappella." She gave Adèle a signal, and they began the exquisite Flower Duet from Delibes' *Lakmé*. Adèle took the servant's part, as befitted her vocal strength in the mezzo range, though Annie was sure she could have handled the higher one as well as her teacher. Still, she was new to the formal study, and Madame must be allowed to display her own undiminished voice.

When the song ended, the room was on its feet, applauding loudly and warmly. Annie couldn't stop her tears and, when she looked at Adèle, saw that she, too, was now weeping, along with most of the women in the room, and many of the men. She sagged with relief. Adèle had been frightened, but she had pushed past the fear and done splendidly. A carafe of water awaited the singers, but as arranged, Julia came out of the kitchen with two flutes and a new bottle of champagne, handed the bottle to Bertrand who smoothly popped the cork and gave each lady a glass.

Annie raised hers and looked around at her guests. "Mesdames, messieurs—let us never let talent go to waste." The room rang with toasts like silvery bells. Adèle and Madame Padilla were engulfed in admirers, and she exchanged a smile with Tallie.

"Well done," Tallie mouthed from across the room.

From a shadow near the entrance, Annie saw the now-familiar figure of Harrison Bird Brown detach itself from the doorway. The guests had resumed their conversations, no one else—she made sure—standing alone and unoccupied. She made her way over to him. He put his hand under her elbow, squeezed it, and kissed her discreetly on the forehead.

"Sorry to be so late—I heard the recital, thank goodness. Forgive my tardiness? The train was held up at Amiens."

"Just this once," Annie handed him a glass. "You're just in time for the unveiling."

Brown's dark eyes widened. "And who are we, ah, unveiling?"

"You'll see."

"You're blushing again. I so enjoy it when you blush."

"Oh, stop!" Annie turned to Julia, who was approaching to greet the artist.

Tallie and Aloysius O'Connor were emerging from the bedroom corridor with an easel on which sat a draped painting. They set it in front of the unlit fireplace. O'Connor withdrew, perching on the edge of Bertrand's sofa. Tallie, left alone, looked terrified. Annie nodded encouragement, but she was feeling similarly.

"Madame Shaw," Tallie began faintly, then her voice strengthened, "agreed to sit to me for a portrait. As it turns out, she has invited you all to the vernissage. I hope you're pleased—dear Annie." With that, she removed the drapery. There stood Annie in her ivory satin gown, in three-quarters profile, her elbow on the Crafts' mantel, as though inviting the viewer to go out with her for the evening. No one would mistake it for a Sargent—it was too strongly colored for that, and the lines owed less to literal representation of flesh and fabric than to gestures that conveyed strength, determination, intelligence, and perhaps sheer presence. But it had undeniable power.

Annie caught Bertrand's eye. He was biting his lip, his head bowed, moved, troubled and pleased all at once. He nodded his approval. His pupil—his lost beloved—had learned well. A murmur of commentary, positive, enthusiastic, had the room humming like a beehive.

Oh, Lord, now I've done it. I'll never be invisible again.

Historical Note

elle Époque era Paris (from the 1870s until World War I) was a magnet for writers, scientists, composers, and artists, drawing expatriates from Europe and the Americas whose creativity thrived in the freedom of its studios and salons. Though the American artists and intellectuals of the Left Bank are better known today, the majority of Americans in Paris were there for business connections, lower costs of living, and the opportunity to live in an older and more aristocratic culture than the one they had left.

The insular and largely wealthy American Colony in Paris, concentrated in the 8th and 16th arrondissements of the Right Bank, flourished from the 1880s well into the twentieth century, attracting such notable long- and short-term residents as the Joneses (Edith Wharton's birth family), the Jameses, the Pells, the Cassatts, and the Goulds. Artists, struggling and otherwise, like John Singer Sargent, James McNeil Whistler, Samuel F.B. Morse (who was a painter before inventing the telegraph), and Henry Ossawa Tanner came to Paris to study at L'Ecole des Beaux Arts and the Académie Julian and to burnish their reputations at home. Henrietta Reubell, daughter of an American mother and French father, was a good friend of Henry James and was noted for the bohemian character and diversity of her salons, which served as a bridge between the more conventional Colony and the transgressive artists and intellectuals of the period.

Among these expatriates were members of the Haggerty, Crafts, and Shaw families. Anna Kneeland Haggerty, later Annie Shaw, this novel's protagonist, was born on July 9, 1835, in New York City and died on March 17, 1907, in Boston. The first surviving child of wealthy Irish American auctioneer Ogden Haggerty and his wife Elizabeth Kneeland, she grew up in New York City and in the family's summer home, "Vent Fort," in Lenox, MA. A younger brother, Ogden, was born in 1837 and died in 1844. Her sister Clemence Haggerty, born in 1841, married pioneering organic chemist James Mason Crafts in 1867 and their union produced four daughters.

Annie met her future husband Robert Gould Shaw around 1860, when he was a clerk in his uncle's business. After his enlistment in the Seventh New York regiment at the outbreak of the Civil War, he served with the Second Massachusetts Infantry before reluctantly accepting the colonelcy of the 54th Massachusetts Infantry, United States Colored Troops, formed by Massachusetts Governor John Albion Andrew as the first Northern Black infantry regiment. They married on May 2, 1863 and, following a triumphant march through Boston on May 28 immortalized by sculptor Augustus Saint Gaudens in a bas-relief which stands on the edge of Boston Common.

Shaw departed for the Sea Islands of South Carolina with his regiment on May 28, 1863. In a doomed attempt to take Battery Wagner on Morris Island in Charleston Bay, he was shot through the heart at the head of his regiment on July 18, 1863. His marriage to Annie had lasted seventy-seven days, of which they had spent twenty-six days together. The regiment's heroism was celebrated in the 1989 film *Glory*, which won an Oscar for the young Denzel Washington and starred Matthew Broderick as Colonel Shaw. It did not, however, acknowledge the existence of Shaw's wife.

After Shaw's death, Annie returned to her birth family, spending the winter of 1867 in Washington, DC. In the early 1870s, Annie and her mother traveled extensively in Europe, with the Crafts family moving there in 1874 when James Crafts left Boston for research in Paris at the École des Mines. Ogden joined them in 1875, traveling between Switzerland and France in hope of finding a cure for what was evidently a heart ailment, but died in Switzerland in 1875 and was buried in Green-Wood Cemetery in Brooklyn, New York.

According to a letter of Henry James from that year, Annie had developed "some cruel malady," a tumor, evidently, while another friend mentions in 1879 that she is "still suffering, but more hopeful of recovery" and spending time in Paris and Cannes. In the 1880s, Paris records show Annie and her mother living on the avenue Henri Martin in the same building as her sister and brother-in-law and their daughters. With her mother's death in 1888 and burial in Lenox, Massachusetts, Annie continued to occupy their Paris apartment.

James Crafts became a professor in MIT's new organic chemistry department in 1891; in that same year, the Haggerty sisters sold their beloved summer home in Lenox to the sister and cousin of J.P. Morgan, but required the Morgans to move the original building to a nearby lot across the street. The entire Crafts family returned to the US in 1892, but Annie stayed on in Paris, where she lived until returning to Boston in July of 1903.

Annie's aunt by marriage, Anna Shaw Greene (renamed Julia in the novel to avoid name confusion) lived in Paris until her death in late 1901. Annie's mother-in-law, Sarah Blake Sturgis Shaw, lived until December 1902; her sister-in-law Josephine Shaw Lowell, a noted figure in institutional philanthropy (the Lowell Fountain in New York's Bryant Park was named in her honor), died in 1905. Josephine's daughter, Annie's niece by marriage Carlotta Russell Lowell, who never married, lived in New York City until her death in 1924.

Several Colony daughters married Continental aristocrats, often trading newly acquired family wealth for prestigious titles. Annie's neighbor Winnaretta Singer, an heiress of the sewing machine fortune, became the Princesse de Polignac in a mariage lavande with Prince Edmond de Polignac and became a notable salonnière and patroness of such composers as Debussy, Fauré, and Ravel. Railroad magnate Jay Gould's daughter Anna married and divorced the Count of Castellane and then married his cousin, the Duc of Talleyrand-Périgord.

The American Cathedral on what is now the avenue George V, formally known as the Cathedral Church of the Holy Trinity, was the Paris home of expatriate Episcopalians. The parish formed in 1859, and its magnificent Cathedral was consecrated in 1886, with the Rev. John Brainerd Morgan, cousin and brother-in-law to the famous financier J.P. Morgan, as its Rector. Annie Shaw, her mother Elizabeth Haggerty, her sister Clemence Haggerty Crafts and other family members were parishioners there, as was in later times the well-known actress Olivia de Havilland, whose funeral took place there in 2020.

Acknowledgments

any years ago I first saw the movie *Glory*, which brought to light the inspiring Civil War story of the heroic 54th Massachusetts Infantry, one of the Union's first Black regiments. Their white colonel, Robert Gould Shaw, was the scion of a prominent abolitionist family. Curious about the history behind the film and about Shaw in particular, I came upon Russell Duncan's *Blue-Eyed Child of Fortune*, a collection of Shaw's Civil War letters with a lengthy biographical introduction.

To my surprise, I learned that Shaw had been married. The movie had written his wife, Anna Kneeland Shaw, completely out of the script. My curiosity about Annie and her life before and after her marriage led eventually to the writing of this novel.

Given its lengthy gestation and the complexity of the historical research involved, I owe thanks to more people and sources than I can possibly remember. With apologies to those I may have inadvertently missed, I offer my deepest gratitude to the following:

Kate W. Thweatt, archivist, and Rev. Lucinda Laird, former dean, of the American Cathedral of the Holy Trinity, Paris;

Dr. Russell Flinchum, former archivist, and the late Jonathan Harding, curator, of the Century Association; Dr. Eleanor Jones Harvey, senior curator of 19th century art, Smithsonian American Art Museum; and Dr. Kenneth Maddox, scholar in residence, Newington-Cropsey Foundation, Hastings-on-Hudson, NY.

Grateful acknowledgment is due to the staff members of the many libraries and museums from which I obtained invaluable assistance with the historic research that underpins this work of fiction, including the staff of the Archives de Paris; Bibliothèque de la Ville de Paris; Boston Athenaeum; Boston Museum of African-American History; Century Association Archives, New York; Family History Library, Church of Jesus Christ of Latter-Day Saints, Salt Lake City, Utah; Green-Wood Cemetery, Brooklyn; Houghton Library, Harvard University; Lenox Library, Lenox, Mass.; Massachusetts Historical Society; Milstein Division of US History, Local History and Genealogy, New York Public Library; National Library of Ireland, Dublin; New-York Historical Society; Staten Island Museum; Staten Island Historical Society; and Ventfort Hall, Gilded Age Mansion & Museum, Lenox, Mass. I never fail to be amazed by the generosity and helpfulness of these custodians of history.

In addition to innumerable internet resources, I relied heavily for factual background on the following texts: Michael Anesko and Greg W. Zacharias, *The Complete Letters of Henry James*; Cameron Allen, *The History of the American Pro-Cathedral of the Holy Trinity, Paris (1815-1980)*; Peter Burchard, *One Gallant Rush: Robert Gould Shaw and his Brave Black Regiment*; Russell Duncan, *Blue-Eyed Child of Fortune: the Civil War Letters of Colonel Robert Gould Shaw; Where Death and Glory*

Meet: Colonel Robert Gould Shaw and the 54th Massachusetts Infantry; Memorial RGS, 1864 (poems and tributes by friends, public figures, and family members); Joseph Alfred Scoville, *The Old Merchants of New York City;* Lorien Foote, *Seeking the One Great Remedy: Francis George Shaw and 19th Century Reform;* Cornelia Brooke Gilder, *Hawthorne's Lenox;* Lincoln Kirstein and Richard Benson, *Lay This Laurel;* Leslie Minturn Allison, *Mildred Minturn: A Biography,* and Jean Zimmerman, *Love, Fiercely: a Gilded Age Romance.*

Many thanks for invaluable advice and feedback to Harriet Chessman, author of *Lydia Cassatt Reading the Morning Paper;* to early readers Alex Brown, Beth Kanell, and Mary Hays; and to writer friends Liz Bedell, Mary Johnson, Maura MacNeil, and Martha Andrews Donovan for moral support and believing in the project when my own energy was flagging. Special thanks to Cornelia Brooke Gilder, author of *Edith Wharton's Lenox, Hawthorne's Lenox,* and the Ventfort Hall docents' guide, for encouragement, hospitality, and leads into the more obscure corners of my story.

The path to publication for unknown authors these days is a steep and stony one. Warmest thanks to Samantha Kolber and all the good folks at Roostock Publishing for believing in this book and bringing it into the world, and a hearty thanks to Tim Newcomb for designing the Paris map.

To Wayne Fawbush, who has lived with Annie Shaw and her story as long as I have and who kept me going when I was tempted to abandon it, more thanks and love than I can ever express. *Portrait of an Unseen Woman* wouldn't have happened without you.

About the Author

oberta Harold is also the author of two historical mysteries, Heron Island and Murdered Sleep. She was born in Glasgow, Scotland, educated at convent schools there, and emigrated to the Washington, DC area with her family in 1965. Admitted with the second class of women to Princeton University in 1970, she graduated with the first in 1973 and went to medical school for a year and a half before admitting that she should have been an English major. This she eventually remedied with a master's degree from Middlebury College's Bread Loaf School of English in 2001.

Moving to Vermont in 1977, she stumbled into a twenty-plus year career in community and economic development which included a stint as state director of USDA Rural Development for Vermont, New Hampshire, and for a time the Virgin Islands. She was appointed director of economic development in the first term of Vermont's first woman governor, Madeleine Kunin, and later worked as an independent strategy consultant for small businesses and nonprofit organizations.

She won the Bread Loaf School of English poetry prize in 1999 and was first runner-up in 2002 in Seven Days' emerging writers short story contest. *Heron Island*, the first in the Dade Wyatt historical mystery series, was a Finalist in the Legacy Fiction awards of the Independent Publishers of New England (IPNE) and its sequel, *Murdered Sleep*, won the IPNE 2015 Genre Fiction award.

She has acted in community theater productions for many years. Favorite roles include Lady Bracknell in The Importance of Being Earnest, Ouiser Boudreau in Steel Magnolias, and Mistress Quickly in The Merry Wives of Windsor. She sings in the soprano section of Rock City, the rock'n'soul chorus of Barre, Vermont. A member since 1978 of The Mother of All Book Groups, founded in 1972, and a founding member of the Bardolators, a Shakespeare discussion group, she lives in Montpelier, Vermont with her husband and cats.

 *We Grow Our Books in Montpelier, Vermont*
Learn more about our titles in Fiction, Nonfiction, Poetry and
Children's Literature at the QR code below or visit
www.rootstockpublishing.com.